THE ART OF CATCHING FEELINGS

"Unfailingly sweet and surprisingly sexy at the same time, *The Art of Catching Feelings* is a home run for Alicia Thompson."

—Jodi Picoult, #1 *New York Times* bestselling author of
Mad Honey and *Wish You Were Here*

"I'm an Alicia Thompson fan first and a human second, and *The Art of Catching Feelings* is a shining example of why. Chris and Daphne's achingly vulnerable, hot slide into love was so masterfully crafted with intimacy and care that I was tempted to go right back to the first page once I finished (fine, and maybe I did). With her signature effortless prose and deeply insightful musings on life and love, this is Alicia Thompson at the top of her already spectacular game."

—Jessica Joyce, *USA Today* bestselling author of
You, with a View

"A soft and sexy riff on *You've Got Mail*, *The Art of Catching Feelings* delivers a beautifully layered look at how intimacy blooms on and offline. I savored the bittersweetness of Alicia Thompson's expertly deployed angst. Whether or not you're a baseball fan, you'll find yourself rooting for Daphne and Chris from the moment of their one-of-a-kind meet-cute."

—Rosie Danan, *USA Today* bestselling author of
Do Your Worst

"Reading an Alicia Thompson book always feels like watching the most elegant of baseball plays—the kind of utter mastery that seems, deceptively, like ease. Explosive, subtle, and quick-witted all at once, Alicia's prose is as sharp as her characters are human, and Chris and Daphne's romance is a stunning portrayal of finding genuine joy and partnership at our lowest points. I didn't think it was possible to love baseball more than I already did, but *The Art of Catching Feelings* manages to capture everything that makes this sport and this genre special: flawlessly executed fundamentals, an impeccable balance of tension and release, and breath-stealing moments that stick in your chest long after the game, or book, ends."

—KT Hoffman, author of *The Prospects*

"On the leaderboard of the handsome, sad baseball men of fiction, Chris Kepler would rank near the very top. Alicia has such a gift for writing characters who are hilarious, thorny, (horny), and fully human—which is also really what baseball's about. *Feelings* is a love letter to the game and the patience and transitions it demands, as well as a love story between characters learning how to find themselves as they find one another. It's as steamy as a day game in August and as exciting as the final out of a world championship. In short, I loved it."

—KD Casey, author of the Unwritten Rules series

"There is perhaps no better title for Alicia Thompson's latest romance: *The Art of Catching Feelings* is such a lovingly constructed tribute to the range of emotions people experience in the modern world while falling in love. I read most of this book with my own heart in a desperate clutch of hope for Chris and Daphne, and when I finished, I sighed with perfect, pure fulfillment. I'm in no way ashamed to be cliché when I say that this book is the romance equivalent of a home run."

—Kate Clayborn, *USA Today* bestselling author of
The Other Side of Disappearing

Praise for

WITH LOVE, FROM COLD WORLD

"One of the most perfect books I've read this year . . . This exquisite book doesn't feel like it was written: It's as though it slowly coalesced, words drifting down like snowflakes until, suddenly, the whomping weight hits you like an avalanche."

—*The New York Times*

"An electric, utterly unique workplace romance that burrowed deep into my heart, starring polar opposites with off-the-charts sexual tension and a truly unforgettable setting that feels like a character in itself. *With Love, from Cold World* is a steamy delight sure to keep you warm all through the winter. I need everything Alicia Thompson writes beamed directly into my brain."

—Rachel Lynn Solomon, *New York Times* bestselling author of
Business or Pleasure

"Alicia Thompson writes stories that are so uniquely real to me, with characters who are flawed and lovable and achingly relatable, alongside writing that balances trauma and humor with incredible skill and heart. I was invested in Lauren, Asa, and the quirky world of Cold World from the jump, and I loved their story every step of the way. A new forever favorite."

—Anita Kelly, author of *Something Wild & Wonderful*

"With this swoony enemies-to-lovers rom-com, Thompson gets in well ahead of the annual slew of Christmas romances, taking readers to Florida's Cold World amusement park, where the winter holidays are celebrated year-round. . . . This will have readers dreaming of sugarplums at any time of year."

—*Publishers Weekly*

"*With Love, from Cold World*, appealing and funny, is a lovely romance, featuring bisexual representation, a cast of quirky characters, and the best kind of happily-ever-after. Somehow cozy and comforting in spite of its chilly setting and sexy scenes, this novel is bound to leave readers with a smile."

—Shelf Awareness

Praise for

LOVE IN THE TIME OF SERIAL KILLERS

"Unique, sexy, hilarious, charming, *Love in the Time of Serial Killers* is to die for: the perfect beach read for anyone who loves witty banter, intelligent plotting, and compelling characters. . . . The true crime is NOT reading this novel!"

—Ali Hazelwood, *New York Times* bestselling author of *Not in Love*

"A criminally addictive romance. With excellent wry humor, lovably messy characters, and so many heart-squeezing moments, this book is sheer perfection from beginning to end."
—Rachel Lynn Solomon, *New York Times* bestselling author of *Business or Pleasure*

"Phoebe is an immensely relatable and likable character, one whose prickly exterior hides a deep fear of vulnerability. It's a joy to watch her realize that the only thing scarier than a grisly murder is falling in love." —Kerry Winfrey, author of *Faking Christmas*

"Smart, clever, and slow-burn steamy, *Love in the Time of Serial Killers* is a fresh, lovable rom-com that tackles facing our fear of not only the worst life can bring but the very best and being brave enough to take a chance on love."
—Chloe Liese, author of *Better Hate than Never*

"*Love in the Time of Serial Killers* is funny, sharp, and thoughtful."
—Sarah Hogle, author of *Old Flames and New Fortunes*

"It's criminal how much we enjoyed *Love in the Time of Serial Killers*, the perfect pairing of intrigue with utterly charming romance and a deeply relatable story of how sometimes life's most complicated mystery is how to open your heart."
—Emily Wibberley and Austin Siegemund-Broka, authors of *The Breakup Tour*

"With toe curling swoons, witty banter, and enough true crime references to make Truman Capote proud, this is not one to be missed." —Sonia Hartl, author of *Rent to Be*

"Fans of Christina Lauren and Rachel Lynn Solomon will adore this ode to true crime and its poignant message of opening your heart to love, even when that's the scariest thing of all."

—Amy Lea, author of *The Catch*

"The perfect blend of romantic comedy and true crime you didn't know you needed. A charming and darkly funny read, this book is a love letter to murderinos, romancerinos, and those of us still trying to figure out who the heck we are."

—Nicole Tersigni, author of *Men to Avoid in Art and Life*

"Thompson's clever premise is a trendy hook for a romance that explores family, grief, and the relationships that define us."

—*Washington Independent Review of Books*

"The fast-paced plot is alternately hilarious and touching, and readers won't be able to put it down. True crime is an incredibly popular genre, and this book is a must-read for crossover romance fans."

—*Library Journal* (starred review)

"Highly recommended for romance readers who enjoy flirty dialogue, pop-culture references, strong female characters, and, of course, true crime."

—*Booklist* (starred review)

NEVER BEEN SHIPPED

ALICIA THOMPSON

BERKLEY ROMANCE
NEW YORK

BERKLEY ROMANCE
Published by Berkley
An imprint of Penguin Random House LLC
1745 Broadway, New York, NY 10019
penguinrandomhouse.com

Book design by Alison Cnockaert
Illustration on page viii by Jenifer Prince

Library of Congress Cataloging-in-Publication Data

Names: Thompson, Alicia, 1984- author.
Title: Never been shipped / Alicia Thompson.
Description: First edition. | New York: Berkley Romance, 2025.
Identifiers: LCCN 2024044546 (print) | LCCN 2024044547 (ebook) |
ISBN 9780593640951 (trade paperback) | ISBN 9780593640968 (ebook)
Subjects: LCGFT: Romance fiction. | Novels.
Classification: LCC PS3620.H64775 N48 2025 (print) | LCC PS3620.H64775
(ebook) | DDC 813/.6—dc23/eng/20241011
LC record available at https://lccn.loc.gov/2024044546
LC ebook record available at https://lccn.loc.gov/2024044547

First Edition: June 2025

Printed in the United States of America
1st Printing

The authorized representative in the EU for product safety and compliance is
Penguin Random House Ireland, Morrison Chambers, 32 Nassau Street, Dublin
D02 YH68, Ireland, https://eu-contact.penguin.ie.

if this flops i stg

AUTHOR'S NOTE

This book contains backstories involving an alcoholic parent, childhood physical abuse, an abusive/toxic romantic relationship, and threatened revenge porn.

PLAYLIST

THREE THINGS ABOUT THIS PLAYLIST YOU SHOULD KNOW:

- Each song pairs with its correspondingly numbered chapter in the book.

- Yes, there are a lot of Paramore/Hayley Williams tracks, but believe it or not this is what RESTRAINT looks like.

- Ten-minute songs are rough on playlists, but let's give an honorable mention to "Konstantine" by Something Corporate and especially the *long blond hair* part.

1: **"JOHNNY BOY"** by twenty one pilots

2: **"SMOKE SIGNALS"** by Phoebe Bridgers

3: **"ROUND HERE"** by Counting Crows

4: **"DEAD OAKS"** by Now, Now

5: **"SO JEALOUS"** by Tegan and Sara

6: **"FAKE HAPPY"** by Paramore

7: **"WE SINK"** by CHVRCHES

8: **"TO BE SO LONELY"** by Harry Styles

9: **"NERVOUS AT NIGHT"** by Charlie Hickey

NEVER BEEN SHIPPED

CHAPTER
ONE

JOHN DIDN'T *NEED* new strings. He could've easily bought them in the month he had before the cruise would set sail, could've ordered them online and had them waiting at the house by tomorrow morning. Hell, he probably had several unopened packets of strings already in his guitar case, or shoved deep in his underwear drawer, or slid carelessly somewhere under his bed.

It was a delay tactic. He knew it, and he didn't care.

The bell on the door to the music shop tinkled overhead as he stepped in, already comforted by being surrounded by instruments—the wall of electric guitars hung up for display, the row of amps to test out, the drum kits and xylophones and keyboards set up where kids wouldn't be able to help themselves when they walked by. The only downside was that his favorite clerk wasn't behind the counter, but that was okay. He'd be in and out.

Except John had never made a quick trip to a music store in his life, and he certainly wasn't going to start today, when the whole point was to put off the inevitable. He wandered over to the guitars, his eyes drawn to one with a sunburst paint job and a fifteen-hundred-dollar price tag. He took it down from the wall and plugged it into an amp.

"Sir?" The freckled clerk—he couldn't have been more than eighteen years old—came over before John even had time to play the *May I help you?* riff. "I'm sorry, sir, you're not supposed to touch the guitars."

John knew that. There was an index card with that very message printed on it, stuck between the strings. Sometimes John played around it if he was just looking to fuck off for a second, other times he removed it entirely if it was interfering with his ability to play.

"Sorry," he said. "Usually I come when Gary's here, and he always lets me get them down myself."

The clerk's face brightened for a second at the mention of Gary's name, then dropped again. "I get it, but customers really aren't allowed to—"

And then the clerk's face changed completely, and John knew with a sinking feeling exactly what was coming. As a teenager, John had been in a band that had released a couple albums, toured the world, and, most memorably, performed a song on-stage at a fictional prom for fictional shapeshifter characters in a TV show that aired at eight, seven Central.

"Wait, aren't you—I mean, weren't you—" The kid wouldn't be able to remember John's name. Probably he'd never known it. But that was the problem with appearing in a single episode of a popular TV show fifteen years ago, and also the problem with having his distinctive black curly hair. John got recognized a few times a year, which wasn't too bad, definitely wasn't as bad as it used to be, but was still a few times too many as far as he was concerned.

There was no point in denying it, though. John had tried that tactic a few times, and it was seldom convincing and only made him feel like a dick.

"John Populin," he said, reaching out his hand to shake the kid's. "I played guitar in ElectricOh! back in the day."

"You played *Nightshifters* prom," the kid said. "That song—"

And then, to John's horror, the kid started *singing* it. "If Only," the one hit from his one-hit-wonder band. The big, surging high notes all came in the bridge, but it was a low note at the end of the first verse that John had always thought was the sneaky hard one to nail. You almost had to half speak it, and done badly it could sound discordant, like you'd made a mistake.

When Micah sang it, it had always sounded like a warm, intimate purr directly in his ears, like he was listening to her voice through headphones even when she'd been projecting to the back of the venue.

"Yup, that's the one," John said now, cutting the kid off before he could get to the lyrics that still felt like a stab to his gut, even all these years later. "Surprised you watched that show. Seems a little before your time."

"Everything's streaming now. And my girlfriend watches all that old teen crap. The one about the brothers who hunt supernatural shit, the one about the brothers who play basketball, the one about the brothers who live in that sick house and the guy with the eyebrows plays their dad . . ."

"That's right, I'd forgotten Ryan got adopted."

The kid blinked down at John. "Huh?"

John didn't know why he was letting himself get drawn into this conversation. "That's a lot of brothers," he said instead, then gestured down at the guitar he was still holding. "Is this the only finish you have in stock for this one?"

"What you see is what we have," the kid said, which of course John had already known. He wasn't in the market for a new, expensive guitar anyway. John got by—he was still living off his royalties from "If Only," which he had a co-writing credit on, and then supplemented that income with various corporate events and weddings he played with one of his cover bands. He lived with housemates to split the rent, he stayed home most nights he didn't have a gig, he kept his wants and needs small enough that they didn't take up too much room.

He set the guitar carefully back up on the wall. The *Please ask a sales associate for assistance* card was a little askew, threaded between the strings, and so John nudged it straight again. *Strings.* He had come there for strings.

He didn't wear a watch and didn't feel like taking out his phone, but he probably only had forty-five minutes before the meeting at the record label's offices started, and he really didn't want to be late. He hated being late.

"Can I just get a couple sets of tens?" he asked the kid.

"Of course," the kid said. "Electric? We have D'Addario nickel-wound, we have—"

"That's fine."

The kid led him over to the front of the store, where he grabbed a couple packets from behind the counter and set them next to the cash register. "What are you playing now?" the kid asked as he started to ring John up. "Let me guess. A custom

Fender? A Les Paul? Wait, wait, one of those boutique brands, like a—"

"A Squier Telecaster, mostly."

The kid reacted to that like John had given him something sour to eat. A moment of surprise, then disgust, and then a badly masked neutrality like he wanted to spit it out but knew it wouldn't be polite. Probably the kid hadn't expected a rock star—even a former rock star—to admit to playing what was essentially a student guitar. The thing had come with a mini amp and a chord book, and had cost three hundred fifty-nine dollars after tax. John should know. It had taken him an entire summer of mowing lawns to save up for it.

He'd never been a rock star—certainly had never *felt* like one. Micah, on the other hand. She'd been a star from the moment he'd met her, with her long, sunset-colored hair and the way she lit up a room and the power she had to put everything she was feeling into her voice until you could feel it, too.

It had been thirteen years since he'd last been in the same room as her. Ten if you counted that concert in L.A.—which he didn't. He had no idea if she still wore her hair long, if she would light up when she saw him or shut all the way down, if she had anything to do with music anymore. But he guessed all it would take was another forty-five minutes or so, after he got his receipt for this transaction that was taking forever, after he jumped into his beat-up Camry and drove across town. After he arrived at the offices for the record label that made more money off his music than he did, which had cast him out like he was nothing after the band had blown up, which wanted him now to smile and play those old songs on a *Nightshifters* cruise in what they'd assured him over the phone was a "great opportunity."

After he sat down at a table across from people he hadn't seen in over a decade, but who'd once been the most important part of his life. After he saw *her*, who'd once been practically his whole life.

And then he'd finally know.

TWO

MICAH COULD TRIP into being ten minutes late for anything, but for this meeting? She'd given her rideshare driver a
generous tip to let her sit in the car for the extra fifteen minutes
it would take to ensure she was *really* late.

When Ian, the band's old rep at the record label, had contacted her about performing on this *Nightshifters* cruise, she'd
initially said no. Absolutely not. No way. She even hung up on
him, although she'd immediately felt bad and blamed it on poor
cell coverage when he'd called right back. He'd assured her that
the focus of the cruise would be on the show's cast reunion, and
that ElectricOh! would only have to perform a few songs for the
ship's "prom night," and that would be it.

"How does that sound?" Ian asked, a thread of desperation
in his voice. "Take a nice beach vacation, catch some sun, sing
a couple old ones, and then you're back on land and can return
to your real life."

"No."

Ian had named the sum of money the band would get for appearing on the cruise, which—even split five ways. Not bad.

It had been enough to make Micah hesitate just a little bit. Her "real life," after all, wasn't nearly as glamorous as people might think. She owned an apartment in L.A., which was something— paid for with royalties from the very song that got her this cruise opportunity in the first place. But the apartment sometimes felt more like Rapunzel's room at the top of the tower, and Micah was the princess who would sleep all day and only venture out at night to roam around a harshly lit drugstore where she could pretend to be a normal person just making an emergency run for tampons.

Micah was mixing up her fairy tales. She couldn't remember the one that involved CVS.

"No, thank you," she'd said to Ian, and then offered a quick goodbye to send the message not to call back.

Of course, the next phone call had been from her father. Or not really her *father*, since he'd called in his capacity as band manager for ElectricOh!. She'd made that mistake before.

"You're doing this cruise," he'd said without preamble. "You need to do something with your life—and before you start, you know Hailey appreciates your help with her salon, but she can hire her own people. That's not where you belong and you know it."

The past few years, Micah had been flying back to Ohio to spend weeks at a time helping her younger sister open her own hair salon. It hadn't been particularly grueling work—slapping a new coat of paint on a wall, organizing supplies, driving around town to drop off stacks of glossy postcards advertising the salon's services. Micah had even let Hailey blow up poster-sized images showing off Micah's hair to put in the shop, which wasn't a hardship because Hailey'd always done a great job and Micah loved her sister . . . but which had still made her feel weird and sad in some indescribable way, seeing her smiling face plastered on the walls.

And that was just about some fucking *pictures* in a hair salon, so how much worse would it be to do this cruise, with all the renewed attention it might bring? But because Micah always felt sixteen again the minute she got on the phone with her father, she'd at least heard him out. "And consider your bandmates," he'd said. "You don't think they might be able to use this opportunity? I know they weren't happy with the way things ended, but this could be a chance to put some of that to bed. Ryder and Frankie are still in the industry, and then there's that boy who practically lived at our house—"

"Okay," she'd said finally, as much to get him to stop talking as because she knew he was right. "Okay, I'll do it."

Since then, the scope of the cruise had ballooned a little—per the contract, they were now committed to *two* performances, a short set and then the one song at prom night, and were also supposed to host "two (2) Activities to be named at a later date, but in no event to last longer in duration than two (2) hours each, with the Band to have final approval over the Activities, such approval not to be unreasonably withheld."

Contracts weren't supposed to be funny, but that line had made her laugh. *Approval not to be unreasonably withheld.* What a joke. She'd scrolled to the bottom to see the digital signatures already added—Steve, their happy-go-lucky drummer; Frankie, the bassist and all-around comforting presence; and Ryder, the lead guitarist and her ex, topping the list of reasons why she hadn't wanted to do this cruise in the first place.

Micah had at least gotten to a point in her life where just seeing his name wasn't a jump scare, so that was something. Publicly, his narrative had become that ElectricOh! broke up because no one else in the band cared about the *music* the way he did, which used to make her blood boil and now just made her laugh. She was glad that their romantic relationship had never been officially confirmed, so she could sidestep any questions with coy non-answers without going into all of it. How stupid she'd been to let herself get caught up in him, how stupid she still felt for not extricating herself earlier, for the sake of the band if nothing else. Maybe she could've cut out the rot before it spread.

The only ones who hadn't signed the contract yet were her and John.

John. He'd been her best friend once. Now she had no idea what he even *looked* like, if he bothered to run a comb through his unruly dark hair, if he'd filled out or if he was still all knobby elbows and too-long legs, if he'd ever managed to grow a beard like he used to desperately want to. "My family's Italian," he'd say. "It's my birthright."

And she would've made an Olive Garden joke because they'd had a whole bit, and he would've grabbed her around the waist and threatened to tickle her, which was such a farce because she knew *he* was the ticklish one, if you could get him around the neck . . .

It had been a long time since she'd allowed herself to think about John like *that*, dredging up the visceral memories that could make her feel like she was right back in seventh-grade homeroom. And it had been even longer since she'd felt like she'd had anyone in her life that she knew that well, who knew her, who she had that kind of shorthand with, who she'd been able to be completely and utterly herself with.

Now the driver spared her a glance in the rearview mirror before making a not-so-surreptitious grimace at the blinking app open on his phone screen. "Uh, miss?" he said. "There are other requests coming in, so . . ."

Micah looked out the window at the nondescript concrete building that housed Tasteless Art Studios, the niche subsidiary of a major record label that had given them their start sixteen years ago. The building hadn't changed at all, which seemed impossible. She hadn't seen anyone walking up to it in a while, which she hoped meant that everyone involved in today's meeting would already be inside.

"One more minute," she said. "Promise."

WHEN MICAH FINALLY walked into the building, she immediately saw everyone there for the meeting through the open glass wall of the main conference room. She would've preferred a more private space—she'd feel like she was in a fishbowl the entire time they were talking—but she supposed there was a benefit to it now that she was on the outside looking in.

Ryder had taken a seat in the center, which she knew he'd done on purpose, and was talking animatedly to a woman with red lipstick next to him who Micah didn't recognize. Must be one of the label reps. Ryder looked exactly as she'd expected him to, but then of course he did—she'd kept up with him a bit, watched a few of his new band's music videos. She told herself she kept tabs on him in a self-defense sort of way, in the same manner you might track a spider you weren't going to kill but didn't want to bite you again. But then she would also sometimes click back and forth between those new videos and ElectricOh!'s old ones, getting a sick thrill when she compared how many views each had. She was positive he'd kept tabs on her in the same way, could probably tell her more about how badly her solo singles had charted compared to her contemporaries than she allowed her own self to admit.

Across from him was someone whose back was to Micah, but who from the big hair and swinging earrings she already knew was Frankie, the band's bassist. Of all the people she'd lost touch with, Frankie was probably the most inexplicable. They'd been close while in the band together, and Frankie had reached out to Micah several times after everything had exploded. Frankie had been collateral damage, an unfortunate victim of Micah deciding to go scorched earth and start completely over. It hadn't been fair, and Micah wondered how things could've been different if she'd just once picked up her phone and texted to say, Hey, thinking of you, let's hang out. She bet Frankie would've.

At one end of the table, as if leading the meeting, was Steve, the band's drummer. She recognized him because he looked exactly the same, just a little softer around the edges and with the ripped cargo shorts he used to wear traded out for a pair of businesslike khakis. Somehow she knew that he'd chosen his seat not because he actually *wanted* to be at the head of the table but just because he was oblivious to any implications a particular seat might have.

John wasn't there, which must mean he wasn't coming. Her heart had been beating fast—not panic attack fast, but close—and suddenly she felt it slow down, almost abruptly, the way a roller-coaster ride flipped you upside down one minute and the next an apathetic employee was lifting the safety bar and ushering you out.

"Feel free to take a seat anywhere," the receptionist said now, smiling at Micah as she led her into the room. "And help yourself to a water, something from the fruit and cheese plate . . . just let us know if we can get you anything else."

Micah thought about grabbing a bottled water, but it felt somehow close to showing weakness. She realized how stupid that was the minute she sat down and immediately wished she had a drink. Ryder must've clocked that she took a seat next to Frankie instead of the open one next to him, and he was smirking at her from across the table. God, he had a punchable face.

It was an attractive face. She could admit that. There was a reason she'd felt pulled to him back when they were teenagers, had let herself get caught up in their relationship even though she knew it wasn't good—not for the band, and especially not for her. He had floppy dark blond hair that fell over his forehead, piercing blue eyes, and the perfect aristocratic nose of the kind of guy who played tennis in the summer and skied in the winter. When you looked like *that* and you played lead guitar in a band, you could get any girl you wanted. And somehow, Micah had been flattered that he'd wanted her.

"Where's John?" Micah asked, and immediately wished the question back. Another sign of weakness.

"He told me he was coming," Frankie said, and why did that send a kick to Micah's stomach, a flutter of . . . what? Jealousy?

Hurt? That he and Frankie were obviously close enough to still talk, to check in with each other?

"He'll be here any minute," the woman Micah didn't recognize said. She couldn't tell if that was an assumption, or something that the woman knew for sure. Either way, she was already starting to pass around a sheaf of papers to each person, leaving an extra one at the empty place next to Ryder. "In the meantime, let's go ahead and get started. I know everyone has a busy schedule."

Micah's schedule consisted of taking this meeting, catching an early-morning flight from Orlando back to L.A. tomorrow, and then sitting cross-legged on her bed, listening to a podcast while making friendship bracelets she kept in an empty guitar case in her closet. The friendship bracelet trend had passed and still she couldn't stop making them—there was something soothing about it, to her, stringing little beads along a piece of nylon, making the same words and color combinations over and over.

"I'm Roberta Dresser, but you can call me Bobbi," the woman said, giving a little wink, like she was somehow letting them into a very exclusive club instead of just . . . introducing herself by the name she wanted to be called. "I'm the publicity coordinator for this *Nightshifter* cruise, and I'll be your main point of contact both off and on the ship. We know we've already been discussing some of these logistics via email, but we figured the best way to make sure everyone was on the same page was to have at least one meeting face-to-face before we set sail. We appreciate Tasteless Art for hosting us here, and all of you for coming out."

In other words, they were concerned about inviting the band

on a cruise ship without verifying that they could all be in the same room together first. Which, fair.

"If you turn to the second page in your packet, you'll see the itinerary for the cruise laid out. Now, there could be minor adjustments made up to the last minute, but this should give you some idea—"

Micah tuned her out as she scanned down the schedule. The parts that ElectricOh! were responsible for were helpfully highlighted on the printout—hosting a bingo game and playing a mini set on the second day, playing in a midnight shuffleboard tournament, and then, of course, prom on the last night of the cruise. It depressed her, how *fun* it all sounded. How much of a blast it probably would've been, had it been under different circumstances. If the band had lasted all this time, if they were the kids who'd started it in the first place, if they were grown-ass adults who'd moved on with their lives but were excited for the chance to live out a nostalgic fantasy.

Of course, maybe some other members of the band were better adjusted than she was.

"Shuffleboard!" Steve crowed, blatantly interrupting Bobbi but seeming not to notice. "Oh shit. That's kinda like bowling, right, because I *kill* at bowling. I scored two hundred just last week with my league."

"Did you have the bumpers up?" Frankie asked with raised eyebrows but no particular malice. Steve laughed good-naturedly, and it gave Micah whiplash, just how quickly they could seem to slide back into their old dynamics.

Bobbi showed her first crack, though, looking briefly uncomfortable while she glanced from Steve to Frankie and then back to the paper. "Well, not all band members are needed for all activities. We need three of you for bingo, but only two of you will compete in shuffleboard, and for the performances . . ."

Micah squinted down at the schedule again. The only song they were performing on prom night was "If Only," and if they were going to perform it like they had on the TV show, that would mean it would be just Ryder and John with her out there, playing their acoustic guitars. Which meant that the entire band had been invited on this cruise . . . to play a few songs on an off night.

"You can absolutely take my spot in shuffleboard," she said to Steve, trying to give him a smile she hoped looked genuine.

"Ah," Bobbi said, "the contract does specify which members are necessary for certain activities. Remember that the—"

"*This* certainly feels familiar," Ryder drawled from across the table. "Just like old times, right?"

Her gaze shot to his, and he pursed his lips in challenge. It had been one of their biggest arguments as a band—probably the one that had been their death knell from the very beginning. As the lead singer, and a girl, Micah had always been singled out for attention from the media, fans, music critics, you name it. She hadn't asked for it, she hadn't wanted it, she hadn't even *liked* it, but there had only been so much she could do about it.

"You immediately finding a way to shit on everything?" Micah said before she could stop herself. "Totally, it's a real blast from the past."

Ryder raised his eyebrows. She'd played right into his hands with that one, and she knew it. He was spoiling for a fight. "Oh, *I* shit on everything? That's funny. The last time we were in this building I seem to remember—"

"Enough," Frankie said, then spoke louder when Ryder kept

talking. "*Enough.* Cut it out. Let Bobbi get through it all and then we can figure out who's responsible for what."

"Frankie's right," Ryder said, as though he hadn't been one of the people being addressed in the first place. "I mean, I know it's some female solidarity thing, the way she's always stood up for you—"

"They," Frankie said.

Ryder blinked. "What?"

"I'm not *she*, I'm *they*."

"Well, how was I supposed to know that?"

Frankie gave him a placid look that seemed to convey simultaneously a supreme peace and also a *do not fuck with me* vibe. Micah wished she knew how to look like that. "I didn't say you were supposed to know it. I simply corrected you so that you would know it now. Anyway, Bobbi, you were saying?"

"Uh." Bobbi licked the tips of her fingers, ruffling through the pages in front of her more like she didn't know what else to do than like she was looking for something specific. *We've broken her,* Micah thought. *Five minutes in the room with us and we've already broken her.* She felt the sudden inappropriate urge to laugh.

"I just think if this is going to be the Micah Presley Show we should all know that going in," Ryder said. "I need to know where to stand so they can cut me out of photos later."

"Oh my god," Micah burst out. "That was *one* magazine cover, *fifteen years ago*, could you please—"

"I'll stand wherever you need me," Steve put in helpfully. "Or sit. Since I'm the drummer. I'm usually sitting."

"Technically, this show is none of ours," Frankie said. "It's a *Nightshifters* cruise, in case you all haven't clocked the logo at the top of these sheets. We played one song on a TV show and now they're asking us to play it again over international waters while people are, I don't know, dressed in shapeshifter cosplay or something. We're not even the main band! I think we could all stand to get over ourselves."

"Easy," Ryder said. "Already done."

Frankie leveled him with a look. "Is it? Can you honestly swear to me that you're over yourself?"

He held up three fingers in a Boy Scout salute. Or else he was doing the thing from *The Hunger Games*. Either way, Micah didn't trust it for a second.

But then Frankie turned to her, and although their face wasn't unkind, it was also very serious. "And you? Are you over yourself yet?"

Oooof. That *yet*. If Micah had wondered if Frankie held any of it against her, everything that had gone down, she supposed that was an answer. They had to, at least a little.

"Yes," Micah said.

"I'm over myself," Steve put in. "I sell laptops at Best Buy and my kid's only three and covers his ears and yells 'No punk music!' if I put on anything in the car that's not a cartoon movie soundtrack."

Frankie smiled. Steve was never the problem, and they all knew it. He had the most easygoing personality combined with the most surprising ability to destroy a drum set with how hard he hit it. "Truly humbling. I can promise—"

And just when Micah was wondering again, *Where the fuck is John?*, suddenly there he was. She'd turned her seat so she could better face Roberta as she spoke, and out of the corner of her eye she saw him burst through the front door of the building, nodding quickly and saying something to the receptionist, who'd half-risen from her seat. He'd always had an almost preternatural *stillness* about him, a way of being able to just *be*, quietly observing without giving away much of what he was feeling. It was only onstage that he seemed to vibrate with energy, lost in his own world as he played his guitar, moving with the music. She felt now like she'd gotten a glimpse of something she wasn't supposed to, able to see him through the glass as he paused for just a moment before opening the door to the conference room. He gave his armpit a discreet sniff, which made her smile. And then he ran his hand through his dark hair—it was still a little unruly after all, the curls grown out enough that they fell over his eyes. *John.*

She was still smiling a little when he opened the door to the conference room, causing everyone to look up. The hair was the same, but he was different in so many subtle ways. He was still lean—he'd been skinnier than she was, when they were kids—but his shoulders were broader, a wiry strength in his forearms and biceps where they strained against the sleeves of his plain white T-shirt. That was different, too. She couldn't remember ever seeing him wear a color other than black, but here he was, the surprise of that white shirt so stark it made her suddenly have all kinds of fanciful thoughts, like that he was an actual angel sent to save her.

An *angel*. Because he'd shown up in a white T-shirt. It was ridiculous, not least because the closer Micah looked, it was obvious that he hadn't even bothered to dress up for this occasion. The shirt looked like one of those that you get out of a pack of five, and there was a smear of something black around the bottom edge. A smear of something on his gray pants, too, which had a rip in one knee. His chest was rising and falling quickly, like he was out of breath, and his cheeks were flushed. Her own lungs felt suddenly tight, which must be a sympathy thing.

"Sorry," he said, glancing around the room. His gaze skimmed over her so quickly she barely even knew if he'd *seen* her, and that suddenly annoyed her more than anything else.

He'd shown up almost an hour late, looking like *that*, and all he had to say for himself was *Sorry*? What about some kind of explanation? What about something more personal, *anything*, that would give her an idea what he might be thinking, if he'd noticed her at all, if he'd thought about her in the years that had passed?

"We were just discussing whether we were over ourselves," Frankie said dryly. "How about it, John?"

He'd stopped by the door where the snacks were set up, reaching for a water. "How about what?"

"Are you over yourself?" Frankie said. "We've got a full commitment from everyone but you so far."

John had to pass by Micah to get to his seat, and she turned her head, holding her breath even though she didn't know why. Because she was waiting to see how he'd answer? Because she was overwhelmed by being suddenly in the same room with him, by having him mere inches behind her chair, when for years he'd felt as inaccessible to her as if he'd lived on the moon?

Probably because he was sweaty and she didn't want to get a whiff. That was all it was.

She let herself exhale when he'd taken his seat, and it was only then that she noticed there was a bottled water sitting right in front of her, where there hadn't been one before. She hadn't seen John place it there, but that was the only explanation. Her gaze shot up to his face, wanting some confirmation, but his head was tilted back, his Adam's apple bobbing as he drank down half his own water in a series of gulps.

Look at me, she thought. *Goddamn it*, look *at me.*

He finally set the bottle down on the table, his bottom lip still wet when he ran his tongue over it. "Yes," he said. "One hundred percent."

He directed his words to Frankie, but then he was catching Steve's eye, returning a smile. Ryder was right next to him, but he didn't turn to acknowledge him in any way, although maybe Micah was reading into that. He glanced over at Bobbi, seeming to understand by process of elimination that she was the one running the meeting. He cleared his throat, sliding the papers in front of him closer.

And then, in a suspended moment that sent a shiver down Micah's spine, even though she'd expected it, even though she'd been trying to *will* it to happen—he looked right at her. She felt the years between them in that one look, was somehow able to flash back to the very first time they'd met in seventh-grade homeroom, then through the rest of it—the friendship and the band and the aftermath and the long, lonely years that had unspooled from there, bringing them back to this moment right here.

"I'm over all of it," John said.

CHAPTER
THREE

JOHN WANTED TO drink her in like the water he'd just gulped down. But he knew he had only about three seconds before he made it weird, so he tried to take in everything at once so he could move on.

Three. Her strawberry-blond hair was tucked up in a bun at the back of her head, a little askew, like maybe she'd been resting against the car seat on the way over here. He assumed it was still long—longish, at least, long enough to put up in a bun—but not the waist-length hair she'd been known for during ElectricOh!'s height. When he'd walked behind her, she'd turned her head, giving him the perfect view of the tendrils that had slipped out, the dandelion tattoo half-hidden under the collar of her shirt, bits of the fluff going up her neck.

Two. Her nails were still ragged around the cuticles and bitten down to the quick, only a few small chips of black to suggest she'd once had them painted. She used to paint her nails all the time on the bus, opening a window to waft out the smell, although it would still linger. She said she did it to stop herself from chewing on them, but it never seemed to work.

One. She was looking right back at him, the directness in her sea-glass-green eyes almost a challenge.

John dropped his gaze first, pretending to study the papers in front of him before his eyes focused and he got pulled into reading them for real. There was a full itinerary for the cruise, which already seemed like too much—the band would play twice, a three-song set and then "If Only" during the prom on the last night of the cruise.

Bingo? he mouthed to himself.

He felt at a disadvantage, coming in so late, because it was obvious that they'd discussed some of this before he got there. He'd had ample time to get to the record label office after leaving the music shop, but then he'd stopped at a traffic light and noticed the temperature gauge in his car creeping over the red line. He'd tried every trick he could think of—changed his route to minimize the number of lights he would hit, turned the heat in the car all the way up and rolled down his windows to compensate. He'd sweated all the way through the nicer button-up shirt he'd decided to wear for this meeting, and then gotten grease all over it when he'd used it like a rag while checking out his engine, which was too hot to do anything with, anyway. Eventually, he'd left his car on the side of the road and walked the last two miles.

"There are other optional activities," the woman with the bright red lipstick was saying. "Like it would be great if you'd make an appearance at the opening-night panel. There will be a section cordoned off for all the talent so you'll be able to watch without worrying about being bothered by anyone. There will be official photographers who work for the cruise company on the ship, taking pictures for the website and other—"

"Oh, Micah loves pictures," Ryder said from next to John. "Don't you?"

John had never been a fighter. He'd spent his childhood trying to make himself as small and quiet as possible, wanting to *avoid* a fight. If his dad could forget that he existed, then maybe he couldn't hurt him. Even times when he'd gotten picked on in school, he'd always found other ways to deal with it. He'd refused to react, ignoring the bullies until they left him alone, or else he'd worked around it, taking another route to the bus stop, finding another place to sit at lunch, whatever it took.

But god, he thought it might feel incredible to punch Ryder right in that smug little mouth. Just once.

He glanced across the table at Micah, expecting to see a storm in her eyes. She'd always had the most expressive face. But she was looking down, intent on some doodle she was drawing on the paper in front of her.

She used to fill in the open parts of letters on every handout a teacher gave them, sometimes in the textbooks themselves. Once she'd gotten in-school suspension for drawing on a desk, and he'd "broken" her out of the classroom where kids were sequestered for that purpose so that she could eat lunch at their usual table. They'd really thought they were getting away with something, but only now did he realize the teacher had probably just been too apathetic to care.

He and Micah had met first. With two last names starting with *P*, they'd been in the same homeroom from seventh grade through sophomore year of high school, which was the last one they'd attended before the band had taken off and they'd finished their education with a combination of virtual classes and tutors.

"Micah Presley—no relation," she'd said to introduce herself, and then, when John hadn't immediately replied, "Elvis? He was a—"

"Singer from the fifties," he'd said. "I know."

"Well, spanning a few decades, technically," Micah had said. "But yeah. And you are?"

Maybe memory had exaggerated his recollection of the awkward length of his silence after her question, when he'd just stared at her, but he didn't think so. It was less that he didn't know about Elvis—although he was nowhere near the expert Micah was, he'd learn later; she was low-key obsessed because of the name thing. And certainly less that he didn't know his *own* name, which he'd been carrying around for twelve years, the junior of another John Populin—very *much* a relation, he was sorry to say, when he had to call the local bar to see if that was where his dad was. It was more that he was so used to sitting in the back of classes, a novel tucked into his textbooks, ignored by teachers and students alike. He could go whole days without saying a single word at school. And here was this strange girl, this strange and almost impossibly beautiful girl, just . . . talking to him?

It had been two weeks before he'd gotten up the nerve to tell her his name.

Micah had met Frankie later, in high school, and had encouraged them to learn the bass specifically because she and John had talked about starting a band. It was a joke at first, mostly an excuse to come up with funny or lewd potential band names, but quickly became serious before they'd even written a song together. They'd found Steve after Micah asked around if anyone knew a really good drummer, and someone had seen him play a basement show with his punk band.

Then it was Steve who'd brought in Ryder, a guy he knew from around the music scene. He'd been the last to join the band but, at three years older than the rest of them, already a senior and with way more experience playing in other bands, it wasn't long before he became the lead guitarist and the de facto leader. John hadn't minded that at the time. He just wanted to play.

"No rehearsal," Micah said now, cutting into his thoughts. He realized he'd missed the last couple minutes of what they'd been talking about, but Micah's pronouncement had obviously come as a shock, because everyone was just staring at her.

She cleared her throat. "We can practice our parts separately, and then find a few hours to rehearse together once we're on the boat. I don't see any reason to do more."

Frankie frowned. "I think we're going to need more rehearsal than that. We haven't played as a group in—"

"To be honest," Steve said, cracking his knuckles, "the less PTO I have to use, the better. Although I don't think I'm getting paid for it. At least not by Best Buy. Wait, does it count as PTO if someone else pays for it?"

"I don't want to do this if we're not going to *sound* good," Ryder said. "I'm not looking to be a joke."

The *again* hung in the air, unspoken. Their last show had been so colossally, excruciatingly awful that John found it hard to laugh about, even after all this time.

"Tasteless Art has a rehearsal room right here that we've reserved," the woman running the meeting put in helpfully. "But

we can book something in L.A. if that would be more convenient for everyone. We just thought, since the cruise is leaving
out of Miami, it would make sense to spend a few days—"

"No rehearsal," Micah said. "That's a dealbreaker for me.
We're only playing a few songs, we can figure them out on the
boat."

Everyone was looking at him now, and John realized he was
the only one who hadn't weighed in. Truthfully, it wasn't like he
had anything going on. He hated agreeing with Ryder on anything, but he also didn't particularly want to sound bad, didn't
want to have this possibly last experience of playing ElectricOh!
songs live be anything but smooth and perfect. On top of all of
that, the original rehearsal location was the most convenient for
John, since he'd somehow come to Orlando for that last band
meeting and had fallen into still living there thirteen years later.

"Fine by me," he said. "No rehearsal."

CHAPTER

FOUR

BY THE END, the meeting felt like eight hours had passed and
also no time at all, both like they covered a lot of ground and
like the whole thing could've been an email. Micah was exhausted and looking forward to getting to her hotel room and
falling into bed before catching an early-morning flight out of
there.

She could sense that Ryder was waiting for her, wanting to
grab a private moment after everyone else had cleared out, so
she went to the bathroom and stayed long enough that she felt
confident he'd given up. She tried to refresh her makeup in the
mirror, only to smudge it worse than before. In the end, she
washed it all off so she could apply it again.

She'd dressed for the meeting very deliberately, like she was
preparing to go into battle. Just enough of the pop star glamour
that she could feel a little powerful, like she could hide behind
the stagecraft of winged eyeliner and platform boots. Just
enough no-nonsense styling—her long hair in a bun, her cloth-

ing modest enough to cover most of her tattoos—that she made it clear she knew this was a business venture first and foremost.

Except her bun had gotten a little messed up on the car ride over, and now she winced when she considered herself in the mirror. Had that been how she'd looked the entire time?

She snagged the elastic out of her hair, letting the strands hang loose around her shoulders. Somehow, over the years, her hair had become more than just *hair*—it was a lightning rod for other people's attitudes toward her, the ultimate expression of her emotional state, one more way that she felt controlled and one more way that she asserted control. She couldn't help a twisted smile, even remembering the time she'd hacked it all off to her chin and dyed it black, just before touring had begun for ElectricOh!'s doomed second album. The record label had actually threatened legal action. Something about a clause in the contract with an amorphous reference to anything that lost "audience goodwill." Over fucking hair.

She ran her fingers through it now, pulling it up into a ponytail and giving herself one last look over before venturing out of the bathroom. The receptionist gave Micah a smile as she made her way to the front door.

"You know, I was a big fan of *So Much Promise*," the receptionist said, referring to Micah's solo record. A terrible choice for a title, because it had made the bad reviews all riff off how Micah had had *so much promise*, and what happened? Which the receptionist undoubtedly knew, judging from the slight emphasis on the *I* in that sentence. *I* was a big fan. An acknowledgment that she knew she was in a select group of people who felt that way.

Hell, *Micah* hadn't been a fan of that fucking record.

"Thanks," she said, reaching into her bag for her sunglasses. "Appreciate it."

A quick scan of the parking lot showed that everyone seemed to have left, and Micah felt her shoulders relax as she pulled out her phone to order a rideshare. But then she noticed John, standing at the edge of the parking lot, his own phone pressed to his ear as he laughed at something someone said. *Laughed.*

He'd been so serious in the meeting. She remembered that side of John, the quiet one that took a while to crack. But she remembered this other side, too, the one that had been slyly funny and quick to break with one goofy look from her across the room. She wondered who was making him laugh like that now, who'd earned the right to his inside jokes and his most private smiles.

She felt suddenly so alone. So obviously, stupidly, pathetically *alone*, hiding out in bathrooms and in her apartment and in all these rules she'd created for herself around her life where she never let anyone get too close. Her last somewhat serious relationship had been with a woman who'd worked a high-powered job in tech, and she'd never understood why Micah had walked away from a career that seemed like a dream. *Because I kept failing*, Micah had said, and Liz had looked at her like she was defective. "Failure is a mindset," she'd said. "I don't believe in failure. Only in opportunities to innovate."

In a perfect world, Micah would've delivered her exit line then, something about how maybe they should innovate their way right into breaking up. But instead she'd just kept dating Liz for another two months, feeling increasingly bad about herself. And then after that relationship had ended, she'd gone on a series of self-destructive dates with anyone who said they wanted to meet up and weren't looking for anything serious, almost like she was challenging them to treat her like she was something disposable, then turning around and feeling hurt when they did.

And now here she was, standing alone in this parking lot, her phone in her hand, and John was over there *laughing* with someone. It made her angry, and she didn't know why.

She slid her phone back in her bag, heading across the parking lot toward John. She caught only a snippet of his conversation—"don't worry about it, it's fine"—before he turned. She tried not to take it personally, the way his face tightened up the moment he saw her, the way his mouth went back to a straight line. But damn.

She took it personally.

"All right," John said into the phone. "I'll let you go." His gaze swept over Micah, from the top of her head where the ponytail was pulled tight down to the tattoo at her neck. Then he looked down at his own shoes, kicking a piece of gravel out of the way. "Yup. I'll see you at home. No, no, don't watch without me. Couple hours, tops."

No *I love you* to end the conversation, but there had been an easy familiarity that still spoke of someone he knew well, and cared about. Someone he lived with, who he shared TV shows with. *I'll see you at home.*

"You live here?" she asked, not meaning the question to come out so snotty but landing somewhere in that vicinity anyway.

"Yeah."

"Convenient."

He just looked at her, and she immediately saw how stupid that had been to say, too. What, like she thought he'd stayed in the same city as their record label just on the off chance that over a decade later, they might schedule a meeting and he'd be able to roll right out of bed and drive a couple blocks over?

"You'd think you'd be able to make the meeting on time, then," she added, suddenly considering that side of things. He'd been the only one of them who *hadn't* had to catch a flight for this thing, and he'd been the one to arrive way past fashionably late. "What happened to putting the *punk* in *punctuality*?"

"What?"

"That's what you used to say, when—" She sighed. "Never mind."

He put his hands in his pockets, rocking back a little on his heels.

"Where are you living now?" he asked. "L.A.?"

There was no real curiosity in his tone, which rankled her. Just a neutral politeness, like he was going through the motions of small talk at a dinner party.

"Still L.A.," she said. "We can't all make big changes, I guess."

His brow furrowed, like he didn't get that, and she gestured toward him. "Orlando," she said. "The white shirt. I'm pretty sure you're taller."

"The white—" He glanced down at himself, like he was only just realizing what he was wearing. She wished she hadn't mentioned it. It felt too revealing, that she'd even noticed. "I doubt I'm taller. *You're* taller."

"It's the shoes," she said, and then before she had time to think how strange it would be to do, she leaned down to unzip the sides, stepping out of them until she was standing in her socked feet on the pavement. She took a step toward John, to where her toes almost touched the fronts of his Converse, the top of her head at his eye level. Micah had always been tall, for a woman—with the shoes they'd been almost exactly the same height, but now he had a couple inches on her five-ten frame.

He didn't smell like sweat. He smelled like . . . John. She didn't even know how to describe it, but it was instantly familiar to her, from all those times they'd sat next to each other on a couch, all the times he'd leaned over her, crossing a song off the set list and writing another one in its place.

All the times they'd slept together. Literally *slept*—Micah had always struggled with insomnia, but for whatever reason she'd had an easier time on the nights when John had opened his hotel room door and let her slide into bed with him. Occasional naps on the bus, curled onto the same tiny bunk. That had all ended, of course, once she'd started dating Ryder. Then she'd always had someone to share a bed with, and yet it had never felt quite the same.

There'd been a time when she could've buried her hands in his hair to mess it up, to brush it out, just because she *felt* like it. She had the strongest urge to do it now, just to reach up and tousle his already tousled curls, to stretch one out and see it spring back into place. She had the strongest urge to run her hands along his broad shoulders, like she was an aunt marveling at how much her nephew had grown since last Christmas, like she was a wife checking the fit of a suit before a big presentation at work. She wanted to know if she could still get him to giggle if she found the spot right under his ear. She wanted to know if he ever let himself cry, the way she'd only seen him do once when they were thirteen and then never again after.

"What else?" John said.

Her mouth was suddenly dry, and she sucked in her bottom lip, running her tongue over it. John tracked the movement, and when his gaze lifted back up his brown eyes looked darker somehow, closer to black. Had he been reading her mind?

"What else what?"

"You still live in L.A., you're still just as tall," he said. "What else hasn't changed? Give me one more."

Micah felt like her life had been stagnant for so long, but put on the spot she couldn't think of a single thing to say. "I still like pineapple on my pizza."

That caused a sudden grin to flash across his face, gone so fast she could've blinked and missed it. But she knew if she closed her eyes she'd see the afterimage, would feel the warm glow of triumph in her chest later.

"I do, too, now," he said. "My—yeah, I came around."

What had he been about to say? His girlfriend? His *wife*? She couldn't help but notice that he didn't wear a ring—she'd fixated a lot on people's hands during the meeting, watching them flip through the papers, gesture while the person was speaking, tap impatiently on the table (that was Steve, so to be fair, maybe less impatience than the fact that he was always tapping on *something*). Steve was the only one of them who seemed to have gotten married in the intervening years, although Micah supposed there was a possibility that some people had gotten divorced, or just didn't wear a ring.

She almost asked John outright, but of course it wasn't any business of hers. So what if he was dating someone. They had never been that to each other, anyway, and for over a decade they hadn't been anything.

"What else?" she asked instead.

"Orlando, white shirt, pineapple," he said, counting them off on his fingers. "Those are my three things."

"Give me three that *haven't* changed."

"My height," he said, which made her roll her eyes. Yes, they'd covered that. "I still play a *mean* guitar, if I do say so myself."

She smiled. "I bet you do." And truthfully, she'd never doubted it. If there was one person she trusted implicitly to keep it all together on the cruise, to stand exactly where he was supposed to and play every note pitch perfect, it was John.

"And I still . . ." He trailed off, staring down at her. His expression had barely changed, and yet she *felt* like something had shifted, but she didn't know what. His lips were slightly parted, his eyes so close she could see the flecks of gold in his irises. She wanted him to say something *real*, something that would crack them wide open, that mattered more than just preferred pizza toppings or where they were living now.

He let out a breath. "I still don't get it," he said. "The thing with Elvis."

She tried to smile at that one, too, but it felt a little twisted and false. "Well," she said. "No accounting for taste."

FIVE

EVEN WITHOUT REHEARSALS, the month between that meeting and the start of the cruise flew by. John practiced every day, holing himself up in his room and running through every song in ElectricOh!'s limited catalog, even ones he knew there was no chance they'd bother to play. It was as much an exercise in remembering as it was an exercise in learning anew, and he was surprised at how *good* it started to feel, playing all these old songs he hadn't let himself think about in so long.

Now, the day before the ship was going to set sail, all he had to do was finish packing. He had three guitars—two acoustic and one electric—and an undoubtedly overkill supply of accessories and extras, from his pedal board to tuners to patch cords to strings. He'd focused so much on the music side of things, he'd barely started packing anything else.

"Easy." One of his housemates, Asa, had wandered into John's room to help, although so far he'd been less than helpful. He was standing in front of John's closet now, pretending to survey the outfit choices even though John had always used the closet more for instrument storage than anything else. It was a disaster at the moment, picked through and piled up and all disorganized compared to how he usually kept it. "For the first day, you're going to want to wear something black. For the second day, I'm thinking . . . hmm, maybe black? Then the third day, well, everyone knows it's good luck to wear black. Now the fourth day is the big show, right? You're going to want to make a statement, so . . ."

Asa turned, his eyebrows raised expectantly. John huffed out a laugh, unable to resist playing along. "Black again?"

Asa ran his hand through his hair, like he was really considering that one. He cycled through hair colors and styles more than anyone else John knew, and right now it was a faded pink he was debating whether to re-dye or grow out. "Could work. Do you have an LBD in here?"

All John's clothes were in his dresser, so he opened the second drawer, sifting through the folded-up T-shirts. "I do wear other colors, you know."

Asa gave a pointed look at the open drawer, which, okay, happened to contain almost entirely black shirts. John came across one that was dark gray, and would've held it up as proof except even he knew that was a stretch.

Hadn't Micah made a similar comment? Something about the white shirt he'd worn to the meeting, almost like he'd betrayed something, changed in some fundamental way. He'd never gotten around to asking her three things that had changed in *her* life. He had just been debating the wisdom of asking her if she was planning to be in town long, entertaining the brief, clearly delusional idea of asking her if she'd want to come to his house for dinner, when she'd reached down to put her shoes back on and ordered a rideshare to come pick her up.

"What's the story behind the name?" Asa asked. "Electric-Oh! Is that a reference to something?"

John grunted as he took the entire bottom drawer out of the dresser, putting it on his bed so he could go through it without having to keep bending over. "That's not in the Wikipedia?"

"I searched you up one time, back when you first moved in," Asa said. "I didn't read all of it."

It was one of the things that John had appreciated most about his housemates, actually. They were all easy to live with—Kiki, who always had ten thousand opinions about whatever show the house had chosen to watch as a group; Elliot, who was a big music fan (they were definitely the one most likely to have listened to ElectricOh! in its prime); and then Asa and his now-fiancée, Lauren. Everybody cared about each other but also minded their own business, seeming to navigate boundaries that hadn't even been spoken aloud, like the way John never really wanted to talk about his past in a band. But now he'd spent the last month playing all those old songs, was about to spend five days stuck on a boat with people he used to spend every waking minute with, and was probably going to have to answer a thousand questions more invasive than *What's the story behind the name?*

"We went to a concert together in high school," John said. "Me and Micah and Frankie, our bassist. And the lead singer was kinda over-the-top showboating—you could just tell he was feeling himself. I think he must've been at least a little blitzed.

He had this billowy white shirt unbuttoned down to his belly button, and he kept gyrating against the mic stand."

"Sounds like quite the show," Asa said. "Who was the band?"

"You know, I don't even remember. They opened for someone else we were there to see. I bet Frankie still has their concert ticket somewhere. They're good at that kind of thing."

"So this isn't a story about how you stole that guy's band name because you were so impressed by his gyrations?"

"Ha," John said. "No. He kept shouting, 'You're electric, Ohio! You're electric!' We thought that was hilarious, so we said it for *months* afterward. Then somehow that led to us calling ourselves Electric Ohio!, which sounded too much like a utility company, and then that became ElectricOh!, and yeah. That's the name that stuck."

"With an exclamation point."

"What can I say, it was the time. We were also trying to adequately convey the unhinged excitement of that guy yelling at the crowd in his pirate shirt. If we had known what a bitch it was going to be, always having the next word autocorrect to a capital letter, we might've made different choices."

There were a lot of different choices they might've made in retrospect. But it was hard to go down that road, because everything affects everything else. It was easy for John to wish they'd never allowed Ryder in the band in the first place, but he could also admit that the band would've never been what it was without him. He might be a dick, but he was a good guitarist and had written some really solid lead lines. And then maybe they would've signed a different type of record deal, if they'd been at all savvy about the way the business worked, wouldn't have given up so much control and locked themselves into a contract that was so easy to get perverted later into something none of them had wanted. Or at least had *said* they didn't want—John still wasn't sure how Micah actually felt about all that.

"And you really haven't played with any of these people since the band broke up," Asa said.

John laughed without any real humor. "I've barely *seen* any of these people since then. Frankie and Steve and I text every once in a while. Happy birthday, here's a funny meme, what do you think of the new album by this band we used to tour with, that kind of thing. As for Ryder . . . let's just say there's no love lost there. Besides, he's busy with his new band—he's the only one of us who's really had a consistent career in the music industry after ElectricOh!, although Frankie still does some session work and Micah had her own thing for a bit."

"Is that—" Asa started to say, then held up, like he was carefully considering how to phrase whatever he was going to say next. John knew the question he wanted to ask and decided to take pity on him. It was what everyone wanted to know. And for all Asa's sometimes playful and flippant attitude, it was a testament to his thoughtfulness as a friend that he'd shown restraint in ever bringing it up before John had opened the subject himself.

"Micah wanted to go solo," he said. "And the way the contract was structured, she really didn't need us—she could fulfill the third album we were signed for on her own. So that's basically what broke the band up."

John wondered if it was obvious just how much heavy lifting the word *basically* was doing there. Because the truth was, there had been a lot of reasons why the band was doomed.

Creative differences—Ryder had always wanted them to get

more radio play, *more* chart domination, but then had somehow seemed to turn on everyone the more popular they got, saying they were betraying their artistic principles. He'd hated that they'd done the *Nightshifters* episode, although John had always suspected that was because they'd performed the one song that Ryder didn't help write. The song that had come together in the middle of the night, when John and Micah had both been unable to sleep and had found each other on the back porch of the rental they'd all been staying in while recording the first album. The song that had gone on to be ElectricOh!'s most successful by far, in part because of the *Nightshifters* connection, in part because . . . well, they'd put everything into that song. At least, John knew he had.

And then there were the personal differences. John didn't know exactly when Micah and Ryder started dating—they'd kept their relationship a secret from the public for its entire duration, or at least as much a secret as possible. There had always been whispers, rumors, blurry candid photos that were posted to the internet and debated on various forums. But they'd also kept it a secret from the *band* for at least the very start, which still had the power to piss John off. And then Micah and Ryder dated—occasionally breaking up, then getting back together, then repeating the cycle again—for the next two years. Through the tail end of promoting the first album, and then into the second album and that disastrous European tour.

"We were all really young," he said now to Asa. He didn't know why, as much baggage as *he* might carry around about the way things had ended, he didn't want Asa to think less of Micah for it. "It was a lot of pressure."

"How old were you?"

"Sixteen when our first album came out, nineteen by the time we broke up."

"Wow," Asa said. "A whirlwind three years."

It had been a maelstrom. And John felt like he'd never fully gotten closure on any of it. Maybe it was impossible to believe he ever would.

But Micah had approached *him* in the parking lot. She could've just jumped into a car and left, but instead she'd chosen to walk over, admonish him for being late, make fun of his T-shirt, take off her shoes and then stand so close to him that he could see where she'd applied her mascara thicker on one eye than the other. He'd always assumed that she was done with him, that whatever had broken their band had broken them, too. Now he didn't know what to think.

Just then, he heard the sound of the front door opening and shutting, the clatter of keys being hung up on the wall where they all kept theirs in case someone had to move someone else's car. It was just past five, which meant it was probably Lauren, home from work.

Asa leaned out John's doorway, the grin on his face already confirming what John had figured. "Hey," he called out. "In here. We're trying to get John ready for this cruise."

Lauren stepped cautiously into the doorway, clearly not wanting to disrupt anything by coming all the way into John's room. She'd only moved in with them last year, and she could still be a little hesitant about asserting herself in any way with the rest of them in the house. John tried to help her feel comfortable as much as he could by including her in all their traditions and activities, filling her in on any idiosyncrasies of the house he could tell she hadn't caught on to yet. But he understood how it could be. It took a lot to feel truly part of a group that had already existed before you.

Asa looped his arm around her waist, pulling her in to kiss her temple. "What do you think?" he asked. "What's the perfect outfit for a day at sea, playing in a band with an exclamation point in its name, with people you haven't performed with since you were all in skinny jeans?"

Lauren eyed the clothes that John had spread over his bed, tilting her head while she seemed to consider the question. "I guess I would say . . ." She bit her lip, and John could tell she was holding back a smile. "You look very nice in black."

IN THE END, John had more luggage than he'd ever remembered bringing on a single trip. Back when ElectricOh! were touring, he'd become an expert on packing light, fitting the bare essentials into a single suitcase, rewearing the same outfits over and over again and letting the roadies handle most of the gear. But now, they had no roadies, and he was petrified he'd forget something important.

If he thought *he'd* overpacked, he couldn't wait to see what Micah had brought. It had been yet another source of contention with Ryder—how many outfit changes she'd always had, all the coverage they'd gotten as people posted roundups of her best tour looks or videos of her showing off her closet on the bus. To John, it had been a stupid thing to hold against her. She was the lead singer, after all. Her look was as much a part of the band's stage show as the images projected behind them or the lights that pulsed to the beat.

But when he saw her, standing over to one side in the area

reserved for the artists to board the ship, she didn't seem to have much with her. A silver hard-shell suitcase, a single guitar case, and a smaller purse slung over one shoulder. She was frowning down at something on her phone, and he wished he knew if she was really intent on whatever was on there or if she was faking to look like she had something to do. There was a time when he would've known.

"Hey," a voice said from behind him, and he turned.

"Hey, Frankie." It was surprisingly instinctual, his move to hug them, and so that was what he did. "Decent flight?"

"Not too bad," Frankie said. "Got in super late last night, so just crashed at the hotel and then woke up in time for the driver to get me here."

Ryder, Frankie, and Micah all still lived in L.A., whereas Steve had moved back to Ohio where they were originally from. John hadn't seen Steve or Ryder arrive yet, but he assumed they weren't far off. "Was anyone else on it?"

Frankie glanced pointedly over to Micah, who was still on her phone. "No," they said. "I assume she caught an earlier one. Have you really not talked to her since—"

"Nope," John said. *She* also hadn't talked to *him* in all those years, he could point out. It went two ways. But that probably opened up a bunch of stuff best left unsaid, parts of their history that had been wrapped up in the band but separate from it, too. "Are you nervous about playing again?"

Frankie shrugged. "Not really. I'm such a better bassist now than I was then. I swear I used to just follow the root notes and was scared to do anything more innovative than that. So I'm ready to have some fun with it. What about you?"

"Yeah," John said. "Same."

He *was* a better guitarist than he'd been then. He might not be writing many of his own songs anymore, but he'd played thousands—maybe tens of thousands, he didn't even know—of other people's songs. It had made him learn chord shapes and techniques he might not have otherwise, made him more precise in where he put his fingers and more attuned to different strumming patterns. Some of ElectricOh!'s first songs seemed almost endearingly simple to him now, clearly the work of kids who wrote around chords that felt natural to their hands and didn't know all the clever little things you could do with music. John had felt like he'd put everything he wanted to *say* into that music, but now he realized how limited his vocabulary had been.

And yet the songs really did say something to him, even now. Maybe more so for their simplicity. *That* part did make him nervous.

"Should we go over there?" Frankie asked, nodding toward Micah again, and John hesitated. He was just about to say *Sure, let's go*, when Steve bounded up toward them, Ryder following close behind.

"The gang's all here!" Steve said, holding up his phone and snapping a quick picture before John even knew what was happening. He'd probably been caught midblink. "Can you believe we're going to be on a ship with Tatiana Rivera? Do you think we'll get to hang out with her or will the TV people and music people be separate?"

Tatiana had been the female star of *Nightshifters* and was definitely the most famous person on the ship, since her male counterpart had been the only cast member to decline the cruise. John wouldn't be surprised if they barely breathed the same air as Tatiana Rivera, fellow "talent" or no.

"I met her at a party in the Hills a few years ago," Ryder said with a smirk. "I'll introduce you."

"Sweet," Steve said. "I just want a picture. So I can show my kids when they're old enough to be impressed by it. You know? Like look at Dad with a real-life celebrity! Tyler would be more impressed if this was a Disney cruise and I got a picture with Donald Duck, to be honest, but what are you going to do."

Frankie gave Steve an indulgent smile. "Not Mickey?"

"It's the way Donald talks," Steve said, before doing an eerily pitch-perfect impression. "He loves it."

This time when John glanced over to Micah, she was looking right at their group, although she tried to look away fast enough that it wasn't obvious. Which, of course, only made it that much *more* obvious. John started to head over there, but Ryder cut him off at the pass.

"I have some things to discuss with Micah before we head out," he said. "Watch my stuff?"

He was already walking off before John had a chance to answer. Micah looked up as Ryder approached, and John tried to figure out how she felt about seeing him, but her expression stayed neutral as he said something to her and she shrugged one shoulder, saying something in response. This time it was John caught staring as Micah's gaze shifted over to their group. But unlike her, he didn't look away, didn't try to pretend he hadn't been watching them.

"That should give the fan sites something to overanalyze for the next two years," Frankie said, and John turned back.

"What do you mean?" he asked. He knew what Frankie meant. He just had a masochistic need to hear them say it.

"Oh, you know. They've dredged up every grainy picture of the two of them together they could possibly find. That one of them all cozy backstage at that festival. The one of her feeding him a Cheeto. The ones where they zoomed in and swore she was wearing a ring with his initials on it on her left hand."

It had been a Cool Ranch Dorito, technically. And the ring had been a twisty kind of design, given to Micah by her younger sister. But yes, John remembered all the analysis when people were trying to figure out if it was confirmed that they were dating. He just assumed all of that had stopped, sometime around when he realized he no longer got the record label's annual holiday card in the mail anymore.

"You're really not online, are you?" Frankie asked.

"Not particularly," John said.

"Bless you," Frankie said. "You might be the last one left."

The conversation between Ryder and Micah actually looked like it was getting a little heated, to the point where John wondered if maybe they *should* intervene. Although they were in a cordoned-off area, they were still visible to part of the line of cruisers that had started snaking around the port, and several had their phones up like Frankie had predicted. But aside from the optics or exposure, it was impossible to ignore that Micah's body language got increasingly uncomfortable the longer Ryder kept talking at her. She'd already tried to interrupt him several times, a pink color rising to her cheeks, no longer as cool and collected as she'd been when he went over there in the first place.

But then an announcement over the loudspeaker made Micah jump, and a woman's cheerful voice told everyone they could start moving toward the gangway. Ryder broke away from

Micah with a few last angry words, grabbing his stuff from John's feet without looking at anyone else in the band. He was already halfway to the ship by the time Frankie let out a huffed laugh.

"Well, okay," they said. "This should be fun."

Frankie and Steve started making their own way toward the ship, but John had to try to gather his stuff, shifting his duffel bag to one shoulder so he could sling one of his gig bags over the other. He'd finally gotten it all under control just in time to fall in step behind Micah, who picked up her guitar case and started walking.

She only made it a few feet before the latches on the case seemed to give way, the top buckling out, suspended for a second that seemed to stretch forever as John tried to react in time. He bent down, trying to catch the guitar before it tumbled out of the case and landed on the concrete with the sickening *thunk* and buzz of vibrating strings that John had heard too many times.

But instead of a guitar, out poured . . . bracelets?

There were so many of them. Hundreds, maybe thousands. Little colorful beaded circles that just kept spilling and spilling out of the open guitar case, John already kneeling on the ground to catch them, his own guitar lopsided on his back, but not sure what to do now. They slipped through his fingers like sand, and he snagged one that caught on his palm.

JUST BECAUSE, it said in beaded letters, surrounded by a pattern of pink, blue, and white, some silver stars bracketing the words.

Micah was crouching down next to John now, shoveling the bracelets back into the case.

"What are—" he started to say, and she snatched the bracelet off his hand. The action caused her fingertips to tickle his palm, like when they'd done fake readings for each other back when they were kids. They'd always ended with the prediction that your house would have a pool, and then you'd have to snatch your hand away fast, before the other person spit in it. Only once Micah hadn't been fast enough, and John had straight-up landed a dime-sized pool of spit right in the center of her hand. He'd felt terrible about it, but she'd just laughed, making him shake her hand. *Now we're blood brothers*, she'd said. *Spit brothers. Whatever.*

"I've got it," she said now, and then, when he tried to pick up a few more bracelets to put in the case, "I've *got* it."

He wasn't going to leave her to clean them up all by herself, so he continued scooping them up and putting them in the guitar case, figuring if he worked fast and without talking she couldn't say anything about it. He glanced at her once, trying to see her face, but part of her hair had fallen out of her ponytail and covered her like a curtain.

When they'd finally picked up the last of the bracelets, John closed the case, double-checking that both latches were secure before handing it to Micah.

"Thanks," she said grudgingly.

Some of that hair was stuck to her cheek, and he had the strongest urge to reach out and brush it away, to tuck it behind her ear. But of course he had no right to do that kind of thing anymore. Instead he just shifted his own stuff back into his hands, trying to get a grip on everything, and gestured for her to go ahead.

"After you," he said.

CHAPTER

MICAH FELT LIKE she didn't fully relax until she was alone in her cabin on the ship, finally done with the early check-in process and the safety briefing and everything else they needed to do before setting sail.

Her room was small, by necessity, but pretty nice. It even had a balcony, with two chairs and a view of the horizon stretching out over the water. Micah's first thought had been *I hope Ryder has a balcony room or I'll never hear the end of it.* Her second had been *Actually, fuck that, I hope they put him in a storage closet.*

He had a lot of nerve, coming up to her and telling *her* that she needed to be on her best behavior on the ship. "We're all professionals here," he'd said. "And people just want to see a good show."

It was condescending that he thought he needed to tell her that, but fine. She didn't disagree. But then he'd touched her arm. "You know," he'd said. "People still ship us."

And then Micah thought she understood a bit better. They

were supposed to *put on a good show* not just on the stage but off it, too—maybe give people a little bit of what they wanted, clandestine moments that gave more proof to the pretty-much-confirmed rumors that they'd dated, that maybe suggested they could date again. Or maybe Ryder expected it to be real, thought that Micah would be able to put everything behind her and pick up right where they left off.

Yeah, *fuck* that.

She collapsed onto the bed starfish-style, lying there for the few minutes it took to get her breathing back to normal. Then she turned her head to the view outside the balcony, her gaze snagging instead on her luggage stacked up in the corner.

She could've done without the embarrassing moment outside, when her guitar case had fallen open and all the bracelets had spilled everywhere. She didn't even know why she'd brought them. Maybe she'd had some thought that she could give them away to people, leave them in various places around the ship, unload all these things that she'd made just to *make* them and now didn't know what to do with them after that. Maybe she'd just wanted her former bandmates to think she'd actually brought an instrument.

She knew they all hated her. It had been pretty obvious, by the way they'd stayed in a little group separate from her. And Micah supposed she couldn't blame them for that. She *had* broken up the band. She *had* been the one to walk away. Or worse—to walk into the rest of their contract without them. Technically, that meant they'd gotten paid for a record they didn't even have to make, but she knew that was no comfort.

Micah rolled over onto her stomach, pressing her face into the crisp white comforter on the bed. She didn't know if John hated her. It was hard to imagine him hating anyone—it had never really been his style. But he was definitely a stranger to her now, and somehow that felt just as bad.

He'd come to a concert of hers once. She'd been playing the El Rey on a tour that had been absolutely miserable, starting with the fact that she could *feel* the disappointment from her entire team that it wasn't going better. So she'd performed at legendary venues that normally would've had her over the moon, and instead all she could think about were the emails that had gone back and forth about how they didn't have "confidence in the numbers" to warrant booking bigger stadiums, what benchmarks she wasn't making for presales, and on and on.

When one of the venue's security team had found her backstage to tell her that someone was asking to see her, she'd snapped a quick *No* before she'd even registered the name. That was what she'd told herself later—she hadn't realized it was him.

But the truth was that there'd been a moment between when she'd said no and when the security guard had left when it had hit her. *John.* There'd been enough time for her to say *Wait. Yes. I do want to see that person. Send him back.*

Instead, she'd let the security guard walk away. And then she'd spent the last ten years wondering what John would've said.

There was a knock at her door, and Micah startled. She had the sudden irrational thought that it was *him*, that she'd summoned him just by thinking his name. But when she opened the door, Frankie stood on the other side, their tight corkscrew curls teased out into an Afro around their face, their dangling earrings giant rainbows with fringe hanging down from the clouds on either end.

"Are you coming to the panel?" Frankie said. "You don't have to, but remember that it's 'encouraged.'"

Their air quotes made Micah smile. To hear Bobbi talk about the cruise at that meeting, it had sounded like everything was absolutely up to them, they were just there to have fun . . . except of course for the quasi-mandatory, if-you-know-what's-good-for-you activities they'd been "encouraged" to take part in.

"Let me just get ready," Micah said. She started to close the door, figuring that Frankie wouldn't want to wait around and she'd meet them out there, but instead Frankie surprised her by coming all the way into the room.

"Your digs are really nice," Frankie said. "A balcony, wow."

Micah felt her stomach sink as she grabbed her makeup case from her bag. "Do we not all have balconies?"

Frankie shrugged. "I can't speak for everyone. John and I are in interior rooms. We don't even have a porthole."

It was a good reminder that no matter how far into their own bullshit they might be, ElectricOh! was far from the main draw for this cruise. There were Tatiana and the other *Nightshifters* cast members, who probably all had balconies and huge suites, and then the Silver Cuties, the main band who'd provided several songs for the show's soundtrack over the years. They were the ones who were playing full sets, not just the mini ones ElectricOh! had been contracted for. They were also still an active band that put out new music and toured. Micah had spent a few hours when the cruise had first been announced watching their music videos and scrolling through their social media with all the excited comments from fans.

Micah had dipped a toe into a few lingering ElectricOh! fan accounts to gauge any response there, too. Her favorite one was an account with only a few hundred followers that captioned every single post with "if this flops I stg" but always managed to dig up older photos Micah had forgotten existed. Most importantly, the account didn't seem to blame Micah for breaking up the band the way most people did, including, she was sure—and with justification!—her own bandmates. Part of cutting things off so abruptly the way she had was that she really didn't know the ins and outs of how they all felt. So far in that initial cruise meeting, they'd seemed almost as over Ryder as she was, so maybe he hadn't been able to poison them against her as much as she'd feared.

Still, Micah wished that they'd at least given every member of the band the same type of room.

"Surprised you came to get me," Micah said, leaning in to apply her lip stain. "Won't they be mad at you for crossing sides?"

She caught Frankie's frown out of the corner of her eye, reflected in the mirror.

"There aren't *sides*," Frankie said. "At least, not in my book. That shit was a long time ago. And yeah, some of it sucked at the time—I'm not saying I didn't hold a grudge for a bit. But in the end, I'm glad everything worked out the way it did. I feel like I'm living the life I want."

Micah was genuinely happy for Frankie if that was the case. They deserved it. But she couldn't deny the kick their words sent to her stomach. *I'm living the life I want.* It sounded so simple, when they put it like that. As if the life you wanted was just out there, waiting, and all you had to do was grab it and put it on like you were applying color to your face.

"I heard the parts you recorded on that *Wondering* album," Micah said. "They slapped. The first track especially."

Frankie beamed. "Thank you," they said. "John said that was his favorite, too. They might go on tour this summer—I'm still in talks to join the live band for the North American leg."

Something about the fact that she and John had both listened to the same record, had responded to the identical song, got to her a bit. It felt like the equivalent of looking up at the same moon or something fanciful like that. It was stupid of Micah to even feel that way.

They used to listen to records together all the time. John would come over, and they'd hang in her room with the door cracked a chaste six inches, no matter how many times Micah protested to her parents that it wasn't *like that*. Calling it "listening to records" was glossing it up, since they'd mostly listened to illegally downloaded songs through the tinny speakers of her computer. But he'd always hear things she didn't hear, point out little parts in the instrumentation or an unusual vocal approach that she'd think about every time she heard the song after that.

She'd never gone to John's house, which had been one of those things they just Didn't Talk About. They'd had several of those.

"Well, they'd be lucky to have you," Micah said now to Frankie, hesitating only a minute before deciding to go for it. "What's he up to these days anyway? John?"

"He plays in a couple local bands," Frankie said. "One is a cover band with a hilarious name—I can't think of it right now. Another plays weddings, corporate parties, that kind of thing."

So he *was* still involved in music, even if not on the same level as he'd once been. Micah didn't know why that comforted her somehow, that at least he hadn't lost that. "Maybe a cover band for us," Micah said. "Call it ElectricOhNo!"

Frankie laughed. "I would pay actual cash money."

"That's not a bad idea," Micah said, finally finishing her makeup and putting everything away. "If we can think of this gig as just like, us covering ourselves. Maybe it would take the pressure off."

"Are you feeling the pressure?"

Aren't you? Micah wanted to shoot back, but apparently not. "No more than usual," she said. "It's always nerve-racking, getting up on a stage. No matter how many times I've done it, I feel those butterflies right before I go out there."

"But then . . ." Frankie smiled, closing their eyes as if in sheer bliss. "God, what a rush."

It really was. There was no other feeling like it on the planet. The problem was you could get almost addicted to it, could *crave* it, and then when you stepped back off the stage your life felt almost depressingly flat afterward. Sometimes Micah thought if she could somehow stay on the stage sixteen hours straight, stumble off just in time to catch some sleep, then go right back to it the next day, she could get through life so much better. Just constant performing, performing, performing with no downtime to think about a single thing outside the lights and the beat and the faces in the crowd and the music coursing through her.

Instead she'd crafted the opposite life for herself, where she was alone with her thoughts all the time and hadn't been on a stage in years. She didn't let Hailey pay her for the work she did for the salon—it didn't seem right, when Micah still made enough from her co-writing credit for "If Only" to keep herself afloat *and* kick in a little extra toward the opening of the salon in the first place. But sometimes Micah wondered if that would've been a better life for herself, one where she'd never gotten a taste of that performance rush, one where she could sweep hair off the floor and answer the telephone and only every once in a blue moon think *Wait, didn't you used to want to make music?*

"All right," Micah said, pressing a hand to her stomach. She was feeling a little queasy, but she couldn't tell if it was the cruise or lingering nerves. She hoped the fresh air would help either way. "I'm ready. Let's go listen to a bunch of beautiful people talk about a show I've never seen."

"Oh, you never watched it?" Frankie said. "I binged all seven seasons. The college years get *insane*. Don't bother with the sixth season—it goes off on a whole tangent where everyone thinks there's a murderer targeting girls on campus, but actually it's just one of the shifters people keep seeing skulking around Greek row? But like, they never do figure out who was murdering all those girls, then. Imagine, three girls turn up dead at the same quaint liberal arts college and they're just like, oh well, best left unsolved. Also there might be a creature on campus, don't worry about it."

"Well, people loved the show enough to give us *this*," Micah said, gesturing out at the people as they stepped out onto the pool deck. As Bobbi had promised, there was a roped-off section where they could stand separate from the rest of the crowd, which Micah especially appreciated once she saw just how many people were out there. The main deck was totally packed, people pressed together dressed in their T-shirts with character images on them, a couple even dressed like the characters themselves—post-shifting, Micah assumed, since their costumes came complete with headbands of furry ears and tails attached to their pants. There were people already in the pool on the other side of the deck, drinking and laughing and seeming like they barely knew a panel was about to start. Then there were people wrapped around the deck above, leaning against the railing to look down at the stage that had been set up with six chairs.

John and Steve had already arrived and were standing over by a stack of chairs, talking. Steve had a brightly colored cocktail in his hand, and John held a cup of something of his own. As if sensing her gaze on him, John turned his head, and Micah slid her sunglasses down over her eyes.

"Why don't you just talk to him?" Frankie asked.

Briefly, Micah thought about playing dumb, saying *What do you mean?* or *Who?* But that would be a waste of time.

"Did he ever mention me?" she asked instead. "When you two kept in touch."

Frankie paused in a way that told Micah the answer before they had to say it. *Don't ask a question you don't want the answer to.* She should've remembered that.

"You know John," Frankie said. "He keeps things pretty tight to the chest."

"Right."

"But you know he would talk to you. He's always been yours."

That made Micah whip her head around. "What does that mean?"

"You were friends first," Frankie said. "Before any of the rest of us."

Oh. Well. That was true.

The wind had picked up, and even under the cover of the overhang above them, Micah could feel it start to slice through.

She wished she'd brought a jacket, but instead all she had was the thin black-and-white-striped T-shirt she'd chosen because she felt like that was the closest to nautical she could get.

The boat was also moving more than she had expected. Wasn't that supposed to be one of the benefits of a cruise? The ship was so large that it was steadier on the water, and you could walk around like you were hanging out on land? Instead, Micah felt like she could feel the sway under her feet, had to brace slightly to keep her balance.

It wasn't too late to bail on the panel. Technically, she'd made an appearance. She was just about to get Frankie's attention when the stage lights kicked on, a roar went up from the crowd, and the cast of *Nightshifters* started filing out onto the stage, waving as they took their seats.

Micah glanced around. No one was looking at her. Probably nobody cared if *she* specifically was there or not.

But she knew there was no getting around it. She was trapped.

CHAPTER

SEVEN

JOHN HAD NEVER felt more trapped in his life. He hadn't been on a cruise before, and he'd already decided he didn't like it. It had been cool when the ship had pulled away from the port and everyone had rushed to the sides, waving and cheering. But now he was very conscious of the fact that the ship was *moving*. And worse than that, he was conscious of the fact that there'd be no getting off it, at least not until they reached the private Bahamian island owned by the cruise company that was their only excursion stop.

He clapped for the last of the *Nightshifters* cast as they took their seats, already scanning around to see if Bobbi was there and would notice if he left or not.

His gaze snagged on Micah, who was standing with her arms crossed, her expression neutral as she watched the panel. Micah's short-sleeved shirt bared most of her arms, and he could see more of her tattoos, although there were others he couldn't see but knew were there. The peony she'd gotten to cap one shoulder, the delicate word etched on the inside of one wrist. She still had a lot of open real estate on her arms, though, and that surprised him—somehow he assumed she would've filled all that by now. From what he could see, she didn't appear to have any *new* tattoos.

But of course there were a lot of different places to get tattoos that he wouldn't necessarily be able to see.

"We knew we had something very special from the first table read," Tatiana was saying on the stage. "And look at all of you now! Obviously we were right."

A huge cheer from the crowd, who were pressing forward, as if wanting to get even a couple inches closer while the cast answered presubmitted questions about the show. John had never gone into music for the adulation—if anything, it had often made him feel uncomfortable, having people look up at him like that while he was onstage. But he couldn't deny that there was something powerful about seeing a whole group of people so united over a shared love of one single thing. Everyone here loved a television show *so much* that they would save up thousands of dollars, take time off work, and subject themselves to these winds and seas just for this moment where they were all in it together. It made him miss it, for a second—being in a successful band. Being part of something that could give people that.

He nudged Steve next to him. "Hey," he said, gesturing toward where Micah and Frankie were standing. "Should we?"

They crossed over to join their bandmates, excluding Ryder. John had no idea where Ryder was or why he wasn't at the panel, but he didn't particularly care. Micah glanced up at him, her eyes still hidden behind those sunglasses, the slight parting of her lips the only sign of surprise.

iteration. That was the word tattooed in lowercase script on the inside of her left wrist. She'd never fully explained to him what it meant, but he'd never asked. He felt like he'd lost any right to ask her about her tattoos after he'd let her down when she got her first one.

"Where's Ryder?" he asked now, which was not what he'd meant his opening gambit to be at all, and which he regretted the moment the words were out of his mouth.

Her mouth tightened. "I don't know."

"He was supposed to introduce me to Tatiana," Steve said.

"Something tells me you'll have ample opportunity," Frankie said dryly. "Not like we have many places to go. Where did you get the drinks?"

"There's a bar over there," Steve said, pointing his drink toward the pool on the other side of the ship. "But there's also people in yellow shirts who'll take your order. This one is something with *Breeze* in the name. It's good as hell."

Steve took another slurping drink up his straw, as if making his point.

"What's yours?" Micah asked John.

"Try it," he said, tilting his cup toward her. He didn't know what had made him say that, either, any more than what had made him ask about Ryder. He felt like his head was all turned around, the sway of the ship making him a little unsteady. They'd shared drinks all the time, picked food off each other's plates, borrowed each other's razors when it came time to shave. Once this had been an instinct, to offer her some of his own drink, but he couldn't say that was what was going on anymore.

She took the cup from him, and he wished he could see her eyes as she brought it to her mouth, taking a tentative sip.

"Fruit punch," she said. She had a subtle line of red above her upper lip now, where the drink had stained her skin.

"Felt right for the occasion."

"So you still don't drink?"

He shook his head slowly. "I said I never would," he said. "And I never have."

Only Micah could guess what that promise to himself meant. They might have shared everything as kids, but he'd never wanted the full ugliness of his home life to touch her. It was the one part of himself he'd kept deeply tucked away, powerless to prevent her getting a sense of the broad strokes but not wanting her to have all the details.

Well. One of the parts.

The ship shifted under their feet, to the point where even the actors sitting on the stage had to brace themselves against their chairs, laughing nervously at the weather, one of them losing a hat that went flying off into the crowd. Next to him, Micah stumbled, still holding on to his fruit punch, and John grasped her by the arms just as the rest of the contents of the cup sloshed all over his shirt.

"Oh my god," she said. "I'm so sorry."

The liquid was already starting to make the fabric stick to his chest, cold and wet, but he was reluctant to let go of Micah. He could feel the way her skin prickled into gooseflesh under his fingertips, and he gave a slight squeeze, wanting to warm her up.

"It's okay," he said. "Don't worry about it."

She looked up at him, giving a shaky little laugh, but he noticed she didn't step out of his touch, either. "At least you weren't wearing white."

"Very fortuitous."

Just then, John felt a hand land heavy on his back, and he turned to see Ryder, who'd just arrived and apparently felt moved to greet John with a quasi-bro hug. Something that they'd . . . probably never done, not even back in high school.

"Hey, guys, sorry I'm late," Ryder said, as if they'd all been waiting on him. He'd already insinuated himself in the group, and John took a step back, letting his hands drop from Micah. "Miss anything good?"

"These Breeze drinks," Steve said, brandishing his now-empty cup. "But the bar is open."

"Your friend Tatiana was looking for you," Frankie said.

Ryder looked so momentarily eager that John had to hide a smile. "Really?"

Frankie rolled their eyes. "No, not really."

Ryder flicked his hair out of his eyes with a jerky head movement. "Well, don't forget we have rehearsal tomorrow morning," he said. "So no getting drunk tonight. Steve? Did you hear that? You're cut off."

"Chill out, man, I've only had one of these things," Steve said.

"And we have bingo after lunch." Frankie pulled out their phone, maybe checking a schedule they'd saved on there. "So tomorrow's pretty packed."

"Don't look at me," Ryder said. "It wasn't *my* idea to save rehearsal for the boat. We could've all been sleeping in or laying out by the pool tomorrow morning."

John glanced over at Micah, but her face betrayed nothing. He still didn't totally understand why she'd pushed so hard for no rehearsals, but he supposed her schedule must be busy. For some reason he thought of those bracelets again, tumbling out of her guitar case.

"We have three songs to run through," John said. "And three hours to do it. We should be fine."

"Hey, if we nail them down early we can still catch some pool time," Steve said, and Frankie reached out to rattle his empty cup.

"What was in this?" they asked. "You *are* cut off. There's not going to be any time to lounge in the pool tomorrow."

"Say what you will," Steve said, "but you and I both know if rehearsal runs long, it won't be because of me."

Knowing Steve, that was an innocent statement—meant more as a cocky self-aggrandizement, or more truthfully as a declaration of fact. Steve had *never* been the problem. He kept time like he had a metronome ticking in his brain, and even when he'd broken or thrown a stick, he had such a smooth way of grabbing another one without missing a beat that John had suspected he did it on purpose as part of his showmanship.

But Ryder immediately bristled, and John could tell he'd taken Steve's comment as a dig. "So I have high standards," he said. "Sue me. I'm not going to let us stop practicing a song until we have it perfect, and if that requires that we play it until all our fingers fall off, then that's just the way it's going to be."

Then he glanced at Micah. "Obviously not *your* fingers. You just have to hold the microphone and look pretty like usual."

There was no missing the flush of color that rose to Micah's cheeks at that dig.

"We all have high standards," John said, his voice low. "You're not the only—"

"It's more my arms than my fingers," Steve put in. "But I've been working out, I joined—"

"I never said I was the *only*," Ryder said, "although your word choice is fucking hilarious. Maybe if you spent less time—"

"*Guys*," Frankie hissed in a tone that suggested they'd said it a few times already. "Guys, seriously. Shut the fuck up."

Steve had the grace to look chagrined. "Sorry, Frankie, we shouldn't be arguing. And I didn't mean—"

Frankie held a finger up to their mouth. "*Shhhh*. For real. Argue all you want, just not when they're starting to talk about season six, okay? I've been waiting years to hear this shit."

Years was a little dramatic for John, but he'd also been curious about that season. The minute he turned his attention back to the panel, he couldn't help but notice out of the corner of his eye that Micah had slipped away from the group, disappearing somewhere back into the ship. He almost followed her. He didn't care about a fictional murderer of some fictional college girls.

But he also had no real right to go after Micah, no expectation that she would welcome his presence. He rubbed the back of his neck, giving Frankie a smile when he caught them looking at him, and pretended to turn his focus back to the stage.

EIGHT

IT WAS EVEN hard to walk down the hallways leading to the rooms, Micah discovered. The ship kept pitching at the last minute, and she had to brace her hand along the wall to keep herself steady.

She wasn't feeling very well. And she didn't know if it was run-of-the-mill seasickness, if it was the onset of a panic attack, if it was something else. She just knew she had to get away from everyone, couldn't stand there on that deck for another second.

Luckily, most people had gathered for that first night's panel, and so the halls were relatively quiet. Still, she definitely caught the few people milling around looking at her—some because they clearly recognized her as Micah Presley, some maybe just because she was staggering like she was drunk. A lot of them probably thought Micah Presley *was* drunk, which would be just perfect, if that rumor started going around. *I've had one sip of fruit punch!* she wanted to shout. She wanted to laugh inappropriately.

The power to shapeshift would be pretty useful right now,

actually. She'd turn into a wolf, and even if it was strange, a wolf tearing down the halls of a cruise ship—even if it was *scary*—she'd be sure-footed and quicksilver fast, gone before anyone could register what they'd seen.

She stumbled a little, hitting one knee on the aqua-and-pink seashell carpet, before standing up. A group of giggling girls passed her by before doubling back.

"Excuse me," one said. "Aren't you her?"

Vague enough that maybe she could get away with acting like she didn't know what they meant. She was worried she'd be sick in front of them, which just could *not* be the cruise memory these girls were looking to make their first night. But she also knew that pictures with anyone even tangentially related to the show were exactly the kind of memories they'd treasure, and she wanted to give that to them, wanted to be that for them.

"Micah Presley," she said. "From ElectricOh!."

"Oh my god," another of the girls said, immediately pulling out her phone. They all grouped around Micah, and she barely had time to put a smile on her face before they'd taken a sequence of selfies and told her that they loved her before moving down the aisle. That word always threw Micah—*love*. Even when she knew it wasn't meant literally, or at least not on a level beyond the way you might say it about anything. You love scented candles, or a book you read, or when a last-minute cancellation frees up your afternoon. The word didn't always have to have as much weight as Micah put on it, but she still found it hard to receive, wanted to shrug it off even when she knew it was only a gossamer thing skimming over her shoulders.

There was another group heading toward her now, and Micah wondered if it would be too obvious if she split off in the opposite direction, even though she was already turned around with no idea if she was taking the most efficient route to her room. She was considering her options when she heard a voice from behind her.

"Hey," John said, but when she turned she realized he wasn't talking to her. He was addressing the group, who were closer now and had already gotten their phones out. "Sorry, we've got somewhere to be, but we'll see you around the ship, yeah?"

They looked confused for a second, like they'd been suddenly redirected and didn't know which way they were facing.

Micah felt John's hand at the small of her back, so light she almost thought she was imagining it, and she wanted to lean back into it just to see if she was. But then he was guiding her forward with a little more pressure, giving a wave to the group as they squeezed past them in the hallway. "Definitely go check out the panel happening right now on the pool deck," he said. "I think they're about to open up on season six."

That got the group chattering among themselves, picking up the pace as they headed in the opposite direction down the hall. John dropped his hand the second they were alone, which made Micah's stomach swoop. She couldn't tell if it was disappointment or just another symptom of being on this goddamn ship.

"Sorry," he said.

"You say that a lot." It was the first word he'd said when he'd walked into that meeting a month ago. The first word she'd heard him say in over a decade.

"Better than the alternative, right?" His gaze caught hers for a moment before it slid away, and she couldn't tell if that was aimed at *her* specifically. God knew she had a lot to apologize for, a lot she'd never said. "Anyway, I wanted to—"

He cut himself off there, knocking his fist gently against the railing like he was testing its strength.

"Wanted to what?"

The hallways were narrow, and she was pressed against John now, close enough that she could feel his body heat against her skin. Or maybe it wasn't fair to blame that on the hallway, when she had ample room to move away. There were more people headed toward them, and John glanced up, reaching like he was going to touch her elbow before thinking better of it.

"You didn't look good," John said, his voice low enough that she had to lean in more to catch it.

"Gee, thanks."

But she knew what he meant. He thought she'd been upset by what Ryder said, which—she shouldn't be. She was certainly used to it by now, coming from him. There had been all these throwaway comments while they'd dated, landing lightly enough that he could tell her it was just a joke, or an observation, calm down, you're putting words into my mouth. And yet somehow they'd landed hard enough to get stuck in her, like little burs she would still come across no matter how many times she thought she'd picked them all out.

She barely had the energy to worry about Ryder at all right now, though. Her stomach was rolling along with the ship, and she wanted to make it to her room with the desperation of someone crawling through the desert looking for water.

John did take her elbow then, his hand warm and firm as he guided her down the hallway, giving anyone they passed a quick nod and a hello but moving efficiently enough that they were gone by the time the person tried to say anything.

"I'm fine," Micah said, although she didn't know why she

bothered. She was very clearly *not* fine, and the truth was that in that moment, she didn't even want to be fine. She wanted John's hands on her, wanted to feel taken care of and like someone else had custody of her body for a few minutes. God, when was the last time she'd felt that way?

"Which one's yours?" he asked when they'd finally reached their deck, and she rummaged through her bag, coming up empty. Finally she pulled her cruise ID card out of the back pocket of her jeans, where she'd shoved it, lanyard and all. She looked down at the card, frowning while she tried to figure out where her room number was listed on it.

"It should be on the blue one," he said. "With the pattern of waves in the background."

That made sense. Making her official Artist badge also have a room number and key card capabilities would've been a colossally bad idea, from a security standpoint. The problem was that when she closed her eyes, she could see the card he was describing very clearly, and it was . . . currently sitting on top of the nightstand next to her bed.

"Fuck," she said. "It's in my room."

She doubled over, resting her hands on her knees. She *really* wasn't feeling well, and she didn't think it was just a panic attack. Although it certainly wasn't helping, the adrenaline coursing through her body even remembering Ryder's words, thinking about rehearsals tomorrow, remembering the girls with the selfie and the screeching.

John slid a blue card out of his own back pocket, touching her briefly on the shoulder. "Come on," he said. "We don't have far to go."

CHAPTER
NINE

THE MINUTE HE opened the door to his room, Micah disappeared into the bathroom, shutting the door behind her. He didn't know what to do—he didn't want to hover, but also wanted to make sure she was okay. He changed out of his own punch-stained T-shirt, pulling it over his head by the back of the collar and swapping it for another clean one, trying to move quickly even though he knew the chance that Micah would emerge from the bathroom in the next five seconds was minimal.

Finally he figured he could make himself useful and called the number printed on his welcome paperwork, asking if there was any way to get some ginger ale, saltines, a packet of Dramamine or whatever else they might have on board. He also explained Micah's lockout situation and was told they could meet her back at her room and let her in to retrieve her key.

John paused, not *trying* to listen but finding it impossible to completely ignore that Micah was currently getting sick in his bathroom. "Maybe later," he said. "Thanks."

Once he'd hung up the phone, he knocked lightly on the bathroom door. He could still hear her moving around inside, but she didn't appear to be actively throwing up anymore, so that was something. "Micah?"

Nothing.

"Everything okay?" he asked. A stupid question. Obviously everything wasn't *okay*. "I mean, do you think it's just seasickness, or . . ."

She groaned, and he wondered if even saying the word was the wrong move right now.

"They're bringing you medicine," he said. "And some other stuff."

"Tell them to bring a horse tranquilizer," Micah said through the door. "One guaranteed to put me out for oh, approximately five days."

John smiled. She couldn't be *too* bad off if she was making jokes like that. He sat down on the floor, leaning his back against the shared wall. "Have you ever been on a cruise before?"

"No," she said. "And if I ever go on another again, it'll be too soon."

"Feeling any better now?"

The door opened then, just a crack, but it made it easier to hear her. "Yes? No. I don't know. Mostly I feel stupid."

John would ask her why, but he could already guess. She would hate that she'd shown this weakness, would hate that she wasn't in control, probably *really* hated that he was the one to see her this way. He hoped that last one wasn't true. There had been a time when he would've been the only one she would've felt comfortable seeing her this way.

"I really thought cruises were supposed to be different," Micah said. "Like because the boat is so big, you don't feel the water or something."

John brought his knees up, linking his hands loosely around them. "I think that's the idea. But it was pretty windy out there. Hopefully it'll calm down soon."

"Nobody ever thinks about those people on the *Titanic* who were feeling sick as a dog, just normal run-of-the-mill seasickness, and then had to deal with an *iceberg* on top of that."

"I think on a cruise you try to avoid thinking about the *Titanic* at all."

"Ah. Good point." She laughed, such a quiet, intimate sound through that single crack in the door that John felt a sudden chill. He rubbed his hands over his knees, swallowing hard.

"You know, it's supposed to help if you're actually *not* down below," he said. "Like if you go up to where you can look at the horizon, breathe some fresh air."

"Well, my room has a balcony." The door opened a little wider then, and he turned to see Micah's fingers gripping the wood before her palm dropped to the linoleum floor. "Sorry about that, by the way."

"Did you request specifically that I not get one?"

Another laugh, this one more of a snort. "No. I just hate when things aren't even."

John leaned his head back against the wall, not sure how to respond to that. Things had never been *even*, but that hadn't been a problem for him. If they only had so many balcony rooms to go around, it made sense that they would give one to her above other members of the band. He just hoped Ryder also got one or they'd never hear the end of it.

"They said they could let you back into your room, if you feel up to it," he said.

Her hand was still splayed on the floor, less than a foot away from him, and he stared at it, as if it could give him some insight into what she was thinking. She had long fingers—part of being tall, and she'd always been a little self-conscious of them. More so because of the nail biting, which he noticed at least looked better than it had at the meeting. She'd clearly gone for a professional manicure, her nails now painted what looked like black but what he could see was a dark navy blue. She no longer wore any rings, not even the twisty-design one from her sister that she'd worn for so many years.

"Not yet," she said. "If that's okay."

He wondered if she'd lost the ring. It was the only reason she would've been without it, back in the day. "It's fine. Take as long as you need."

There was a knock at the door, and John pushed himself up to answer it, accepting the bag with ginger ale and crackers and medicine from a guy with an unnaturally wide smile. John almost shut the door before remembering that he was probably supposed to tip, and he dug through his pockets, trying to find money but only coming up with a guitar pick and a crumpled receipt.

"It's good," the man said. His badge said he was from New Zealand. "Not to worry."

Something about the way he phrased that—the extra formality in it—made John even more determined. "No, no, hang on," he said. "I know I have—"

"In my bag," Micah said from the bathroom. "It should be by the door."

Sure enough, the black cross-body bag Micah had been carrying was slouched over on the floor where she must've dropped it on her way in. It felt somehow invasive, going through Micah's stuff, but she'd clearly meant for him to. He rummaged through a few items—pens, a small notebook held shut with a stretchy band, a bottle of medication—before he hit upon her wallet. There was a five-dollar bill sticking out, and he grabbed it by the corner to hand to his friend at the door, who gave him a beaming smile.

"I'll pay you back," John said once he'd shut the door and hung Micah's purse on the handle where she wouldn't forget it.

He could hear the water running in the bathroom, and when she emerged she had droplets still on her chin where she must've rinsed her mouth out in the sink.

"Why?" she asked. "It was all stuff for me."

He glanced inside the bag. "What do you want first?"

She held out her hand, and he gave her the entire bag. She took the bottle of ginger ale out first, uncapping it too fast and letting out a little fizz, which she ducked her head down to lick off the top before it started spilling everywhere. John glanced away, shoving his hands in his pockets.

It was weird, how easy it was being with Micah again. How much it felt like no time had passed at all, like they still had the natural rapport they'd always had as kids, once John had gotten up the nerve to talk to her again in homeroom. At the same time, it felt impossibly difficult. He'd always had this *awareness* of her, even back in those days, but he'd shoved it down. So deep, he told himself he didn't feel it. But now here she was, sitting tentatively on the edge of his bed, her head tilted back as she took a swig of the ginger ale, and even when he wasn't look-ing directly at her he still always knew she was *there*.

They'd been each other's first kiss. It had been when they were thirteen, one of those *Should we? Just to get it over with?* type of deals. At least that was how Micah had framed it.

"How are you feeling?" he asked now.

"I don't know yet," she said. "Should I take the medicine?"

"Couldn't hurt." He paused, wanting to mind his own busi-ness, but also having a sudden thought about the medication bottle that had been in her purse. "Unless it interacts with any-thing else you're taking?"

She'd already put a single tablet on her tongue and swished it down with a sip of ginger ale. "That stuff in my purse is for panic attacks," she said. "I don't take it all the time—just if I feel one coming on or know I'm about to be in a situation that could trigger one."

He smiled. "Like this entire cruise?"

"Believe me, that's why I made sure I'd refilled the prescrip-tion before I got here," she said. "But it makes me a little drowsy sometimes, so I was trying not to use it if I didn't have to."

He wanted to ask her more about the situations that trig-gered those feelings, what had happened to make her realize she needed medication in the first place. But it was definitely none of his business.

The ship moved again, the feeling somehow more unset-tling for the fact that the room was completely enclosed without even a glimpse of the water outside. It felt like being *inside* a stomach, which was definitely not the kind of thought to share with Micah, who still looked a little pale.

"Fuck," she said. "This sucks."

"Lie down if you need to," he said. "Maybe it'll make you feel better."

"This is *your* bed."

It was still made up with crisp white hospital corners, a towel folded into an elephant resting atop the pillows. "I haven't used it or anything. It's clean."

She let out a huff of a laugh. "That's my point. It's *yours*."

But he could see suddenly just how tired she looked, how spent. He didn't share that observation with her—he knew how little she'd appreciate the reminder that she wasn't looking her best, that he'd noticed, that maybe other people had, too. They could always call back down to guest services on the ship, get someone to meet Micah outside her room and let her back in. Get someone to tell her what her room number was in the first place. But looking at Micah, the way she was curling her hand around the cap to the ginger ale bottle, then opening her hand back up to see the circular imprint left in her palm . . . he knew that would probably be the last thing she'd want to do.

"Just rest," he said. "I'm going to go back out, maybe take in a bit of the show if it's already started."

"Oh yeah. I wanted to see that."

The Silver Cuties had done several songs on the *Nightshift-ers* soundtrack, and they'd been the main band booked for the cruise, with a full concert tonight and then another on prom night. John didn't know any of them personally, but he took a professional interest and generally enjoyed what music of theirs he'd heard.

"Come out later," he said. "If you feel up to it."

She stared up at him. The room was dim, with only the overhead light by the door switched on and no window to provide extra illumination. And yet John felt like he could see how pronounced the dark circles were under her eyes, maybe just because he knew what to look for.

"Why are you being so nice to me?" she asked, her voice almost a whisper. "Don't you hate me?"

He thought about all the reasons he *should* be mad at her. She'd broken up the band—that wasn't just some Yoko Ono blame-the-woman type shit. One minute they'd been taking a brief respite after a rocky European tour, trying to figure out whether to get back in the studio or keep touring, and the next minute she'd bought the rest of them out of their contract, saying she was going solo.

She'd disappeared from his life after that, had left so many of his texts on read, had completely erased all these years of history like they didn't mean anything to her, when they'd meant everything to him. And then the one time he'd tried to see her, she'd turned him away.

"I don't hate you, Micah," he said. "I could never hate you."

"I hate myself."

He believed her. She wasn't just *tired*, he realized, she was *unhappy*. And he wondered how long she'd felt that way.

"I wish you wouldn't," he said. He reached over to grab the towel animal off the pillow, setting it carefully on the nightstand before turning down the covers. "Come on, get in."

She hesitated. "Turn around," she said, then gave him a crooked smile when his brow furrowed at her demand. "I've been traveling in these clothes. I've been on your bathroom floor. I don't want to contaminate your bed."

John dutifully turned his back to her, trying to ignore the

swish he knew was her pulling her shirt over her head, the hiss of a zipper and then the crackling slide of her jeans down her legs. In the mirror on one wall, he could see a flash of ankle before he looked back down at the carpet. He could hear her getting into the bed, the rustle of the covers, and still he stood there long after the sounds had stopped.

"You can turn back around," she said, a smile in her voice. "I'm decent."

It had always done something to him, the image of her in his bed. He'd just tried to ignore it. But how many nights had she burrowed under the covers right next to him, never consciously touching but sometimes waking up to find that they'd crept closer to each other in the middle of the night?

Now he could see the sharp line of her collarbone, that peony tattoo capping one shoulder, the straps of her black bra peeking over the white covers. He tried to bring his gaze back to her face, but that was worse—something about her expression, so vulnerable and expectant, made him not want to walk away. It made him want to take his own clothes off and crawl in right beside her, hold her while they both drifted into sleep.

"Get some rest," he said gruffly. "And we can catch up more later."

CHAPTER

TEN

MICAH DIDN'T THINK she'd be able to sleep at first, no matter how tired she was. For one thing, she still didn't feel right—lightheaded and somehow empty, every movement of the boat swaying through her like she had nothing to hold her up.

For another thing, it was strange to be in John's bed. It wasn't the bed itself, which was standard issue for these cabins and which, as John himself pointed out, he'd never even slept in. But she couldn't help but be conscious of the intimacy of it, the fact that this was where he *would* be sleeping, that she was surrounded by his things, from the gallon Ziploc she'd seen in the bathroom with his deodorant and toothpaste to the shirt he'd been wearing earlier draped over his luggage. It had been the one she'd spilled punch all over, so he must've changed into another of his seemingly never-ending black band T-shirts while she was in the bathroom.

How strange, to have been out of each other's lives for so long, and then to have both gotten semi-naked within feet of the other within the span of the last hour. She wondered if John had ever gotten any tattoos, like he once said he wanted. She hadn't seen any, but then there were a lot of places to get tattoos that you wouldn't see.

They'd gone to get their first tattoos together when they were seventeen years old. Technically too young, but they'd *felt* more than ready. That was one thing about being in a band from such a tender age—you grew up so fast. You still couldn't vote, or smoke, or gamble, or drink, and yet you'd traveled the country with very little adult supervision playing to crowds of people, many of whom were old enough to do all those things you couldn't.

She stretched her toes under the covers. John had even pulled the bottom of the top sheet out from under the bed, apparently remembering how much she hated having her feet constricted while she slept. She would often kick the covers off her feet entirely, letting them out in the open air while the rest of her body was cocooned warmly in blankets.

It wasn't the most comfortable, sleeping in a bra. She reached around to unhook it from the back, sliding it down her arms and dropping it on the floor next to the bed. And there was that first tattoo she'd gotten, on her ribs right under her left boob. If she'd known that was supposedly one of the most painful places to get one, maybe she wouldn't have done it.

It definitely felt intimate, rolling over until she was lying on her stomach in John's bed, her breasts pressed against the crisp white sheets. She still felt lightheaded, but she no longer felt as empty, and when she closed her eyes it was no time at all before sleep pulled her under.

CHAPTER

ELEVEN

JOHN WAS GRATEFUL he'd thought to grab a hoodie from his room before he'd left. The wind was still biting, rocking the ship a bit every time it gusted against the side. He put his hood up, hoping to block some of the wind and maybe also decrease his chances of getting stopped by anybody as he made his way toward the mezzanine above the pool deck, where the show would be going on.

He shouldn't have thought about that first kiss. It had been such a small moment, in the scheme of things—probably Micah didn't even remember it. He didn't like to remember it, because then it was like playing the recursive notes to a song that would get in his head and stay there, looping over and over.

They'd been hanging out in her room, like usual. The door cracked six inches, like always. Even her dad yelling at her about that six inches had been enough to make John break out into a full-body blush back then, although Micah had always yelled something back about "C'mon, Dad, it's *John*."

He couldn't remember how they'd gotten on the topic of

kissing. Maybe someone in their class had been bragging about a recent encounter. Maybe Micah had been reading one of those magazines she'd liked, featuring a pop star on the cover and lots of tips about how to rock a smoky eye and nude lip, or neutral eyes and a red lip, whatever the trend was. But eventually Micah had asked him if he'd ever kissed anyone.

He'd hesitated. He didn't know why his instinct had been to lie to Micah, to tell her that he had, because he never lied to her. Or at least, only by omission. "No," he said finally.

"Me neither." She'd rolled over onto her back, staring up at the ceiling. "I wonder how you know how to do it, when the time comes. Like your lips touch and suddenly, boom, you're just . . . kissing?"

"I guess," John said. "That's how it looks in the movies."

She'd turned to him, propping her head up with her hand as she considered him. He could still see her so clearly in that moment—the bend in her wrist, the way her fingers were lost in her strawberry-blond hair, how clear her green eyes had looked as she'd glanced down at his mouth, not even making any bones about it. That had always been one of the things that had gotten him about Micah—the way she just *went for it* sometimes, the way she seemed willing to jump without knowing where she would land. She was looking right at his mouth, and he knew what she was going to say before she said it.

"We should try it," she said. "Just to see."

He wanted to kiss Micah. God, how he'd *wanted* it. But it seemed like she was just coming up with the idea right now this very second, whereas he'd had a year to want it. He'd felt like they weren't caught up.

"I don't know," he'd said. "You're my best friend."

"And you're mine," she said. "That's why it's perfect. We'll get our first kiss out of the way together, so we can say we did it. Then when it comes time to kiss someone for real, we'll be ready."

"Your dad—" John didn't fear Micah's dad, not really. When he got mad, he reacted in a very predictable way. There'd be some yelling, maybe grounding, more likely the *threatening* of a grounding that would never actually happen. The worst, Micah would say, rolling her eyes, was when he made you sit down and listen to him lecture at you for an hour straight, and god forbid you broke eye contact or cracked a smile because he'd start all over.

John hadn't told Micah what it looked like when *his* dad got mad. It was different every time. That was the worst part about it.

"He's watching the game," Micah had said, sitting up then. "Come on, Johnny, get up here. This will only take a minute."

John had been sitting on the floor at the foot of Micah's bed, her copy of *Twilight* in his lap even though he'd barely been reading it. He knew that he could say no and she'd drop it. But he didn't want to say no. He set the book carefully back on the bottom shelf of her bookcase, then climbed up to sit cross-legged on Micah's bed, facing her.

She chewed her lower lip, the corner of her mouth tilting in a smile. "I don't really know how you get started."

"That's not in your magazines?"

"I guess you just . . ." She leaned forward, planting a kiss somewhere closer to his chin. Even that small touch sent a thrill down his spine, and he'd rubbed his palms against his jeans, feeling where they'd gone sweaty with anticipation. Suddenly *he* wanted to kiss *her*, wanted to be the one to make the jump for once.

"I think it's more like . . ." He touched her face, just the barest graze so he could hold her in place while he pressed his lips more firmly against hers, feeling her intake of breath against his mouth.

And then she did something he hadn't expected. Her lips parted, opening for him, and he felt her tongue slide briefly against his before he pulled back.

He stared at her, still breathing hard. Her mouth looked a little pinker to him, a little swollen, but surely that couldn't be—they'd barely kissed.

"That's how they do it in the movies," she said, and he realized there was the suggestion of an apology in her voice, like she thought he hadn't liked it. He was still trying to gather the words to explain that wasn't it—god, had he *liked* it. He just hadn't seen it coming. He needed a minute.

She'd given a little laugh, rubbing the back of her hand against her mouth. "Well, now we can say we've done it. And I'm sure it gets better, with the second and third and fourth and whatever. Once you get used to it."

Had she not thought the kiss was *good?* John felt suddenly embarrassed. If there was one thing about first kisses, it was that they were supposed to be memorable, right? And now that would be hers, that she'd remember for the rest of her life, and it hadn't even been good.

Wait, wait, he'd wanted to say. *Give me your second and your third and your fourth and whatever else, I can make it better.* But she was already rolling off the bed to cross over to her computer, scrolling through her music library until she found an old blues record she liked.

Maybe that was why now he *hoped* Micah didn't remember

it, if that had been her experience. And it had never been weird between them after that—they'd gone right back to being friends like they'd always been. John had been there to hear Micah talk about those second and third and fourth kisses with a guy she dated freshman year, more kisses than he could possibly count as she'd dated various other people after that. And he'd done his share of kissing, too, although he'd never shared any of the details with her.

"Hey." He heard Frankie's voice behind him, and he turned. They were hard to miss, with their big hair and distinctive style, but from the groups of people they'd left in their wake talking excitedly and scrolling through their phones, he assumed they'd taken a different approach than he had. Less of a "try to fly under the radar" and more of a "walk around openly, sign autographs, then keep going." He'd always admired the way Frankie moved through the world.

"Hey," he said. "You recognized me."

They gave him an incredulous once-over. "You're not exactly incognito. I mean, yes, every guy here has a black hoodie. But you have a very distinctive introspection about you. The minute I saw someone standing with his hands in his pockets, looking out over the water, I knew it was you. This isn't a situation where I have to start removing my boots and telling you I'll go in after you, is it?"

John smiled. "Why is *everyone* referencing *Titanic*? Can't we all agree not to talk about it for the next five days at least?"

"Sure," Frankie said. "Add it to the list. Where's Micah?"

In my bed. "Resting. She wasn't feeling well."

"Yeah, she didn't look great. I hope she's better by tomorrow morning."

"I think it was just a bit of seasickness," John said.

Frankie regarded him in a way that immediately made him squirm. It felt like they'd always seen through everyone from the very start, going all the way back to high school when they'd once spotted Micah making out with a girl by her locker and they'd turned to John and said, *This must be* killing *you*.

"You really didn't keep in touch, all these years?"

John shrugged. "I reached out a couple times." He could've tried harder, and he knew it. But what was he supposed to do, if she didn't answer his text messages, if she turned him away the one time he'd tried to make contact in person? He wasn't going to force it.

He'd said he didn't hate her, and he meant that. He wasn't even angry anymore. But there had been a time when he *had* been, when he hadn't been able to understand why she'd detonated something that had blown up in all their faces. Why she hadn't *talked* to him about it before, or even afterward. He knew that the prevailing theory among fans—hell, the prevailing theory among the *band*, since they'd never been told otherwise—was that she wanted a solo pop career so badly she'd stepped right over them to get there. That was what John had believed at the time, with no evidence to believe anything to the contrary.

But the more time that passed, the more he saw how that just didn't make any *sense*. Micah had never talked about wanting to be a star on her own. If anything, she'd always seemed genuinely grateful to have a group around her, had gone out of her way to share the spotlight even when the record label and the press and everyone else seemed determined to shove her out front and center as the main face of the band.

"How about you?" he asked.

"Yeah, I also tried. I sent congratulations when her record came out, which in retrospect she probably thought was sarcastic, but I really meant it. And of course I texted her when she did *Playboy*, just to tell her the spread was hot and check to see how she was doing. She did say thank you to that one, but not much else."

John felt his face heat, and he turned back toward the water, letting his hood block Frankie from view. Micah had done an interview with *Playboy* only a few months after the band's breakup. It had been the first official announcement that the band was done, which had caused quite the stir—along with the photos.

He'd never seen them. He'd gone out of his *way* to never see them, although he'd found a text-only version of the interview on a fan page for the band, the one and only time he'd ever visited that kind of site. The tone had been . . . defiant. There was a very *fuck it* quality to Micah's answers that had seemed at the time to back up the idea that she was done with her old life, was ready to start completely over.

There had been one answer that had gotten to him. He could still remember the exact phrasing. *ElectricOh! gave me a lot of firsts. Those will always mean something to me—some of them more than others.*

Some of them more than others? What was that about?

"I always thought the timing of that interview was odd," Frankie said.

"How so?"

Frankie pursed their lips, tilting their head. "It was what, a year before her solo album came out? Maybe more? There was nothing for her to promote. It would've made more sense to do a big feature like that closer to the release date, to build buzz. She got to announce the band breakup, but to what end? We could've done that with a press release."

"Well." John placed his hands on the railing of the ship, letting the cold metal sting his palms until he withdrew and put his hands back in his hoodie pockets. "Micah always did whatever she wanted."

There was no bite to his words, and he hoped Frankie knew how he meant it. That had always been one of Micah's best qualities, to him. He could admire it even when he'd been hurt by it.

But Frankie had a point. The timing of doing such a big, splashy interview, the photos that seemed *designed* to be incendiary, that defiant tone . . . yeah, it did seem strange.

He tried to remember when exactly she and Ryder had broken up. If the start of their relationship had always been shrouded in a bit of secrecy, the end had its own mystery surrounding it. In his mind, it had happened almost simultaneously with the breakup of the band, but it must've happened either *before* or *after*. And suddenly it seemed like the answer to that question could unlock all of it.

"Who ended things?" he asked. "Her, or Ryder?"

"To hear Ryder tell it, he did," Frankie said. "But you know that doesn't mean much."

It didn't mean shit. But then, maybe none of it did. It had all happened so long ago.

The lighting changed, going dark before a cheer went up from the crowd on the deck below, a burst of colored lights sweeping over the ship that indicated the Silver Cuties were about to take the stage. There were people lined up against the railing that looked over the stage below, so John and Frankie had no chance of getting any closer, but they at least turned around so they could face the show. The air was still bitingly cold against John's cheeks, making the tip of his nose feel numb, but at least the ship wasn't moving as much as it had been earlier. He wished suddenly that Micah *would* come out to see the show. She'd always loved watching live music. It had been one of their most formative bonding experiences.

"Do you remember that pit at the Warped Tour?" John said to Frankie.

"Oh my god," Frankie said. "I thought we were going to die. Like, were all the steel-toed boots and spiked bracelets *necessary*? Didn't you get a black eye?"

"No, but Micah—" John started, then remembered. That's right. He *had* blamed the black eye on the show. "That was the most scared I've ever been in a pit."

"She put us in so many situations that looking back now, I'm like uh-uh. No *way* would I try even half that shit. Hell, these days my ideal show involves assigned seating and a preposted schedule of the exact time each band will go on."

"Ha," John said. "Seriously."

But he was thinking about how he didn't know that he even had an ideal show anymore, couldn't remember the last time he'd gone to a concert where he hadn't been playing. Back then, his ideal show had always been getting as close to the stage as possible, less because he cared about that and more because Micah did, and he loved standing next to her and watching the lights play over her face while she sang along to all the lyrics at the top of her lungs.

He stayed for the Silver Cuties' entire set, and they put on a great show. But there was something *missing* from the entire experience, and the more time John spent on this ship, the less he felt like he was going to be able to pretend he didn't feel it anymore.

IT WAS PAST midnight by the time John quietly let himself back into his room. The darkness was unrelenting the minute the door shut behind him, and so he switched on the bathroom light and cracked the door, hoping it wouldn't wake Micah up. He could see the shadowy outline of her under the covers, but she hadn't stirred, which led him to believe she was still asleep.

As much as he'd genuinely wanted her to get rest, he hadn't really thought all of this through. There was a chair shoved into one corner, barely enough to toss some clothes on, much less for all six feet of John to curl up on to *sleep*. But he also wasn't about to just climb into bed next to her without asking her first, even if it was *his* bed.

He took his time brushing his teeth, changing into the cheesy Batman pajama pants Asa had gotten him for Christmas one year—John had no idea why, when he'd never expressed any particular affinity for Batman. Maybe all his moving around in the bathroom woke Micah up after all, or maybe it was just that she'd already been sleeping for five hours, but by the time he emerged he could see that her eyes were open but still drowsy, staring at him as he stood in the doorway to the bathroom.

"Hey," he said.

"Johnny," she said, her voice barely a whisper.

The bass for the concert had been loud, and the stage had

transitioned for a DJ set directly after for those who wanted to keep partying on the first night of the cruise. That must be what John felt in his chest, then, the low reverberations still pounding through his skin and muscle and bone.

He cleared his throat. "How are you feeling?"

She licked her lips like they were dry. "Better. I'm sorry I—"

"Don't worry about it." He grabbed her bottled water from where she'd left it on the dresser, handing it to her before retreating to a safe distance at the bathroom doorway.

"Thanks," she said. When she sat up in bed to take a sip, she held the covers to her chest, but he couldn't help but notice that her back was bare. Christ, was she *naked* under there?

"They should still be able to get you into your room," he said. "If you wanted to call down now."

She looked at him. Her hair was still half in the ponytail she'd lain down with, half pulled out and haloed around her head in wisps that caught the bathroom light. "You want your bed back."

"I would've taken the chair," he said. "But yeah, now that you're awake, the bed would be more comfortable."

"So get in."

He felt a traitorous twinge in his dick at the very suggestion. If he wasn't careful, he'd *have* to get under the covers quickly, if for no other reason than to hide his reaction to her. But that was the very definition of *out of the frying pan, into the fire*.

"Come on," he said. "Don't you have a balcony? Imagine waking up to that view."

She shifted the covers under her armpits, and he had the sudden thought *Imagine waking up to* that *view*. Which immediately made him that much more desperate to get her out of his room. Hell, if she felt so bad that he hadn't gotten a balcony, maybe she'd be open to switching.

"I'm really tired," she said. "And tomorrow is a big day. If you wouldn't mind . . . I mean, it's fine with me, if . . . can I just stay?"

John had an urge to tell her *absolutely not*, to gather up her clothes and march her out of there like a scene out of a soap opera. But he could see how much it had cost her to even ask. And truly it didn't have to be a big deal, if neither of them made it a big deal. They'd slept together countless times before.

But that was before, he thought, and then he didn't know what to make of that. Before *what*?

He switched off the bathroom light, climbing into bed next to her. It was already warm and toasty under the covers from where she'd been wrapped up in them for the past few hours, and her body gave off heat like she'd been charging that whole time. He was cold from being out above deck for so long, and it was tempting to snuggle closer to her, toward that heat source, but he stayed on his edge of the bed.

"Thank you," she said.

"Don't worry about it," he said again. At this point, he wondered if he knew how to say anything else. Meanwhile all he was doing was *worrying about it*.

He tried to put everything from his mind—the nearness of her body, the apparent *nakedness* of it—and concentrate on getting some sleep. He'd need it. But he was still wide awake when he heard Micah's voice behind him several minutes later.

"Nice pajama pants," she said.

He grunted.

"I didn't know you were a Batman guy."

"I'm not."

"But you—"

He punched his pillow, rolling over until he was facing her. It was too dark to make out any details of her expression, but he could hear her breathing.

"My housemates gave them to me," he said. "One of them, anyway."

"Your housemate?"

"Yeah," he said. "I share a house with some other people—Elliot, Kiki, and then Asa and Lauren. Asa gave me these, and knowing him it was some kind of joke, although I have no idea what the punch line was supposed to be. Just that I look goofy in them? No clue."

"You're kinda mysterious like Batman," Micah said. "You have an alter ego. I don't know. I don't think you look goofy."

John didn't know what to say to that.

"So that's . . . who you watch your TV shows with?"

She must still be half-asleep, because she wasn't making much sense. "My housemates? Yeah, we watch TV together sometimes."

"Ah," she said. "That's nice."

It *was* nice, not that John thought about it much. He supposed it was the kind of thing you took for granted after a while—having people you could hang out with, share things with even if they were as superficial as a dating reality show you were all invested in watching together. Somehow it didn't feel superficial, when you had people who looked forward to you coming home and wanted to hear your opinions on whatever had happened. It was friendship, in a way that John realized he hadn't had since those days of hanging out with Micah in her room, going to shows together, talking late at night after everyone else had gone to bed just like this. That had felt so comforting then. It felt dangerous now.

"Let's get some sleep," John said. "You said it yourself, tomorrow's a big day."

CHAPTER

TWELVE

WHEN MICAH WOKE up, it took a minute for her to orient herself to her surroundings. For one thing, it was *dark*. For another, there was a strange sound in the air, almost more an absence of sound than a sound itself. It was like being inside an echo.

But the main thing was that she'd woken up next to a man. And not just any man, she realized as everything came rushing back to her at once—*John*. Her onetime best friend, her bandmate, her biggest regret. She'd shared a bed with John last night.

And this morning, he had an arm casually draped over her shoulder, his hand palming her bare breast.

She could control the amount of touch just by breathing. Inhale, and she swelled to fit his hand, the contact warm and all-encompassing, feeling like he *meant* it. Exhale, and it was barely a tickle, her nipple hard and wanting against his palm, begging for more.

And speaking of hard and wanting . . . she could feel him against the back of her, the ridge of his erection unmistakable where it pressed against her ass through the thin fabric of his pajamas, her underwear. She wanted to press back, to push against him just to see what would happen. She wanted to take his hand and close it around her breast, give it a decisive squeeze that said *Yes, this is real.*

But she knew that none of that was a good idea. If John woke up now, no doubt he'd be mortified to be caught in this kind of position—it wasn't like he *wanted* it. They'd just drifted toward each other while sleeping, and then his body had taken over . . .

God, his body could take her all the way over. She suddenly wanted John to fuck her with a desperation that was almost painful.

This was *John* she was having these thoughts about. It had to just be the shock of being near him again, after all those years, the way he felt like the same boy she'd always known and like a man who was a complete stranger to her. Even the weight of his arm felt different, the ridges of veins over the muscle of his forearm, the light dusting of dark hair. She wasn't meant to be noticing all of these new details about him.

She had to get out of his room. She had to get out of his *bed*.

Micah slid out from underneath his arm, listening to hear if she'd woken him. But he was still breathing the heavy, deep rhythm that told her he was out. She felt along the carpet next to the bed until she came across her bra, then shuffled carefully forward until she was able to grab the rest of her clothes and disappear into the bathroom to freshen up. He'd helpfully looped her bag on the handle of the door leading back out to the hallway, and she double-checked to make sure it had everything inside, including her phone, before opening the door to make her escape.

The strip of light from the hallway illuminated John on the

bed, his tousled black curls spread out over his pillow, the covers pushed down to where she could see the back of his elbow. She wondered if he'd notice that she'd left, if there was a chance he'd been dreaming of her. All fanciful thoughts, and she shut the door before she could get lost too far down a labyrinth of them.

BY THE TIME Micah was due to the Starlight Theater for rehearsals, she'd gotten herself back under control. She'd found someone to let her into her room—to locate her room in the first place. She'd showered, changed into new clothes, and sat out on her balcony with a cup of tea just in time to watch the sun rise. It really was incredible, that this time yesterday she'd been sleeping in a Miami hotel and now here she was, on a ship in the middle of the ocean watching the first light of day come over the horizon.

The ship seemed to have stabilized from the night before, which she was grateful for, and although it was still a little chilly, it had been pleasant enough for her to enjoy the balcony with her cardigan on.

She felt like she could still *feel* the weight of John's hand on her breast this morning, was conscious when she breathed of her bra abrading against her nipple in a way that reminded her of his palm. It was so stupid, to have thoughts like that, and she had to figure out a way to put it out of her mind before she faced everyone at rehearsals.

But overall she was feeling good. She and John seemed better now—more like the friends they'd always been. And if she'd briefly entertained *more than friends*-type thoughts about him, well, he didn't have to know that. The extra sleep really had helped her, and she was feeling like maybe there was a chance they could perform well on this cruise. More than that, maybe they could have some fun.

She was sitting in one of the folding chairs set up on the Starlight's stage alongside all their instruments and equipment, chatting with Frankie, when John walked in. He did a bit of a double take when he saw her, almost like he didn't expect that she'd already be there.

"Putting the *punk* in *punctuality*," she said, grinning at him.

He made his way over to his guitar, not bothering to sit down as he lifted the strap over his neck and plugged in, pressing one of his pedals down with the toe of his Converse while he started tuning up.

"I stole that," he said after a minute. He hadn't been looking at her when he said it, so she couldn't tell at first that he was talking to her.

"What?"

"From Henry Rollins," he said. "I think I read it in some interview."

Micah's jaw literally dropped open. She couldn't believe what she was hearing. All those years, she'd thought he'd come up with that phrase. "You let me believe it was yours."

"I know," John said. "You thought it was so clever."

"So why—"

He did glance up at her then, and there was something almost shy around his eyes. For a minute, she thought maybe he'd been semiconscious that morning after all, that he was thinking of his hand on her bare skin the way she couldn't stop thinking about it. But that was impossible. He had definitely been sleeping.

The problem was that *she'd* been wide awake, and now it was hard to watch his hand as it wrapped around the neck of his guitar, his fingers easily fretting a chord that she could tell he wasn't even thinking about. *He could play me like that*, she thought, and then had to look away.

What the fuck was *wrong* with her?

The doors to the theater burst open, and Steve and Ryder entered in such a performatively noisy way it was like they were trying to kill the mood. Which was fine, obviously. There wasn't any mood. Micah busied herself messing with the microphone, humming a few notes into it before holding it farther away to sing a line from "If Only." She had already done her usual vocal warm-ups in the shower, and as shitty as he'd been in the *way* he'd said it, Ryder wasn't wrong—she didn't have nearly as much to do as the rest of them, since she didn't play an instrument onstage.

To get ready for a full tour, she'd had an entire workout regime—she had a small trampoline in her apartment, and she would jump on it for hours, practicing belting out her biggest notes without getting out of breath. The old man who'd lived downstairs had eventually asked her, very nicely, if she wouldn't mind doing that only from the hours of ten to two o'clock. She'd been happy to oblige, and after that he would sometimes bring her up a steaming bowl of noodle soup, claiming it was good for the vocal cords. It had always made her feel warm and cared for, and she swore her voice got stronger, her pitch more precise. As far as she was concerned, that soup had been magic.

"All right," Ryder said once he had his guitar, like he was calling a meeting to order. "We can start with 'Sunflares,' since it's a little faster, and then 'Open Mouth,' and close out with 'Anesthesia.' That also makes sense because—"

"We're playing 'If Only' as one of the three," Micah said.

Ryder shot her an impatient look, glancing at Steve and rolling his eyes as though they'd been over this. Micah had been feeling pretty good about this gig only a few minutes ago, and now she was already having her doubts. Surely Ryder couldn't have turned Steve against her that soon?

Or should she have said turned against her *again*? Maybe still.

"'Sunflares,' 'Open Mouth,' and then close with 'If Only,'" Micah said firmly.

"We're already playing that fucking song on prom night," Ryder said. "We have to show we're not just some one-hit wonder—"

"On this cruise, we *are* a one-hit wonder," Frankie cut in. "Micah's right. They're here to hear that song. We should play it every chance we get. And prom night will be acoustic, whereas this one will be electric. It'll feel different enough."

Ryder slapped his guitar so hard the sound buzzed through his amp. "*No*, it won't—"

"We have to play 'If Only' both times," John said. "It's in the contract."

Micah had barely read the contract, if she was being honest. She'd skimmed it enough to get the gist, had checked to make sure there was nothing in there about having to spend any alone time with Ryder, and then had signed on the bottom line. But if she trusted anyone to have read the entire thing from top to bottom, it was John.

Ryder looked ready to argue, but John just kept tuning his guitar, strumming a chord until he apparently liked what he heard. "I have a copy of the contract in my room," he said. "I can get it, if you want."

"Let's just run through 'Sunflares,'" Ryder muttered, and Micah bit back a grin.

It took them three tries to even get through the first chorus. That shouldn't be a surprise—it could be difficult to get into the right rhythm, even when they all knew their individual parts. Micah was just starting to panic, though, worried that she *had* tanked them with her insistence on waiting to rehearse together until they were all on the cruise. Now they had to play later that night, and they could barely get through the first song.

"Hey," John said when they took a brief break after the third try. "You've got this. There's no need to rush through it."

Because that was the worst part. It was definitely, unmistakably Micah's fault that they kept fucking up. She went too early into that chorus, and then somehow the syncopated guitar riff threw her off, and she could never catch up. It was like jumping into the middle of a game of double dutch, and thinking for a second you had it, until all of a sudden the rope tripped you up and you were face-first on the ground.

"I think I know what I'm doing wrong," she said.

He shook his head. "Don't think. *Feel* it. You know you can feel it."

God, could she feel it. That was part of her problem. She was trying to look anywhere but at John's hands, but her gaze kept getting pulled toward that direction, and then suddenly she was right back in that bed, him warm and hard against her.

"Micah?" She realized John had been talking to her for the

last few seconds, but she'd been off on some other planet. Some distant, horny star. What she needed was to find twenty minutes to herself where she could take care of these feelings, and then she could go back to normal.

"Hmm?"

"You okay?"

John had always been good at seeming to tune out the conflict around him, to focus on the task at hand. It had made him an ideal bandmate when things had been at their most tense and fractured, because she could always look to him to help ground her onstage, could take strength from his calm presence even off the stage. She'd wondered about his home life when they were kids, knew deep in her bones that there was stuff going on there that had made him turn inward the way he had, like rough waters smoothing down a rock. She thought leaving at a young age to play music would give him a respite from that, but then she supposed it had just introduced a different kind of strife. She wished she'd been a better friend to him in those years.

"Last night—" he started, but she never got to hear the rest of what he was going to say, because Ryder rejoined the group, draining what was left of a beer. It was nine thirty in the morning, but what did she know.

"Let's go again," Ryder said. "Do we need to slow it down for you, Micah?"

He stretched out the words, saying *slow it down* like she wouldn't possibly be able to understand. In a perfect world, she would've nailed it on her next try, and Ryder would've somehow cut his hand open on a guitar string and needed to be helicoptered off the boat for emergency care.

In this extremely imperfect world, Micah fucked up again. And again.

"I can't believe this shit," Ryder said, taking off his guitar and practically throwing it on the ground. He'd always been about the rock-star dramatics, but this one seemed especially stupid, since they only had so many instruments on board. Presumably he would need that guitar in one piece.

"I'm sorry," Micah said. She could feel tears stinging at the corners of her eyes, and willed them not to fall. "Maybe it's the song, maybe we move on to—"

But Ryder was already halfway down the aisle toward the door to the theater. "I'm taking ten," he said over his shoulder. "I suggest you take the time to search up *basic four-four time signature* and see if anything on YouTube can help you out."

Steve stood up, too, twirling one drumstick in his hand before setting both on top of his kit. "The jump from three to four in the chorus is tough," he said. "But you've done this before."

Frankie gave Micah a sympathetic shoulder squeeze, but they left with Steve. Micah knew that a break was probably a good idea, that there was no point in continuing to push through if it just wasn't working, but she also couldn't shake her panic that time was running out and they were no closer to having a tight set than they'd been half an hour ago.

Only John remained behind, sitting on his amp, one leg crossed over the other while he idly strummed his guitar.

"I *have* done this before," she said, pacing back and forth, chewing on her thumbnail. It tasted horrible because of the nail polish she'd had applied before the cruise in order to prevent that very action, but not horrible enough to stop her. "I'm a professional. Or at least I *was* a professional. I haven't performed in eight years—did you know that?"

"Why did you stop?"

She barked a bitter laugh. "I didn't get another record deal," she said. "*Soft sales*—that was the phrase they used. And no record deal, no tour. They're not looking to sink money into an artist that isn't going to have anything else come out."

"But what stopped you from doing anything else? Something on your own. An indie project, featuring on another artist's song, whatever."

She paused in her pacing, turning to look at him. "Join some cover band, play the local bar scene? That's what you did, right?"

It came out nasty, the way she said it. And maybe she'd meant it to. She was frustrated—at her incompetence, at the seemingly infinite number of ways she could let people down. She was frustrated by the way John could just sit there, playing his guitar with such quiet skill, could slot himself into any band he wanted without missing a beat. The way he could fade into the background, providing the foundation of the music without needing to take center stage. It could be just him and his guitar against the world. He didn't even know what a gift that was.

"Why not?" John asked. "You could've made a killer Elvis impersonator at a fast-food joint." His brown eyes were steady and serious, staying on her as he started strumming a song she immediately recognized. *"Chicken tender, sour and sweet, never let me go . . . you have made my life complete, and I love you so."*

He sang softly, his voice barely projecting over the guitar, which was still playing through his amp. John had always been self-conscious about his voice—Ryder and Frankie had done all the live backup vocals. Micah didn't entirely see why. He might not have the strongest voice—she wouldn't know, since she'd barely heard him use it. But he could carry a tune reasonably well, and there was a low warmth to it that she liked. Or maybe that was just because it was *him*.

"Keep going," she said when he stopped after that verse.

He laughed, slapping the strings of his guitar in a way that she knew meant he wouldn't be singing any more. "That was supposed to get you to smile."

It had objectively been hilarious. She'd probably crack up later, thinking of how he'd turned the lyrics of "Love Me Tender" into a song about chicken nuggets. But for now she was caught in the spell of his serenade, and she just didn't want it to stop.

"What kind of cover bands are you in?" she asked.

"Ah," he said. "This'll definitely make you laugh. I answered a Craigslist ad to join a band that plays the Offspring's greatest hits all around Central Florida. Want to know what it's called? Guess."

Micah could already feel the smile tugging on her lips, but she shook her head. She had nothing.

John raised his eyebrows, like he knew what a bomb he was about to drop. "The Knock-Offspring."

That did surprise a laugh out of her. "Oh my god," she said. "No way."

"*Way*," he said. "Although we haven't been able to practice much lately. Our drummer Eric's back went out."

"The Kids *Aren't* Alright," she quipped, and John started playing the distinctive riff that opened that song.

"Eric's cool," he said once he'd stopped. "Pretty Fly—for a White Guy."

"I guess he's got to Come Out and Play," Micah said. "Once his back is feeling better."

John grinned at her. "In the meantime, he's Gone Away."

Micah searched her brain for more songs by The Offspring. She could remember "Why Don't You Get a Job?" but couldn't quite think about how to slot it into this conversational back-and-forth. John watched her face until he started playing another song she vaguely recognized as by that band but couldn't place.

"You're Not the One to play this game with me," he said. "I promise you I can go longer."

She arched her eyebrow at him. "You think you can out-last me?"

She wasn't talking about some nineties band anymore. And from the way he missed a note in the tight palm-muted riff he'd been playing, she thought he knew it. Whether he had any memory of what had happened between them this morning, he was surely aware of what had been between them the night before. All that tension couldn't have been only in her head, the feeling of him sliding under the sheets next to her, the way he'd seemed to hold his body unnaturally still while pretending to already be asleep. She knew he hadn't fallen asleep that fast.

Micah was so close to doing something stupid, like just asking him about it, when the door to the theater opened again and Ryder, Frankie, and Steve entered together, their hands full of drinks. Ryder and Steve each had beers, which was *interesting* to Micah, given that it was Ryder who'd been so insistent on their professionalism at rehearsal just the other day, and Frankie had a couple bottled waters, which they handed out to John and Micah once they reached the stage.

"Did y'all bring a reusable water bottle?" they asked. "I don't like putting all this plastic out into the earth."

Micah held up the water bottle she'd brought with her to rehearsal.

John glanced between hers and Frankie's. "I'll buy one," he said.

"Good man," Frankie said, giving him a pat on the head.

Micah was jealous of that simple, casual touch. She'd almost touched him that morning, smoothed out his hair, put a hand to his cheek. But it had been dark and she'd been trying to be quiet, and she was sure she would've ended up poking him in the eye instead.

"Now, are we ready to do this, or what?" Ryder asked once he'd plugged his guitar back in.

Micah glanced at John, bringing her microphone up to her mouth. *"Chicken tender, barbecue, all my dreams fulfilled . . . "*

He grinned at her, and that was when she knew that the rest of rehearsal was going to go just fine.

"What?" Ryder said. "Chicken what?"

"Nothing," Micah said. "I'm ready."

CHAPTER

THIRTEEN

JOHN DIDN'T EVEN know how he got through that rehearsal.

At first, it had just been *bad*. They were all out of sync, with Frankie playing behind the beat just a bit and Ryder's and John's guitars sounding like they were talking over each other instead of being in conversation. And then Micah was clearly nervous and in her head about it, and the more she fucked up, the more nervous and in her head she got.

He'd barely been able to look at her when he'd arrived. He'd been disappointed when he woke up alone, only the slight imprint on the pillow next to him giving away that Micah had been there at all. But he'd been relieved, too. Because he'd had a *hell* of a dream about her, and had woken up so hard it was painful. Thanks to the total darkness of his room, he'd also overslept, which meant he hadn't had time to do anything about it before he had to run to rehearsal.

Which was another reason it had been difficult to get through the last couple of hours—he just couldn't stop thinking about

Micah in ways he really shouldn't be thinking about her. Her hair was back in its usual ponytail, but he couldn't help but remember the way it had been last night, messy and undone from rolling around in bed. She was dressed casually today, in a black T-shirt with the words THE SAME SONGS OVER AND OVER printed in white block letters, and jeans that perfectly formed to her ass when she bent over to move the mic cord out of the way. And he found himself thinking about that expanse of bare back when she'd sat up in bed the night before, how much he wanted to put that entire peony tattooed on her shoulder in his mouth.

And then there had been Ryder, who just seemed determined to be every asshole stereotype he could fit in before lunchtime.

"Hey, man," he said to John now, clapping him on the shoulder as they packed up the gear, some of which cruise officials would take care of later. "I know they didn't need two guitarists for bingo, and since you don't like public speaking—or hell, private speaking—I think it's smart that you're sitting this one out."

Micah was required to be one of the hosts for the bingo game, of course, and John had happily conceded one of the other two spots to Frankie, who seemed really excited to do it. Ryder wasn't *wrong* about John's antipathy toward public speaking, so it had been an easy decision to make. Ryder was the logical third person to round out the hosting duties, and even though John and Steve were supposed to sit up in the balcony seats of the theater to still be "around" and "participating," somehow he knew that Steve was going to sneak out halfway through for that pool time he was determined to get.

It had been a no-brainer to opt out of bingo, but then John

had to watch from the balcony while Ryder made a show of pulling out Micah's stool onstage and helping her up. And suddenly John felt like he wanted to go back in time and insist that he could've hosted the shit out of some bingo, actually.

"Who's ready to play some games and win prizes and hang out with ElectricOh!, am I right?" the host from the cruise ship said into his microphone, gesturing over toward the small table on the stage where Frankie, Ryder, and Micah were seated on their stools. Micah gave an awkward little laugh, raising her own microphone to her mouth.

"Well, three fifths of ElectricOh!," she said. "The rest is up there where they can heckle us."

The crowd below swiveled to look up toward where John and Steve were sitting in the balcony seats, and Steve put two fingers in his mouth and let out a loud whistle.

"We'll let security handle them if they get too rambunctious," the cruise host quipped, then gestured up toward the screen behind the stage where all the bingo numbers were displayed. "I know I don't need to explain how this game works, but . . ."

He went on to explain how the game worked, which John tuned out while he watched Ryder place his hand on Micah's waist, leaning in to say something in her ear. She laughed, but John could tell it was for show.

Who *had* ended things between them? And when? John hadn't allowed himself to think too much about Ryder and Micah's relationship. It had been like a mild case of tinnitus the entire time they'd been together—always there, always annoying, but much, much worse if you actually focused on it.

John wondered which floral tattoo was for Ryder, if she'd gotten one for him at all. He knew that was the story behind

Micah's tattoos—the ones he knew about, anyway. She'd gotten a different flower for different people who were important to her life somehow. The dandelion on her neck was for her younger sister; the peony was for her grandmother; and she had a rose on her thigh that was based on one that could only be found at Graceland or had been named after Graceland, he couldn't remember.

They'd gone to get their first tattoos together, when they were still technically underage. They'd flipped through books of the artist's flash work, trying to decide what to get, suggesting more and more outlandish options for the other one. Finally, Micah had closed the book, looking up at him with an expression that was more questioning than triumphant.

"I know what I'm doing," she said.

"The pizza slice on roller blades?"

"I don't think we're at the *matching* tattoo phase yet," she said, nudging his shoulder.

It had been a joke, clearly, and yet he felt something catch in his throat. "So what is it, then?"

"You can see it when it's done," she said. "I'll show you mine if you show me yours."

But even after they'd taken Micah back to another room, John kept turning the pages of the book, with zero idea what he wanted to commit to putting permanently on his body. And when they'd called his name and he'd stood up, catching a glimpse of the couple people laid out on tables in the main area of the tattoo shop, artists bent over them with needles buzzing . . . he couldn't do it. He'd shaken his head, sitting back down.

"I'm just waiting for someone," he said, even though he'd filled out the same forms that Micah had, had clearly put his name down for an appointment. The shop must have been used to people bailing at the last minute, though, because the guy with the gauged ears and tattoos covering half his face had just shrugged, going back to the computer to click through a few screens.

When Micah had finally emerged from getting her tattoo done, he couldn't see any wrapping or bandages visible on her arms or legs. "Well?" he asked. "What did you get?"

Her gaze was also sweeping over him, and she seemed to register that he didn't have anything wrapped, either. "You first."

He ran his hand through his hair, embarrassed to be caught out. "I, uh—"

Her eyes had widened. "You didn't do it?"

"I don't think I like needles?" he said. "I didn't know that about myself until I saw all these needles, but yeah. Is there an option without the needles?"

"John Lorenzo Populin Jr.," she said, and he winced. He hated it when anyone said his full name aloud, and she must've remembered that, because her face softened slightly even as she turned and left him standing there in the middle of the tattoo parlor lobby.

"Well, don't think you're getting to see mine, then," she said. "Until you've fulfilled your side of the bargain."

And he never had.

Steve brought him back into the present when he accidentally sloshed a bit of drink on John's shoe. John could've sworn that Steve had sat down with no drink at all, so he had no idea where the brightly colored cocktail adorned with a festive umbrella and slice of pineapple on the rim had come from.

"Sorry about that, mate!" Steve said. At the height of the

band's fame, they'd played a festival in Australia *once*, and that experience had been all it took to get Steve obsessed with calling everyone *mate*. There was something so endearing about the fact that he still did it.

"I think rehearsal went okay," John said. "All things considered."

Steve leaned in, obviously trying to hear John over the bingo numbers being announced and the noise from the crowd. "Oh yeah! Once Micah figured out that transition, it was a piece of cake. Like riding a bike. Hey, want to see a video of my kid learning to ride a bike?"

"Sure."

Steve handed his drink to John, reaching into his back pocket to grab his phone. He scrolled through a bunch of pictures, stopping to show John several—Tyler with birthday cake all over his face, Tyler at the playground wearing an Elsa costume, the back of Tyler's head at the zoo, the back of Tyler's head reading a book. Finally he handed his phone to John, switching it out for the drink as a video already in progress continued to play of Tyler riding a bike with training wheels down a suburban driveway.

"That's awesome, man," John said, handing the phone back once the video was done. "He's really got the hang of it."

Not that John had any idea what made a kid *good* at riding a bike at that age, but it seemed like the thing to say. And it worked, because Steve beamed like the proud father he was. "He does. Little speed demon. Remind me, do you have any kids? Wife, girlfriend, kid on the way, anything like that?"

"None of the above," John said. "Just haven't had time."

Steve nodded, like that made sense, but truly it was just

something John had *said*. It didn't actually make any sense at all. He'd had nothing but time. He didn't even know if he wanted kids, didn't know if he felt any particular pull toward "settling down" just to do it. But he couldn't blame it on time. He thought about his days spent playing in various local bands, hanging out at the music store when his favorite clerk was on duty, eating cereal on the couch while watching a TV show. And suddenly it felt like such a *waste* of a life. Was that all he'd been doing?

Down on the stage, someone had brought props for the band members, and now Frankie had a lei around their neck and Ryder was hamming it up with a pair of cruise-branded sunglasses over his eyes. Micah had a cute little sailor hat she'd perched on top of her head, and it kept almost falling off every time she laughed, until she had to hold it with one hand. Frankie had said something to make Micah legitimately, full-on lose it, and John caught himself smiling, too. It was good to see her laugh like that, especially after the way she'd looked yesterday.

"B-4!" the host announced, and a roomful of papers shuffled as everyone checked to see if they had that one. Frankie, Ryder, and Micah had each been given a few cards themselves, and Micah leaned over Frankie's shoulder, trying to see if they had that number.

"I need to step it up *before* I lose my ass," Micah said into the microphone, and Frankie grinned at her.

"You should've thought of that *before* you challenged me," they shot back.

"Ladies, ladies," Ryder said, looping his arm around Micah's shoulders. "We can all go back to *before*, don't you worry."

And with that, he planted a big kiss right on Micah's cheek, knocking the sailor hat down to the stage.

Even from up in the balcony, several yards away, John could see the way Micah tensed up. The problem was that the crowd *loved* it. There was a collective, almost involuntary *aww*, followed by whispering that gained volume as people got more and more excited. Several people had their phones up for the entire bingo game, so John had no doubt this entire thing would be on YouTube later, filled with comments about how cute they were together or how people had called it, they *said* they weren't done yet.

Micah played along, smiling and continuing to make the occasional comment into the microphone, but once the bingo game was over she was the first one off the stage. Sometime in the middle of everything, Steve must've also found a way to sneak off for the pool time he'd desperately been wanting, so John was alone as he made his way down the stairs. He kept getting stopped, and he scribbled his autograph on several bingo cards just to be able to climb up onstage and make his way behind the curtain to try to find the rest of his band.

"*Ladies?*" Frankie was in the middle of saying. "Come on, you're such a troll."

"It's a word," Ryder said. "And it was just a *kiss*, Christ, Micah, don't be such a drama queen about it. Everybody was into it."

"*I* wasn't," Micah said. "*I* wasn't, and that's the most important part. Ever hear of consent, you dirtbag?"

"Oh, like you asked for our *consent* before you completely snaked our album deal out from under us?" Ryder said. "I don't recall being asked how I felt about that."

John expected Micah to fire back after that, but she didn't. Instead she just grabbed her own pair of cruise-branded sunglasses, setting them on her face before pushing past John toward the exit. He barely had time to decide whether to follow her or stay when she'd already gone.

"What the fuck?" he asked Ryder. "You owe her an apology."

"I don't owe her shit."

"Your pathetic career isn't her fault."

Ryder stretched his arms wide, as though encompassing the entire ship. "Look around you, Johnny boy," he said. "This is *all* her fault. The fact that we're some one-hit-wonder joke, the fact that we're one step above a cruise ship talent show act when we should be selling out stadiums by now, the fact that we can't get through a single one of these events without being at each other's throats. And I'll play your stupid fucking song tonight, but never forget that while you're so busy looking out for *her*, all she cares about is looking out for herself. Call *me* pathetic? It's your fault that you've never been able to see that."

Once again, John felt the overwhelming urge to punch Ryder right in his pretentious, arrogant face, but once again he felt powerless to do anything but stand there. Ryder shoved past him hard enough to jostle his shoulder, and still John just took it.

Frankie looked at him sympathetically once Ryder had gone, leaving only the two of them. "She mentioned wanting to get some air," they said. "I bet you could catch up to her."

CHAPTER

FOURTEEN

MICAH WAS SITTING on one of the deck chairs on the very top level of the cruise ship, the one reserved for only the artists and any entourage they might have brought with them. She'd already spotted Tatiana looking fierce in a tiny bikini, surrounded by a few other women she assumed were part of her group. If the situation of this cruise had been any different, maybe she would've tried to flirt with Tatiana a bit, just to see if she was all the way straight or if she was a little curious.

But that was the last thing on Micah's mind now. She just had to figure out how to get through the next four days without wanting to throw herself—or Ryder—off the ship.

"Anyone sitting here?" John said from behind her, gesturing at the chair next to hers.

"No."

He sat down at the end of his, tilting it forward with his weight. He had to catch himself from falling with one hand down on the deck, and he laughed a little when he settled himself more securely, rubbing two of his fingers that had stopped his fall.

"Are you hurt?"

He examined his fingers, which looked normal at least—not bent or scraped up or anything like that. "Nah," he said. "I'm fine."

She thought of his fingers playing the guitar. She thought of them against her nipple this morning, what they would feel like inside her. She cleared her throat. "I think you're going to need those."

"I'll try not to be so clumsy in the future," he said. "I'll be all right."

The wind had started back up a bit—not as bad as the day before, thankfully, but enough that it kept whipping strands of Micah's ponytail onto her cheeks, sticking against her mouth. She gathered her ponytail with one hand to hold it out of her face.

"He's not wrong, you know," she said. "I did snake the album deal right out from underneath all of you. And I never apologized for it. But I *am* sorry. You have no idea how sorry I am. I should've apologized a long time ago. To everyone, but especially to you."

Why especially to me? she thought he might ask, and then she'd have to decide just how honest she wanted to be. But instead he shifted on the chair, leaning back into it so he was reclining, not even looking at her.

"Ryder shouldn't have thrown that in your face," he said. "Not now, and definitely not as a way to deflect from the fact that *he* was the one who was being a jackass. He shouldn't have kissed you like that, in front of everyone, when he knew you wouldn't like it. The band had a lot of problems, and was probably doomed in a hundred different ways that had nothing to do with you."

That was kind of him to say, but Micah didn't believe that. She could think of a number of the band's problems, and unfortunately she seemed to be at the center of all of them.

He did turn to look at her then, squinting against the sun. "I never did get to hear your side of the story when that all went down," he said. "I feel like it's my fault that I didn't ask."

"You were angry with me," she said. "You all were."

"Well, I'm not angry now. And I'm asking now. What happened, Micah?"

Just that question, the gentle way he'd asked it . . . She felt tears already starting to leak down her face, and she wiped them away, hoping he hadn't noticed.

"Things weren't great between Ryder and me," she said finally. "You had to have noticed that. I know it was adding to all the tension in the band, because we were fighting all the time, and then the whole band was fighting all the time . . ."

That last European tour, it had felt like they couldn't agree on *anything*. Ryder hated the sequencing of the set list. Frankie kept having technical issues with their rig and because they were overseas with limited equipment, they kept trying quick fixes that never seemed to solve the underlying problem. Steve had wanted more time to party and see the sights and had rebelled against itineraries that he said were hampering his ability to enjoy himself. Micah had been exhausted—physically, mentally, emotionally. It came out in her voice, which she couldn't even stand to listen to in video recordings from that tour. It sounded so raw, it broke when she tried for certain notes, and she could just *hear* the way she was barely hanging on by a thread.

And as for John . . . well, he'd been withdrawn. She felt like she'd lost him, ever since she started dating Ryder, and she felt like she couldn't blame anyone but herself. He was still around, still steady, reliable John. But ever since she'd made the mistake of telling Ryder the story of the night she and John had written "If Only" together, he'd gotten it into his head that John was a huge threat to their relationship and possibly to the entire band. The only way Micah could mitigate that was to spend less and less time with John, and so that was what she'd done.

"God, it's such a cliché, right?" she said. "Romantic relationships fucking up a band. Except No Doubt and Fleetwood Mac were able to work through it, become *better*, even. I don't know why I started dating him in the first place, I always—"

She broke off, not sure how honest she wanted to be. There was giving John the closure he deserved, and then there was just opening up a bunch more doors that were probably best left locked up tight.

"He can be very charming," John said. "When he's not being a complete dick."

Micah choked on a laugh. "Yeah," she said. "I guess that was it. I was young and stupid, I don't know. We were all spending so much time together, it was this pressure cooker that nobody else understood . . ."

"So you two broke up before the band did," John said, like he was prompting her to continue but also like he was clicking something into place for himself.

"Like the week before," Micah said. She paused, wanting to feel John out on one of the few things *she'd* always had questions about, that had been an open wound all these years. "Did Ryder ever show you anything?"

He frowned. "Show me anything? Like what?"

It was possible he was playing dumb, but she didn't think

so. It was also possible he just didn't remember, in which case she wasn't looking to jog his memory. "Nothing," she said. "It's not important. The point is, Ryder and I broke up—for good this time—and it was messy and ugly and I just didn't see any way back from it. Not to him, and definitely not to being in a band with him."

"I would've kicked him out so fast," John said. "I was dying for an excuse."

She believed that *now*. But then, everything had been so topsy-turvy that she legitimately hadn't known what to believe. Ryder had said things that made her feel like the band would be on *his* side over hers, if it came to that, and she didn't know if she could take it.

"I wouldn't have wanted you to do that for me."

"For *you*? The guy tunes his guitar with the capo still on, I would've done it for *me*."

That got Micah to laugh, and John must've heard something in the phlegmy sound, because he glanced over at her, reaching out to grab her hand and give it a quick squeeze.

"Hey," he said. "I'm sorry you went through all that. And I'm sorry you didn't feel like you could talk to me about it. You can always talk to me."

She *should've* talked to John about it then. For years and years, he was always the person she'd gone to. But then she'd pushed him away when she started dating Ryder, and she felt like she had no right to ask him to come back. She didn't know that he would.

"Well, instead I talked to my dad," Micah said. "I was talking to him as my dad, but he was listening as our band manager, and . . . I guess the label had already expressed that they weren't really happy with us, that they didn't have a vision for that third record on our contract. It sounded like they weren't going to give us any support to record it or promote it or anything. I asked my dad what that meant, if we were going to lose our record deal and have to pay back any of the money, and he said . . ."

She swallowed, knowing this was the part where she really sounded like a piece of shit. There was no way around it. She could've taken all of that information to the band, and let them decide together what to do with it, if anything. They could've waited it out, called the record label's bluff, let them put whatever meager resources they were willing to into the third album and then walked away with the freedom to decide what to do with their careers next.

She could feel John's gaze, steady on her face, but she couldn't look up at him.

"He said you should do the third record on your own," John finished for her. "And you saw it as your out from the band, as your chance to get away from Ryder, and you took it."

"I took it."

And then she hadn't wanted to answer any questions about it, hadn't wanted to have to explain. She knew they were angry with her, and she'd been angry at *them*—some of it irrational, some of it misinformed and confused from stuff Ryder had told her over the years, but some of it a legitimate resentment toward people who she felt would always think of her in this one narrow way. Micah Presley, the lead singer of ElectricOh!. She didn't want to *be* that anymore.

Legally, the whole process had been almost depressingly simple. The other band members received their cut of the contractual advance and bonuses for that third record . . . they just hadn't had any part in making it. Behind the scenes, they'd been bought out.

"But then after," John said, "why didn't you take my calls? I even came to one of your concerts once, it was—"

"The El Rey," she said. "I know."

"You were really good," he said.

"I was fucking miserable."

"You put on a great show."

She sighed, looking over at him. She'd applied sunscreen earlier that morning, but not the amount she would've if she'd known she'd spend the afternoon sitting out on the deck like this. She could feel the sun warming her cheeks, the tip of her nose, her forearms where they rested on her lap, but she couldn't find it in her to move.

"I was so ashamed," she said. "I just couldn't face you."

"Ashamed?"

Micah swallowed. She couldn't even get into all that, or she knew she'd *really* lose it, start openly sobbing right here on the deck where Tatiana and her posse could probably see the whole thing. She already felt better for having talked to John about a lot of this stuff, but there were still parts of their history that felt so raw, even now.

"Can I ask you a question?" she asked.

"Sure."

He said it so quickly, so easily, but still she hesitated. She knew he wasn't expecting what she was about to ask him. She had no idea how he was going to respond.

"Your dad," she said. "He . . ."

"He died," John said. "About four years ago."

That definitely hadn't been what Micah expected him to say. For one thing, she figured he had to know that she knew that already. Hailey had called to tell her that they'd sent flowers for the funeral, which had upset Micah because it was the first time she was hearing the news that John had lost his dad, much less that there'd been a funeral and it had already passed. Micah liked to think she would've flown back for that, although maybe that was giving herself too much credit. She'd started several text messages to John, thinking she'd reach out, tell him she was sorry, see how he was doing . . . and then she'd wonder what made her think she had the right to text him at all, and she'd delete whatever she'd written.

"I heard," she said now. "I'm so sorry."

"Yeah."

This was such a bizarre situation to have this conversation in. Probably she should drop it—wait until they weren't lying out in the sun in this seemingly idyllic cruise setting, the sapphire-blue water catching the sun and sparkling in the distance, the breeze ruffling John's hair and giving him a windswept appearance that reminded her of when they'd been teenagers and his hair had always been a mess. It *felt* like they were teenagers again, somehow, both dressed in their jeans and black T-shirts, him with his Converse, her with her platform boots, like two emo kids dragged on vacation by their parents but determined to stick to their aesthetic.

"You know he was an alcoholic," he said. "And it did a number on his liver, in the end."

"I'm really sorry to hear that." That hadn't been what she was going to ask, either. She *had* already known that about John's dad—a few things John had said over the years, the one time she'd met his dad and noticed the bloodshot eyes, a few things her own father had insinuated here and there. And then there was John's promise to himself, to never let a drop of alcohol cross his lips, because he said he knew that stuff could be genetic and even if the odds were good that he could drink in moderation and never have a problem, he'd be damned if he'd take the chance. *I treat it like a peanut allergy,* John had told her once. They'd gone to a party freshman year where she'd had a single beer and gotten so tipsy John had carried her on his back all the way home. She remembered admiring his conviction.

But she remembered other things, too. Like the time they'd been in band together, and one day John's clarinet hadn't been where it was supposed to be in the classroom cabinet. They'd looked everywhere, but eventually the teacher had called home to tell John's dad that he'd owe a hundred and fifty dollars to have the clarinet replaced. John had missed the next two days of school, which wasn't like him—and when she called his house, there had been no answer until finally someone picked up the phone and then hung it up immediately, as if just to stop it from ringing.

"Oh," the teacher had said to Micah the second day John was out. "Tell your friend that his clarinet was located after all. It was in my office."

When John finally came back the next Monday, she was excited to tell him the news. "In his *office* the whole time," she'd said. "Like he never thought to look there? What a loser."

She thought he'd laugh with her about that, but instead he'd sat down on the curb and just started to cry. They weren't small tears, either—they were big, racking sobs that shook his whole body. She'd never seen John cry like that. She'd never seen a *boy* cry like that. He put his head between his knees and just kept hiccup-sobbing while she stood there, not sure what to do. Until eventually she sat down next to him and rubbed circles on his back until he calmed down. Afterward, she tried to ask him what was wrong, if he was okay, if it was about the money or if he was mad at the teacher, or—

But he never wanted to talk about it.

And apparently he didn't want to talk about it now, either, because he just looked over at her, his gaze dipping briefly to her mouth—so briefly she thought she might've imagined it, or conjured it in some wishful thinking. His eyes were dark and a little sad when he gave her a smile. "You ready for ElectricOh!'s big reunion show tonight?"

She smiled back, wishing she could always feel his gaze on her like that, warm and kissing her skin like the sun. "Ready as I'll ever be."

CHAPTER

FIFTEEN

THEY'D HAD ALL these preshow rituals, as a band. Steve always downed a Mountain Dew in five seconds and crushed the can in his hand, giving a rebel yell that he said hyped him up for the next two hours. Micah had her vocal warm-ups. John would sit quietly with his eyes closed, as if he was meditating, but mostly he was thinking about one tricky transition he had to do between two pedals on their opening song, switching between clean and distorted and back again.

Right as they were about to go on, they'd stand in a circle, their arms around each other, and yell, "You're electric, Ohio!" It had been incredibly cheesy and cringey. It had been the best John had felt in his entire life.

Now they didn't do any of that. Steve was scrolling through his phone; Ryder was smoothing down his hair, trying to catch a glimpse of his distorted reflection in a metal pole; and Frankie's fingers were moving as if they were playing bass, clearly running through their parts.

Micah was pacing back and forth, chewing on her thumbnail.

She kept passing right in front of John, and he wanted so badly to snag her around the waist, to pull her toward him and just whisper in her ear *It's going to be okay*. But instead he looked down at his shoes, waiting for the moment when the cruise staff member told them it was time to go on.

She was dressed in an outfit that was half eighties-inspired, half a nod to the *Nightshifters* TV show. Tight, shiny black leggings and a loose shirt that hung off one shoulder, patterned in bronze-and-black stripes that looked vaguely like werewolf fur. Her hair was in her usual ponytail but teased out, with three tight braids close to one side of her scalp. When ElectricOh! had been a band, they'd had stylists for photo shoots, TV appearances, that kind of thing, but she'd always done her own styling for tour performances. It blew his mind, especially when his "getting ready" consisted of deciding *which* black shirt to wear.

"Electric?" the cruise staffer said, poking her head in. "You're up!"

All their equipment had been set up toward the front of the stage, in front of the equipment for another band who would go on after them. It wasn't an unusual setup for an opener, especially one who was only going to play three songs, but it meant that they didn't have as much room to move in. John was only a few feet away from Micah, who grabbed the microphone and raised one arm in the air, the action revealing a glimpse of the pale skin at her waist, her long fingers silhouetted against the lights that were shining down on the stage.

"Nightshifters!" she yelled out to the crowd without bothering to bring the microphone to her mouth. "Let's fucking gooooo!"

These were all the parts that John had forgotten, that came back to him like no time had passed at all. The sheer adrenaline rush of playing those opening chords, the crowd moving like a wave as people started jumping and dancing and singing along. The way he was immediately lost in his own world, cocooned in the insular soundscape coming through his in-ear monitors, the way he felt immediately part of something bigger than just him, the energy of the crowd and his bandmates lifting him up.

And Micah. She might've been pacing and chewing on her fingernails only a few moments before, but now you *believed* she was a rock star. She was spinning and tossing her head, her ponytail whipping in the wind, she was stepping up on one of the monitors at the front of the stage and holding the microphone up to let the crowd repeat a line back in a call-and-response. She could save the universe. She could do anything she wanted.

She made the transition to the chorus no problem, her foot stomping along to the beat from Steve's kick drum, leaning into the mic as she delivered the last line the way she always had live, half singing, half a yell. She turned to John only briefly then, shooting him a quicksilver grin and letting her tongue hang out in a message he got loud and clear. *Holy shit*, her dancing eyes said. *I did it. We're doing it.*

And then two seconds later, she was spinning toward the front again, coming in hot with the next verse. They finished "Sunflares" in what felt like a blur of seconds, and then they rolled right into "Open Mouth." It had always been one of John's favorite songs to play live, with this low, pulsing rhythm that built to a crescendo toward the end. Although Ryder had written his own lead guitar line, it had been on a foundation that Micah and John had written together, and the song structure was a little strange in the way they could've only managed when they were too young to know any better.

He caught Frankie's eye, and couldn't help but smile as they mimicked the way he was leaning into his guitar, rocking his body back and forth. He exaggerated his movements even more, which led to them exaggerating theirs, and after all the work of practicing these old songs for the last month, the near-miss nightmare of rehearsal earlier that day, he was surprised to find he was having *fun*. He was having a fucking blast. He turned his back to the crowd, playing toward Steve as the drummer smashed into that big buildup that John had been waiting for.

When John turned back around, he bumped into Micah, who was much closer than he'd expected with their limited stage area. It happened sometimes during live shows, and you just had to keep playing, make sure that you didn't miss a note and then you could compare bruises later. But then Micah crashed into *him*, like they were fourteen and back in the pit again, and when he looked at her there was a playful challenge in her eyes. She slid her hand along the back of his neck, which he knew was slick with sweat, and he felt her fingers tangle briefly in his hair before she pushed off him. She hunched over the mic as she belted out the final lines of the song, getting lower and lower until she was on her knees, her ponytail flipped over, the tip almost touching the stage. John played the final chords under Ryder's closing lead line, but inside he felt like something wouldn't stop vibrating.

He could still feel her hand on his neck. And had she *pulled his hair*?

After the song was done, Micah set the mic back in its stand, carrying the whole thing up with her to the front of the stage.

"You're electric!" she yelled out to the crowd, and they responded in a roar of noise that had John reaching to remove one of his in-ears just so he could hear it. It had always been one of Ryder's complaints about Micah, that she talked too much in between songs, and considering this was supposed to be a tight three-song set, John knew there was an argument that she shouldn't be doing it now. But this was the first time they'd played together in over a decade, and it might be the last time they ever did—at least like this, plugged in and the five of them all on the same stage. He couldn't begrudge her a little talking.

"Thank you so much!" she said now. "Seriously, this is . . . wow, this is amazing. We're in the middle of the ocean."

A cheer from the crowd, and Micah laughed a little. "Right? The middle of the fucking ocean. Wild. It's wilder still just to be up here, I never—"

She turned back to face the band, like she was asking their permission. Or maybe like she was apologizing. But then her face cleared, and she turned to face the crowd again.

"If you don't know us, we're ElectricOh!," she said. "And we are *so* excited to be here. If you'll indulge me for five seconds, I wanted to introduce some of the people up on this stage, just so you know who you're looking at. On bass, we've got the *very* lovely, *very* talented . . . Frankie Simons!"

Frankie played a quick scale on the bass that made John smile, because he got it for the inside joke that it was—it sounded much more impressive than it actually was to play, and it had always bothered Frankie when movies included moments like that as a sign that a musician could hack it.

From the grin on Micah's face, she got it, too. "I think they can handle it, Junior," she said, then swept her hand toward

Steve. "And behind me, we have the baddest-ass drummer on the planet, he can *still* hit even if his kid doesn't like punk music . . . Steve Gerding!"

Steve twirled his sticks before playing a quick, staccato drum solo.

"Don't worry, Steve," Micah said, tilting the mic stand to one side before catching it with her foot to set it upright again. "All kids go through a rebellious phase."

That was the other thing about Micah. She owned the stage no matter what she was doing on it—when she was singing, when she was just riffing between songs. When John looked out over the audience, he could see that she had them in the palm of her hand.

He was so busy looking outward that he almost missed that she was talking about *him* now. She was talking *to* him.

"That's right," she said, laughing. "You know it's true. Go ahead and play us a little something."

He wished he'd caught whatever she said at the beginning. He blanked, couldn't think of a single impressive riff he could play. He plucked out the notes for "Hot Cross Buns," the song they'd learned on their first day of band in middle school. The crowd laughed, someone in the back giving a loud whistle.

Her face softened. "A classic," she said.

And then she was moving on to introduce Ryder. Smart, leaving him last. That would satisfy his ego a bit. He played a little solo and then gave a modest wave afterward.

"Okay," Micah said. "That's enough of that. Now—"

John didn't have a microphone in front of him. Sometimes he sang along to parts of the song as he played it, but nobody needed to hear his voice amplified as part of the mix. So he had to walk up to Micah to catch her attention, leaning in to talk into her mic. He could tell he'd taken her off guard, because all she could do was tilt the microphone toward him, like she was interviewing him for the news.

"You didn't introduce yourself," he said.

She gave a self-deprecating eyeroll, but the crowd had already started to cheer, and she took the microphone back. "I'm Micah Presley," she said.

"No relation," John put in.

"No relation," she agreed. He had no idea if anyone could even hear what they were saying, between the sound of the crowd and the fact that neither of them was speaking directly into the microphone anymore. He put his guitar pick between his teeth, freeing his hands so he could clap for her as the crowd went wild. When he glanced over at Frankie, they were also clapping, and Steve started hitting the snare with a steady, even *crack* until the applause morphed to trace the same beat.

"All right, all right," Micah said, giving John a playful shove. "Places, please. We all know why we're here. Nightshifters— this one's for you."

If John thought the crowd was loud before, it was nothing compared to the sound they made when Ryder played the opening notes of "If Only." John should've put his in-ear back in before the song started up, because now he had to come in with that first chord, and it was still dangling around his neck, but he found he didn't care. He liked the experience of being able to hear more of what was going on around him, the mix still in the one ear monitor he did have in.

Micah left the microphone in its stand for this one, and even with a view of her back John knew she had her eyes closed.

She'd told him once that she got self-conscious, making eye contact with someone in the crowd while singing a particularly romantic or intimate or revealing line. She usually kept her eyes closed through the entire first two verses of this song, which led him to wonder which line in particular made her feel that way, or if it was all of them.

People in the audience had started putting their phone flashlights on, swaying back and forth like they were holding up lighters. John could tell the moment Micah opened her eyes, too, because he heard her breath catch, an almost imperceptible hitch on the last word that sounded like she'd meant it to be there. *Are you gonna come over?*

"This is your part," she said to the crowd, turning the microphone toward them to let them take over a couple lines of the chorus before she finished out the rest herself. John could see people in the first few rows crying—actual *tears* streaming down their faces—and that used to be the kind of thing that made him uncomfortable. He'd always looked down at his guitar, turned away, tried to ground himself in his own experience without worrying about anyone else's. But now he felt like he might cry himself.

And then there was Micah, arms outspread, belting out the huge building notes of the bridge that felt like they could fill the entire ship. He'd taken all of this for granted, after a while. The crowd, the music, the people on the stage, *her.* He'd forgotten how special it all was. When the song was over, he almost didn't know what to do with himself. It took Frankie, gesturing him over for a quick collective bow with the rest of the band, to get him to remember to move.

"Holy *shit*," Frankie said once they were off the stage. "That was incredible. Seriously. I've never felt energy like that."

"Well, we're playing to a crowd of die-hard *Nightshifters* fans," Ryder said. "Consider the audience."

"I wish every audience was die-hard *Nightshifters* fans," Steve said. "Remember Hamburg?"

Frankie leveled a glare at their drummer. "Steve."

"What?"

"Read the vibe, *please*. Nobody wants to talk about Hamburg right now."

Steve held up a finger like he was about to argue, before thinking better of it. "Tell you what I do want to talk about is a ham-*burger*, because I'm flippin' famished."

"All right, let's grab food. Anyone else?"

Ryder immediately jumped in, which meant that Micah, predictably, declined. John took one glance at Micah and turned down the offer of food, too. He could hear Frankie still talking as the three band members walked away—"I can't get used to this new Steve who doesn't curse. It freaks me out."

When they left, John looked over at Micah. She was actively trembling, he realized, her hands shaking so much she was having trouble raising her water bottle to her mouth.

"Hey," he said. "Rest for a minute. Catch your breath. It's okay."

She sat down on one of the amps that was stowed in the alcove where they'd been hanging out before the show, and he urged her over so he could squeeze onto the spot next to her. He took the water bottle from her.

"Open up."

She gave him a helpless look, a *Really? You think I can't handle it myself?* type of expression, but she did as he told her, opening her mouth and letting him squirt a stream of water in.

He wanted to smooth the strands of hair that had escaped from her ponytail away from her face, wanted to pull her onto his lap and hold her until she stopped trembling. She'd touched him during the show, but that was different—that had been the heat of the moment, part of the stagecraft. He didn't know what was allowed here.

"Do you need your medicine?" he asked.

She shook her head. "It's the adrenaline," she said. "I'll be fine in a minute. I just—"

"You were incredible out there," he said. "But I get it. It was a lot."

"It was a *lot*, right?"

"A fuckton of a lot," John agreed. "But in a good way."

She smiled at him. Her eyeliner was a little smudged, and it made her look like a tired party girl at the end of the night. "You were incredible out there, too, you know."

"ElectricOh!'s still got it," John said. "Who would've guessed."

Micah snorted. "Not *Pitchfork*."

John laughed himself, rubbing his hand over his face. "God, no, certainly not *Pitchfork*. What did they give our second album? A five point something?"

"Four point five. They called it *lighthearted but shoddily constructed*."

"Which made no sense," John said. "If anything, the album was a bit of a downer but *impeccably* constructed, in my opinion."

"It was front-loaded."

"Well." John looked down at his hands. His fingertips were

all calloused from playing the guitar as much as he did, but still somehow he'd managed to nick the side of his hand on the strings while playing so hard tonight, and he had a thin scratch to show for it. He noticed that Micah was staring at his hands, too, and he picked up her water bottle again, intending to hand it back to her.

But instead she opened her mouth once more, and he squirted another stream of water inside. Some of it dripped down her chin, and she wiped it away, her eyes on him the whole time.

"We probably should get food," he said, then backtracked when he heard how that sounded. "I mean, not together—just that we should both eat. Separately."

She smiled, her lips still bright and shiny from the water. "Why not together? I don't know if I can handle being around a ton of people right now. Why don't we each go back to our rooms, shower, freshen up, whatever—then I'll order room service and we can eat it on my balcony?"

If things didn't feel so *weird* it was exactly the way John would've wanted to spend his night. Just the two of them, hanging out, postgaming the show or talking about everything but the show as they decompressed. But things did feel weird.

"Please?" Micah said.

Then again, they didn't have to feel that way. Ever since they'd cleared the air somewhat on the upper deck earlier that day, John felt like there was a chance of them being friends again. Maybe not the way they were—maybe they could never get that back—but at least where they could be in each other's lives. A simple dinner together was a good way to start.

"Okay," John said. "Give me an hour and I'll come over."

CHAPTER
SIXTEEN

MICAH ORDERED PRACTICALLY one of everything, because she was famished and assumed John must be, too. She also realized she didn't know as much as she once had, about his likes and dislikes—whether he still picked the pickles off his burgers, if he still preferred to dip his fries into honey mustard if they had it.

"Oh, and do you have pineapple and ham for the pizza?" she asked before she got off the phone. "A couple slices of that, please."

The food arrived before he did, and for a minute Micah had a panicked feeling that he'd changed his mind, that he wouldn't show after all. She even checked her phone for a text before remembering that she'd changed her number in the intervening years, and he wouldn't have her new one. She didn't know why this was feeling somewhat like a *date*, but she had to shove that out of her head. He'd given no indication that he thought of this as a date.

And if it had been one, it would've been unconventional.

She'd thought about changing into another outfit after her shower, but she actually hadn't brought that many with her, and she felt like being as comfortable as possible. So instead she'd changed into her pajamas, which consisted of a spaghetti-strap tank top and boy shorts underwear. But then when she'd glanced at herself in the bathroom mirror, it looked a little *too* revealing—the amount of leg on display, the way her nipples pebbled against the thin fabric of the tank.

There was a soft knock at her door, which jerked her out of her thoughts.

"Just a minute!" she called, rifling through her suitcase until she found an oversized shirt. She'd pulled it over her head and was still twisting it to lie straight when she opened the door to John.

"Hey," she said.

His gaze flickered down her body, and for a minute she thought he could see all of it—her nipples still straining against the fabric, the heat that suddenly pooled at the bottom of her stomach just from having his eyes on her, having him standing so close. But then he just cleared his throat, gesturing toward her shirt.

"Why am I not surprised," he said.

She glanced down. It was one of her favorite comfort items of clothing, faded black and washed to premium softness, a black-and-white image of Elvis singing into a microphone emblazoned across the chest, the screen printing worn away in places. She'd cut out part of the neck, because she hated shirts that felt too tight around there, and it hung loose and long enough to hit her midthigh like a dress.

"Come on in," she said. "The food's getting cold."

She'd opened the sliding glass door to the balcony, which probably hadn't helped, although the weather had warmed up considerably over the course of the day. She wondered where they were now—they were supposed to make their port stop tomorrow at the cruise company's private Bahamian island, so she didn't know if they were still actively sailing or if maybe they'd stopped, only miles away from land. It was weird, not knowing. It also felt kind of nice, like maybe this was some in-between state where she could exist for a while without having to think about any parts of her real life.

They shifted food around until they could make up their own plates of random bits of all of it, like they were at a buffet. She noticed that John did place one of the cups of honey mustard next to his fries, which made her oddly proud, like she'd accurately guessed a difficult question at trivia.

"Thanks for ordering all this," he said once they were sitting on the balcony chairs, their plates on their laps.

"It was fun," Micah said. "I know this will sound random, but it felt like being Macaulay Culkin in that second *Home Alone* movie, you know what I'm talking about? Like having the ability to order whatever over-the-top thing you wanted and they'd just bring it to you."

"I know *exactly* what you mean," John said. "Asa is obsessed with those movies. He makes us watch them every year. Sometimes twice, if he gets it in his head to do a Christmas-in-July-type thing."

Micah smiled. She liked hearing him talk about his house-mates. She liked the way she could tell there was obvious caring there, that these were people who were important to his life. She liked the way he'd dropped the descriptor *housemate* from in front of their names when talking to her, as if he already included her enough in his life to assume she'd know who he was talking about.

And she couldn't deny it—she liked knowing that these were the people he went home to, rather than a wife or girlfriend or whatever else she might've assumed when she first heard him on the phone that time.

"How long have you lived there?"

John looked up, like he was thinking about the answer, but also giving himself time to swallow the bite of pizza he'd just taken. "A few years," he said. "I stayed in Orlando, after the band . . . I had an apartment but broke the lease early when I had to move back to Ohio for a few months. I guess I could've gotten another apartment when I came back, but the experience soured me on the whole corporate landlord thing, and so when I saw an ad for a house looking for an extra housemate, it just seemed like, okay. Let's try this out."

There was so much in between those details, questions that Micah had and then things that she could assume. From the timing, she could figure that he'd returned to Ohio because his dad got sick. She also felt like she heard a little bit of loneliness behind the words—like his decision to live with other people had less to do with corporate landlords and more to do with wanting to not be *alone* anymore.

But maybe she was projecting.

"What about you?" he asked.

"I have an apartment in Silver Lake," she said. "Mostly so I can walk around the reservoir."

"By yourself?"

She knew he was asking more about the apartment than the

walking, but it didn't matter, since the answer was the same. She also wondered if that was his way of asking if she was seeing anyone, if that was the kind of thing he'd care about.

"Yeah," she said. "It's the converted upstairs of a house, and this old man lives underneath me. He's a riot, to be honest. Like for a while I thought he hated me, because he'd always be out walking his dog and if he caught me coming or going he'd just stop and glare at me, like I was doing something wrong. I racked my brain—like had he seen me with a woman and he was homophobic? But I barely brought anyone back to my apartment. Was he still mad about the time I overfilled the garbage can and it tipped over? Because I was pretty sure I'd cleaned everything up from that."

John was watching her face, the ghost of a smile around the corner of his mouth. "So what was it?"

"It was my hair!" Micah smiled herself, just remembering. "He said he couldn't figure it out. What color it was supposed to be, if it was even real. He sounded legitimately upset by it, like it was new technology he couldn't quite get."

John's gaze went then to her hair, still wet from the shower and plaited into a simple braid. It had been resting on her shoulder, and she realized that the tip had dripped a damp circle on her shirt over her left breast. The fabric was a slightly deeper shade of black there, and the water made the outline of her nipple clearer even through the double layers she was wearing. She flipped her braid back, sliding down in the chair to rest her feet against the balcony railing.

He glanced at her bare feet before he bent down to place his empty plate on the floor next to his chair. She felt a surge of triumph when she saw him lean over to untie his own shoes, slipping them off, and then his socks after that. So he was staying a while.

"Is it hard for you?" he asked. "The fame part."

Micah considered the question. "Not nearly as bad as it used to be," she said. "I mean, I get recognized if I'm out and about. But it's L.A.—there are celebrities everywhere, and I'm hardly the biggest one."

"True," John said. "I saw Tony Hawk on Sunset once."

She raised her eyebrow at him. "That's your biggest celebrity sighting?"

He shrugged. "What can I say, it was cool."

The moon was bright enough that it reflected on the dark waves, the only way you might be able to see that there was a whole expanse of ocean out there. But you could hear it, when you were quiet—the gentle lapping of the water against the ship.

"I don't know why I said that," she said finally. "If anything, the fame stuff is worse. I don't get recognized as much but when I do, it makes me feel . . ."

She expected him to finish her sentence for her, wanted to hear what word he'd supply so he could tell her how she felt. But he just sat there silently, waiting patiently for her to go on.

"Like that person out on the stage tonight? That's not me. Not the real me. That's a persona I play, a projection. It's like a costume I can put on. I'm Batman in my mask and my cape, I've got all my gadgets, I can fight any bad guy I'm faced with. But catch me without that stuff, and I'm just . . . I'm a joke. An impostor. Not only am I not wearing my mask and cape, but worse than that, they feel so *stupid* to me. A cheap Halloween version of the real thing. But I can see in people's eyes how badly they *want* it to be real, and I just don't know how to be that, I don't know how to be what people want me to be."

Micah could feel the weight of his gaze on her, but she couldn't look at him. She brought her hand up to her mouth, gnawing on the nail of her middle finger, then studying it like it was important that she monitor the progress she'd made.

"I think the thing about Bruce Wayne is that he was *also* kind of a badass," John said. "In a super-rich-dude sort of way. So that might not be the best example."

She did glance at him then, and he gave her a tentative smile that didn't quite reach his eyes.

"I thought you weren't a Batman guy."

"Doesn't mean I haven't seen the movies."

She laughed. "Okay, yeah."

He didn't say anything for a few minutes, and she thought maybe they were going to drop the topic. She was relieved, in a way—she'd already said more than she meant to. But then she heard his voice, so low she almost had to strain to hear it over the sound of the water.

"Trying to be what other people want will fuck you up every time," he said. "And you had a lot of pressure on you from a pretty young age in that regard. But, Micah—that person on-stage *is* you. It's another part of you. It's honestly a gift, that you share it with other people. And then the part of you that's three days unshowered, standing in the snack aisle at Whole Foods, tired and irritated but trying to connect with a fan because you can see how important it is to them . . . that's a gift, too. You have to trust people to see that. And if they don't, well. Fuck 'em."

Micah could feel the burn at the corner of her eyes, but she

would do anything not to cry. It was just that it was such a release, hearing words of kindness, hearing them from *John*, who
she knew she didn't deserve them from. It was like wrapping
your hands around a warm cup of tea after you'd been out in
the cold.

"Were you having me followed?" she said, trying to make
her voice light. "That Whole Foods imagery was *very* specific."

"As soon as I said it I was like, ah, fuck, should've gone with
Trader Joe's."

There was something erotic about seeing John's bare feet.
They were long and straight and when he moved she could see
the bump of his ankle bone peek out from the bottom of his
jeans.

She shifted in her chair. *Christ.* She was acting like it was the
Victorian era and a glimpse of a well-turned ankle could give
her the vapors.

"You getting cold?" John asked. His gaze swept over her legs
in a way that broke her out in full-on goose bumps, even though
she knew he was probably just clocking the fact that she was
underdressed for being outside on the balcony. The truth was
when she stopped to think about it that she *was* getting a little
cold. But she was also loath to break this up, worried that if they
went back inside he'd wish her a good night and head back to
his room.

"Not yet," she said. "Let's just stay out here for a few more
minutes. It feels good to get some fresh air."

SEVENTEEN

IT COULD STAND to be a little colder, in John's opinion. He was way too aware of the expanse of smooth skin of Micah's legs, that grayscale rose tattoo on her thigh so close he could reach out and squeeze it. The T-shirt she wore covered her as well as any dress, but she didn't seem to appreciate how *loose* it was, how it rode up when she slid down in her chair to reveal a sliver of ass cheek peeking out from her boy shorts, how when she'd bent over to grab some silverware he'd gotten a glimpse right down her top.

It hurt him to hear that she felt that way about herself—that she saw herself as some sort of fake superhero. But considering he also had very complicated feelings whenever anyone brought up the band, or his past career, he couldn't say he didn't get it.

"I was embarrassed," he said, "the first time I took the stage post-ElectricOh!. I was temporarily filling in for a local band's guitarist who'd moved out of state. I saw the ad on a music store bulletin board and contacted them to arrange a tryout and everything. And I didn't want to be a dick about it, like *Do you know who I am?*, but it also felt . . . humbling. Just showing up at some random guy's house and being like, *Hey, I play guitar, I'll be in your band for a few months until you find someone else.*"

"Like it's embarrassing if they know who you are," she said. "And it's embarrassing if they don't."

John ran his hand through his hair. "Exactly. There's a pause, after I introduce myself, where I can't decide which outcome will be worse."

"So why did you do it? It couldn't have been for the money."

John laughed, thinking of the fifty-dollar share of the door he was lucky to get for most shows, the free beers he was offered and turned down that were the more common mode of payment. "Definitely not the money. I just really wanted to play music, and not alone in my room. I wanted to play with other people again."

"Why not start another band of your own?" Micah asked. "Like Ryder did. Or even advertise yourself as a session or touring musician, like Frankie."

John had never fully put into words why he hadn't gone those routes, even to himself. It felt like pushing on something sensitive, like he had a tooth pain he could ignore if he just didn't press on it.

"I don't know," he said. "Didn't feel right, I guess."

She shivered, tucking her knees up to her chest and pulling her whole shirt around them. It struck John as such a middle school move, so reminiscent of the way she used to hug her arms to her chest inside her sweatshirt in science, which always ran about ten degrees colder than any other classroom. It gave him that ache in his stomach again, when he thought about who they'd been then, how far they'd come since to get *here*, two people on a cruise ship who hadn't talked in over a decade. But at least who were talking now.

"You're cold," he said. "Let's head back inside."

He grabbed his plate and then hers, too, stacking them on top of one another to set them back on the room service tray. He was planning to turn to her then, to thank her again for dinner but make some comment about how he really should be going (to do what?) or he was tired (he was wide awake). But she'd already followed him inside, closing the sliding glass door to the balcony behind her, and he saw that his shoes and socks were still out there. It would've taken ten seconds for him to go and retrieve them, but for some reason those ten seconds made him decide to stay.

"I read some of your private messages once," he said. "When we were in maybe ninth grade? I always felt guilty about it, so I thought I'd tell you while we're clearing the air."

Her face brightened, like this was the most delightful bit of news he could've possibly told her. "What do you mean, you read my messages?"

He felt the tips of his ears heat. "We were hanging out in your room, and you had to go do some chore your parents were nagging you about . . . and I went to pause the music we were listening to, and your inbox was up, and . . . yeah, I skimmed through and then I opened one."

"Such a little hacker," she chided. "Anything good?"

It had been the mention of his own name that had gotten him to click on one. It had turned out to be a fairly innocuous mention—she was telling someone about a group project they'd worked on for school. And then he'd realized, what exactly had he been hoping she'd been saying? And how easy would it have been to stumble upon something he *wouldn't* have wanted to see, like if she'd been complaining about him or listing his most annoying traits?

"Not really," he said. "It was mostly about school."

She sat cross-legged on her bed, looking up at him. "What was the song?"

"'Lonely Nights.'"

"One of my favorites."

He knew that. It was the reason why he'd paused it, so she wouldn't miss it when it came on.

The way she was looking at him, it made him wonder if she'd put that together. "I still feel like I'm getting away with something if I listen to that whole album without turning down the chorus of the fourth track."

It was actually one of the records that John had a hard time going back and listening to now, because it made him too nostalgic and sad. "Your dad *hated* the cursing."

"But it was like, how do you think I know *exactly* when to turn it down and back up? I'm just singing the words in my head."

"I guess at least he didn't have to hear them," John pointed out. "It's a respect thing. I get it."

"I used to cheat off you in science," Micah said. "While we're clearing the air."

John blinked. "Oh, I knew that."

"Stop, you did not."

"Micah, how do you think you could see my paper so well? I pushed it over toward you and made sure my arm wasn't covering it. Of course I knew."

She gave an incredulous little laugh, grasping her knees and rocking forward on the bed. "Oh my god," she said. "I thought I was being so slick."

"You knew I would've let you if you'd asked, anyway."

"Yeah, but it's better if you weren't in on the plan. That way you couldn't be held responsible if we got caught."

"Like they would've tortured the information out of me? Come on, give me more credit than that."

She laughed again, then patted the bed next to her. "You can sit down," she said.

He hesitated. It wasn't like there were many seating options in the small cabin. She had a chair in one corner, too, the same way his room did—and hers was a little bigger, in fact. But that was where they'd stacked the trays of room service, so it was out of commission. And then there was a small countertop in another corner with a round stool tucked underneath. It was clearly where Micah had been doing her hair and makeup, because she had a bunch of products spread out on the counter. John still could've gotten the stool and pulled it out far enough to sit, except now that felt awkward to do once she'd offered the bed.

"You're looming," she said. "It's distracting."

He took the spot next to her, stretching out his legs and crossing his feet at the ankles. When he glanced over at her, she was looking at his feet, and then her gaze flickered to his before she looked away, her cheeks a little pink.

"Your turn," she said.

"For what?"

"Clearing the air," she said. "Airing our grievances. Whatever this is that we're doing."

He didn't even know what to call it. But it felt good to talk to her, so he was willing to keep playing.

"Uh, let's see . . ." He racked his brain for something else he could confess. "When I was going through that phase where I thought I'd wear eye makeup onstage, I borrowed your eyeliner pencil a few times."

She elbowed him in the ribs. "*I* knew about *that*," she said. "John, you asked me! I'm the one who taught you how to do it!"

He remembered that. Of course he remembered that. She'd been very patient with him, and very *close*, her breath warm on his cheek as she carefully applied eyeliner to one of his eyes while he watched, and then handed him the pencil and talked him through the steps to do it himself. "Yeah, but after," he said. "Before I'd bought any of my own stuff."

She waved that away. "I didn't care."

"Those magazines you always read said that was one of the worst things you could do," John said. "Share eye makeup. It was only a couple times."

"And the magazines were probably right on that one," she said. "Along with the tip to rinse your hair with cold water, which I *still* do. But they also told you to eat strawberries before a date so your lips would be naturally red and to pop a wintergreen breath mint before a blow job to really blow his mind, so. I didn't live my life by those magazines."

He couldn't tell if she meant that she'd never tried those techniques, or if she had and they hadn't worked, but he definitely wasn't going to ask. He just wished his body hadn't had such a stereotypical response to even hearing her say the words *blow job*, because now he wished he was under the covers instead of on top of them.

"Well, so far I invaded your privacy and could've given you an eye infection," he said. "And you only copied off my tests, which I was one hundred percent letting you do, so I don't think we're even."

"I stuck my tongue in your mouth when you didn't ask for it," she said. "I think that might give me an edge."

John didn't know what shocked him more. That she'd referred to that kiss at all, or that she'd referred to it like *that*, which was far from his memory.

"Micah," he said. "*I* kissed *you*."

She'd had her own elephant made from a folded towel on her bed, and she picked it up now, turning it over in her hands. "Only technically. I made you do it. And then I came on way too strong, and ruined your first kiss."

He almost didn't know what to say to that. There was so much he could say, and yet he didn't know how much he should. But he also couldn't just leave her thinking that.

"It was perfect," he said. "You didn't make me do anything, and you didn't come on too strong."

"*Pitchfork* would give it a ten?"

He could tell she was trying to make a joke out of it to lighten the mood, but the fact that she'd brought it up at all meant that it had to have bothered her some, over the years.

"You know *Pitchfork* is stingy with those," John said. "But maybe a nine point eight."

She looked at him. "Where did I lose the two tenths?"

"You could've given me a second to recover so I could kiss you back."

She pulled at the towel elephant's ear, and the entire thing unwrapped in her hands until she was holding a balled-up strip of terry cloth. "Oh," she said, laughing a little, and he couldn't tell if she was referring to the elephant or to what he'd just said. Either way, this conversation was starting to feel like a mine-field, so he pushed himself off the bed, standing up.

"Well," he said. "I should—"

"Are you dating anyone right now?" she burst out.

"No." He paused. "Are you?"

"No."

For a minute those short words just hung there, like that was the end of the conversation and there was nothing more to it. Micah was looking at him, her lips parted, like she was about to speak, or maybe waiting for him to. He didn't know what she wanted him to say.

"It's weird," she said finally, "to think of all the people we've been with since we saw each other last."

John spent a lot of energy *not* thinking about that kind of thing, but he thought he knew what she meant. Weird to think about these whole relationships that might've played out, first dates and anniversaries and fights and breakups, in these years when they'd been out of each other's lives. He raised his eye-brows in a way that he hoped read as jokey and light, not like he was being sincere or, god forbid, trying to flirt.

"Are you asking for my body count, Micah?"

She flushed. "No," she said. "Or I mean, you can tell me if you want. That's something friends talk about."

John *had* been flirting, at least a little. Because the wild part was that he was pretty sure Micah had started it, had maybe started it the second she'd opened the door wearing that over-sized T-shirt falling off her shoulder, although he couldn't think why he'd gotten that feeling. Even the show had felt a bit like foreplay. The revelation of that first kiss, so long ago, was still knocking around his brain, making him wonder if they'd both carried around wrong impressions from that false start that had affected everything after.

"Let's not talk about it," he said.

He'd meant that he didn't know if he could be that kind of friend to her, one who listened to all her sex and love stories and pretended they didn't eat him alive. He'd meant that he didn't know how open he wanted to be about his own relationship history, worried it'd help her read between the lines in ways he wasn't ready for.

But from the sudden light in Micah's eyes, he wondered if she'd read something else into his words. Something more like *Let's not talk about it, let's do something about it*. His gaze dipped briefly to the rise and fall of her chest before he brought it back up to her face, where she was still watching him.

"God," she said after the silence stretched uncomfortably long. "I'm just so *horny*. Aren't you horny?"

Hearing her even say the word sent a rush to his dick. Of course he was horny. He thought of his dream that morning, how *real* it had felt, the softness of her bare skin against his hand.

But he also felt . . . he didn't even know what the word was. Not quite disappointed. Not quite resigned. *Hopeless*, he guessed. Hearing her say that word made him feel a little hopeless.

"Sure," he said. "That's probably why I'm going to go back to my room and jerk off before I go to bed."

"I always wondered," she said, "how you did that while we were on tour. The bus didn't give a ton of privacy."

She'd *always* wondered? What did that mean? "Shower," he

said, then cleared his throat. He couldn't believe they were having this conversation. "I would do it in the shower. I assumed that's what everyone was doing."

She shook her head, and he closed his eyes. He wasn't going to ask. He wasn't—"Not you?"

"I mostly abstained. I'm, uh . . ." She bit her lip, giving him a smile that was such a perfect blend of shy and sexy that something in his stomach flipped. "Not very quiet."

Something he *really* didn't need to know about Micah, because now he wouldn't be able to get it out of his head. Although now that he knew that, it did make it interesting that he'd never overheard her and Ryder, because that had always been one of his biggest fears while they were dating. They'd stayed in more hotels on that ill-fated European tour, which had provided some separation at least.

"I don't think sex is a good idea," he said, cutting to the chase. He'd given her an out, to backtrack and pretend that wasn't what she'd been talking about, but somehow he knew she wouldn't do that.

"Why not?"

He found that the go-to answers on his tongue didn't really apply anymore. Because it would fuck up the band? What band. Because it would fuck up their friendship? If he was being honest—what friendship. They'd been out of each other's lives for so long that he supposed it proved that they could be out of each other's lives for even longer, if it came to that. But he still felt a knee-jerk panic at the idea of losing Micah in any permanent way, and he worried this was one thing they couldn't come back from. He didn't know if *he* could.

"Because if I touch you . . ." He swallowed, not sure how to finish that sentence. The dream of her was one thing. He wanted it to be real. But like, he wanted it to be *real*.

"So don't touch me."

He bit back a smile. "That's a loophole and you know it."

She sat back against the pillows, rubbing her feet along the covers. Even that small rustling sound shot straight to his dick.

"Well, I'm not going to beg," she said. "Unless you want me to."

Maybe it was the blood quickly leaving John's head and going straight to his lower body, but suddenly he wondered if maybe *this* had been the ticking time bomb in their friendship from the very start. He'd always been aware of Micah in that way. He'd thought never acting on it was the only way to keep things stable, but maybe he'd gotten that all wrong. Maybe it was a building pressure that needed a release valve or it would never go away.

He leaned on the bed, his fingers splayed against the sheets, his face close to hers. He could tell he'd taken her by surprise by the way her eyes widened and she drew in a shaky breath, and for a second he saw beneath all the bravado she had on the surface to the woman who was actually scared as hell to put herself out there like this. It was that glimpse that made him suddenly decide *Fuck it*.

"If I wanted you to, huh?" he asked.

She nodded slowly, her gaze steady on his. "Just tell me."

John could get off on the potential alone—the possibility. How many times had he watched the way she moved during a show, had he sat so close to her he could smell her shampoo, had he touched her in casual ways he had to pretend didn't mean anything?

"Undo your braid."

She reached up to pull the elastic off the end of it, her fingers a little clumsy as she untwined the strands, running her fingers through them until her hair was splayed out over her shoulders.

John wanted to reach up and touch it, but he felt weirdly like he'd made a promise—not to her even, but to himself. So he settled for just looking at her hair, letting his gaze run over it from the top of her head to where a strand swayed slightly every time she took a shallow breath.

"You really do have uncommonly beautiful hair," he said. "I can see why it confuses people."

"It's just hair."

He made a sound in the back of his throat that was meant to be a rejection of that. "Put your hands in it," he said. "And say *Fuck*, I have beautiful hair."

A smile played around her lips as she shook her head. "I'm not doing that."

He raised his eyebrows. "Oh? Are we at your limit already?"

She rolled her eyes, but she reached up to bury both hands in her hair, gripping it around the scalp and scrunching it a little. "*Fuck*," she said, putting the same emphasis on the word that he had. "I have beautiful hair."

"Hmm," he said. "That was pretty good. But I didn't *feel* it. Try again."

She seemed to get that he was serious then, that he wasn't going to move on until she said the words right. She slid her hands into her hair again, her grip gentler this time, more sensual. "*Fuck*," she breathed, "I have beautiful hair."

He waited for her to open her eyes again. "Perfect," he said. "You should own that, you know."

She was staring at him almost like he was a stranger, like she was seeing him for the first time. "What about when I cut my hair and dyed it black and looked like Prince Valiant?"

He smiled. "Then I'd make you put your hands in it and say *I'm a sexy Prince Valiant.* I know it's just hair, but it's okay to admit it's gorgeous."

Her gaze went up to the top of his head, then back to his face. "I want to touch yours so badly."

He remembered the show only a few hours ago, that slide of her hand, the way she'd tugged. "That would be breaking the rules, though," he said. "Wouldn't it."

He saw the pulse jump in her throat, but she didn't say anything in response. His gaze traced the line of her jaw, that tattoo at her neck, the hint of the one at her shoulder showing next to her exposed collarbone from the loose collar of her shirt.

"Pull your shirt down," he said.

EIGHTEEN

IT WAS THE specificity of the command that got to Micah. Not *Lift your shirt up* or *Take your shirt off*, which would have made more sense, but *Pull your shirt down*. It was the first indication that something was happening, something more than just John admiring her hair. It was the first indication that maybe he had certain fantasies, too, the same way she had.

She tugged on her shirt until it was completely off her shoulders, stretched taut under her breasts, which were still covered by the tank top underneath. Her nipples felt so tight it was almost painful, and there was no missing the way they strained against the thin fabric of her tank. She assumed John wanted her naked, but she waited, wanting to follow directions to the letter.

Something flared in his eyes as he looked from her chest back to her face. "That one, too," he said.

It was easy to slip the straps down her arms, and then she was completely bared to him, her breasts pale and proud in the dim light of the room. She'd switched on one of the lights next to the bed earlier but left the overhead one off, and now she was grateful for that little bit of mood lighting as John looked down at her.

"So fucking beautiful," he said.

She tried to smile, but she felt like it was shaky. "You gonna make me grab these, too, and say it?"

"Don't tempt me."

She *wanted* to tempt him. She wanted him to touch her so badly she almost couldn't stay still, had to writhe a little on the sheets to relieve some of the tension in her body. From the way he watched her, he knew exactly what she was doing, knew the effect this was having on her.

He blew gently on one of her nipples, making it pucker more and sending a shock wave of shivers through her body. She gasped, arching her back. "*Fuck.* Do that again."

He could've pointed out that he was calling the shots here, but she didn't know that was entirely true. It felt like a push-and-pull, a dynamic they'd always had, where she was the one who wanted to jump and he was the one who gave her the bravery to actually do it. He blew another stream of air on her nipple, and she whimpered.

"You're really not quiet," he said. "What sound would you make if I put my tongue on you right now, took your tits in my mouth?"

If she could've arched her back enough to put them there, she would've. "Do it," she said, her voice breathless. "And find out."

She never would've guessed John was a dirty talker, or that he would be so good at it. She wouldn't have guessed much about John at all, when she thought about it—he'd always been almost maddeningly opaque about anything to do with sex or relationships, even when the subject had come up. There'd been *one* time, when Steve had made some comment about third base—she couldn't even remember what—and John had given a bashful smile before catching her eye and looking away. There'd been something in the tail end of that smile, something knowing and wicked, that she'd found herself thinking about for a while after.

"Touch yourself," he said now. "Show me how you like it."

She reached up to roll her nipples between her fingers, watching him watching her until it became too much and she had to close her eyes. She pressed her thumbs into her nipples, then pinched them, hard, until the sting became an ache and she finally let go, panting a little.

"You like a bit of pain, don't you?" He was talking so matter-of-factly, but there was a rasp to his voice that let her know this was getting to him the same way it was getting to her. It made her wonder what *he* might've noticed about *her* all those years, what conclusions he might've drawn about what she'd be like in bed. If he'd thought about it at all.

He leaned over her, his mouth so close to her ear that his breath stirred her hair, his body so flush with hers it felt like a fever. "How do you make it better?" he asked.

The words came out before she had time to think about them. "Spit on me."

He looked at her, his eyes dark. Then he bent his head and spit directly on one nipple before giving the other the same treatment. "Rub it in," he said.

Micah massaged John's spit in circles over her nipples, feeling the touch almost like it had a direct line down to her clit.

Holy shit, was she about to *come*? Just from this? She wanted to give in. She wanted to hold back, make him work harder for it.

As if reading her mind, John's gaze went to her legs, bent at the knees and spread open. She wondered if he could see the way she pulsed through her underwear, if it was obvious how wet she was.

"Take those off," he said. "I want to see you touch yourself everywhere."

She lifted her hips, sliding her underwear down her legs in record time, moving to kick them off when they got tangled around her feet. But John reached down to grab them first, balling them up in his hand.

"I thought you weren't allowed to touch me," she said.

"And I haven't," he said. "Have I?"

She'd felt the ghost of his fingertip tracing one ankle bone, *knew* she'd felt it because she was so attuned, like a stringed instrument picking up vibrations from across the room. She felt like he'd done it on purpose, like he knew full well that he'd technically broken that rule, but she wasn't about to say it aloud if he wasn't.

"No," she said.

"Good," he said. "Now let those legs fall open for me, honey."

She'd been clenching her knees together without even realizing she was doing it. Her shirts were still tangled around her waist, and she reached down to lift them both over her head, tossing them onto the floor until she was completely naked. John's gaze was on the bounce of her breasts from the action, but she saw when it snagged on the tattoo she'd gotten all those years ago. His hand came up, almost like he was about to touch it, before he clenched it in the sheets instead, his knuckles so close they grazed her rib cage.

"That's what you got?" he asked.

It was the chord shape for A minor, the grid of the fretboard and then the Xs and Os showing the strings you muted and the ones you played open, three filled-in dots showing where you placed your fingers.

She'd assumed he already knew that. She'd assumed he would've seen the pictures in *Playboy*, one in particular where she was lying on her side, her arm over her head, the motion lifting her breast almost as if she was trying specifically to show off the ink underneath. She felt like she had been. She'd *wanted* him to see it, had looked at the pictures herself when the magazine came out and tried to see them through his eyes.

She realized how excited she'd been to show it to him even back when she got it, had imagined his gaze on her when she lifted her shirt to reveal it. She'd kind of regretted that she'd said she wouldn't show it to him unless he got his own tattoo, which she knew might never happen.

"You didn't exactly keep your side of the bargain," she said, her voice a little shaky.

He reached up to smooth her hair back, tucking some of it behind her ear. That simple touch was so unexpected, felt so *good*, that she closed her eyes and let out a sigh that cracked in her throat.

"I know," he said. "I'm sorry about that."

She felt something rise in her chest, some emotion expanding her lungs that she didn't want to stop and analyze. She did let her legs fall open then, reaching down to touch one finger to the crest of that most sensitive spot. She couldn't help the moan that escaped the moment she felt that pressure—fuck, she really did think she could make herself come in a matter of seconds if she wanted to.

"Goddamn, Micah," John said. "You have such a pretty pussy."

"Touch me," she said. "*Please.*"

His eyes were almost black as he watched her rubbing her clit, pinching it between her fingers the way she'd done with her nipples earlier. When she slid a finger all the way inside, she could see that he had to reach down and adjust himself in his jeans. She knew this was killing him, too, so why wouldn't he just *touch* her?

"Please, John," she begged, not even caring how she sounded. "*Please,* holy Christ, I'm about to—I'm—I want—"

"What do you want?"

She wanted it all. She wanted everything. But for now, in this moment, all she could think of was the way he'd told her he'd take her tits in his mouth, the way he'd covered her nipples in his spit. "Your mouth," she gasped. "Please, John, please, kiss me—"

He moved until he was between her legs, his hands coming up to squeeze her thighs, his fingers digging into her rose tattoo as he adjusted her legs over his shoulders. She was so grateful just to feel his *hands* on her skin, to have that connection that meant she wasn't out here alone, a live wire dancing on the ground. When she felt him put his mouth on her she seized up almost immediately, clenching her body to try to hold back the wave she felt rising within her. She could feel every tiny sensation of his tongue dragging up her slit, the way he placed hot, open-mouthed kisses right on her wet center, the low groan he made in his own throat as he tasted her.

And then she couldn't hold on any longer. The wave crested and broke, and she buried her hands in his curls as she let out a guttural cry, the orgasm sending sparks through her body that had her arching and spasming under him.

He made his way back up her body, those calloused fingertips skimming her hips, her rib cage, over her breasts, her shoulders. Until he was eye level with her, and she wrapped her hand around the back of his neck, and pulled him down for a kiss.

It was strange, to think this was their first *real* kiss. Their second, if you counted that one in her bedroom when they were teenagers. It had all the crackle of a first, but there was something so right about it that it felt impossible to believe she hadn't been kissing John this whole time. She could taste herself on his lips, and she was hungry to taste everything he had to offer. She opened her mouth, pressing her tongue against his so hard she heard him grunt, but just when she thought maybe it was too much, her coming on too strong again, he took her cheeks between his hands and deepened the kiss. He took her full bottom lip between his teeth, tugging on it just enough to send that spark of pleasure-pain to her clit again, before he slid his tongue along the same spot.

She could feel the hard ridge of his erection through his jeans, rubbing right against her where she was still hypersensitive, and she rocked her hips against him. She'd been doing it more for *him* than for her, but she was surprised at how quickly the action brought another rise of sensations in her, and she was only aware of the breathless panting sounds she'd started making when John pressed back into her.

"That's it," he said. "Use me. Grind that pussy on me."

"*Fuck*," she said, clenching his biceps as she came again,

even harder than the first time. He swallowed her cry with his mouth, kissing her until she was lying boneless and prone underneath him, barely able to move. It didn't seem fair that she'd come twice and he still had yet to come at all, and she tried to reach down with her shaky hands to undo the button of his jeans.

"Micah—"

"Tell me to touch you," she said. "Tell me how to touch you."

He groaned, almost like he was going to refuse her, but then he reached down and flicked the button so easily it made all her attempts look like a joke, sliding his zipper down and taking his cock out. It was so hard it was almost literally throbbing, and there was a drop of precum on the head of his dick that she swiped and then sucked off her thumb.

He gave a full body shudder. "Fuck, Micah. I'm not going to last long if you—"

She licked down the palm of her hand, leaving a wet trail from her tongue, before wrapping her hand around his cock and giving it a squeeze. His jaw clenched briefly before his mouth fell open, and he was off like a rocket, warm stripes of semen splashing her skin. His arms were trembling slightly as he held himself up over her, looking down at where he'd just come all over her belly.

"That was . . ."

"Yeah," she agreed, even though she didn't know what word he was going to say. She wished she'd let him finish his sentence. *Incredible?* It *had* been incredible. She tried to think of the last time she'd come that hard and drew a blank. *Surprising?* It had been a surprise, in the best definition of the word. But then she also felt like she could say it had felt *inevitable*, like they'd ended up right where they always knew they would eventually. In that way, it didn't feel like a surprise at all.

A part of her wanted to stay beneath his weight forever, didn't even care that she could already feel his come drying on her skin. But another part of her knew that she had to get up, and it would only be harder if she didn't do it now. She shifted beneath him, waiting until he'd carefully lifted himself off her before she rolled off the bed and shut herself inside the bathroom.

It took her a long time to pee. She was still so overstimulated down there, it was a few minutes before she was even able to. She was washing up when she glanced at herself in the mirror. It was impossible not to—the bathroom was small but the mirror took up the entire wall above the sink. She also couldn't help her first impression, which she tried to shove away as soon as it came. Her hair was tousled and flipped over to one side, but in a sexy way, and even in the harsh lighting of the bathroom it looked like it glowed a little. Her mouth was very pink, her lower lip puffy, and her eyes were wide and green as she took in the rest of herself. The soft swell of her breasts, her nipples a slightly darker shade of pink than her mouth, a shadow of a bruise from where she'd pinched one hard.

I am *beautiful*, she thought, and then immediately felt ashamed and stupid for even thinking of herself that way. She turned the faucet off before opening the door.

John was sitting on the end of her bed, tying his shoes. Her stomach dropped, even seeing that he'd gone out to get them, that he'd gotten all the way to putting them on before she could stop him. She didn't want him to go.

He was still bent over his shoes when he glanced up at her. In her entire life, she didn't know that she'd ever been more naked than that moment, standing in the bathroom doorway while John's eyes traveled over her entire body, stripping everything away until she was sure he could feel her heartbeat in his own chest, could know every single thing she was thinking. There was something bottomless in that look, and she felt herself falling into it.

But if he could read her mind, he wouldn't be putting his shoes on. She grabbed her Elvis shirt from the floor, tugging it over her head.

"Well," she said, hoping she achieved the right casual tone. "Definitely better than masturbating separately in our own rooms, wouldn't you say?"

He was still staring at her, his forearms now resting on his thighs. He had a way of making a look *feel* like a touch, as he'd just amply demonstrated, and she felt this one tingle all the way down to her toes.

"Definitely," he said, then hesitated. "Are we good?"

"Great," she said, and now it had to be obvious how much she was overcompensating. Her voice sounded unnaturally high. She knew John heard it, too, because he frowned at her.

"I'm sorry," he said, "for—"

The last thing she wanted right now was one of John's fucking apologies. "Seriously, we're great," she said. "And don't be sorry. You were the one who said sex didn't seem like a good idea. I was the one who pushed it. Like I said, I was feeling horny, and now I'm less horny, so . . . yeah. I'm great. What about you?"

He was still looking at her, like he didn't believe her. "Great," he said finally, and she couldn't tell if he was answering about his own state or just responding to her babbling characterization of her own.

He stood up then, and for a second she thought he'd give her a hug goodbye. Her body tensed, anticipating it, *craving* it, but he seemed to clock the tension and read something else into it, because he just shoved his hands in his pockets.

"We're due for shuffleboard soon," he said. "And I should probably—"

He'd need to change clothes, if nothing else. She remembered the way she'd ground against his jeans only minutes before, and willed her gaze not to drop past his waist. She'd also completely forgotten that the shuffleboard tournament had been scheduled for midnight, which was undoubtedly supposed to be part of the *Nightshifters*-themed fun but now just seemed like poor planning to have to participate in a sport they didn't know how to play on a dark, cold ship.

"I'll see you out there," she said.

"Great," he said, and that was fast becoming one of her least favorite words. She watched him as he went to the door and opened it, the quick glance down either side of the hallway reminding her *Oh yeah, maybe we don't want anyone to know that we did this.* She waited for him to glance back at her one last time, had the smile she'd give him all prepared, but he didn't. He just walked out, shutting the door quietly behind him.

CHAPTER

NINETEEN

SURELY ON A list of sexiest sports, shuffleboard would be somewhere near the bottom. And yet John was still so turned on, he could barely follow a single word of the instructions the cruise director was giving them about how to play the game.

At the last minute, they'd told Ryder and John they would be the two representatives from ElectricOh!, playing against Tatiana Rivera and another cast member from *Nightshifters*. John had assumed Micah would be playing in his place, so he was caught unprepared—shifted suddenly from being in the background to being in the hot seat. He sought out Micah among everyone gathered for the tournament, trying to figure out if the change had come from her or from up above.

She was still wearing the Elvis shirt, although she'd thrown leggings on underneath it, and then an oversized cardigan that covered the whole outfit. Her hair was back in the braid she'd had it in post-shower. The whole look should've been too casual, maybe, borderline sloppy, but Micah had a way of making anything look stylish and purposeful. Still, John found himself wondering if that was always what she'd planned to wear. Somehow he didn't think so, and then he didn't know if there was any significance to that. She had to know at this point he would have a Pavlovian response to that fucking Elvis shirt.

He should've stuck around her room longer. He'd felt the *What does this all mean?* swirling around his head, and the more time she stayed in the bathroom, the more he started to doubt he actually wanted the answer to that question. When she'd emerged, she'd been fully, unapologetically, *gorgeously* naked, and it had taken his breath away. Not just the sight of her— although, Christ, the *sight* of her—but the fact that he was seeing her that way at all. It felt profound, somehow, sacred. He'd felt momentarily unable to speak.

Then she'd made that crack, which he supposed had answered the question he'd never asked.

This was exactly why he'd known it would be a bad idea, to give in to the temptation to be with Micah. For her, it had obviously been an impulse, something she wanted to do so she did it. *I was feeling horny, and now I'm less horny, so . . .* For him, it had opened a Pandora's box he'd kept so tightly locked away. And he didn't know if he could get everything back in that box. He didn't know if he wanted to.

It took a moment for John to realize that Ryder had come up to stand next to him, and that he'd been talking now for a couple minutes.

"Sorry, what?"

Ryder sighed, flicking the hair out of his eyes in a practiced gesture. "I know we've all had our differences. But Frankie and Steve say they could be in, depending on what it would look like. A limited run, probably. Dates in a few major cities. Maybe one of the big festivals. There's that one in Vegas, it's all nostalgia—"

"Wait," John said, still trying to catch up. "Are you talking about *getting the band back together*?"

"Why not?" Ryder said. "We all agreed that tonight's show went off without a hitch. Just like old times."

There were a lot of hitches in the "old times," John wanted to say, *you being the biggest one.* "And Micah's into this?"

"Not yet. But she will be, after you talk to her."

John glanced over at where Micah was standing with Frankie, her arms crossed, her face animated as she said something that made Frankie laugh. The idea that Micah—the same woman who'd walked away from the band in the first place, the woman who only a month ago had said *no rehearsals* because that was how little she wanted to spend time with them—would now want to reunite seemed like something to laugh about. And yet John found himself considering it, wondering if *he* would want to do it, if it meant spending time with her again. If it meant they could be on the stage like they'd been tonight, some magical alchemy happening that made them feel bigger than their individual parts, if it meant they could have private moments offstage that would bring them closer again.

He'd say yes for *her.* He wondered if she'd do the same for him.

The cruise director called for all their attention to begin the tournament. He explained that a member from each team would stand on either end of the court, and Ryder was quick to claim the head end. It was clear that he thought it was yet another way of asserting his superiority, but it backfired when Tatiana chose to be at the foot end with John. He could tell that Ryder wanted to be the one next to the actress, but instead he was stuck with her very handsome co-star whose IMDb credits weren't as impressive.

"Hope you're bringing your A game," Ryder said as they split off to their different ends.

"I've never played shuffleboard in my life," John said. "My game is going to be pass/fail, hate to tell you."

Tatiana was already standing at their end of the court, and John offered a handshake as he approached, introducing himself. On *Nightshifters*, you could always tell what season you were watching by how curly Tatiana wore her hair, and now it was flat-ironed to season one levels. It was surreal how exactly the same she looked as she did on TV, from her wide smile to the distinctive mole on the tan skin of her cheek.

"I caught your show last night," she said. "You were very good."

"Thank you," he said. "I caught all seven seasons of your show, and *you* were very good."

"Except season six?" she said, her brow arched, but her eyes were sparkling.

"Even season six," he said gallantly.

After that, they had to focus as the game started. Ryder went first, using his stick to push one of their yellow discs out onto the court. It didn't pass over the middle line, which meant John had to walk up and remove it from game play.

"It's all good," he said to Ryder, which he meant sincerely but realized only after it came out that it was the worst possible thing he could've said. Ryder was fuming.

"Bit of a hothead, that one," Tatiana said to him once he'd taken his place back next to her.

"You have no idea."

Her teammate took his turn, and she clapped supportively, although afterward she leaned into John and said, "He is so drunk right now, I don't know how he's standing up."

That made John laugh. It was weird, how easy it was to talk to Tatiana—arguably the biggest star on the ship. Maybe it was because he didn't want anything from her, not validation that they were on the same level the way that Ryder did, not even an autograph or picture the way that Steve did.

He glanced over at Micah, but she was examining her nails, probably daydreaming about chewing on them and trying to remind herself not to. Every once in a while she interacted with someone in the crowd, leaned back to be in a selfie, or signed a CD case someone held out to her. Gratifying, that people still had CD cases, that they'd brought them all this way. Frustrating, that Micah wouldn't even look at him.

Ryder sent another disc skimming down the court, lightly tapping Tatiana's team's black disc. John could already tell that Ryder's main strategy was going to be *hit the other team's discs*, whether that was the best move or not, and he had to remind himself that he didn't actually care who won this game.

When they tallied up their points at the end of that round, they were tied up at eight apiece, and Ryder gestured toward Micah.

"Why don't you update the chalkboard?" he said. "You're good at keeping score."

The cruise director started to interrupt to say that wasn't how it was done, but Micah grabbed a piece of chalk. "I always thought that was *your* strength," she said. "But I'm happy to."

"Ooof," Tatiana said. "They used to date?"

John wondered if she brought it up because she already knew, or solely based off the animosity between them now. "Yeah," he said. "Back in the *Nightshifters* days."

"And what about you?"

John glanced at her. "We're just friends."

"Hmmm."

He wondered what *that* meant, but he had to take his turn. He surveyed the yellow discs, trying to figure out what the strategy for an opening shot even was here. For the first time, he was very conscious of the crowd that had all gathered to watch, circling the court, up on the mezzanine of the deck above, a section of contest-winners seated on chairs to one side.

"Don't hold your stick like a sword," the cruise director called from the other side of the court.

Just what he needed to be told in front of everyone.

"Loosen up, think of it as an extension of your hand. Your thumb should be up here, like this."

John adjusted his grip, trying to follow what the director was saying. When he glanced up, he caught Micah watching him. She didn't smile, but she didn't look away. And suddenly he knew, as clearly as if she'd whispered it in his ear—he'd be goddamned if she was any *less* horny than she'd been earlier. He might not know where they stood, friendshipwise; he might not know how she felt about him beyond that. But she'd liked what they'd done earlier, and she was just as desperate as he was to do it again.

Maybe there was no strategy at this point. He took a couple steps toward the disc, sending it sliding down the court.

He was supposed to look at Ryder for confirmation of where it landed, but he found himself looking over Ryder's shoulder to

Micah instead. *Nice shot*, she mouthed, and he grinned back at her.

"Just friends," Tatiana said, lining up her own disc. "Okay."

"I'm in love with her," John said, and Tatiana's stick ended up going crooked, sending her disc flying toward the crowd. They gasped and moved back a few inches as if in a wave, picking up their feet to avoid getting hit.

"You did that on purpose," she said, but her voice held no real censure.

John was as surprised as she was. Not about the way he felt—that part had been there for so long, he didn't even know who he was without it. He was just surprised he'd actually said it out loud, to *Nightshifters* star Tatiana Rivera, of all people, in the middle of the night in the middle of an ocean while playing shuffleboard in front of a crowd that included several werewolf masks.

"And how does she feel?" Tatiana asked.

"That," John said, setting up his next shot, "is the million-dollar question."

"She's jealous as hell right now," Tatiana said. "I can tell you that much."

This time John could've been the one to accuse *her* of doing that on purpose. He sent his disc ineffectually down the court, where it landed almost dead center on the line. Not out of play, but worth nothing unless it got knocked into the scoring zone later.

"No, she's not," he said automatically.

"Trust me, she's practically *green*. She keeps glancing over here when you're not looking."

In normal circumstances, John prided himself on his discretion, and there were many reasons to be extra discreet around whatever was going on between him and Micah. At the same time, he couldn't help but want more of Tatiana's insights now that he had her here. God knows he couldn't talk to the rest of the band, and the terrible reception on the boat made any chance of a long conversation with any of his housemates back home impossible.

"We hooked up," he said. "But I couldn't tell if it was just physical for her or if it meant more than that."

"How long ago did you hook up?"

John glanced at his watchless wrist in a gesture that probably looked like a joke, but had just been a vestigial instinct. "Two hours?"

Tatiana laughed, then seemed to get that he was serious, and laughed even harder. "Oh my god," she said. "This is too good."

There was a sharp whistle from the other side of the court, and John and Tatiana both glanced over to see Ryder gesturing at them. "We gonna play or what?" he yelled.

"Patience," Tatiana called back, "is a virtue."

The crowd cheered, obviously loving the banter, and Tatiana turned to wink at John. "So how did things go afterward," she said, leisurely setting up her next shot. "Two hours ago."

But the crowd had spooked John. He and Tatiana had been talking in low voices, and they were far enough away, but it occurred to him that having this conversation surrounded by people recording on their phones probably wasn't a great idea. Besides, he was pretty sure they were supposed to be hamming it up more, actually putting on a show instead of just quietly talking to one another and playing shuffleboard. The show-manship part had never been his strong suit.

He also had no idea how he would answer Tatiana's question, because he wasn't sure *how* it had gone. He glanced over at Micah again. She was leaning against the scoreboard, waiting for the end of the frame when she could add more points to the running totals. She was playing with the end of her braid, flipping the comma-shaped bit over her fingers and then pulling it through. He remembered that moment in her room—*undo your braid*. From the directness of her gaze when she looked back at him, he thought she might be remembering the same thing.

"I think I'm about five seconds away from forfeiting this game," John said, sliding one of the yellow discs into position to take his turn. "But you said patience is a virtue, so here we go."

CHAPTER

TWENTY

MICAH WISHED SHE had her phone on her so she could quickly search *how the fuck long are shuffleboard games supposed to go actually*. It felt like this one was taking a million years.

Heading into the final frame, ElectricOh!'s team had taken the lead by seven points, but Micah didn't even care who won. She'd felt like she'd taken a million pictures, she'd signed a million autographs, she was cold, and she was sick of watching Ryder's over-the-top celebrations whenever he scored.

John took his turn, which landed neatly right in the middle of the eight-point section, and Tatiana squeezed his arm in congratulations. Okay, Micah wasn't too proud to admit it. *That* was another reason she was looking forward to the game being over. Hadn't they just met? How were they already so . . . chummy? They'd spent practically the entire game talking, laughing, touching, and it was driving Micah crazy.

She knew she had no right to be upset about it really. She and John hadn't discussed what exactly they were doing—had it been a onetime thing, a *what happens on the cruise stays on the cruise* type of deal? Had it been the start of a friends-with-benefits situation? Micah didn't even know where they stood on the *friends* part, much less the *benefits* part. Had it been something more than that?

"Would you sign my CD?" She heard the voice come from over her shoulder, and she turned around, pinning a smile on her face.

"Sure!"

It was ElectricOh!'s first album, which was titled *Self-Titled*. Not the band's name to make it an actual self-titled record, but literally *Self-Titled*. What could she say, they'd thought they were so clever at sixteen.

The picture on the cover was the five of them, standing behind a chain-link fence that had a triangular warning sign in the upper left corner—yellow with a black lightning-bolt arrow, indicating that the fence was electrified. They'd thought that was clever, too. Her four band members were standing in various poses—hands in pockets (John), arms crossed over chest (Frankie), hand running through hair (Ryder), looking down and laughing (Steve). Micah was the only one touching the fence, her fingers curled through the chain link, one eye partially obscured, the other staring directly at the camera.

God, they looked so *young*. The kids on that CD had no idea what was coming. They had no idea what they were getting into. They were on the other side of the fence and couldn't see the warning sign.

Micah used the woman's Sharpie to scrawl her jagged signature on the plastic case, adding an *X* over her *i* like she always used to do. Her handwriting certainly hadn't improved since she was a teenager. If anything, it had devolved.

"Could you get Ryder to sign it, too?" the woman asked.

"Tell you what," Micah said, giving the woman a wink. "I can get you the whole band. Give me a second."

It was a terrible idea, not least of which was because if Micah did this for one person there would soon be a whole crowd of people requesting the same thing. But she wanted to have an excuse to approach John, and she figured this was as good as any.

She went to Frankie and Steve first, since they were hanging out on the sidelines, chatting with a few members of the Silver Cuties who'd shown up. Then she went to Ryder, who was predictably annoyed to be interrupted in the middle of the game, even though as far as she could tell all he was doing was standing there watching discs slide toward him.

"You don't have to do everything a fan asks you to," Ryder muttered while he scribbled a huge *R* that took up most of the remaining empty space. "They're called boundaries, Micah, you should look into them."

"When I want to set a boundary," she said, "I do. *You* should know that better than anyone."

His gaze flickered up to hers, and for a second she saw— what was that? Guilt? Fear?

But no, she was projecting. Ryder was too self-centered to feel emotions that took other people into account. He thrust the CD case at her, turning back toward the game in a dismissal that made her feel like *she* was the fan trying for an autograph. Maybe she'd draw devil horns on his picture on the cover. For a laugh.

Then it was time for John. The shuffleboard court suddenly felt longer than it had seemed only a few moments before, and she felt strangely exposed and self-conscious as she headed toward him. It felt like walking the plank.

No, that wasn't right—it was an analogy that had occurred to her only because they were on a ship. It was more like when the teacher called on you in class and you had to head up to the board to work out a math problem in front of everyone, and you could feel all their eyes on you.

But that wasn't right, either. She did feel like everyone was looking at her, but she found she didn't care. The only person she cared about was John, who'd been in the middle of talking to Tatiana but broke off when he saw her heading toward him. Now he was watching her, an expression on his face that looked almost . . .

It felt like walking down the aisle.

Sailing had been much smoother since that first night, thankfully, but Micah still stumbled a little as she approached them, and John's hand shot out to steady her.

"You good?" It was a variation of the same thing he'd asked immediately after they'd hooked up earlier—*Are we good?* She was starting to think that an honest answer to that question might be the scariest thing of all.

"Yeah," she said. "Sorry. I was just—"

It seemed so silly now, coming all this way so he could sign a CD. She *did* feel like the fan, putting herself out there. She was also conscious of Tatiana standing nearby, and even if she might've entertained a very tiny, she-didn't-want-anyone-to-get-hurt-actually fantasy of the beautiful actress somehow falling overboard only a few minutes before, she wasn't about to be rude.

"Hi," she said. "I'm Micah, from ElectricOh!."

"I know who you are," Tatiana said. "It's so good to meet you."

And then she did the most surprising thing. She ignored Micah's outstretched hand and gave her a big hug instead, squeezing her like they were long-lost friends. It was the only thing that got John to drop his own hand, which had still been clutching the back of Micah's elbow.

Fuck. Tatiana was super *nice*. Micah didn't know exactly what she'd planned when she'd approached them—as much as a primal part of her had wanted to stake her claim on John somehow, she knew she couldn't do that. Any public display of affection was too public, and anyway, what claim? And whatever her private feelings, she wasn't about to be snarky toward some woman just for having the gall to enjoy John's company.

But Tatiana was so beautiful, and so fucking nice, if it weren't for the fact that Micah felt impossibly depressed by the thought, she'd almost ship them herself.

"Let's get the three of you together," a voice said from behind them, and Micah turned to see one of the official cruise photographers, gesturing for them to get closer for a picture. Micah tried to let Tatiana take the middle, because she figured that was how the photographer would want it, but Tatiana ducked around so that Micah was in the middle instead. She barely had time to register John's hand at the small of her back, a flash of a camera, and then the moment was over.

John had always hated taking pictures, but at some point there was no getting out of it. She had so many photos with him from when they were younger, an almost incalculable amount—promo shots, press coverage, a few candid ones that meant more to her than any of the posed ones. She thought suddenly of the creased photograph she still had stuck in the pages of a book in her apartment, of the two of them sitting outside the band room in high school, Micah cross-legged in the grass and in the middle of saying something, John leaning back on his hands with his legs stretched out, laughing.

"You wanted me to sign that?" he asked, pointing to the CD case in her hand.

"Oh," she said. "Yes. Sorry, I'm holding up the game."

She handed the CD to John, who started trying to sign it with the shuffleboard cue still in his hand, then crouched, bringing his knee up to give himself some support.

"Here," Micah said, reaching out to grab the stick, then turning around to present her back to John. "Use me."

There was a pause before he lifted her braid, setting it over her shoulder. She felt the whisper of his hand over the back of her neck, like he was pushing stray tendrils of hair out of his way, but she knew he hadn't had to do that. And then she felt the pressure of the CD case against her shoulder blades, heard the squeak of the marker as he must've signed his name. He'd always signed *John P.*, which she found cute for some reason— why the last initial? There was no other John in the band. He also carefully wrote out every individual letter, which was more than anyone else did. It really didn't look like a rock star's autograph. It kind of looked like how you might sign a polite note to your neighbor.

When he was done, she turned around. He was holding out the Sharpie and the signed CD, but his gaze slid from the askew neckline of her T-shirt to her mouth before he finally smiled at her. "There you go."

What had that look been, if not staking a claim? She glanced at Tatiana, who was practically *beaming* at them. Truly, was she the nicest person on the planet?

"Are we ready to keep playing or what?" Ryder yelled from the other side of the court, making Micah jump a little. She'd been so wrapped up in the moment that everything else had fallen away, and she was almost shocked to remember the crowd, the cruise, the entire context for why they were standing there in the first place.

Micah handed John back his shuffleboard cue, then gave Tatiana a little salute she knew would haunt her nightmares later. "Good luck," she said. "May the best person win and all that. Talk after?"

She aimed that last part at John, hoping it sounded casual enough. But his eyes briefly shadowed, which made her stomach swoop.

"Yeah," he said. "There's something I have to talk to you about."

That didn't have to be ominous. *She* was the one who'd brought up having a conversation, after all. And yet she still found herself dreading whatever he was planning to say. Something about his face suggested it wasn't going to be anything she liked.

"Great," she said. That fucking word again.

ELECTRICOH! ENDED UP winning the shuffleboard tournament, which became extra thrilling when they got presented with a kitschy trophy and vouchers for the casino. Steve was excited for the trophy, but he was *really* excited for the casino vouchers, and he gave Micah a high five so hard it made her hand sting.

"I want to find a poker table," he said. "Who's with me? Do they have poker, or is it all just slots?"

"Only one way to find out," Frankie said, snatching their voucher from Steve's hand like they didn't trust him to give it up of his own accord.

"Technically, John and I are the ones who brought the trophy home for ElectricOh!," Ryder pointed out. "So I think the prizes are supposed to be for us."

Frankie shot him a withering look. "There are *five* of them, you cartoon. The intent is very clear."

"That's not how it works?" Ryder asked with a look of wide-eyed faux innocence. "That's how writing credits apparently work."

Micah knew on some intellectual level that had been a dig meant specifically for her, more commentary on "If Only," which she and John shared writing credit on because they'd written it together, just the two of them. But she found she didn't care about all of Ryder's little comments. She was too busy watching John and Tatiana standing off to one side after the photographer and crowds were starting to clear out, still talking and seeming to take their sweet time wrapping it up.

"You go ahead without me," she said. "I'm pretty tired."

"So that means we can have your voucher?"

She couldn't see herself going to the casino on this trip, but something made her reject the idea of being completely left out of the fun. She plucked one of the vouchers from Steve's hand, giving him a grin before taking one more.

"I'll claim my prize, thank you," she said. "And I'll make sure John gets his."

"Gets my what?" John said from behind her. She turned, expecting to see Tatiana there, too, but the actress was gone.

She wondered if John had any plans to meet up with her later. She knew it was none of her business.

"Your prize for winning shuffleboard," she said, handing him his voucher. "Who knew you were such a ringer."

"My competitive spirit ended up coming out," he said, looking at her.

Why did that single look set her on fire? *So did mine*, she thought, thinking again of Tatiana. She felt suddenly breathless, and like everyone would be able to tell. "You didn't want a repeat of the great MTV *Guitar Hero* fail?"

John's brows drew together. "That game is nothing like playing actual guitar," he said. "The timing's all wrong. They penalize you for hitting the note too early, but in real life you have to—"

Micah had heard this exact rant several times before. It had been one of her favorites to tease out of John, because she knew he usually *hated* getting competitive, hated getting that emotionally invested in the outcome of something that really didn't matter or worse, was out of his control. But he'd lost a *Guitar Hero* match that had been filmed for a charity special to some BMX guy, and he was still salty about it. It was adorable.

She put a finger to John's lips to stop him from talking. Her first thought was how soft his mouth was, how hard it had been on her earlier when she needed it to be. Her second thought was that his eyes were wide now, lips parted in a way that tempted her to slide her finger inside.

Her last thought was *Oh fuck, that's right, I shouldn't be doing this in front of everyone.*

She withdrew her hand with a laugh, hoping to play it off. "We don't need to hear those excuses again, am I right, Frankie?"

Frankie's gaze went from Micah to John and back again, and something like a smile started to curl at the corner of their mouth. "Definitely not."

"Just admit you're bad at *Guitar Hero*, bro," Steve said. "I rock at it. You should see me on those DragonForce songs. The *precision*. The grace. It's like watching a ballet."

He lifted his hands to play an air guitar, banging his head as if to an unheard beat.

"I would've kicked that bike guy's ass," Ryder said, which was unfortunately also a familiar rant, just not one that Micah found as cute. At least he hadn't seemed to clock her sudden touchiness with John, which was a small blessing. Ryder had always been disproportionately, unattractively competitive, and she knew nothing would bring it out more than seeing her and John together, even though Ryder had zero claim on anything she did anymore.

"As much as I'm loving the opportunity to relive a *Guitar Hero* competition from over a decade ago," Frankie said, "are we going to hit up the casino, or what? Some of us want to wake up early enough tomorrow to actually enjoy the beach."

"Hey, I want to enjoy the beach," Steve said, like he was somehow affronted by even the implication that he wouldn't. "But I got a bit of gambling in me first."

"I'll get mauled in there," Ryder said, which was probably *true* but still managed to emphasize where he felt he ranked in comparison to Steve and Frankie.

Frankie turned from him without justifying that with a response. "Micah already said she's out," they said, directing the words to John. "How about you?"

The way his gaze slid to hers made her remember what he'd

said earlier. *There's something I have to talk to you about.* It had sounded specific. It had sounded bad.

"I'll probably just turn in," he said.

"Looks like it's just me and you, Steve," Frankie said. "Let's go do some damage."

Once the others split off to go their separate ways—Steve and Frankie toward the casino and Ryder toward she-didn't-care-where—Micah was left with John. The shuffleboard court had mostly cleared out, but there were still a few people hanging around. Luckily, there was a roped-off section where they could head back toward their deck without anyone following them, and Micah started walking in that direction, figuring that John would stay a few steps behind until they'd reached somewhere more private.

What she didn't expect was that the minute they'd rounded the corner, he slid his hand up her wrist, gripping her forearm to pull her into an alcove. And then his hands were on her face, in her hair, and he was kissing her, god, he was fucking *kissing* her.

TWENTY-ONE

EVERY KISS WITH Micah counted, as far as John was concerned.

There'd been that first one, when they were too young and inexperienced to even know what they were doing. A single press of the lips, that terrifying, thrilling touch of tongues.

Then there'd been their kisses earlier that night, which had been hot and dirty and just a little aggressive, like they were both still fighting something with each other, with themselves. He hadn't wanted to kiss Micah so much as he'd wanted to consume her, to take in everything she was offering and give it back to her in a way that let her know that he was hers, that she was *his*.

But this one was different. It was deliberate. It was slow and aching and everything John had wanted to say all night but hadn't been able to. He pressed his fingers to Micah's jaw, to her cheeks, to the line of her throat. She tasted vaguely of cherries—it was probably her lip balm—and when she finally stopped to take a breath he was right there to swallow it.

"I thought," she said, panting around the words, "we were supposed to be talking."

"I can multitask," he said, his breath hot against her ear as he kissed the sensitive skin behind it. "Let's talk."

He was supposed to be bringing up band business with her, convincing her to do some sort of reunion tour that everyone else apparently wanted, but in that moment he couldn't think of anything he cared less about. Then she'd said she wanted to talk, and he'd wondered if it was going to be about *this*, whatever was happening between them, if she'd say she regretted it or that it couldn't happen again. But then she'd pressed her finger to his lips, and suddenly the idea of *talking* had flown right out of his head.

Micah tilted her head back, giving him more access to her throat. When she laughed, he could feel the vibration of it against his mouth.

"Have you always been like this?" she asked.

Always like what? If she meant the way he'd been back in her room, the way he'd told her what to do, how to touch herself, then the answer was no. He'd never been like that before. If she meant the way he was now, grabbing this moment for a public display of affection like they were two teenagers in high school again, then no, he'd never been like that, either.

But if she meant had he been like *this*, hungry and desperate for more of her, then the answer was yes. Always yes.

"Have you?" he asked.

She took his hand, sliding it up her rib cage to press it against her bare breast, her nipple hard against his palm. He'd suspected she wasn't wearing anything underneath her shirt when he'd seen her in it, had had a vision of her at one point bending to pick up one of the discs off the court, giving him a view right down the front. He'd been able to picture it so clearly—the soft curve of her breasts as they hung down, the sharp point of her nipples from the cold—that he'd had to close his eyes and tell himself to get it together.

She was sliding her own hands up inside his shirt now, clenching the muscles of his back while she arched into him. "Earlier tonight," she said, "you were going to apologize for this. But I don't need it. I'm not sorry."

"I'm not sorry, either," he said, nuzzling into the warm space between her neck and her shoulder, pressing an open-mouthed kiss to her collarbone, huffing a small laugh. "I was just going to apologize for finishing so fast."

He felt her smile against his forehead. "Don't. I was flattered."

"And for coming on your stomach," he said. "Without asking first."

"John, you can come anywhere you want to on me."

He groaned, his hands tightening on her breasts. He pinched her nipple, pressing her back against the wall with a kiss that made her sag a little in his arms, until he slid his hands around her shoulders to hold her up.

"You can't say shit like that," he said.

"Why not?"

Because it makes me lose control. But who was he fooling? He hadn't been in control from the moment she'd told him she'd beg if he asked her to.

He reached down to cup her ass in his hands, shifting her up a bit against the wall. The alcove was private enough that they *felt* alone, but of course he was conscious of the fact that they were still technically on the deck of a cruise ship, that there were doors marked Staff Only right next to them that someone might go into or come out of at any second. But from the way Micah's breath hitched as his fingers slid into the waistband of her leggings, barely less than an inch, he knew that this was all part of what got her off.

"You'd have to be quick," he said.

"I can be quick."

His hand skimmed over that smooth skin below her waist, pausing for a moment before he went any further. "You'd have to be quiet."

"I can be quiet," she whispered.

He bit her earlobe. "You'd have to beg."

She shifted under his hand, tilting toward him like she was trying to urge him to touch her where she wanted it. "*Please*," she said. "I want to come so bad."

"How bad?"

"It's all I've been able to think about," she said. "John, please. Touch me."

He slid a finger inside her, and she leaned her head back against the wall, her mouth open slightly as she panted her need. He could've watched her like that all night, the play of emotions over her face as he curled his finger, as she let a little more of her weight sink down onto him. But they did need to be quick, and so he brought his thumb up to press against her clit, giving it a hard rub.

"Fuck," she breathed, clutching his forearm with a grip so strong it almost hurt. "*Yes.* I'm so close already, please."

He could tell. She was so wet, and he could feel her clenching around him, could hear her breath quickening. He rubbed circles over her clit, his fingers patient and already slick with her.

"Inside me," she said. "I want to feel—"

He used two fingers this time, pumping them inside her while continuing to rub her clit with his thumb, and he felt her tense up just in time to bring his other hand up to cover her mouth.

"Shhh," he said into her ear. "You promised to be quiet."

When she did cry out, the sound was muffled, her breath hot on his palm. Her eyes were squeezed shut, a sheen of sweat on her forehead even though there was a chill in the night air. She gripped his biceps, and he realized she was partially holding herself up that way. He removed his hand from her mouth to brace her at the waist, bringing his other hand up to suck her off his fingers.

She opened her eyes. There was something so vulnerable and unguarded in Micah's expression, post-orgasm, that made John's stomach flip. When she looked at him like that, he thought there was nothing easier than being together, the two of them, just like this.

"You have very dexterous hands," she said.

"Do I?"

She smiled, biting her lip. "I've been watching them a lot," she said, stretching hers into an F chord shape on his forearm like it was the neck of a guitar. "The way your fingers move. It's been a little hard to focus."

He'd taught her guitar, back in high school. That chord had been her biggest struggle—it required the most stretch, and she'd flatly refused to learn any song that used it until one day it had just clicked. He remembered having her eyes on him even then, but he'd known not to read anything into it. She was just trying to learn. But now he wanted to ask *Since when?*, wanted to know if she'd ever looked at him in those days the way he'd looked at her.

But maybe it didn't matter. She was twining her fingers in his now, and it felt good just to hold her hand.

"Especially after I slept in your bed," she said, "and woke up this morning with you touching my boob."

He groaned, leaning his forehead against hers. "Oh god," he said. "I thought that was a dream."

"Not a dream," she said. "And don't you dare apologize. I was into it."

He kissed her. "Okay," he said. "Then I'm not sorry."

They were still kissing—slow and languorous and exploratory, almost textbook definition *making out*—when a throat cleared next to them. "Excuse me," a man holding a pile of towels said. "I need to get to that door?"

John felt his face heat almost like they *had* been caught doing more than just kissing, and he was quick to move away from the alcove, his hand still holding Micah's.

"Sorry about that," he said. "Uh, have a good night."

They were halfway up the stairs toward the next deck before Micah started laughing. "Have a good *night*?" she said.

"What else was I supposed to say?"

"It was the *way* you said it. You sounded so guilty! Remind me never to rob a bank with you."

"You need a reminder for that?"

She dropped his hand when they finally reached the top deck, which he tried not to read anything into. It was probably best if they flew under the radar with whatever this was between them, and they hadn't exactly done a bang-up job of being discreet so far. It was a beautiful night—clear enough to see the stars, a crispness in the air that reminded you that you were *alive*. They settled up along the rail, looking out over the water.

"Wait, have we already stopped?" Micah said, leaning out a little. "I think I see lights over there."

"It would make sense," John said. "If there are excursions leaving first thing tomorrow for swimming with dolphins or whatever else."

"What time is it even?"

John didn't know, and he didn't particularly care. Time on the ship stretched and contracted. He was vaguely aware of being tired, in that pleasant way where you knew you'd fall asleep the second you sank into your bed, but he could've also stayed out there with Micah forever.

"Let's walk to the other side and see if we can make out more of the port," John suggested.

They strolled along the deck of the ship, and John almost reached for her hand again. Instead, he shoved his hands in his pockets, tilting his head back so he could see the stars. It was hard to believe that only a day had passed since he'd been walking along the deck in a similar way after the Silver Cuties show, except alone and thinking about Micah asleep back in his bed. Their history was so long and this one day felt somehow like the longest part of it.

He could tell she was similarly in her own head as they walked, and he wondered what she was thinking about. But then he didn't have to wonder, because she took a breath and asked the question that had obviously been on her mind.

"What did you want to talk to me about?" she said. "Back at the shuffleboard game."

The last thing he wanted to talk about was ElectricOh!, but he couldn't put it off indefinitely. "The band was discussing a potential reunion tour," he said. "And wondering if you'd be into it."

She stopped for a second, looking at him. "A reunion tour."

John ran his hand through his hair. He really wished he hadn't agreed to be the person to bring it up with her. For one thing, he knew less about it than anyone else—it hadn't been his idea.

"I don't know how it would work," he said. "Tie it to the anniversary of an album? Play a couple festivals? That's all the kinds of stuff we could figure out, I guess, but yeah. Get ElectricOh! back together, at least for this one specific purpose."

She was standing very still, and everything that had felt so open to him only a few minutes ago now seemed totally closed off. "And you want to do it."

He didn't know what he wanted. He certainly hadn't signed on to this cruise with any hope or even desire to get the band back together again. But it *had* felt magical, being back onstage, playing their songs. And if it meant an excuse to see more of Micah, well, that also sounded pretty good to him.

"I think it's interesting," he said. "Worth some consideration, at least."

She pressed her lips together, giving a nod like he really had given her something to think about. But John knew before she even spoke that whatever those thoughts were right now, they weren't good.

"The band discussed this," she said. "The four of you. The band. Whose idea was it? Let me guess—Ryder's?"

Since John hadn't been present for those initial discussions, he had no idea, but he would put money that Micah was right.

Frankie and Steve both seemed satisfied enough with the way their lives were going after ElectricOh!—Frankie had their session work, Steve had his family and his job at Best Buy, and he could see them going along with the idea but not coming to it themselves. Ryder was the one who had a chip on his shoulder about everything and would want a chance to try to rewrite their legacy. Normally, John's knee-jerk reaction to anything that originated with Ryder was to reject it, but this was such a big decision, he didn't want to act too rashly.

Some of what he was thinking must've shown on his face, because Micah's eyes narrowed. "He asked you to talk to me, didn't he? He knew if he tried it I'd just say no. But he knew if it was you . . ."

John felt something slipping away, but he also knew there was no point in being anything less than honest. "Yes," he said. "He asked me to talk to you."

She crossed her arms over her chest, looking out over the water. A strand of her hair was blowing across her eyes, but she didn't seem to care. "Was that what this was all about?" she asked. "The—what we just did? You figured you could seduce me into going along with it?"

The very idea was so wrong, so *ugly*, that John was struck speechless. That had never even crossed his mind, and he didn't know whether to be more anxious to reassure her or more angry that it had crossed *her* mind in the first place.

"That's what you think of me," he said. "After all this time."

She swallowed, and it could just be the shadows on the dark ship, but he thought he could make out a small purple mark he'd left on her pale throat, next to her dandelion tattoo. She still wouldn't look at him, and he felt himself veering toward angry, which was an emotion he *hated* feeling. He hated it more directed toward Micah, because he'd so rarely felt it with her. He hated it because he knew there were other emotions underneath it, deeper still, that were even harder to look at head-on.

"If you don't want to do it, say no," he said. "I don't really care. But just remember that at one point, Micah, we were a *band*. The five of us. We were a group of people who made something together, who supported each other, who rode the highs and lows together. Maybe we can't get that back. Maybe we shouldn't try. But I'm not going to erase what we had then, either. It's too important, it's—"

Now it was his turn to take a hard swallow. It wasn't just the band, obviously. It was *them*. Even before they'd had the band, it had always been *them*.

"It's probably four o'clock in the fucking morning," he said. "And I'm sure we're contractually obligated somehow to be on that beach. You can think about it and let everyone else know your decision. I'm heading to bed."

He waited a second, to see what she might say. Only a few minutes ago, he'd assumed they'd be sleeping together that night—not even having sex necessarily, just sleeping together in the way they'd done so many times before. He'd been looking forward to it. The ability to snuggle up against her if he wanted to, to hold her if he wanted to, to open his eyes the next morning knowing she'd still be there.

But all she said was "Okay. Have a good night."

The echo of his earlier words had to be deliberate, and they only frustrated him more. That and the fact that she'd directed them toward the water, and not toward him.

"You, too," he said. And then he walked away, heading toward the interior part of the ship. Right before he disappeared through the door, he glanced back once to see her still standing there, a lone figure dressed in black, her hair bright in the moonlight. She was still staring out at the ocean, and he felt a sudden pang of . . . what? It wasn't as easy to name as the anger. It was a feeling that could pull him under if he let it.

John realized they'd never gotten to see the port. At this point, they'd see it in daylight, and they'd do it separately. He opened the door, and left her behind.

CHAPTER
TWENTY-TWO

MICAH FELT HUNGOVER, and she hadn't even had a drop of alcohol on this cruise so far.

For one thing, the sun was so bright. She'd woken up later than she'd planned but still way earlier than she would've liked, and she'd made her way down to the cruise company's private island. It was a gorgeous, perfect beach day—warm wherever you were in the sun, just chilly enough in the shade to feel like a relief. The sky was clear and blue, and the water literally sparkled like something out of a tourism commercial.

And the sun was way too fucking bright, giving Micah a headache even though she'd put her sunglasses on.

Frankie and Steve must've gotten there early enough to claim a couple chairs, because they were already lying out, looking lazy and comfortable. She didn't see John anywhere, but she assumed he must be around, since he was the one who'd brought up the beach last night.

She knew she shouldn't have said what she did. The minute

it left her mouth, she'd known it was wrong. But she'd been angry and blindsided and ready to lash out, and so that was what she'd done. Self-sabotage had always been a specialty of hers.

She was already halfway to feeling completely sorry for herself, debating whether she should just go back to her room and take a nap, when she heard someone call her name.

"Micah!"

It was Frankie, bracing against the back of the chair with one hand, the other hand curled around some kind of tropical cocktail. "Come over here!" Frankie yelled. "We've been waiting for you."

Had they? Micah took off her sneakers to make her way toward the chairs, the white sand burning the bottoms of her bare feet a little. Frankie tried to shoo Steve off his lounger, telling him he needed to be a gentleman about it, but he looked so comfortable lying there with his eyes closed that Micah hated to be the one to disturb him. She perched on the edge of Frankie's lounger instead.

Frankie gave Micah a look over their sunglasses. "Jeans and sneakers?" they said. "At the beach?"

Micah glanced down at herself. It was about as beachy as she got—she was wearing a bathing suit, at least, a one-piece that was plain and lifeguard-y except in dark purple instead of red. But over that, she'd layered a loose pair of ripped jeans, her knee and a glimpse of her thigh tattoo peeking out from the shredded places.

Frankie, on the other hand, looked like they were born to be in a tropical paradise, with their silver-and-teal bikini and gauzy sarong cover-up.

"Watch John be in a full-out T-shirt and jeans," Frankie said. "He'll be wearing the exact same thing he wore for the show last night. Where *is* John?"

They asked like Micah would be the one to know, and she cleared her throat. "No idea," she said. "Maybe he slept in."

"Maybe he went snorkeling," Steve put in. "I want to go snorkeling. You think it's too late to sign up?"

"You should go check," Frankie said.

Steve drummed his hands on the sides of the chair, taking a second for some internal debate before he finally sprang up as though he'd been given a timer to complete his task. "I'll be right back," he said. "Micah, save my seat."

"You're delusional if you think I'll give it up," Micah said, settling onto the now-vacant lounger. "Move your, lose your."

The words had flown out of her mouth before she'd had time to think about them, but man, did they bring her back. It's what they always used to say when they were kids—it had started out as *Move your feet, lose your seat* and had morphed over the years to the simplified *Move your, lose your.* Once they'd had a whole library of sayings and phrases and jokes like that, a lexicon that was all their own.

Micah scanned the people on the beach. Everyone was in their little groups, having a good time—splashing in the water, spread out on towels to catch some sun, and there was even a game of volleyball that had broken out. It occurred to her that this cruise was maybe a little stressful, and not just for the people working it like ElectricOh! and the cast of *Nightshifters* and everyone else. Although it was a vacation, it also had an intense itinerary, featuring nonstop opportunities to see panels and music and play trivia and attend group activities. This was the first time she'd seen people just seeming to *relax*.

She still didn't see John anywhere, and she was starting to wonder if he was going to come down to the beach at all.

"You really don't know where he is?" Frankie asked, seeming to clock Micah's search and understanding the reason for it.

"Why would I?" Micah asked.

Frankie glanced over with an *Are you kidding me?* expression. "You two have always had vibes, but ever since we got on that boat you have had *vibes*. I just assumed you'd spent the night together."

They said it so casually, like it wouldn't be the kind of event that would completely explode everything. Then again . . . would it? What was there now to explode?

"We didn't always have vibes," Micah protested. It sounded weak, even to her ears. "We were friends."

Frankie pressed their lips together and pushed them out. "What's that saying? Love is friendship caught fire? I've been waiting about a billion years for this one to catch."

"I already made the mistake of dating someone in the band," Micah said. "I wasn't about to make that mistake again."

"Your mistake was dating *Ryder* in the first place," Frankie said. "Fuck whether he was in the band or not. I mean, objectively I see it, in the way that people keep telling me Captain America is hot and I have to nod and pretend I see anything other than a red-white-beige-and-blue blur. But I never did understand why you went for him at all, if I'm being honest."

Ryder had had that kind of charisma you could have in high school just by virtue of being a couple years older and being reasonably attractive. *He'd* pursued *her*, which had felt so flattering at the time. They'd played a late-night show, and afterward he and Micah had both gotten drunk, John having already gone back to his own hotel room sober as a judge like he always was. She'd wanted to join him, had known that if she knocked on his door he'd let her slide under the covers like she had so many times before. But she'd also felt reckless and out of control and she hadn't wanted John to see her that way, hadn't wanted to risk somehow tainting him by even letting him around it. When Ryder had kissed her, she remembered feeling a drop in her stomach, less a swoop of anticipation and more one of dread, like she knew what she was doing was wrong and yet she was going to do it anyway. She barely remembered that first night they'd been together, but after that they were suddenly a couple, and she'd figured it was best to keep everything going as best as she could. First, by not letting the rest of the band find out. Then, by trying not to let any of the cracks show. And finally, by cutting the band off when she cut Ryder off, to try to make it as clean a break as possible.

Which was a laugh, of course. These past couple days, she'd been confronted over and over with all the jagged edges of that break.

"Capricious youth," Micah said.

"Sounds like a band name," Frankie said, then smiled as their eyes caught on something behind Micah. "Hey! There you are."

Micah knew without turning around that it would be John. She really did feel hungover—tired, clammy, a little sick to her stomach. She ached everywhere, including a throbbing between her legs that she knew was as much anticipation as it was a reminder of what they'd gotten up to yesterday. She already missed the way they'd been then for a few precious hours, the way she could touch John any way she wanted, the way she'd begged him to touch her. She missed the way they'd been before that, all those years ago when there were most definitely always *vibes*, when she could tell him to lay his head in her lap so she could play with his hair.

Frankie had been wrong about John at the beach. He hadn't come in his usual jeans and black T-shirt—instead, he was wearing proper swimming trunks, showing off his legs dusted with dark hair, his bare chest, the flat brown circles of his nipples, and another trail of dark hair from his belly button disappearing into his waistband. Even after all they'd done together, she realized this was the most naked she'd ever seen him, and it felt suddenly wildly intimate, like she couldn't believe she was seeing him *now*, in public, like *this*.

Luckily, Frankie spoke, because Micah didn't know that she could. "You own a bathing suit!" they said.

He gave them an odd look. "I live in Florida," he said. "I go to the beach all the time?"

"Of course, of course, that makes sense. I keep forgetting that you live in that hellhole."

John rubbed the back of his neck, the action causing his biceps muscle to flex. "I guess I can tell how much it feels like home to me now by how annoyed I get when other people call it a *hellhole*. It's hot, the politics suck, but there are a lot of good people there and a lot of things to fight for and to love about it."

He glanced at Micah before glancing away, like he was embarrassed to have said so much.

"There are legit alligators, though," he said. "That's not only

in memes. I saw one in a retention pond just outside my neighborhood."

"Stop it," Frankie said. "You were almost selling me and now
I'm all the way out again."

John was also holding a book in his other hand, like he'd
planned to go off and read by himself instead of hanging out
with them, and Micah wished she could ask him about it. John
felt as inaccessible to her now as if he was miles away in the
middle of the ocean.

"You need someone to get your back," Frankie was saying.
"Micah can do it."

Wait. What?

John's gaze slid to Micah again, and this time the eye contact caught and held. *If you don't want to do it, say no*, he'd told
her last night about the reunion tour, as if it were that easy, just
to figure out what you wanted and then to tell other people what
that was. He seemed to be saying something similar with his
eyes now, something along the lines of *You don't have to*. Or
maybe he didn't want her to touch him, but speaking up went
both ways. She'd let him say that if it was how he felt.

She scooted back on the lounger, straddling it to leave room
right in front of her for John to sit. "Sunscreen?" she asked, holding her hand out.

Frankie gave her the bottle, and Micah tried to smile in a
way that seemed friendly and unbothered, that acted like last
night had never happened. "Come on, Florida boy," she said.
"You don't want to burn."

He hesitated only for a second before he lowered himself
onto the lounger, straddling it, too, so he could shift closer to
Micah. She had a sudden core memory of a time they'd been

like this, only their places had been switched, and he'd had his chin on her shoulder. *It's going to be okay*, he'd said in her ear, and she could remember the way he'd said it, the way she'd believed him, even though she could no longer even recall what event had necessitated the assurance.

She had the strongest urge to put her chin on his shoulder now, and hug him tight, but of course she couldn't do that. So instead she just squirted some sunscreen onto her fingers, and touched them to the spot at the top of John's spine.

He tensed, relaxing as she started rubbing the sunscreen onto his skin.

"Cold?" she asked.

"A bit," he said. "It's fine."

When she went back for more lotion, she warmed it between her hands before touching John again. She spread her palms over his shoulder blades, unable to resist digging in a little as she worked the lotion in. His skin was so warm, his shoulders so broad, she wanted to touch him like this forever. *I'm sorry about what I said last night*, she tried to say with her hands. *I didn't mean it*. She slid her hands all the way down to his lower back, where she used her thumbs to rub sunscreen into the twin dimples there. *Come back to me.*

John gave a grunt, and she paused, her hands still near his waist.

"Everything okay?"

He cleared his throat. "You almost done?" he said. "Seems like you got everywhere."

While she'd been lost in her own thoughts, enjoying this chance to touch him, he'd probably been counting down the seconds until the whole ordeal was over. She spread the lotion that was still on her hands along his rib cage, wanting to ensure she really did get everywhere but also unable to resist one more opportunity. Then she lightly slapped his back, like it was the trunk of a car she was telling to move on.

"There you go," she said.

He glanced at her over his shoulder. "Thanks."

He grabbed his book from where he'd set it next to the chair, and she didn't want him to leave yet. She held the sunscreen out to him.

"Do me?"

She thought she'd done a decent job of slathering it all over herself before she'd come out there, but of course there would be places she couldn't reach. It wasn't just that she wanted John to touch her . . . but that was most of it. She could've easily asked Frankie, and would have if John hadn't come up when he did.

For a second she thought that was exactly what John was going to suggest—that she just ask Frankie to do it instead. But then he took the bottle from her hand, gesturing for her to turn around. She awkwardly brought her leg up and over, practically falling into John's lap until she was seated sideways on the lounger, John next to her. She pulled her ponytail over her shoulder, presenting her back to him.

Either John had learned from her (probable) or he was just naturally more considerate than her (confirmed), because the minute he touched her, his hands were warm and sure. She did get a shiver down her spine when he ran his hands down the length of her back, but she couldn't blame that on the sunscreen. She felt like she could feel every callus on his fingertips, every tiny adjustment of pressure as he ventured slightly under the outline of her bathing suit. John was very thorough. But then, she knew that.

He was working under the straps of her bathing suit now, and she slid them partway down so he had better access to her shoulders, holding the front of her bathing suit up just in case it got any ideas. His hands felt so good, and when he squeezed the place where her shoulder curved up to her neck she couldn't help but moan.

"Did you already get here?" he asked, brushing a featherlight touch across the half circle of skin that showed where her jeans hung loose on her hips, revealing the cut of the swimsuit.

She *had* already taken care of that part, had put sunscreen all over her legs even though they were mostly covered because she burned easily and hadn't wanted to take any chances. But she didn't want this to be over, so she shook her head.

John squirted more sunscreen into his hand, rubbing it in circles across the exposed skin at her hips, his fingers sliding under the waistband of her jeans to ensure he didn't miss a spot. It reminded her so much of what they'd done the night before— his hand down her pants, his other hand over her mouth, that fast, desperate orgasm—that she had to clench her thighs against the sudden pulse in her clit. One of the most erotic experiences of her life and then she'd gone and ruined it all afterward.

The sound of the bottle cap snapping shut made her eyes fly open. She'd barely been aware that she'd closed them in the first place.

John was already getting up from the lounger, and the shift from his weight lifting almost sent her toppling forward, except he reached down to steady her by the shoulder. Almost as soon as he'd done it, he drew back, like somehow even after he'd just had his hands all over her *this* was going too far.

"I'll see you both later," he said. "Maybe after—"

But Micah never got to hear what he was going to say, or figure out if she would've been brave enough to follow him and ask if they could talk. Steve and Ryder walked up at exactly that moment, talking animatedly about something.

"Oh good," Ryder said as he approached. "Everyone's here. What do you think makes more sense—to celebrate the anniversary of an album that flopped, or one that actually sold some copies?"

"Fifteen is a round number, though," Steve said. "Anniversary stuff is always around a round number."

"Nobody cares about the *number*," Ryder said. "They care about the *music*, and if they didn't care about the music then, they won't care about it now."

Micah's stomach clenched. "What are we talking about?" she asked, even though she already knew. She just wanted to make him say it.

Ryder glanced down at her. Her bathing suit straps were still halfway off her shoulders, she realized, and she reached up to adjust them. His gaze on her made her skin crawl. She stood up, not wanting to be lower than him for this conversation. They were almost the exact same height—in heels, she towered over him, which was why he'd never liked her to wear heels.

"Move your, lose your!" Steve declared, jumping onto the lounger.

"I thought John was going to talk to you," Ryder said, shooting an irritated look John's way. "We were discussing the possibility of getting ElectricOh! back together, just for a limited tour."

"No."

"Or a couple festival dates. There's one in Las Vegas that—"

"No."

Ryder held up his hands, like he was trying to get her to calm down, even though she hadn't raised her voice. She remembered that move from when they'd dated. She'd always hated it.

"I know you think you alone get to make *every* band decision," Ryder said. "But we get to have a say in our careers, too. And if we say we want to do this, then—"

"She said no," John said. "And whatever we do, it has to be unanimous. If she says no, then it's a no."

"That's always been your problem, hasn't it?" Ryder said with a smirk. "You've never known how to turn a *no* into a *yes*."

John just looked at him. There was something in his eyes that she'd never seen there before. He could shut Ryder down in an instant, of course, could tell him all the ways he'd had her saying *yes* as recently as a few hours ago, could play right into the alpha bullshit Ryder had always introduced into the band dynamic. Sometimes she thought that so much of what had happened would've never gone down if he hadn't been a senior when they were freshmen, but they weren't freshmen anymore.

"That," John said, "is an extremely fucked-up thing to say."

Frankie was glancing between the two of them, taking a long sip from their cocktail that ended in the ragged slurp of an empty cup. "All right," they said. "We don't need to go down this road."

"I wouldn't care if you did ElectricOh! covers with your new band," Steve said. "That could be cool."

"I'm not going to do *covers* of my own songs!" Ryder yelled, before seeming to remember that they were on a beach with other people, some of whom had turned around to see what was going on. "I want to know how everyone would've voted—not because of what anyone else said, but based on what you actually want as an individual member of the band. Obviously I'm a vote for *yes*. Steve?"

Steve looked uncomfortable to be put on the spot. "Yes?" He glanced at Micah apologetically. "I mean, I'm also fine not doing it. But yeah, if it were up to me, I think it sounds fun. Not for a long tour. I don't want to miss my kid growing up or anything. But yeah. Sounds fun."

He clamped his mouth shut, as if to stop rambling.

"Frankie?" Ryder prompted. "Not based on anyone else. Just what *you* want. You said last night you thought it would be a great opportunity."

"I know what I said last night," Frankie said dryly. "I can remember back that far, thank you very much. I thought it could be fun, but suddenly I'm reminded why it might not be. And John's right—if one of us is out, then it's a non-starter. We can't do it without Micah. This cruise has been a good send-off. I say we leave it here."

Ryder turned to John then. "Well?" he said. "And please, for the love of god, don't just say what you think *she* wants to hear. Take a stand for once in your life."

Micah closed her eyes. She obviously knew what John would say—last night, he'd seemed interested in the idea. And no matter what Ryder seemed to believe, she wasn't *trying* to take anything away from anybody. She simply couldn't do it.

"Take a stand?" John said, stepping closer to Ryder. "All right, I'll take a stand. I don't want anything to do with Electric-Oh!. Not a reunion tour, not a festival date, not a single god-damn group photo as long as *you're* in the band. You're toxic. And if you think you're a good enough guitarist to make any of this worth it, you're not."

Micah opened her eyes again, staring at John. She could count the times she'd seen him truly angry on one hand. The band had had many arguments, all those years ago, but he'd been more the type to hang back and listen to what everyone had to say, then weigh in with some reasonable compromise after everyone else had shouted themselves out. Now his voice was low but hard, and Frankie and Steve hung back, seeming to understand that this was a fight that had been brewing between the two of them for a while.

Ryder made a scoffing sound. "Says the guy who's been playing dive bars for the last ten years. That tip jar's bound to run dry, wouldn't you say?"

"I don't give a fuck about the money," John said.

"Let me guess, you only care about the *music*," Ryder said derisively, making it clear what he thought about that. "Bullshit. You're a hack. Go get your songbook to play nostalgic slow jams at second-rate weddings. And Micah?"

She looked over at him, even though she realized Ryder was talking about her rather than to her.

"Calls herself a musician when she can barely play an in-strument," Ryder continued, his lips twisting. "It's a joke. She was there for novelty and for some sex appeal, and in the end she couldn't even deliver that, huh? Funny how that works."

"That *is* funny," John said. "Because it's no coincidence that the best song we ever wrote was without you."

John's retort came fast, but Micah barely had any time to process it because Ryder's fist quickly followed. He punched John right in the face, sending John reeling back. Micah saw red—literally, because there was blood on John's mouth, but also in that this was the absolute last shit she was going to take from Ryder. She acted on instinct, without any care as to whether people were watching or if she was putting herself in danger.

And she punched Ryder square in his nose.

It made a sickening crunch, and then Ryder's hands went up to his face, which was now pouring blood from both his nostrils. She was surprised by the amount of blood, and how quickly it came. She was also surprised by the sounds now coming out of his mouth, more animal than human.

She was *shocked* by how much her hand hurt, and yet how good it had felt.

"What the fuck?" Ryder said, holding his hand over his nose. He'd stumbled after she punched him, and he'd let himself fall back into the sand, sitting awkwardly splayed out while he assessed the damage. "I'm going to sue you for assault, you bitch."

"Try it," John said, "and I'll sue you for assaulting me first."

Micah had a sudden, out-of-control urge to laugh. *You should've seen the other guy*, she thought. John didn't look too bad, at least—he had a split lip, and touched it gingerly only to come away with blood on his fingers. But Ryder looked awful, and she couldn't say she was too sorry to see it.

"I don't think *you* want what could come out if I let it," Ryder said to her, and she flexed her hand, wondering if it was too soon to punch him again.

"I'm done feeling shame about any of that," she said. "But *you* should be ashamed. I wasted so much fucking time and energy on you, none of which you deserved. You wonder why you're miserable? Because you're miserable to be around. Our relationship was one long pit in my stomach. You think you're god's gift to music but you would be a hell of a lot better served just trying to be a halfway decent person."

His eyes narrowed, and she could tell he was going to make another crack, something designed to humiliate her in front of everyone else. She didn't particularly care about humiliating him, but she did care about shutting him up, and she knew one thing that would. She crouched down, her voice low so only he could hear it.

"I faked it every time," she said. "But I'm done faking anything."

Looking at Ryder now, she couldn't believe she'd let him have such a hold over her for so long. Not just their relationship, but for the years afterward when she'd carried so much baggage from it. He was nothing.

She glanced back at John, who was standing tense and ready, like he was waiting to see if Ryder would try anything else. She had always been her truest self with John, and more than anything she regretted the way that the whole mess with Ryder and the band had warped that. She wished she could somehow go back in time, travel to when she was sixteen and do it all over again, but this time with different choices. But she couldn't, and maybe it was time to make peace with that part.

She stood up, clenching her fist at her side, her knuckles still sore. She wanted to say something to the whole band—to Frankie, who was looking at her with concern; to Steve, who still looked a little shell-shocked; and most of all to John, who she'd hurt last night for no other reason than she was scared. But she didn't know what to say, so instead she just gave them all a grim smile and walked away.

TWENTY-THREE

WHEN JOHN FOUND Micah, she was sitting out on the beach, right on the line where the ocean met the shore. She had her arms linked around her knees, the bottom of her jeans darker where they'd gotten wet, her bare feet covered in sand. He lowered himself to sit next to her, and for a minute they just stared out at the ocean without talking.

"I brought you some water," he said finally, placing a cup on the sand in front of them. He placed another cup right next to it. "And some extra ice."

"Thank you."

He hadn't been surprised that Ryder attacked him. That had been a long time coming—he was almost relieved it had happened, was glad that the tension had finally erupted. He *had* been surprised when Micah punched Ryder back. He knew that had been an even longer time coming, that she obviously had more reasons to hate Ryder than any of the rest of them, but it had felt a little bit like she'd done it to stand up for *him*, too. And he was surprised how good that had felt.

Still, he felt like there was a lot more to that story than she'd ever said, and suddenly that seemed like the key to all of it.

"When you asked me yesterday if Ryder had ever shown me anything," he said, "what did you mean by that?"

She gave a jagged, humorless laugh, rubbing her eyes with her uninjured hand. "He has pictures of me," she said. "Compromising pictures."

That revelation in and of itself wasn't that shocking. It was something people who dated did, John supposed. But the way Micah said it, he knew it was only the tip of the iceberg, and so he stayed silent, waiting for her to go on.

She glanced over at him, as if assessing his reaction to that before she continued. "When I broke up with him that last time, he threatened to release them," she said. "He said it would be good for the band, actually. Get us some publicity. He said if I was going to use sex to sell our music then we may as well go all the way with it."

John curled his fingers into his fists until he could feel his nails biting into his palms, and he had to make a deliberate effort to loosen his hand and stretch his fingers back out. He wished he *had* punched Ryder, after all. He wished he'd shoved his face into the sand so hard it would take days to get all the grit out of his eyes and mouth. The sudden violence of the fantasy was jarring to John, but for once he didn't shy away from it. He let the scenario play out in his head, trying to control his breathing until eventually he was able to speak.

"That thing he said, about you being there for sex and novelty." John turned to her, wanting to make sure she heard him, not just his words but really *heard* him. "It's not true. You never needed anything to sell our music. You have an incredible voice. A once-in-a-lifetime, sends-chills-down-my-spine voice. You're so goddamn talented, Micah. As a singer and a song-writer. That's what got us as far as we got—not any of the rest of it."

She rubbed her hands over her legs, like she was cold, even though it was fairly warm in the sun. "It's complicated, though, isn't it?" she said. "Because I know that the way I look, the nov-elty of me being a *girl* . . . it is part of it. If I wear a shirt onstage where you can see my nipples, then that's the big story after-ward. But also I chose to wear that shirt, I *wanted* to wear it, it made me feel powerful and sexy and like I could do anything. It's part of the show, and I love to put on a show. But then I'd get off the stage, and I'd feel . . . I don't know. Dirty. Pathetic, like I wasn't good enough to stand on my own without the extra the-atrics. Silly, like I was making a mockery of what we were doing, of the *music*. But for me, it was all wrapped up together. I loved the music, I loved how it made me *feel*, but no matter how I tried to express that, it felt like I was wrong somehow."

John knew the exact show she was referencing. They'd played an outdoor festival, just after their second album—the weather had been suffocatingly humid, and they'd been scheduled in the middle of the day. Micah had worn a one-shouldered tank top, no bra underneath, and every article about the show after-ward had included the same picture of Micah, her hair damp with sweat, leaning back, holding the microphone with both hands, the outline of both nipples clearly delineated against the thin fabric of her shirt.

It was an incredibly hot picture. He should know—he'd looked at it enough. But it was made all the better for its *context*, as far as he was concerned. He could hear Micah belting out that note, could feel the energy of the crowd, could still channel the adrenaline that had coursed through him when they'd taken their final bows and run off the stage. He'd never thought Micah was wrong in any way she'd chosen to express herself with music. She'd always done it in a way that had lifted him up and put him right there with her.

"Here," he said, pulling a wadded bunch of napkins out from where he'd stashed them in the pocket of his swim trunks. He grabbed a few ice cubes from the cup he'd brought and wrapped them up in the napkin, reaching for Micah's hand. Her knuckles were a little red and swollen, and she winced slightly when he pressed the ice to the area, but he didn't think anything was broken.

"I hate that you felt that way," he said. "I mean, I know a lot of it is systemic shit that's bigger than both of us, but I especially hate that Ryder ever made you feel that way. And I'm sorry if I didn't see it, or if there were ways I contributed to it."

She shook her head. "It was never you," she said. "And some of it was Ryder, but a lot of it came from inside *me*. Like I allowed myself to feel those things. I'm angry with myself for that most of all."

"I think," John said, "that we should give ourselves permission to let all that shit go. All the things we wish we'd done differently. I feel a lot of tenderness for those kids back then who thought they knew everything but still had so much to figure out."

She'd been watching where he'd been ministering to her hand, but now she looked up at him. "You do?"

He swallowed. "Yeah," he said. "Don't you?"

"I have a lot of regrets."

"Such as?" Maybe naming them would take away their power somehow, would make them not loom so large in her mind.

"I shouldn't have broken the band up the way I did," she said. "I should've talked to you all, figured out a way to either go on or end things on good terms."

He regretted the way that had gone down, too, wished he could've done something else to make her feel like she could've talked to him. He hated to think of her going through all that and feeling so alone.

"None of us were at our best then," he said. "And I think we were all in survival mode. There was a lot that we missed."

"I probably shouldn't have done that *Playboy* spread," she said. "At least, not in that way. It was very reactionary, and I wish I had done it for a different reason."

He wanted to squeeze her hand, but he didn't want to hurt her, so he settled for rubbing his thumb along her palm. He remembered what Frankie had said, about the timing of that interview being odd, and now he understood it so much better. She'd been spooked by Ryder's threat, and she'd decided to get out ahead of it, to put out her own pictures that she had agency over before he could beat her to the punch. It was a savvy move, because it took most of the sting out of anything he could do to her. But it also meant he'd still had the opportunity to get to her, in a way.

"Were you happy with the pictures?" John asked. "Do you like how they came out?"

She seemed to think about that for a minute before she smiled, a private, sexy smirk at the corner of her mouth that made John's heart speed up.

"Yeah," she said. "I do like them. You really never saw them?"

He started to bite his lip before remembering that he had his own injury, and that move hurt. "I read the interview online," he said. "But I didn't think . . . I don't know. It didn't seem right to look at the pictures without your permission."

"I mean, my *dentist* saw them," she said, "which I could've done without him bringing up while he had his hand in my mouth. They were public."

"I know," John said. "Still."

It hadn't seemed right, and it had seemed *dangerous*, to even allow himself to see Micah that way.

"I wanted you to see them," Micah said. "You, specifically."

Now his heart was going a mile a minute. "Yeah?"

"I thought about it a lot," she said. "What you'd think of them. I even had—"

She laughed, cutting herself off, and he held his breath until he couldn't take the suspense. "Had what?"

Her eyes cut to his, a little shy, before she looked back down at where their hands were still touching. "I had a fantasy that you'd try to get back in touch with me afterward," she said. "Like maybe you'd see the A minor tattoo and it would be the perfect icebreaker to get you to talk to me again, when you finally saw what I'd gotten. I don't know, it's stupid."

He could point out that communication went both ways, and that if she had been dying for him to reach out to her so badly, *she* could've certainly texted him at any time. He'd never changed his number. But his last text to her had been sent only a few months before that interview had come out, sitting like a stone at the bottom of their long text chain. What the fuck, Micah? He could see how that wasn't a message that exactly inspired a response.

Or when he'd shown up at her concert, a couple years after that, she could've allowed him backstage. But he'd also known there were other ways he could've gotten hold of her, if he'd been committed enough to try. How many times had he driven by her parents' house when he was back in Ohio, thought about ringing the doorbell and just asking for her new number? They'd both made mistakes in that regard, and he really was feeling like it was time to let them go.

"I wish I had," he said.

She rolled her eyes. "I should've known you'd be someone who'd read *Playboy* for the articles. Jesus, John."

"I'm no saint."

"Never thought you were," she said. The way she looked at him, he knew she was remembering the night before just the way he was. She turned her hand over until she was holding one of the half-melted ice cubes, and she reached up to touch it gently to his bottom lip. "Does it hurt?"

He shook his head slightly, not wanting to speak and disrupt what she was doing.

"I'm sorry I—" She swallowed. "That thing I said about you seducing me. I didn't mean it."

Everything she'd told him about Ryder made that make more sense, too. There was a lot of trust involved, sending naked pictures of yourself to someone. There was a lot of trust in letting someone touch you, in letting someone in on a fantasy or allowing someone to get you off in public. *Have you always been like this?* Micah had asked him, and the truth was that to the extent he was like anything it was because it was *her*, and he trusted her. He hoped she felt the same way about him, but he understood if she had hang-ups in that regard, after everything she'd been through.

"It's okay," he said. "I could've handled the reunion tour discussion better. My timing's always been shit."

The smile she gave him was more in her eyes than her mouth, which was parted as she dragged the ice cube from his lip down the side of his throat. "I've listened to a million hours of you playing guitar," she said. "You have impeccable timing."

"Well, I hope so," he said. "Because that's kind of the perfect segue."

She was still watching the path the ice cube was making down his throat, a cold drip sliding down and getting caught in his clavicle. But her gaze pulled up to his at those words, a quizzical line between her brows. "Segue to what?"

He took her injured hand again, gently flexing her fingers, monitoring her face for any sign of pain. "We seem to be down a guitarist," he said.

Her eyes widened. "Oh my god," she said. "Did I hurt him that bad? I mean, don't get me wrong, I'd do it again in a heartbeat, but . . . shit, I never meant to take him out."

John shook his head. "He's fine," he said. "He'll need to have his nose reset, maybe—frankly, I'm not losing any sleep over it. But he's not coming back on the cruise. He's going to arrange a boat to take him to Nassau and he'll fly back to the States from there."

"Whoa," she said. "That's . . . over a broken nose? Don't they have medics on the ship?"

"They do," John said. "And they're probably helping him right now to make him more comfortable for his boat ride. But it's the funniest thing, he also happened to have a family emergency that meant he had to leave right away. Don't worry, Steve and Frankie are making sure he gets all packed up and arrangements are made to ship his gear back to him."

He could see the moment when it dawned on her, what he was really saying. "You guys kicked him out."

"I would argue he brought it all on himself," John said. "But yes, we kicked him out."

"You . . ." Her eyes were a little shiny, but it wasn't until she laughed that a single tear leaked out and spilled down her cheek. "I don't know what to say."

John linked his fingers with hers, careful not to jostle her hand too much as he gave a gentle squeeze. "Well, that's why I'm hoping your strumming hand will be in decent enough shape by tomorrow night. How would you feel about playing the rhythm part for 'If Only' at prom?"

TWENTY-FOUR

PLAY GUITAR ONSTAGE? In front of everyone, at arguably the most iconic live performance of their entire career?

"But you play rhythm," she said stupidly, still trying to catch up.

"Normally," John said. "But I'd take over Ryder's lead part, and let you play rhythm. You know the song, Micah. You *wrote* the song. We'd have the next twenty-four hours to practice, and I know you could do it. What do you say?"

Despite what Ryder had loved to charge her with, it wasn't that she *couldn't* play any instrument. She'd written songs on both guitar and piano, after all. In high school, she'd played flute in the marching band, so long ago that she barely knew that she'd be able to play "Seven Nation Army" like they'd once performed. But she'd definitely never felt confident enough to play live, in front of people, while also trying to sing at the same time.

"Frankie would probably be a better choice," she said.

Frankie might primarily be a bassist, but the instruments were close enough—Micah knew they could do it.

"Frankie's ready to step up if we need them to," John said. "But we agreed that we thought you'd be perfect. We can practice, at the very least, and see how it goes. I'll be right there with you, every step of the way."

"You'd have to do the harmonies," Micah said. "On the chorus. If we were really going to make it good."

She could tell from the expression on his face that he hadn't thought that far ahead. But his gaze settled on hers, and she could also tell that there wasn't going to be any getting out of this. "I can do that," he said.

She touched his bottom lip, which looked tender and swollen but had already started to scab over. He sank his teeth into the pad of her thumb, giving her a wicked grin. "Let's do it," he said. "Just the two of us."

It had always been the two of them, hadn't it? Playing guitar in her room, trying to figure out chord structures to their favorite songs. When she'd introduced John at last night's show and called him the beating heart of the band, she'd meant it. He'd always been the one holding everything together.

"*We* wrote the song," she said. "I'm in."

THERE WAS SO much to do that it was only after Micah was back on the ship that she realized they'd never even gotten to swim in the ocean. She almost wanted to go back, but she knew they didn't have time.

John walked with Micah to the medic so she could get her hand looked at, and then he split off to go see about reserving the Starlight Theater for rehearsal space for the night. There hadn't been anything on the schedule after a trivia event that had been hosted there earlier that day, so they were hopeful they could secure it as a private area to practice the song. Regardless, they made plans to meet back up in front of the theater in an hour so they could figure out next steps.

Micah was a few minutes early to their rendezvous point, but still she saw John already leaning against the doors, looking down the hallway like he thought she'd come from the other direction. How many times had he waited for her, just like that, standing outside a classroom with his backpack, leaning against the bike rack in front of the school, pausing at the bottom of the stairs as they ran off the stage after an encore? Suddenly she *did* feel tenderness for the kids they were then, but even more she felt an overwhelming ache for the people they were now. She'd known John so well back in those days, but she wanted to know more about the man he'd become. She wanted him to know *her*.

"I still can't believe that Henry Rollins shit," she said as she walked up. "All this time, I thought you'd come up with that."

He turned around, giving her a smile that made her heart skip a beat. "Good artists borrow, great artists steal," he said. "And that one *is* mine. How's the hand?"

She held it up, showing where they'd wrapped a bandage around her knuckles. If the medic had noticed that one of the members of ElectricOh! had a broken nose and another one had busted-up knuckles, she didn't say anything. She'd given Micah the okay on her hand, since Micah could make a fist, could move all her fingers, and felt more of a dull ache than any sharp pain. "Just some bruising," she said. "Should be fine. Are we all set for rehearsal?"

"Right this way," John said, opening the doors for her.

John must've gotten the cruise to sign off on them using the theater fairly early, because he'd already had time to set up all their equipment on the stage, including two chairs, various guitars, and a small boom box.

"In case we want to listen to the recorded version, or play along to it," he said, seeming to catch Micah's gaze. "It might help."

"Makes sense." He really had seemed to think of everything. She felt bad that she hadn't been able to contribute anything herself. "I feel rude showing up empty-handed. Like the least I could've done was pick us up a pizza or something."

John gestured toward a cooler at the corner of the stage. "I, uh, had them package up some chicken and fruit and stuff like that. I didn't know how long we'd be here."

Micah was touched, not only that he'd thought about dinner already, but that he seemed to remember how carefully she used to eat while they were touring, to preserve her voice. She'd already forgotten all those ways she used to take care of herself, but *he* hadn't.

She climbed the stairs to the stage, circling the equipment gathered in the center. There were two acoustic guitars, which she'd expected—that was how they'd play tomorrow night, after all. But there was also his amp and pedalboard and electric guitar, all set up, and she stopped when she saw them.

"I know we probably won't need to do anything with those," he said. "But again, I figured it couldn't hurt. Better than wishing we had them and them being stowed away somewhere below deck. Plus, I don't like to be too far away from my emotional support Haunting Mids."

She looked at him, and he nudged the toe of his Converse against one of the pedals on his board. It was black, with a little white ghost printed on it. "Haunting Mids. That's the name of the pedal. It pairs well with fuzz, especially—"

"Is that my guitar?"

She'd barely clocked the guitar he'd been playing since he'd arrived on the ship—it was black with a white pick guard, a common enough Telecaster. But now that she saw it on its stand, now that she was walking behind it, she saw the distinctive Amnesty International bumper sticker she'd placed on its back sometime after he'd given the budget-version guitar to her for her fourteenth birthday.

"Oh," he said. "Yeah."

"How do you—*why* do you . . ."

She wasn't mad that he had it. She couldn't remember the exact chain of custody, but she had no doubt that she'd given it to him once they'd started touring and she realized the chances that *she'd* need an electric guitar would be slim to none. Either she'd given it to him to borrow—he'd always said it had a surprisingly good tone, for such a cheap guitar—or she'd given it to him to work on and set up and get back to her. Regardless, she had no doubt he'd gotten more use out of it than she ever would've. She was just surprised to see it here.

"I guess it was my version of your tattoo," he said. "My fantasy that you'd reach out, when you wanted it back."

She didn't know what to say to that, but he didn't seem to want her to say anything. He gave her a rueful smile, like *Dumb, huh?* And then he sat down on one of the chairs, bending to pick up a piece of paper and a Sharpie.

"So these are the chords to start," he said, writing the word

VERSES in all capitals and then scribbling down a series of letters underneath. "And for the chorus . . ." He wrote the word in all caps as another label before transcribing those, too. "And then the bridge . . ." He looked up like he was thinking for a minute, and she could tell he was running through the bridge in his head, trying to recall what his muscle memory already knew.

"The bridge starts on F," she said. "I remember that part."

She watched him write those chords down on the sheet of paper, and it was like they were right back there, when they'd written the song together. The band had all been staying in a rental while they recorded at the Orlando studio, a soulless stucco house in a neighborhood filled with copies of the exact same place, to the point where Micah sometimes accidentally started to turn into the wrong driveway when she went for walks to clear her head. It had been the only place they could find with enough bedrooms for all of them. Recording that first album had been fun, for the most part—they were still energized by the fact that they had a record deal at all, that their dream was actually coming true. But Micah had already started to feel the pressure, and she was having trouble sleeping, too keyed up every time she lay down, her mind going a mile a minute with critiques of what she'd done that day, ideas for what she'd do differently tomorrow.

She'd gone down to the kitchen one night to refill her glass of water when she'd looked through the window and seen John sitting on the back porch, leaning over his guitar while he played a tune she could only barely hear but didn't recognize.

"What is that?" she'd asked when she'd come through the sliding glass door to join him.

He'd stopped playing abruptly. "Just something I got in my head."

"Play it again."

It started in A minor, which had always been her favorite. She knew that D minor got credit for being the "saddest" chord, but for her it had always been A minor—darker, a little more solemn. There was something poignant about the way John played the tune, though, something that dropped her heart into her stomach but lifted it back up again. She couldn't explain it. But that was the thing about music. Sometimes it could speak in a way that words couldn't.

They'd stayed up for four hours on that porch, crafting the verses and chorus, Micah humming a melody over his guitar until she started scribbling down some lyrics that she felt could fit. She'd never had a song come together in quite that way before—where it truly felt like a conversation, like everything John did made her think of a way she'd want to respond. When she'd asked if he had a name for the song, when he'd first started figuring it out, he said, "If Only." And even though she'd already written out most of the lyrics and that phrase never appeared in them once, she knew it was the right title. It perfectly fit everything she'd been thinking, too.

She sat down now, reaching for the acoustic guitar closest to her. John had already made sure it was in tune, of course, and she easily found the position for that first A minor chord on the fretboard, strumming gently with her fingers. It felt good, sitting with a guitar again, feeling its weight on her, the press of her fingertips against the strings. She'd missed it, she realized, which was not something she'd known until that very second.

John pushed one of the open guitar cases toward her with

his foot, indicating a bunch of differently colored picks piled up in one of the pockets. "Later, I'll set one of the mic stands up with a pick holder," he said, "and have you practice grabbing another pick midsong, in case you drop the one you're using. It happens sometimes, especially if you're nervous and your hands are sweaty. Honestly, that's probably the only thing you'll have to worry about—I know you won't have trouble with the song itself."

That was more confidence in her abilities than she had, but she appreciated it and was grateful once again that he'd thought so far ahead. Dropping her pick while she was in the middle of playing hadn't even been on her short list of things she was anxious about.

She reached down to grab a pick from the case, letting out a choked laugh when she read the words printed on it. *"Flick It Good?"*

John looked up, his brow furrowed, until something seemed to click and he grabbed for the guitar case to slide it farther away from her again. But she'd already come up with a whole handful of the colorful picks, and was turning them over in her hands, reading them one by one.

"Go Pluck Yourself," she said. *"Give Me a Lick. I Love Your G String. Put Good Wood on It.* John, these are filthy!"

She didn't think she'd ever seen his face so red. It was delightful.

"They were a present," he said. "A gag gift from Asa. He—"

"Between the Batman pajamas and these, I'm starting to think Asa doesn't exist," Micah said. "He's like your Canadian boyfriend. Your fake Floridian housemate you blame whenever I find out something embarrassing about you. *Shake That Bass*— a bit of a homograph problem there, right? Is that what you would call it? *You Rock My World. I'm Good at Fingering*—well, *that's* certainly true. *It Isn't Going to Spank Itself. Touch My*—"

She broke off, unable to even get the words out, she was laughing so hard.

John had a smile playing around his own mouth now, and he was watching her face instead of looking at the picks. "Touch my what? What does it say?"

She shook her head, her laughter having ascended to that plane where no sound was coming out of her mouth, where her stomach muscles almost hurt and there were tears in her eyes. "*Touch My*—" she started to say when she thought she'd gotten control over herself, but then the laughter started all the way back up again, until eventually John was laughing, too. She held the pick out to him, and he turned it over to read what it said.

"*Touch My Whammy Bar.* That's pretty good. I'll definitely be using that one."

"If you say *any* of this stuff to me during sex, that's it, party's over. I'm putting my clothes back on and you can touch your own whammy bar."

"I don't know. They're not all terrible. Like *Give Me a Lick.*"

Okay, she had to agree that one wasn't bad. In fact, something about the way John said it, that *K* sound in the back of his throat, suddenly wiped away any desire to laugh and replaced it with another desire entirely. She set her acoustic guitar carefully back in its stand.

"What are you doing?" John asked, but in a tone that suggested he knew *exactly* what she was doing.

"We need to focus," she said. "And I feel like we're going to have a hard time focusing." She lifted her shirt over her head, dropping it to the floor next to her. Then she reached behind her back to unhook her bra, letting it fall down her arms to join her shirt.

"I have excellent focus," he said. She could swear his eyes were darker than they'd been a second ago, more pupil than iris.

"I know you do," she said. She slid down to her knees, crawling the two feet until she was kneeling between his legs. When she touched his thighs through his jeans, she could feel his muscles clench, could feel his body heat. She could see where he was already hard, and it made her mouth water.

He was still holding a guitar pick between his fingers, and he flicked one of her nipples with it, making it tighten into an almost painful bud. She arched her back, leaning into the sensation.

"The door's not locked," he said. "Anyone could come in."

It wasn't a rebuff or a rejection. It was a test, a question where he cared about her answer before moving forward. But he also had to notice the way her breath caught, the way her hands tightened on his thighs as he worked her other nipple with his guitar pick, almost casually, like she'd watched him play a thousand times before.

"They won't," she said.

His hands skated along the tops of her shoulders, coming up to cradle her face. "What do you want?" he asked, his voice low. Something about the way he said it, she didn't even think he was only talking about sex. But she didn't know how to answer *that* question, which was much bigger than this moment and which had the power to unravel everything. All she knew was the way she wanted to feel right here, right now.

"I want to see you," she said. "All of you. I want to touch

you. I want to taste you. I want you inside me. I want it all, John, everything you'll give me."

He shrugged out of his hoodie, then yanked off his own shirt, until he was bare-chested in front of her. She'd had the chance to look at him on the beach, but even with her sunglasses on, she'd been conscious of staring too long. Now she was able to drink in the sight of him as much as she wanted: the sharp line of his clavicle, the dusting of dark hair on his chest, his puckered nipples that she touched with one finger.

John closed his eyes briefly before opening them again. "I want everything, too," he said.

She reached up to the button at the fly of his jeans, glancing at him to make sure he was okay with it. The knuckles of her uninjured hand brushed his stomach, the trail of hair leading into his waistband, and she felt him suck in a breath as she worked his zipper down. The rest was difficult to do with one of her hands partially bandaged, and so he lifted his hips off the chair to pull his jeans down his legs, kicking them and his underwear away until he was completely naked. She pulled her own pants and underwear off so she could join him.

"I want to touch you everywhere," she said, running her hands up his calves, his thighs, the jut of his hip bones. She touched him everywhere but his dick, at least with her hands. Her eyes were greedier, unable to look away from the evidence of how turned on he was by her touch.

"Micah—" he said, his voice a little choked as she deliberately let her breasts brush his knees, the insides of his thighs.

And then she took him in her mouth, and he let out a hiss, his hands sliding into her hair. She'd left it down for once, and he gathered it into a ponytail in his fist, tugging slightly to get her to look up at him.

"You don't have to," he started to say, but she moaned, knowing he felt the vibration from the way his dick pulsed in her mouth. She knew she didn't *have* to do anything. She wanted to. Fuck, did she want to.

She took him deeper, sucking and licking until she grasped the base of him with her hand, slapping his dick against her tongue.

"God, that feels so good," he said, his hands still in her hair, his thighs braced so tense around her that she thought he might explode in her mouth at any second. "You're so fucking good."

She felt his words like a heartbeat between her legs, the strength of it taking her by surprise. She'd known about her pain thing, knew she liked it when it hurt. She hadn't thought praise would do anything for her, that she could like it nice as well as mean.

She'd found her rhythm, was so intent on what she was doing that she flinched a little when she felt his fingers gentle on the back of her neck.

"You've gotta—" He twitched under her as she snaked out her tongue for one final lick. "If you want everything, you've gotta give me a chance here, Micah."

She couldn't help her smug smile. "I have you right where I want you."

"You do," he said, dragging his thumb along her wet, swollen lower lip, and suddenly she wasn't smiling anymore. "I promise you do. It's not a competition, but you're winning. I surrender."

She liked seeing her effect on John, liked knowing all the

ways she got under his skin. But she knew that he deserved to know all the ways he got under hers, too, that maybe they could've figured this out much earlier if she hadn't always felt the need to hide behind her own bravado.

"I've been dreaming of having you inside me," she said. "Ever since I woke up in your bed the other morning."

She'd dreamed of being with John like this before then, but it had always been in a more distant way, like she couldn't actually think too hard about what it would be like or else she'd rewire her brain permanently, maybe ruinously. It'd be a way he would grunt while he was helping Steve carry his drum kit, and she'd think, *I wonder if that's the sound he'd make when* . . . Or the way he'd put his pick between his teeth and she'd think, *That mouth could* . . . The way he'd been the few times she'd seen him with a girlfriend, and she'd feel a flush of jealousy, a sudden impulse to say *Mine*, even when she knew she had no right to say that. She'd always had rationalizations to help explain away those feelings, or talk herself out of them, but she was done with that. She'd given herself over to it all, and it *did* feel so good.

She shivered, and John reached down to grab his hoodie, draping it over her shoulders. Her reaction had been more about the sudden overwhelm of the situation—them, together like this—than the cold, but she accepted the hoodie anyway, sliding her arms into the sleeves.

He grasped the front of the hoodie to pull her up toward him, pressing a hard kiss to her mouth. "I don't have any condoms," he said. "I thought about buying some, actually, while I was gathering up all the gear, but—yeah, I didn't want to be presumptuous."

"I *love* when you're presumptuous," Micah said. "For the record. But I have an IUD, and I get tested regularly, just to make sure, so . . . I mean, I'm okay not using one, if you are."

"The last time I got tested was over a year ago," John said. "But I also haven't—it's been a long time. Longer than that."

Micah swallowed any comment she might've made to that revelation when she saw the look on John's face. He seemed mildly embarrassed, or shy maybe, like that information had been hard for him to share. But she didn't want him to be embarrassed about anything. He hadn't held any of her past against her, and she certainly didn't intend to hold any of his against him. She stretched to kiss him, opening up to let his tongue invade her mouth. She almost bit down on his lower lip, before she felt the bump there with her tongue and remembered to be careful.

"Let me fuck you," she said against his mouth. "I want it so bad."

John's hands tightened where he held her around her rib cage, his fingertips just brushing the underside of her breasts. He lifted her onto his lap, his thumbs now shifting to rub her nipples in rough circles that made her have to bite her own lip to stop from crying out.

"You have no idea how long I've wanted it," he said.

She was already so wet, and he was still slick with her spit, so it was easy to slide right down onto his dick until she was completely filled with him. She'd always thought descriptions of your eyes rolling back in your head were a little melodramatic, but that was how she felt, sinking down on him like that. Like she'd suddenly lost any control over her body, her facial expressions, anything except for the sensation of what it felt to have him inside her. He shifted so she sat a little deeper on him, her legs hooked around the back of the chair, and her breath hitched. She could feel him all the way in her stomach.

She opened her eyes to see him watching her, his eyes hooded, his own breath coming sharp and shallow.

"Is this weird?" she whispered. "In a good way."

The corner of his mouth lifted, and it did something to her heart, to see him smile at her like that while their bodies were joined so intimately.

"In the *best* possible way," he said.

TWENTY-FIVE

WHEN MICAH STARTED moving on him, John thought he might actually die. It was all too overwhelming—the feeling of being buried deep inside her, the way she looked wearing only his black hoodie, unzipped and gaping open to show her breasts bouncing every time he thrust up into her. He gripped her hips so hard he worried he was hurting her, and he removed his hands only to have her lift them and put them right back where they were.

"*Fuck*," she said. "You're getting me so close."

"You like doing this on the stage, don't you?" he asked, his mouth close to her ear. "You like when you think someone might see."

She moaned, rocking against him. "Yes," she said, as if the word was torn out of her. "I do—I like it."

"I spent *years* watching that ass move around the stage," he said. "It drove me crazy. You in those tight pants, bending over, dancing, the way you'd roll those hips." He slid his hands down under her ass, hitching her up on top of him, gratified by the way she arched her back, her breaths coming in short, desperate pants.

"You like thinking about me watching you, don't you?" he asked. "You like thinking about what I might do if I saw a naked picture of you."

He could feel the orgasm roll through her—the way her muscles clenched around him, her stomach tensed up, the way everything her body seemed to be coiled so tight and then, with a final guttural cry, she relaxed against him, breathing hard.

"Fuck," she said again, but this time there was a different tone to her voice. It was half matter-of-fact, like *Okay, that happened*, and half full of wonder, like *Whoa, that happened*. He pulled her toward him, kissing her until he felt his own orgasm edging closer, his dick still hard and aching inside her.

After a few minutes, she lifted herself off him, and even that sensation, the sudden rush of cold air on his dick, still wet from *her* . . . When she lay on the stage and pulled him down on top of her, his moves weren't quite as graceful as he would've liked, his knee bumping her thigh, his elbows on her hair, spread out on the wood floor.

"Sorry," he said, shifting his weight after she tried to lift her head and winced a little.

"'Salright," she said, wrapping her legs around his waist, her heels digging into the dip of his lower back. "You can make it up to me."

He knew he'd never forget any of it. Not those small moments of awkwardness or humor, intimate in their own way. Not the way she looked, his black hoodie parted to show her perfect breasts, her nipples tight and wet from where he'd had his mouth on them. Not the sounds she made—high, breathy gasps until he thrust harder, and then it'd be a low moan, ripped from somewhere in the back of her throat. Not the way she *felt*, shuddering around him as she came again, his mouth pressed to hers in a hungry kiss, her hands tangled in his hair.

And then she was splayed out on the floor, her body loose and spent, and he reached up to encircle her wrist with his hand, as if to hold her in place. It wasn't until she linked her fingers in his that he realized he was trembling, and she gave his hand a squeeze.

"I want you to come inside me," she said. "*Please*. I want to be filled up with you."

It was those words that did it, as much as anything else. John thrust inside her until he could feel his orgasm build at the base of his spine, bursting out of him in a series of shocks that vibrated through his entire body. John had never been particularly loud or quiet when he came—he'd never really thought about it before—but this time he couldn't help the ragged, drawn-out expletive he half yelled as he spilled inside her.

Afterward, he lay on top of her, their bodies touching everywhere from where her breasts pressed against his chest to where she was rubbing her foot along his ankle bone. He braced himself on his forearms, not wanting to put all of his weight on her, and played with her hair that was spread out on the floor.

"You rock my world," he said, able to keep a completely straight face until she swatted his arm, and then he couldn't help but break.

She was laughing, too, covering her eyes with her hand. "New rules," she said. "You can't say any of those phrases to me during sex *or* for the ten minutes afterward, especially if you're still inside me."

"Ten minutes? That seems harsh."

"Five, then." She grinned up at him. "Except the whammy bar exception, which extends for twenty-four hours in either direction around any sexual encounter."

"Oh, so I can never say it," John said. "Just put that into the rules if that's what you mean."

He was definitely being presumptuous. He was conscious of the fact that they were on borrowed time—there were less than two days left of the cruise, and then what? They lived across the country from each other. They'd discussed the past but hadn't discussed any sort of future. He didn't even know what a future could look like.

"I like not having too many rules," Micah said, twining her fingers in the hair at the nape of his neck. "Except one I always follow is using the bathroom after sex—is there one in here, do you think, or do I have to go back out to the hallway?"

John knew she had a point, and they couldn't stay like that lying on the stage forever. Still, it was with a little reluctance that he finally lifted himself off her, reaching down a hand to help her up.

"Let's go look together."

THERE WASN'T A bathroom in the theater, but there was one right outside, so they'd both gotten dressed and made their way separately to the facilities. John made it back to the theater before Micah did, and he took a seat in the front row, staring up at their equipment still set up on the stage. He wanted to hang on to the euphoria from the last hour, the way it had felt, being with Micah. But the minute he'd started thinking about the future, his mind couldn't seem to get off it, and now it tripped through a thousand different anxieties and doubts.

They still had to actually rehearse their song, but he wasn't worried about that. The music part had always been easy between them, natural, a way of communicating that seemed so much less fraught than actual words. He knew that Micah had insecurities about playing guitar onstage, but it really was a fairly simple song. He had no doubt she'd be great. He was excited to see her do it.

His singing part got him a little more nervous, but even that he assumed would be fine. Micah would be able to coach him, and worst-case scenario he'd ask them to turn his mic down even more than they normally would for backing vocals. He'd be there to provide a little depth to the choruses but wouldn't worry about his voice coming through too much.

The bit he couldn't figure out was all *this*, the stuff outside the music. After so many years of pining for Micah, of dreaming about her, of telling himself all the reasons why they couldn't be together and it would never work . . . it couldn't be this easy, could it? To simply *be* with her?

And how did she feel? She got presumptuous herself, about the sex part. He *loved* when she got presumptuous. He loved when she talked like everything they'd done had been inevitable, and it was a foregone conclusion that they'd keep doing it. But he didn't know where she stood on anything else, if this was all fun for her, a way to relieve some tension, or if it meant something more. He didn't know if he could trust her to be honest with him about her feelings, because he sure as hell hadn't been honest with her about his. Lies of omission were still lies.

He was so lost in his thoughts that he only heard Micah approach when she was practically all the way to his seat, and he tried to give her a smile, not wanting her to see all that was going through his head. "Hey," he said.

"Hey."

She sat on his lap, facing him by straddling his legs, which he knew he shouldn't encourage. They really did need to practice, and the longer they stayed like that, the more chance there was that they'd just end up fooling around again. Especially since Micah still wore his hoodie, zipped up this time, and he was pretty sure she wasn't wearing anything underneath it.

But he also didn't want to go back to anything real just yet.

She touched his bottom lip, frowning a little. "You're bleeding again," she said. "We must've opened it up, when we were— I'm sorry, I was trying to be careful."

He ran his tongue over the wound, tasting the metallic tang of blood. He'd noticed it'd flared back up when he was in the bathroom, and he'd dabbed it with some paper towels, hoping that would take care of it. He knew it wasn't a bad injury—he didn't need stitches or anything—so he wasn't too worried about it.

"You tried to ask me about my dad," he said. "A couple days ago."

Her gaze was very serious, as she looked down at him. He knew she knew. She had to know. He figured she'd always known. But it seemed important, suddenly, to actually tell her.

"Was he a violent man?" he asked. "Did he drink too much? Did he hit me? I guess those might be your questions. And the answers would be yes, he was violent, yes, he got worse when he was drunk and he was always drunk, yes, he hit me. Pushed me, shoved me, kicked me, threw things at me, whatever he needed to do to feel better about himself after something had set him off."

Micah reached out to touch his face, her hand on his cheek. "Why didn't you tell me?" she whispered. "I mean . . . I'm not trying to blame you. But I would've . . ."

He smiled, wanting her to know he appreciated the sentiment even if he knew it would've been futile. What could she have done? She could've told an adult, he supposed, but he hadn't wanted that. He'd wanted everything to be different. He'd also been scared to have anything change.

"When I was really little," he said, "I didn't tell anyone because I thought it was normal. I didn't know anything else. But it didn't take long for me to realize that it *wasn't* normal, and that my survival depended on me keeping it a secret. At least, that's how it seemed. I can see now how if anything the opposite was true."

"I worried about you all the time," she said. "But I didn't know what to do, if you didn't want to even talk about it. Like that time with the clarinet, you didn't answer the phone, I thought—"

John knew the exact incident she was talking about, because it had been one of the worst ones. His dad had flown into a rage at the prospect of possibly having to pay money for John's mistake, and he'd beaten John so badly he'd stayed in bed for days afterward. He'd known it was Micah calling, and he'd also known he couldn't talk to her. He'd picked up the phone and hung it up, hoping she would get the hint.

"He broke all my CDs for that one," John said. "To pay for the lost clarinet, he said."

Which hadn't made any sense, of course. He could've taken

the CDs to a used record store and gotten maybe thirty dollars out of them, depending on their condition. John had always taken very good care of his music. But the point had never been the money—it had just been to hurt, and destroy, and John would be left angry with himself for caring about anything enough to even let his dad get to him that way.

"I'm so sorry, John," Micah said, her eyes shiny. One reason he'd never told her was that he'd thought he couldn't take it if she started looking at him with pity. But he realized that wasn't what this was. She was looking at him with pain, yes, but it was *caring*. She cared about him, and she hurt when he hurt. It felt good, actually—to share all this with her and let her carry just a little bit of it, too. "I'm sorry I didn't do more back then."

"You did everything," he said. "You were my friend when I most needed one. Those times, just hanging out in your room, listening to music . . . they meant everything to me. And then once we started the band, I knew—I *knew*—you'd get me out. And that's what you did."

She smiled down at him, but it looked a little wobbly. "That's what *we* did."

"That's what we did," he agreed. He grasped the zipper at the top of the hoodie, unable to help himself from sliding it slowly all the way down. He didn't intend to start anything. He just wanted to see her, to touch her. He couldn't get enough of it. He pressed his fingertips onto the chord shape tattooed on the smooth skin under the swell of her breast. That chord had always been her favorite—something about it being the saddest, she used to say. So of course it had been the one he'd had to use to start the song he'd written for her. Written *about* her.

"If only," he said. "Ready to crack this song wide open?"

CHAPTER

TWENTY-SIX

REHEARSAL WENT SURPRISINGLY smoothly, once they finally got down to it. Playing the song in this new way got her excited about it in a way she felt like she hadn't been in years—not that she didn't appreciate the song, because she always had. But it was their biggest hit, and a more standard love ballad, unlike the faster, more punk-inspired songs that had filled the rest of their albums. There'd been a time when she'd been embarrassed by the fact that it was the one the band was the most known for, when it was the least like their other songs. It was almost painfully sincere.

But playing it like this with John, actually strumming the chords, singing along to it together . . . it made her realize that it was just a beautiful fucking song. She was proud of it. She was proud of what it had meant to people, what it meant to *her*.

And she loved hearing John sing. He didn't have the range to trace the higher harmony the way Ryder had, but he had a nice falsetto, which made him actually blush when she told him that. In the end, he sang the chorus straight-on, the way she always would've performed it, and then she took the higher parts. It opened her up to do more with that part of the song—add a few little vocalizations and runs, leaning into her pop background a bit. It was different. It was a lot of fun.

They finally broke for dinner way after they probably should've, both too focused on the work to register that they were hungry until they were full-on into *If I don't get food I'm going to be sick* territory. They spread out the contents of the cooler on the stage and ate in silence for the first few minutes, their only priority getting to a point where they felt more human again.

"This feels like a date," Micah said at last, reaching for the container of fruit so she didn't have to see John's reaction to that. "We did things a little backward, maybe. But here we are having a picnic. I don't know, it just feels a bit like a date."

He was in the middle of chewing, so there was an awkward beat where he didn't respond, and she thought maybe she'd spoken out of turn. But then he swallowed, wiping at the corner of his mouth with a napkin.

"I was definitely thinking of this like a date," he said. "Feels weird to have our first date be a working one, I know, but. If I'd had more time, I would've done this picnic right—gotten us a blanket and some flowers or something."

She liked the idea of John planning things out to that level. "Well, second date," she said.

He raised his eyebrows at that, and she popped a grape in her mouth, letting him think about it for a minute.

"Last night?" he asked.

"I mean, I ordered all that food," she said. "That took some effort! And sitting out on the balcony, looking over the water—

come on, the vibes were *right*. I didn't have any expectation about how the night would end, but I definitely had my hopes."

He laughed. "I had no expectations *or* hopes," he said. "Maybe we should try having a date where we actually both know we're on one."

"Let's start now," she said, leaning back on her hands to look at him. He was so familiar to her, so *John*, but she tried to see him as she might if he was just some guy she'd made it to a second date with. She'd think he was hot—that mess of curly dark hair, those deep brown eyes, the soft pillow of his lower lip. She'd fixate on the way his forearms flexed every time he reached for something, she'd wonder when he'd reach for *her*. "What do you do, John? What are you into?"

"Oh no," he said. "Not *those* questions."

"I'm sorry," she said, "what else do you lead with on a date? We're in our early thirties; the 'What do you do?' question is inevitable."

"You're right," he said. "I just dread it. Uh, I play guitar in a couple bands. And no, they're no one you would've heard of, unless you've spent time around Union Hall in Lakeland."

"Have you played guitar in any bands I would've heard of?"

He rubbed the back of his neck, and she could tell that, all joking aside, this line of questioning *was* making him a little uncomfortable. Which was interesting, given that of course she already knew the answers.

"This is where I would say *I don't know, what bands have you heard of?*" he said. "And then let you list a bunch that I could say no to before you give up. That's only if you haven't Googled me beforehand, in which case then usually I try to dodge a bunch of questions about what happened to the band, why we broke up, et cetera, because I never know if it'll end up in a Reddit thread somewhere later."

"Why don't you just say you were in ElectricOh!," Micah said. "It's not bragging or admitting something bad. It's a fact about you. As much a fact as saying you play in the Knock-Offspring."

"Well, I try not to admit *that*, either," he said, "because I can't keep a straight face. And I never liked talking about ElectricOh! with random people. It felt like such a long time ago. It felt like it had nothing to do with who I was anymore. And yet it has everything to do with who I am now, there's something about it that's . . ."

"Too personal? Vulnerable?"

He nodded. "And sacred, too. Something I want to hold to myself, and not share with anyone else."

That made sense. Micah had also never liked talking about the band with anyone, although she was rarely in a situation where someone *didn't* know about that part of her past. She had a few glib jokes prepared that she would make about the band's breakup, and then she'd find a way to change the subject.

"What about you?" he asked. "What do *you* do?"

He was right. The question was awful—she had no idea why everyone still used it as an opening gambit on an early date. Maybe knowing someone's job told you a lot about them as a person, how they spent their time, what they were good at, how they earned their living. But maybe it didn't tell you anything except whatever rut they were currently stuck in.

"Just coasting on royalties, baby," she said, waggling her eyebrows.

John frowned. "Wait, is that really what you say?"

"Why not? It's true."

"It sounds . . ."

"Like I'm a lazy, privileged person with no purpose in life? Like I'm a failure, a washed-up has-been still reaping the benefits from her glory days? Like I'm an anxious-depressive quasi-recluse who stays up all night, sleeps all day, and then gets my groceries delivered because I don't know if I want to deal with leaving my apartment?"

"I was going to say *reductive*." John looked at her, and she wished she hadn't said any of that. It was way too revealing— not what she would've said on a second date with *anyone*, and not what she wanted to say on a second date with John, who'd been practically beaming at her all evening, making her feel like her ability to transition smoothly from one chord to another made her some kind of guitar god. *Micah, that is fucking* tight, he'd said to her at one point, and even the memory sent a pulse to her core.

"You know what happened with your career isn't your fault, right?" he asked.

She rolled her eyes. "It is very explicitly my fault," she said. "I was in a successful band, which I blew up. And then I had the hubris to think anyone wanted a solo album out of me. *So Much Wasted Promise.* That should've been the name of it. The songs got warped so much in the studio that they barely felt like mine by the time they were done, and then I had to tour with them. I would read all these terrible reviews and comments on the internet, and then I'd put on my costume and my makeup and go out on the stage and try to pretend I didn't agree with half the shit those people wrote."

"But that's the machine, though," John said. "The songs got

warped because record labels don't give a fuck about what you're trying to *say*, they care about making money. If they think a dance beat will get you more radio play, then they'll slap a dance beat on it and who cares if it fits the song or not. If their algorithms push songs with *heart* in the title, bam, suddenly every single song is *heart heart heart*."

"I know," she said. "But good songs come out every day—music that people can be proud of, that *still* manage to sell records. So it is possible—I just couldn't do it."

"But they didn't even give you a *chance*," John said. "Stars are not made based solely on talent and hard work, I promise you that. If that were the case, I could name about a million people who should have the career that Adam Levine has had. Record labels decide who they want to try to break out, and then they *push* to break them out. Those people work hard and have talent, too; I'm not trying to take away from that. But they also get that push, and you never got that. The label got you a producer who wrote a few cookie-cutter hooks, rushed the album out, scheduled a limited tour, landed you a single magazine placement and one late-night show performance, all so they could say they'd done it. And then they washed their hands of you. None of that was *your* fault."

Micah realized she'd been holding the same strawberry in her hand for the last five minutes, but she just found it impossible to eat. She didn't know how she'd swallow around the lump in her throat.

"So many people would *kill* for the opportunities I got," she said. "So many other people would've done more with them than I did."

"Yeah, okay. There are a ton of systemic issues in the music industry—in *any* industry—and there's a lot we can try to do about them. Ways we can be more thoughtful in how we spend our money, who we give attention to, who we boost up and choose to work with. But taking on those issues as a personal failure, as somehow a *moral* one . . . I just don't think it's helpful. You are not a failure, Micah. You're someone who took a few cheap shots, got knocked down, but you're more than capable of getting back up again. God knows the world doesn't *need* our music, it doesn't need shit from us. You want to talk about hubris, who are we even to think that anyone cares? But *I* care. And you should care. Not for the record sales or the concert crowds or any of that, but because you love music and there's such rare, special, precious joy in being able to make it."

He was breathing hard now, like that speech had taken something out of him. It had stolen *her* breath, made it difficult to even speak.

"Damn," she said finally. "All right."

He gave her a crooked smile. "Believe it or not, one of the biggest complaints I've gotten on early dates is that I don't talk enough. Sorry about that."

"No, don't apologize. I've been trying to decide whether I would sleep with you at the end of this date and I think I made up my mind sometime around when you started raging against the machine. It was hot."

"That's what does it for you, huh?"

"Well, it certainly wasn't the Knock-Offspring," she said. "That was almost a dealbreaker."

"I knew I shouldn't bring it up. Bad Habit."

She grinned, enjoying the callback to their little game from before, even though she was still full out of any additional song titles to bring up. Turned out, he *had* been able to outlast her.

He took the strawberry from her hand, popping it in his mouth with a cheeky look that told her he was thinking back to that conversation, too. "So you're from Ohio?"

"That's cheating," she said. "You wouldn't know to ask me that."

"You gave yourself away with the accent."

Her jaw dropped in mock offense. "I do *not* have an accent."

"You mostly don't," he allowed. "But it comes out every once in a while, on certain words. The way you just said *hot*. It's cute."

"Okay," Micah said, picking up another strawberry and holding it in front of his mouth, making him lean forward and nip at it in order to get a bite. "You got me. I'm from Ohio."

His eyes crinkled at the corners. "What a coincidence," he said. "Me, too."

"Do you miss it?"

He took longer to answer that question than she'd expected him to, like he really had to think about it. She'd assumed he'd say no, maybe even *Hell no*. Between what had happened with the band and what he'd confirmed about his childhood, she couldn't blame him if most of his memories were bad.

"I miss seasons," he said. "The dandelions in late spring, the leaves changing color in fall, the snow even though it was a pain in the ass. I miss riding our bikes in the winter and it being too cold to feel our hands, even through the gloves, the way that the smoke from all the chimneys made the air smell like a fireplace."

The way he'd said *our* broke their game a little bit, if they hadn't broken it before. But Micah wasn't about to point it out.

It was comforting, hearing him talk about their hometown like this. It made her own nostalgia that she'd been feeling lately sharpen into something real, an emotion she could take out of its box and turn over in her hands.

"I miss the people," she said. "I haven't felt very close to my parents, especially my dad, after—" She bit back the rest of her words, less out of concern for any continued pretense that this was just an initial date between two people who didn't know each other very well, and more because of course this was stuff he already knew too well firsthand, and she didn't need to get into it now. "And there's my sister, too. I just think of how much better our relationship could be if I lived closer and could see them more."

She automatically reached to twist the ring on her finger, before remembering that she'd lost it recently. She'd worn it every day since her sister had given it to her for her sixteenth birthday, and it still felt weird not to have it. John tracked the movement, smiling a little at her when she glanced up at him.

"How is Hailey?" he asked.

Her sister had always *loved* John, had monopolized his attention whenever he came over to introduce him to every single one of her stuffed animals like he hadn't met them the last time he was at their house. And he would sit there patiently, letting her stack them higher and higher in his lap, asking the occasional question. *What's this one's name? Oh, Giraffe-y, that makes sense.*

"She's doing great," Micah said. "She got her cosmetology degree a few years ago and opened her own salon."

"God," John said. "That makes me feel old."

She quirked an eyebrow at him. "What does that make me?"

It had been a running joke between them, when they were kids. They'd been in the same grade, but Micah's October birthday had made her four months older, and she'd loved to hold it over John's head for that short time. *It must be for a more mature palate*, she'd say when he didn't automatically rave over the new album she'd put on.

He reached for the last strawberry before she could, holding it up to her mouth in order for her to take a big bite, a line of juice sliding down her chin.

"I've always had a thing for older women," he said.

"Oh, you have, have you?"

He ran the strawberry lightly along her lower lip, his eyes dark as he watched her finally take the rest of it in her mouth. He leaned forward to kiss her, his tongue warm and tasting of strawberries, too, his teeth gentle as he nibbled at the corner of her bottom lip.

"These do make your mouth very red," he said, sucking a bit of the strawberry juice off her. "And *extremely* kissable. Your magazines were really onto something with that one."

THIS TIME, MICAH got all the way dressed afterward, putting her bra and T-shirt back on and giving John back his hoodie since she had her own cardigan. They started packing up the guitars and the rest of the equipment, seeming to agree without having to say so that they were done rehearsing for the night.

"I think there's a dance party happening right now," Micah said. "On the main deck. I kind of wish we were just normal people on a *Nightshifters* cruise where we could enjoy that kind of thing."

He slung the case for his electric guitar—*her* guitar, technically—over his back, picking up the hard case for one of the acoustics after she'd grabbed the other one. He'd said there were people who'd helped get the rest of the equipment to the stage, and he could call them to get them to stow it back away where it belonged. He seemed to be thinking about what she'd said, and when she started to walk away, he pulled her back with one finger hooked in the belt loop of her jeans.

"I have an idea," he said, pressing a kiss to her hair. "Let's keep this date going."

They dropped the instruments off in his room, and then John disappeared for a few minutes, coming back with two masks. One was a wolf mask that went over your entire head, while the other was a cat mask that covered the front of your face held up by a rubber band.

"Best I could do," he said. "But I got these off two *Nightshifters* fans in exchange for autographing a few things and promising a picture with the band if they found us at prom. Which one do you want?"

Micah selected the wolf, thinking both of covering up her hair but also of that strange, random vision she'd had her first day on the ship, of being able to shapeshift into a wolf and make her way through all the crowds. Already that seemed like a lifetime ago. John put his own cat mask on, pulling up his hood over his hair.

"This will never work," she said.

"Worth a try, though, right? I always hit the clubs on a second date."

She smiled, although she already had the mask on and so

she knew he couldn't see it. "Not the first? What's the matter—not confident enough in your moves?"

"My moves are too intimidating for a first date," he said. "I wouldn't want you thinking I'm some kind of animal."

"Well," she said, pulling at his cat mask to snap it gently back against his cheek. "No, we wouldn't want that."

Another thing she wouldn't have known about John—he actually *could* dance. And what's more, he seemed to really enjoy it. The minute they got out onto the main deck of the ship, the music throbbing from the DJ up on the stage, he grabbed her hand and led her out into the middle of the dance floor. They were far from the only people wearing masks or costumes, so it wasn't nearly as weird as she thought it would be, and it only took a few minutes before she felt herself relax, knowing that no one was paying any special attention to them at all.

John was still holding her hand as he gave her a spin, and then he was dancing closer to her, his hands on her waist, her hips, her ass as he moved her to the beat of the music. She'd done her fair share of dancing—she'd built a *career* partially on it—but she felt like she had nothing to do but move with him, letting the bass thump through her entire body, seeming to vibrate especially in her chest, which almost hurt suddenly with the force of it. She linked her arms around John's neck, pressing against him even though it slowed them down, made them move as if underwater while the faster electronic music pulsed all around them.

Johnny, she thought. *My Johnny. It's always been you, hasn't it?*

He leaned in, holding his mask a little off his face to give more room to speak. "What?"

She hadn't realized she'd said that last part aloud. She shook her head, suddenly grateful for the mask that blocked out her words, hid her face from his view. She spun in his arms so she was facing away from him now, unabashedly grinding her ass against him until she could feel him getting hard. His hands on her hips were a little rougher now, a little more insistent—*Yes, keep doing that*—and she danced like she wasn't even aware he was there, even though she'd never been aware of anything more in her life.

She split off before they got too hot and bothered, dancing with a group of women who'd been shrieking and scream-talking while they jumped along to the music. They were clearly having the best time, and Micah had a blast dancing with them, pumping their fists to an anthemic chorus, standing half-crouched in anticipation of an epic breakdown, moving in a burst of energy once that beat dropped. When she glanced back at John, he was still dancing, rolling his shoulders, swaying his head back and forth until his hood dropped completely off, showing the way his damp curls now stuck to his neck. But he was watching her, too, and he danced over to her when he saw her attention on him.

"Are you done?" he asked, leaning in so she could hear him, his hand resting lightly on the bare skin at her waist where her T-shirt had ridden up.

She *had* been done, had started to become conscious of how hot it was inside the mask. But suddenly she didn't want this to be over.

"Not yet," she said. "Dance with me."

TWENTY-SEVEN

JOHN COULD'VE DANCED with Micah for hours. He loved watching her move, loved having her body pressed up against his. Dancing was one of those things that he forgot how much he enjoyed until he was actually doing it, feeling the music pulse through him and letting his body move to it in a way that felt natural and free and like an expression of something he normally kept to himself. And yet John felt like he'd somehow never danced before a day in his life, not like this.

He could tell when Micah started to flag a little, though, and he put his hand at the small of her back, guiding her through the crowd to see about finding them some water. When he looked up at the stage, he noticed that the DJ appeared to be one of the members of the Silver Cuties—the bassist, if he was remembering correctly. And there were a few other band members on the stage, together with some of the *Nightshifters* cast, including Tatiana.

"Come on," he said, taking off his mask and letting it dangle from his wrist.

He slid his artist badge out from his back pocket, presenting it to the security standing by the steps to the stage, and then he and Micah were up with the rest of them. Micah had removed her mask, too, and he had no idea if this meant that their cover was totally blown. They'd be at least somewhat recognizable now unless they went back to their rooms for a full outfit change, maybe not even then. At least it had been fun while it lasted.

That also meant that he probably shouldn't touch Micah anymore, stand too close or in any other way suggest that they might be together. Despite all their talk of dates and rules, he had no idea what he and Micah actually were to each other, especially in a public way.

"John!" Tatiana said, holding her arms open to give him a hug as he approached on the stage. "And Micah! My shuffleboard nemeses."

"Hey," Micah said, "*I* had nothing to do with that. I promise you if I'd have been playing, ElectricOh! wouldn't have stood a chance."

"That's what John kept saying about himself, but then he turned out to be a hustler," Tatiana said. She reached down to grasp Micah's injured hand, holding it up to examine the bandaged knuckles. "What happened here?"

Micah grimaced, but John found himself grinning. "Ryder's face is what happened."

Tatiana lifted her eyebrows, her mouth forming an almost perfect O. "Good for you," she said to Micah. "He had it coming."

Micah snorted at that. "You have no idea."

There was an open cooler on the stage, stocked with bottled waters that were dripping with condensation from the half-melted ice. John reached down to grab one for Micah and one for himself, uncapping his and downing three quarters of it before stopping to wipe his mouth. "Don't tell Frankie," he said. "About our continued plastic usage. We'll make up for it."

"I won't," she said, her gaze on him until she seemed to realize what she'd said. "I mean, I won't tell them. Not that I won't make up for it."

She was looking at him strangely, and he touched his tongue to the corner of his mouth, trying to figure out if he'd missed a spot. "What is it?"

She opened her mouth to answer, but then he heard her name being called from over his shoulder, and he turned to see one of the members of the Silver Cuties waving her over. She lifted her hand, acknowledging them without making any move to join them, and he pressed the cold bottom of his water bottle to the bare skin at her hip, smiling at her when she gave a yelp.

"You should talk to them," he said. "They're cool."

If she'd continued to hesitate he would've offered to go with her, but something told him that this was better for her to do on her own. It had felt like they were in the middle of a moment, but this entire cruise had been one long string of moments—he had to trust that there would be others.

"Okay, okay," she said. "But if it gets too industry-talky I'm giving you a sign to come rescue me. I'll start hoedown dancing in place or something."

"I think that would effectively rescue yourself," he said, and then ducked out of the way as she reached up to press her own bottled water to his neck. He was still laughing a little as she headed toward the Silver Cuties, their arms outstretched in a hug to receive her. When he turned around, he saw Tatiana watching him the way he'd been watching Micah.

"You still haven't told her, have you?" she asked.

He didn't pretend not to know what she meant. "That obvious?"

"I guess the question is *why* haven't you told her?"

He glanced back over at Micah. She was standing with her arms crossed, smiling at whatever the drummer for the Silver Cuties was saying, getting that slight dimple she got in the crease around her mouth when she genuinely found something funny. The colored lights from the stage made her hair glow a bright red, and for a second he flashed back to that time he'd seen her on her solo tour, out there in her makeup and short lacy dress. She'd always had the most expressive face, but she was also a performer, and he wouldn't have known how miserable she was on that tour if she hadn't told him.

Meanwhile, he'd thought she could see right through him. She *had* to know how he felt about her, he'd figured, if not the full dimensions of it then at least its general shape. When he was first teaching himself guitar, he used to call her up, playing her little chords and riffs over the phone. Sometimes he'd think there was no way she could make out the tune over such a scratchy connection, the distance he was sitting from the handset on his bed, how quietly he was playing to not disturb his dad. Sometimes he knew she got distracted, could hear her in the background telling Hailey to cut something out, getting called away by her parents for dinner.

But she'd always bring the music back up again, even if it took her until the next day—humming a bit of melody, asking him questions about what he was working on. She paid attention. And if she paid attention . . . then he figured she had to know.

Whatever this was with Micah, it felt like it depended on a certain level of float. It was a ship on rocky seas, it was a cupped handful of water that could drain away as quickly as you scooped it up. If he tried to name it or define it, if he tried to set any actual *rules* and not just joke ones, he didn't know what would happen to it. And he just had to ask himself if he was okay with that.

"We're on a date right now," he said, then flushed when he realized how that must sound, how that must *look* when he and Micah weren't even standing in the same vicinity. The night was cool but the dancing had gotten him warm all over, and he shrugged off his hoodie, feeling suddenly in need of some fresh air on his skin. "It's . . . we're not being public about it."

"Ah," Tatiana said. The way she said the word, it was as if she knew that bothered John, which he felt self-conscious about, like he had to rush to explain. The fact that Micah's entire on-again-off-again relationship with Ryder had also played out in secret wasn't lost on him.

"There's a lot of scrutiny," he said. "You know how it goes."

"God, do I," Tatiana said. "I just started dating Library Dead Girl a few months ago. We talked about her coming on this cruise with me and then were just like, no *thank* you. People would lose their minds."

It took John a second to catch up. "Wait, the one who was in the season six premiere? Whose friend didn't show up for the study group and so she walked home alone? Library Dead Girl?"

Tatiana rolled her eyes with a little smile. "Well, obviously Library Dead Girl was how she was credited. I call her Mallory like a normal person. But yeah, that's the one."

"People really would lose their minds," John said. "I'm losing my mind. But that's awesome. I'm glad you stayed in touch or reconnected or whatever."

Tatiana glanced over at him. "There's something special about it, isn't there? Being with someone who knew you in a different period of your life, who can help you knit together who you were then and who you are now."

Over a brief break in the music, John heard Micah laughing, that throaty sound that turned into a full-out cackle by the time she got going. From the way her mouth formed an O, her eyes shining as she looked from one member of the Silver Cuties to another, he imagined that there had been some gentle trash-talking between them to get her to react like that. She must've felt him looking at her, because she caught his eye from across the stage, her face still midlaugh. She shimmied her shoulders and moved her thumbs in a short approximation of a hoedown dance before pulling a face like *Just kidding, don't worry about it*. He grinned over at her.

He'd almost forgotten that Tatiana was still standing next to him, which was unforgivably rude, but she didn't seem to mind. "Go on," she said, waving toward Micah. "Enjoy the rest of your date."

CHAPTER

TWENTY-EIGHT

MICAH HAD FORGOTTEN how much she enjoyed talking to other musicians—the common language of gear and production and personnel, the excited appreciation for fellow artists who were crossing genres. Somehow she'd gotten it into her head that every interaction she had with anyone in the industry would have this giant elephant sitting right in the middle of it, like she wouldn't be able to look anyone in the eye without seeing her own failure reflected back at her. But when the Silver Cuties' drummer asked if she'd ever consider doing some vocals on one of their songs as a feature, she didn't automatically jump to assume the question was in bad faith, that he was making fun of her somehow. And even if she knew her *maybe* was just a soft way to say *probably not*, still. It had felt good to be asked.

By the time John made his way over to her, one of the members of the Silver Cuties had already moved on to get another drink and the conversation was coming to a close anyway. She smiled at John as he approached, and there was a brief awkward moment when it would've been natural for him to put his arm around her or lean over to give her a kiss. She could tell he wanted to. She *wanted* him to, wanted to pull him closer herself. She'd been watching him out of the corner of her eye, the whole time he'd been talking with Tatiana. At one point, he'd shrugged out of his hoodie, and she couldn't help but track the motion, taking in the flex of his biceps under his T-shirt, his exposed forearms lightly dusted with hair, the knob of bone at his wrist.

At the same time, there was still an entire day left on this cruise, and she didn't know if it made sense to introduce this new variable into the mix. With their fellow bandmates, with the audience, even with themselves. She was trying to hit all the right notes.

So she settled for keeping things casual. "Did you smooth out all your differences after shuffleboard?" she asked.

"For sure," he said. "And you will *not* believe this, but Tatiana has been dating Library Dead Girl for months now."

Micah searched her brain for what that could possibly mean. "That has to be the name of some performance artist or something, right, because you don't look sufficiently weirded out if that's literal."

"I forgot you're not the hardcore *Nightshifters* fan I am," John said. "She's an actress who was in one episode as a girl who got murdered on her way home from the library—Mallory something."

"Ohhh," she said, less because she remembered anything about the episode John was referencing and more because she finally got what he was saying. "Damn, that's cool. People would lose their minds."

"That's exactly what we said." He grinned at her, like he was proud of her for reaching the same conclusion he and Tatiana had. It wasn't even like it was that big a deal—it was an extremely easy conclusion to reach—and yet she still felt his approval like a warm glow.

"I didn't realize she was . . . gay. Or bi, or pan. In a same-sex relationship. I only remember hearing about past boyfriends."

"I don't know how open she is about it," John said. "So we'll just keep it to ourselves to be on the safe side."

"Definitely." Micah had been out as long as she could remember—she'd admitted to crushes on girls as far back as fourth grade, and she'd matter-of-factly told her parents because at the time she didn't even think there might be a reason why she might not want to. She'd been fortunate to have a loving family who didn't blink at something like that, who never made her feel like she was different or wrong or anything other than just . . . a person who happened to be attracted to more than one gender.

"Does it bother you that I'm bi?" she asked John now, the words flying out of her mouth before she could think about taking them back.

His brows drew together. "No . . . I hope I've never given you any reason to think it would."

"No," she said. "But some people . . . I don't know. I've dated people who seemed confused by it, or intimidated by it, or who didn't even believe it was a 'thing.'"

She probably didn't have to tell him that Ryder was one of those people. He vacillated between fetishizing her sexuality, when it suited him to picture her with another woman, or erasing it, when he tried to convince her that she probably wasn't *really* bisexual.

"I've always thought it was cool that you knew yourself that way from a relatively young age," John said. "I'm glad you felt safe enough to share it with people. It doesn't confuse me or intimidate me, and I do believe it's a real thing. I also believe in climate change, while we're laying all our cards on the table."

She knocked her shoulder against his, the closest she could get to a bit of PDA while they were literally on a stage surrounded by hundreds of people. "I believe in climate change, too," she said. "But speaking of cards on the table . . . I think I have an idea for our next stop."

THE SHIP'S CASINO was a cacophony of flashing lights and various electronic sounds, and it was hard to get through the crush of regular people, much less the ones wanting an autograph or picture. But Micah was gratified when she saw the top of Frankie's tightly curled hair behind one of the machines, and she assumed Steve was nearby, too. She'd thought she might find them there.

"How do you feel about group activities on a date?" she said into John's ear, trying to get the volume right to where he'd hear her over the din but she wouldn't be blowing out his eardrum.

He raised his eyebrows. "Normally I'd save that for the sixth, maybe seventh, but I can be adventurous."

She pinched his arm, wishing she could linger over that spot, rub the wound she'd just inflicted. But instead she separated herself from him more, pulling ahead as she led him over to where Steve and Frankie were standing in front of a couple slot machines.

"Heyyyy!" Steve yelled when he saw them, stretching out

the word in a way that suggested he was definitely at least a little lit.

"Still spending your vouchers?" Micah asked.

Frankie gave Steve an indulgent look, like he was a child who'd been on the same carousel all day in a theme park full of rides. "Those ran out a long time ago."

Micah wanted to bring up what had happened with Ryder, wanted to thank them for taking a stand against him. But she didn't know how to mention it without getting emotional in the middle of the casino, which would be a jarring experience on multiple levels. So instead she just patted Steve on the back.

"What's the damage so far?"

"I'm pretty sure I've broken even," Steve said. "House money."

"You have *not* broken even," Frankie said. "And you don't know what *house money* means. What have you guys been up to?"

For some reason Micah's brain went first to all the X-rated stuff she and John had gotten up to, all the things she absolutely could *not* tell her bandmates about. There were several beats of silence while she just stood there, trying to figure out how to even answer that question.

"We were rehearsing 'If Only' for prom," John said finally, and of *course*, that was the thing to say. She felt her cheeks heat and just hoped Frankie didn't notice.

"I think it sounds really good," Micah said. "I'm excited about it."

"I imagine. This performance is going to be iconic." Then they seemed to hear what they'd just said, and they quickly backtracked. "In a non-pressurey kind of way. Iconic like it'll just be a bird floating on the breeze, not a care in the world.

Iconic like one of those crop circles that just naturally happens without anyone needing to do any of the work for it."

"Those are made by aliens," Steve put in. "I watched a documentary."

"The point is," Frankie said, "I'm sure it'll be great."

Even a couple days ago, Frankie's words *would* have made Micah freak out. She was aware of the stakes of tomorrow night's performance, the fact that they had been scheduled to provide the climactic moment of the cruise, four minutes that were meant to be the most magical of the entire trip. But she really didn't feel nervous about it anymore. She was looking forward to being on that stage with John, to showing everyone what they could do.

Micah slid her and John's casino vouchers from her back pocket, holding them up. "Now," she said. "How do we go about using these?"

A few minutes later, they were both set up on slot machines—not because Micah particularly enjoyed the experience of pushing a button over and over, or because she cared about the extremely low odds of winning anything, but because they were open and it was something to do. John took a turn on one, the lights flashing across his face while he waited to see what images the machine would land on.

"I don't even know what I'm looking for," he said. "Three cherries in a row? Isn't that the usual thing?"

"I don't see any cherries," Micah said. "But number seven is lucky, right? And the diamonds look promising."

She kept hitting the button, and random things would light up and tell her when she'd won some kind of bonus, but it truly was baffling to figure out what was happening. Steve stood over her shoulder and tried to tell her when she'd hit a multiplier, but she didn't know what that meant and then she quickly lost it again.

"I hate gambling," John said. "I never do it. I don't even like white elephant gift exchanges and stuff like that. They make me so uncomfortable."

John liked certainty. She'd always known that about him, and now that she knew a bit more about what he'd been through as a kid, it made even more sense to her—that he wouldn't like that feeling of not knowing what to expect.

"I'm not big on it, either," she said. "Although I will admit to occasionally buying a Powerball ticket if the prize is really huge. I don't know why—it's not like I dream of being a billionaire or anything like that. I just get weirdly superstitious about the idea of passing up such a once-in-a-lifetime opportunity."

"And yet you're sitting on a Powerball ticket every day," he said. "And you never cash in."

He said it gently, with no particular sting, but she felt his words like a kick to the solar plexus nonetheless. He had a point, of course. She'd always imagined that she'd spun the wheel and lost big, and so the last thing she wanted to do was spin the wheel again. But it was beginning to seem more and more that she'd built that belief on a faulty premise to start with. Not only did she not have to fear the wheel, but she wasn't sure that she *had* lost on the first go-around. At least, not as devastatingly as she'd always thought.

Steve and Frankie had both moved away to check out other machines, and John took the opportunity to reach over and give her thigh a quick squeeze.

"I'm sorry," he said. "I'm not trying to get on your case."

But she realized that maybe that was *exactly* what she'd needed, all this time. She needed someone who cared enough about her to look at her life and not see what she wanted them to see, a woman living the dream of coasting on money and accomplishments from a decade ago. She wanted someone who cared enough to help her face the future but without making her feel terrible about all the ways she'd fucked up her past. She thought about that one woman she'd dated, the inspirational life hack-y quotes she was always throwing at Micah, and wondered why that had never felt like encouragement so much as impatience. She realized it was because she'd never felt like that woman cared about *her* as a person, so much as about her résumé for when she was being introduced at dinner parties.

"I appreciate you getting on my case," she said, smiling over at him. "Get on my case all you want."

He looked over at her, and for a moment their eyes hooked on each other, like there was an invisible string that wouldn't let them glance away. She could tell John was getting tired, the slight shadow under his eyes, the way his eyelashes drooped a bit at the corners. But she also knew that he wasn't going to call this night before she would, like they both knew they were on borrowed time and they were trying to make as much of it as they could.

Then something flashed on his screen, and he glanced back. "Holy shit," he said. "It *was* all about the diamonds."

Frankie had wandered back over to them, and they let out a whoop when they saw John's screen. "Dude, you just doubled that voucher."

"I have to cash out, right?" John said. "I'm up too much. I can't keep going."

"I don't know," Frankie said. "You're on a lucky streak."

But he'd already closed out, getting up from the machine. "A real man makes his own luck," he said.

Frankie stirred the cocktail in their hand with the little umbrella that had been added to the rim. "A *Titanic* reference, John, really? You're the one who said those were off-limits."

"What can I say?" John grinned at both of them, but Micah swore there was an extra hitch at the corner of his mouth when his gaze slid over to hers. "Things change."

WHEN JOHN CAME back, Steve and Frankie had moved on to take pictures with a group of *Nightshifters* fans who had clearly just come from the dance party, still clad in their full costumes. John leaned over Micah at her machine, resting his chin on her shoulder, nuzzling into her neck and taking a big inhale before he pressed a quick kiss to the spot. It unlocked that memory she'd been thinking of earlier on the beach, that *It's going to be okay.*

They'd been scheduled to play a Battle of the Bands that was a huge deal for them. Up until that point, ElectricOh! had only played some house parties, a coffee shop that offered an open mic night and was ill-equipped for a full five-piece band to play, a few thrilling shows at a local punk record store that John thought was the pinnacle of cool. But when they'd seen an advertisement for a statewide Battle of the Bands showcase, they'd thought, why not, worth a try. They were still in the faking it stage of making it and hadn't been prepared for what would happen if they actually got selected to play.

There was a *real* stage, not just a small DIY riser that shook if you turned your amp up too loud. There were actual *people* in the audience, and not just family or friends or kids who wanted an excuse to get out of the house and drink and make out and didn't particularly care what music was on in the background. Micah had never really suffered from stage fright before—if anything she felt *more* comfortable while she was performing than anywhere else. But she'd felt it that day.

She'd been waiting in the wings, chewing on her thumbnail, trying not to give in to that roller-coaster feeling when she saw the band slotted before them play their last notes and take their bows, heading offstage. She loved roller coasters, but still she always felt the same panic when she reached the top of a long, slow summit that she knew preceded a big drop. *Wait. Stop. I want off. I can't do this.* She felt that way then, the sudden urge to turn to the rest of the band and say *Sorry. Maybe next year.*

But John had come up behind her, his hand brushing her waist, a ghost of a touch she could still feel. He'd rested his chin on her shoulder, and then he'd said *It's going to be okay,* like he knew those simple words were all she needed to hear.

And maybe they were. They hadn't won the Battle of the Bands, and yet it had been what landed them their record deal, and then the rest was history.

Someone had immediately taken over John's slot machine, so he leaned on the back of her chair instead, watching her play a few more rounds. When she ran out of money, she looked up at him to smile.

"We can't all be so lucky, I guess," she said.

"That's why I doubled mine," he said. "So it'd be covered."

"Oh, is *that* why you did it. What foresight."

"I'm not about to let my date lose big," he said. "Not very chivalrous on my part."

"You would've kept going until you won the giant stuffed bear, wouldn't you," she asked, thinking back to the time they'd gone to a carnival and she'd had to pull him away from a darts game she knew was rigged. That rare competitive streak had come out, even then.

"Absolutely," he said. "Forty-eight dollars later, I would've shown them who was in charge."

They'd had a few people approach them for pictures and autographs, and there had been a time when Micah had been playing and a small crowd had gathered to watch, but she was grateful that for the most part people had been very respectful and given them some space. And when she did have encounters with anyone, they were all positive—just an excited fan who wanted to talk about what a particular song meant to them, sometimes even deeper cuts on the album that Micah was surprised to hear them mention. She'd feared this cruise for a number of reasons, one of which had been the crowds, but they'd turned out not to be so bad.

"Can I ask you a question?" John asked, and she tilted her head back to look up at him. Her stomach got that roller-coaster flip, wondering what it could even be.

"Okay."

"What's the deal with the bracelets?" he asked. "You don't wear any. And there were so many, they couldn't just be for you to wear?"

It took a second for Micah to remember what he was even talking about, and then she almost wished she hadn't, because it made her flash back to that terrible, awkward moment when they'd first boarded the ship, when the guitar case had opened and spilled bracelets everywhere. She'd wondered then what John had thought of her, and she couldn't be surprised that obviously he'd *still* been thinking about those bracelets even days later.

"Do you remember that trend, where everyone was making friendship bracelets all the time?"

His brow crinkled. "I think so," he said, but she could tell he didn't. He looked at her, his expression clearing. "No, sorry, I have no idea what you're talking about."

She huffed a laugh. Sometimes she forgot just how *offline* John was, and maybe his internet circles wouldn't have intersected with this anyway. "The point is, I bought a kit and I started making them, too—just for fun at first. I don't know, it was something to do. I would listen to podcasts and make twenty, thirty bracelets at a time."

"Jesus," he said. "Running your own sweatshop."

"It made me feel good to *make* something. Even though I knew they were kind of pointless, because what would I even do with that many bracelets? And then when I found out we would be doing this cruise, I thought, okay, maybe this is my opportunity. I could give them away to people on the ship or something. The ones I made for myself had random Elvis song titles on them—*don't* laugh, it's just what I could think of—but I started making ones that said *Youre Electric* or *If Only* or *Nightshifters* or *ElectricOh*. No exclamation point, because my kit didn't have one, and I tried to scratch off part of the I to make my own but it didn't look right."

"I'm sure people would still be excited to get a bracelet,"

John said. "Even without the exclamation point. You should give them away, that sounds like a great idea."

"It'd be awkward," she said. "What would I do, just walk around with my case, stopping people to open it up and present my wares? It's stupid."

John looked over to where Steve and Frankie were still standing by the entrance to the casino, talking with the same group of people they'd been taking pictures with before. Micah envied how easily they seemed to move through the crowds on the ship—even with things not being nearly as bad as she feared, Micah still found it a little nerve-racking, the idea of just being out among everyone.

"All right," John said finally. "New *new* idea. Follow me."

TWENTY-NINE

THE BRACELETS MIGHT'VE inspired John, but he was excited to do this regardless of anything to do with them. It felt right. It felt like the best possible send-off they could give ElectricOh!, if this cruise was in fact the last time they'd ever play together.

There were couches set up in the main interior lobby of the ship, near the concierge desks, which had been strategic on John's part because he thought it wouldn't be a bad place to be on the off chance his idea ended up backfiring in some way. He sat on one of the couches, reaching down to flick open the guitar case containing all the bracelets at his feet.

"I want one," Steve said, bending to sift through the bracelets, turning them over to read the words. "Oooh, *ElectricOh*. This one doesn't have an exclamation point, though."

"Take as many as you want," John said, unpacking his own acoustic guitar from its case, holding his pick between his teeth as he grabbed the second acoustic and handed it over to Micah.

"Why would I—"

"What did Elvis use to say," John said. "About how he only knew four chords and he only played three? He admitted that his guitar was a prop for him at first, a security blanket, but he still managed to get by. I think you should try getting used to holding one for a while and just see how it feels. That way if you feel moved to play along to anything, you can, and if not, no problem, you'll still look sexy as hell."

"Mmm-hmm," Frankie said as they settled onto the arm of the couch next to Micah. They hadn't brought an acoustic bass on the trip—because, why would they have?—and they said they only wanted to hang out for a few songs, anyway. Steve had a mini set of bongos because that just seemed like something Steve would travel with no matter what.

John glanced at Micah, giving her an exaggerated *whoops* face at his slip, but she just grinned at him.

"I'm worried people are going to think they're supposed to *give* us bracelets," Micah said. "Like it's a tip jar or something."

"We've been doing quite well for ourselves, if that's the case," John said. "But that's an easy fix." He rifled through his stuff until he found the paper he'd written the chords for "If Only" on earlier, together with the black Sharpie. **TAKE ONE** he wrote in large capital letters on the back of the sheet, and propped it up on the guitar case.

"Listen to this tech for Halloween," Steve said. "You get a bowl, and you dump a single small bag of some fun-size Kit Kats, that kind of thing. Then you put a sign on it that says *Take One*, but the candy runs out super fast, right? Only people don't think that's on you for not putting out enough candy, they think it's on everyone else for being too greedy to read the sign and taking too many."

"Look at you, finding ways to rig suburban Halloween," Frankie said. "You can't cash one of your ElectricOh! checks to afford a couple big variety packs?"

"Also, why put any candy out at all, in that case?" Micah said. "You could just put out the sign and have everyone blame greedy people from the start."

"For the *realism*," Steve said, then did a little drumroll on his bongos. "And I'm not saying I've actually done this, I just think it could be a good idea. If you were low on candy."

John strummed a chord, adjusting one tuner a final time before he strummed it again. "Are we ready?"

There was already a small crowd of people forming, trying to figure out what was going on, but no one had approached to take a bracelet. John didn't know why he was suddenly nervous about this—more nervous than he even was about their big performance tomorrow night—but he was.

They'd agreed that they wouldn't play "If Only," since it was already slated for prom night, but other than that, any Electric-Oh! song was fair game. John started with "Open Mouth," since they'd already rehearsed and played that one the night before. Still, they weren't used to playing it acoustic, and it took a minute for them to all settle into it together even though it was a song they knew every tiny nook and cranny of. Micah performed it in the most straightforward way possible, the way she might have sung a song around a campfire, and Frankie backed her up when the song built and wanted to get bigger.

By the time they rolled into another song, even John found himself singing along, which made Micah skip a lyric as she smiled at him. She occasionally tapped the guitar, playing percussion along with Steve, but didn't otherwise move to strum it. He noticed she also smiled every time someone came up to grab a bracelet or two from the guitar case, which meant she was smiling a lot, because there really was an obscene amount of bracelets and they seemed to be unending. The crowd gathered around got bigger and bigger, and eventually they were all singing along to the songs, too, until John forgot to feel self-conscious about his voice or worry about whether Micah was having a good time or any of it. They were just hanging out and playing music. It really could be as simple as that.

Someone requested a particular song that John couldn't remember as well, and so he was trying a couple different notes, traveling up the fretboard until he could find the right key.

"I think it was—" Micah strummed a chord, and then played the next until she'd figured out the entire first verse. "Now see if I can remember the lyrics, they went like—"

But that was where it was great to do this here, like this, because there were people in the crowd who seemed to know the lyrics better than they did. They started singing the first line, and then it was Micah who was singing along with *them*, making a cute little face the couple times she flubbed a word.

Steve and Frankie stayed longer than they originally said they would, but still they peeled off sometime around two in the morning. There weren't any bracelets left in the guitar case, which was a shame—John realized he'd meant to grab one for himself, and hadn't.

"You're not wearing your voice out, are you?" he asked Micah. "You've been using it a lot today."

"Nah," she said. "I have one more in me, at least."

They'd already graduated to playing some non-ElectricOh! songs, mostly nostalgic ones from around the same era or crowd-pleasers he knew everyone would know the words to. But now John started playing a fingerpicked tune, watching Micah's face as she realized what it was.

"That's *my* song," she said.

The closing track off her solo album, technically. It was a somber song, and he'd always thought it interesting that she'd chosen it to close out the record on such a down note. He supposed it was possible she hadn't had control over the sequencing of that, but somehow he knew that had been her choice. It had seemed almost prescient, to have this album full of danceable hits end on a song that seemed to be all about regret, the final recorded song Micah would ever put out. At least so far.

"It's a good song," he said.

"Kind of a bummer to end the night on."

He tilted his head, listening to the music. It *was* sad. But it was hopeful, too. There was something in the way the lead line just repeated and repeated at the end that had always made John think, strangely, of a time-lapse video of a flower blooming. It felt like the song was a bud held very tight, but in the last few seconds you got the sense that it might open up.

He started singing, barely even using his voice, more a suggestion of the words than a full-out vocalization. He let himself drop off once Micah took over, and for the next few minutes it was just her voice and his guitar. The people who had stuck around to keep watching were silent, and somehow John knew it wasn't because they weren't familiar with this song, but because they knew they were watching something special, and it was better to let Micah handle this one alone.

He played those recursive notes at the end, only he just kept playing them, reluctant to let the song resolve all the way.

"Thank you for hanging out with us," he said to the crowd. "Really, I mean it. Thank you."

"Who's excited for prom?" Micah asked, and it was the exact right thing to say, because a whoop went up so loud that she started laughing. "All right, all right. Us, too. We'll see you there?"

John took that as his cue to finally finish the song, sliding his pick between the strings of his guitar as he packed it back away in its case. They stuck around to take a few more pictures, and then it was just them again, heading as if by silent agreement back to the deck with their rooms.

"That was the best date I've ever been on," she said, leaning against his arm. The lights were bright in the elevator, and he could see that she was tired. He almost felt guilty for a minute, like he shouldn't have kept her out that late when he *knew* they had a big day tomorrow, but then he remembered that they could sleep all day if they wanted to. And he hoped she was tired in the same way he was—in that loose, pleasant way where he looked forward to snuggling up with her in bed and letting himself fall down into the deepest sleep.

"I want to take you on a date where I can *touch* you," he said. "I want—"

He broke off, because he realized the impossibility of what he was about to say. They were about to return to their homes on opposite sides of the country, so there was no point in dreaming about some big future that couldn't exist.

"What?" she asked.

He also realized how silly it probably sounded, the fantasy

he'd had since he was a teenager. Something as simple as watching a movie with her, being able to put his arm around her shoulders, having her feet in his lap, ignoring the movie to make out slowly, leisurely, like they had all the time in the world because they did.

He laughed, picking the guitar case back up when the elevator stopped on their floor. "I want a shower, and then I want to go to bed. How about you?"

"Sounds perfect."

They ended up in his room for the illogical reason that it was the first one they arrived at, and if they'd had any ideas about getting up to anything in the shower, they were laid to rest by what a comedy of errors it was to even fit the two of them in the narrow cubby. John carefully unwrapped the bandage around Micah's hand, holding her wrist gently to avoid bumping her as they shifted around in the tight shower. She had to practically hug him in order to spread soapy water all over his body, and he returned the favor by massaging shampoo into her hair and helping her rinse it out. When they finally got under the covers, they were both naked and every time Micah moved he could smell the body wash they'd both used.

"I can't believe how much I was dreading this cruise," she said, turning in his arms so she was facing him. He couldn't make out a single detail of her face, that was how total the darkness was in his room, but her voice was low and filled with something like wonder. "Like, I *really* did not want to do it."

"Why did you?"

She was quiet so long that he almost thought she wasn't going to answer, but then she ran her hands up his arms, her fingers featherlight on his skin. "I wanted to see you," she said. "I knew I had to see you."

"Not just me."

"No," she allowed. "I needed that closure with everyone. But you . . . it was different with you. The minute my dad even brought you up, how much time you used to spend at our house, I said yes so fast. At the time it was more like I wanted him to stop talking, didn't want to hear him even say your *name* because of the way I knew it would make me feel. But it was also because of the way it made me feel that I said yes. Do you know what I mean?"

He knew exactly what she meant. And yet he didn't at all, had no idea if they were singing the same song but in a different key.

"Luckily there was no need to say my name," John said. "Just *SECOND GUITARIST*—all caps, of course, except there was one time when *guitarist* was misspelled, I don't know if you caught that—where the second guitarist will participate in two, parentheses number two, cruise-sanctioned activities including but not limited to—"

She squeezed his biceps. "Not only did you bring the contract with you, but you memorized it?"

"Oh, it's somewhere back home buried under a bunch of other mail. I just said that to get Ryder to shut the fuck up. But now I'm going to put it in my cruise scrapbook, so I can remember what brought us back together."

She rolled over again, snuggling back into him as he put his arm over her.

"I'm glad it did," she said, pressing a kiss to his palm before

putting his hand directly on her breast. He tweaked her nipple, liking something about being able to touch her even in
these small ways that didn't always have to lead to anything
more.

"Me, too," he said. "God, me, too."

CHAPTER

THIRTY

MICAH HAD NO idea what time it was when she woke up. Without any glimpse of the sun outside, it was impossible to tell. It might be early afternoon already, although her internal clock told her it was still the middle of the night.

What she did know was that she awoke feeling warm and cozy and secure, and it was only when she reached her arm over to the other side of the bed that she realized it was empty. "John?"

His name came out as barely a whisper, so it was no wonder that he didn't hear her. He was sitting on the edge of a chair in the corner, partially lit only by his phone resting on top of a small amp, which she could see was on from the red glowing light. He had his electric guitar plugged in, headphones on as he played through what she could tell was the lead line for "If Only."

He'd spent so much time today making sure that she felt comfortable with her part, and then working on his vocals, that it hadn't even occurred to her that maybe he'd be insecure about the fact that *he* was also taking on a new guitar part he didn't normally play. And John had always been a bit of a perfectionist—it drove him crazy when he missed a note live or if he didn't get the tone he was going for in a recording.

"John?" she said again, her voice cracking a little. She sat up, and it was that motion that caught his attention. He lifted one of the padded sides of the headphones away from his ear.

"I hope I didn't wake you," he said.

"You didn't."

"I don't want to fuck up."

"You won't."

In the shadows, she didn't know how much of her he could make out, but she felt like he could see everything as his eyes swept over where her hair was tangled and still slightly damp down to her bare breasts over the rumpled covers of the bed. Her nipples tightened even from that one look.

"Come on, Johnny," she said. "Come back to bed."

He leaned the guitar against the wall, reaching over to switch off the amp and turn his phone light off. He'd dressed in his Batman pajama pants again, which she really did find ridiculously cute, but hadn't bothered with a shirt. She ran her hands over his chest as he crawled up her body, stopping to brace himself over her.

"We never got to go to our prom," he said.

It was true. By the time their senior prom rolled around, they'd already been fully committed on a national tour to support their album. She tried to remember what city they'd been in on that date, sure that they would've marked it somehow, but it was a blur.

"I would've asked you," he said.

"I wouldn't have needed to be asked," she said. "I would've assumed we were going together."

He smoothed the hair off her forehead. "Unless you were dating someone at the time," he said. "Then you would've gone with them."

She wanted to deny that. It was impossible to believe now that she would've wanted to spend that night with anyone other than John, even if it was just in the capacity of friends. But she knew that was revisionist history. If she'd been dating someone else, of course it would've been a foregone conclusion that they'd be her prom date. The only part she was absolutely confident about was that there was no way she would've had more fun than if she'd spent the night with John, however they'd needed to do it.

"Where would you have taken me to dinner beforehand?"

"Taco Bell," he said, and she burst out a surprised laugh that she could tell made him smile, even in the dark. "I'm just keeping it real. Plus you loved the Crunchwrap Supreme."

"It's the superior Taco Bell order, and I'll die on that hill. It has the soft tortilla, the bit of crunch, the cheese, the sour cream . . . a truly perfect culinary delight."

"What would you have worn?" he asked.

She thought about that, casting back to remember her style sense then. "Maybe a ballerina pink dress with a floaty skirt, paired with my combat boots so you knew I was still punk. I would've made sure you knew the pink was *ironic*, because I didn't know how to admit back then that I just liked the color. And I would've tried to get you to wear a white suit like Elvis from the '68 comeback special, but I know you would've gone with black."

"I would've worn whatever you wanted me to."

"Probably ill-advised to eat a Crunchwrap Supreme in a white suit," she said.

"I don't know that I would've had much of an appetite. I would've been nervous at the idea of dancing with you later."

"You're a very good dancer," she said.

"That's not why I would've been nervous." She could hear him swallowing in the dark, and his voice sounded a little ragged, like maybe he was nervous even now. She thought about waking up to find him practicing that song, wanting to make sure every tiny thing was right, and she squeezed his forearms, trying to let him know that it would be okay. "What's the song we would've slow-danced to?"

"Well, it would have to be Elvis, if you were wearing the suit." She took a minute before she answered, like she had to think about it, but it was just for show. She'd known the song the minute he'd asked the question. "'Can't Help Falling in Love.'"

He stroked her cheek. "Ah, Micah. I'm no fool, and I never rush into anything. I've been in love with you since I was twelve years old."

Her entire chest felt tight. Her first instinct was to deny his words, wanting to tell him all the ways that wasn't possible. He only *thought* he was in love with her. He loved her as a friend, maybe, which was no revelation—there had always been love between them. She knew he'd had a crush on her at various points, she'd crushed on him at other points, but it had never gone beyond that because they knew it couldn't. Not without risking the friendship, which Micah would protect at all costs. It was too important.

But she also knew immediately that he meant what he'd said, that it was the truest thing he'd ever said to her. Hearing him speak the words aloud felt simultaneously like the biggest surprise and like the most beautiful, inevitable thing.

"Micah Presley, no relation," he said. "I think I was half-gone for you the minute you introduced yourself. And then sometimes I think I fell the rest of the way two weeks later, when I finally got up the nerve to talk to you and you just rolled with it like no time had passed at all in between. You've always known yourself in this really special way, in this way that invites other people in. You're so brave, and you make *me* brave."

She shook her head, wanting to refute all of that. Hadn't he been listening? She'd spent the past few years hiding out, licking her wounds, making fucking *bracelets* instead of making music, not wanting to face anyone, least of all him. She was the opposite of brave.

"You are," he said, his hands warm and strong on either side of her face. "I know it's been hard, since the band broke up. And I know that everything that came afterward did a number on you. But I have no doubt that, when you're ready, you can do whatever the fuck you want. You've always been able to. And I have no doubt that whatever that is, it's going to be great. You have such power, in the way you feel things, in the way you can make other people feel them, too—with your lyrics, with your voice, with who you are."

It was a good thing it was so dark, because Micah thought that was the only thing saving her from completely losing it, from wanting to hide her face or run away, not wanting to let John hold her and tell her all these things she felt she didn't deserve to hear. That she *needed* to hear.

He tucked a strand of her hair behind her ear, his hand trailing down her jaw. "That's why the world fell in love with you in ElectricOh!," he said. "But I fell in love with you before that, because you've always been the person I most want to talk to, I most want to make laugh, who can make *me* laugh, who makes me feel like no matter what else happens there's always a safe place to go back to, and that safe place is you."

She had so much she wanted to say, so much that his words stirred up. But there was a lump in her throat and no matter what he'd said, she didn't know that she was brave enough to say any of it. She didn't know that she knew how.

So instead she tugged him down to her, pressing a hard kiss to his mouth that was a little clumsy, starting somewhere closer to his chin before he tilted his face to meet her. She felt a sob rising up, but she swallowed it back down, her hands greedy as she clutched the bunched muscles at his shoulders. The action caused a slight throb in her injured knuckles, but she ignored it, not wanting to stop touching him. His hand was on her breast then, giving it a squeeze, dragging his fingertips over the tight bud of her nipple. It seemed like a waste, that they hadn't been touching each other like this all those years.

"John," she said. "*John.*"

She was asking for something, but she didn't even know what it was. She didn't know what more he could give her than he'd already given.

He reached down, his hand between her legs as he found that pulse that was begging for its own release. He rubbed her clit in slow, patient circles, his breath hot on her cheek as he kissed her jaw.

"You have no idea what this does to me," he said. "Just touching you like this, making you come apart like this."

She *wanted* to come apart, could feel her body inching toward it, but then every time she got close he backed off, stroking another part of her until she was angling her hips toward him, trying to get him to touch her in the way she most craved.

He slid a finger inside her, and she made a choked sound in the back of her throat, grabbing his forearm to hold his hand there. She didn't want him to move just yet, she didn't know if she could take it—she just wanted to feel him inside her body, wanted to know that he was touching her in the most intimate way possible.

Eventually she relaxed her grip, and he started working her with his finger before he added another, and then another. When he pushed against her clit with his thumb, she let out a low, keening sound that didn't even sound like it came from her.

"I love stretching you out like this," he said. "I could spend hours with my fingers inside you, just feeling how wet you are, how you tighten around me."

Yes, she tried to say, but it came out more like a moan. When he started fucking her with his fingers, she brought her knees up to her chest, wanting to give him the most access possible. Her hands were on his biceps, his back, his shoulders, his throat, until he gave a strangled grunt that made her drop her hands, worried she'd hurt him somehow.

"No," he said. "Do it again, and squeeze."

She brought her hand up, feeling the ridge of his Adam's apple under her thumb, pressing her fingers into the hollow at the base of his throat. And then she wrapped her fingers around him and did exactly as he'd asked, applying enough pressure that she knew he'd feel it, not enough that it would risk cutting off his breath.

"Harder."

She clenched her fingers around him, rewarded by the shudder that went through his body, the way his hand briefly paused in its ministrations inside her, as if he lost focus for a moment. He had such excellent focus, and she loved to wreck it. But it was almost like he wanted to punish her for that, because then he withdrew his hand entirely, leaving her feeling empty and wanting.

"*Fuck*, Micah," he said, rubbing those agonizingly slow circles over her clit again. "I can't get enough of you."

He'd moved now so he was farther away, out of her reach, but to where he'd have a perfect view of everything he was doing to her if only there was any light. She was grateful for the darkness, grateful that he couldn't see the way she was so open and vulnerable to him. Even knowing he was so close made her legs tremble, to where she almost couldn't hold them up anymore.

"Please," she said. "Please fuck me. I can't take it."

He flipped her over, pulling her by the hips until she was flush against him. The move was so unexpected that she still hadn't fully recovered from it when she felt him push inside her. She was already on the edge from everything he'd put her through up until that point, but he held her in place, like he knew that any movement would make her fall off the cliff.

He brushed her hair off her neck, leaning over to press a kiss there. "You can take it," he said. "You *will* take it. You'll come for me, won't you?"

His fingers dug into her hips as he slammed her back against him, and then he was fucking her fast and hard just the way she'd wanted it. Eventually he reached down between her legs, pressing against her clit as he continued to rail her from behind.

"Come for me, honey," he said. "Just let go."

The way it was building inside her, it was almost painful, too much sensation, too much pressure, too much *him*, too much, too much. When it finally ripped through her body, she couldn't stop the guttural scream that was torn from her mouth at the same time, the way she could feel everything clench and spasm and release, leaving her boneless and weak as she felt John holding her up, his own body shuddering as he came inside her.

"Fuck," he said.

And then she started to cry. She had no idea why—she was embarrassed by the suddenness of it, the *force* of it, the way there was no hiding it. She cried harder than she'd cried in years.

"Hey," John said, wrapping his arm around her. "Hey. Oh god, Micah, I didn't hurt you, did I?"

She shook her head, unable to say anything more, even though she wanted to assure him that he definitely hadn't hurt her. She knew this was a disproportionate response to sex—she didn't even know exactly what it was a response *to*, if it was a by-product of having the best orgasm of her life, all those chemicals coursing through her body, or if there was more to it than that. She reached up to grab his hand and gave it a squeeze.

He'd been stretched out over her back, and there was something comforting about the weight of him like that, holding her down. But her knees were still tucked beneath her, and she had to shift to stretch out her legs, which felt wobbly and tingly and incapable of anything remotely close to walking. He rolled off her until he was lying next to her, their bodies pressed together as he rubbed circles on her back.

"What is it?" he asked as she started to calm down, her tears mostly stopped, only the occasional sniffle to remind her of that wave of emotion. "Talk to me."

She was still lying on her stomach, and she turned her head on the pillow, so she'd be able to look him in the eyes if it weren't so dark that she couldn't see. She imagined that she'd see his love for her there, that maybe she could've always seen it, if she'd only thought to look. He hadn't hurt her, but she was worried she'd hurt *him*, because she'd never seemed to figure out how to do the romantic stuff. She wanted to be better at it for him, wanted to be better at it *with* him, but she was scared that she didn't know how.

"I'm good," she said. "It's all good. It's just . . ."

She didn't know how to finish that sentence, how to even put everything into words. She didn't know if there *were* words. She was grateful when this time he did step in to try to give her some.

"A lot?"

"A fuckton of a lot," she agreed, and she could feel his smile, knew that he caught her reference back to what he'd said after their first show on the cruise. His hand was resting on her back now, no longer moving, just a steady, warm reminder that he was there.

"I don't want to break any of your rules," he said. "Do you need me to carry you to the bathroom?"

She laughed, but it only reminded her of what a mess her

face must be, tears still wet on her cheeks, her nose starting to run. "I can do it," she said. "Just give me a second."

He touched her temple, his fingers finding the hair that had stuck to her face in the dark, carefully combing it away until he could cup her cheek. There was such tenderness to the gesture she almost started crying all over again.

"Take your time," he said.

THIRTY-ONE

WHEN THEY WOKE up for the second time, it was well into the last full day of the cruise, and suddenly the event that had seemed so far away now felt like it was coming up too fast, before they had the chance to get ready.

Micah went back to her room to start her own preparations—apparently some designer she knew had supplied the dress for her to wear, and it was being held somewhere else on the ship where it would be steamed and altered in any way she needed it to be.

And John had his own things to do to get ready, which helped keep him occupied so his nerves couldn't get to him. No matter how much he'd assured Micah that they were good, that their performance was going to go off without a hitch, he couldn't help the butterflies in his own stomach when he thought about that night.

He also was very conscious that no matter how close he'd felt with Micah, no matter how easy they'd left things when they'd parted to meet up later at prom . . . he'd told her that he loved her and she hadn't said it back.

He wasn't sorry that he'd told her. It was past time, and it had felt good to get it off his chest, to know that everything was out in the open. He'd been prepared for the possibility that she wouldn't feel the same way, and had told himself it was still worth it to say the words even if they only ever went in one direction.

John finished his last errand and decided to stroll the deck of the ship, already feeling a bit of that painful nostalgia that hits when you haven't yet left a place you know you're going to miss. He'd spent the past four days on a cruise and had barely had the chance to scrape the surface of what it offered. He hadn't hit up the soft serve machine once. Maybe he should book himself on another cruise, once this was all over, one where he could just sit by the pool and stare out at the ocean and sit in the back row of the Starlight Theater to watch someone else put on a show.

"How late did y'all sleep?" Frankie asked, coming up on him. They'd ended up at the shuffleboard court, he realized, although nobody was playing.

"I don't even want to admit to it," he said. He realized that he'd probably already admitted to something, just by responding in that way to their query. But he'd gotten the impression last night that Frankie already knew about him and Micah, and that they weren't bothered.

"Piece of shit o'clock?" Frankie said, grinning at him. It's what they'd used to call it, when they slept past noon while on tour, even though there was almost no way around a fucked-up sleep schedule in those kinds of conditions. With Micah, especially. She'd always been able to stay up the latest of any of them, and he'd always wanted to hang right there with her.

"Piece of shit thirty," he said. "What about you? Did you head to bed right after you left?"

"I could barely keep my eyes open," Frankie said. "I know I'm going to have to get used to it again, if I end up doing that summer tour after all, but for right now this millennial likes to be in their pajamas and watching their programs by nine o'-clock."

"Well, I hope you do the tour," John said. "If there's a date in Orlando, you know I'll be there."

"Not L.A.?"

He smiled but didn't have anything to say to that. "Do you think there's a way to make music and not have it get warped somehow? Like a way to make something and share it with people, but avoid all the pitfalls of record labels and critics and sales and promotion and all that?"

"No," Frankie said, the answer so quick and deadpan he couldn't help but let out a surprised laugh.

"Okay," he said. "Fair enough."

"I mean, there are different paths," Frankie said. "Like if we'd had more time to just be a *band*, and had signed to some tiny indie label, sure. Everything would've been different. But no, I don't think you can ever avoid all of it. The minute you take a song from your bedroom to a record where anybody can hear it, it doesn't belong to just you anymore. And that lets a lot of people in, all the voices that tell you it's not good enough or not selling enough or not as good as your last one, or worse sometimes, telling you that it's brilliant."

John rocked back on his heels, thinking about how true *that* was. The praise could fuck you up as badly as the criticism; that was one part he hadn't been prepared for. He thought about those people crying in the front row at the concert the other night, how many years it had taken for him to feel grateful for that instead of uncomfortable and weird.

"You can keep everything small," Frankie said. "And then you let fewer people in. But the flip side is that you let fewer people in. And what's the point of music if you're not sharing it with other people?"

He thought back to the night before, how *good* it had felt just to play songs and sing them with his friends, no microphones, no set list, nobody carefully arranging the schedule so they played three hits, recorded a radio bumper—*This is Electric-Oh!, and you're listening to THE Ninety-Seven X, Home of Tampa Bay's New Rock Alternative*—and then moved on to the next thing.

"It really didn't fuck you up, did it," he said. "What happened with the band?"

"Hell no," Frankie said. "For a few years it was an absolute *dream*. We got to fly across the world! When we couldn't even legally drink yet! And then the shine started to wear off, and yeah, I was mad when Micah blew it all up, but I was relieved, too. It freed us all up so we could do our own things. I've never been sorry we started the band, and I've never been sorry that we ended it, either."

Hearing Frankie put it that way, it seemed obvious. John felt almost stupid for all the years when he *had* been fucked up by everything that went down. The band had been fun. Until it wasn't. Simple as that.

Frankie touched his arm. "It was always more emotional for you," they said. "And for Micah. We knew that."

"Well, I'm glad we did it with you," he said. "And with Steve . . . and even Ryder, when he was on his best behavior and not being a complete prick."

Frankie made an exaggerated expression of confusion, their brow furrowed, looking up to the sky. "My memory must be going," they said, "because I'm having a hard time accessing ones of Ryder *not* being a prick. But maybe he gave ElectricOh! the edge that everyone wanted it to have, who knows. I guess sometimes you write a discordant note into a composition on purpose."

"And then sometimes you write it out," John said, thinking back to the moment yesterday when he, Steve, and Frankie had all joined together to tell Ryder they wanted nothing more to do with him. It had been one of the most satisfying moments of his life.

"I don't think she ever loved him," Frankie said. "There was some sort of toxic thing there, and as long as they were in the band together she was going to find herself drawn back into it. That's why in a way I wasn't surprised when she blew it all up. On some level I was proud of her for doing it."

He was proud of Micah, too, even if he wished it had all gone down differently. But he definitely understood it now more than he had then.

The sun was starting to get low in the sky—not touching the horizon yet, but not too far off. People were already gathering on the main deck, some in full *Nightshifters* costumes, many others in formal prom gear. It was supposed to kick off at sunset, with him and Micah to perform a couple hours in after night had taken hold. He knew he didn't have much time before he needed to be ready, and he had something he needed to pick up first before he made his way to Micah's room.

"It was good doing this with you," John said. "Talking, I mean, but also the whole cruise. I'm glad we did it."

"Me, too," Frankie said, cuffing him good-naturedly on the shoulder. "Now go do your thing, and I'll see you out there."

AN HOUR LATER, John stood outside Micah's room, adjusting the left cuff of his shirt. He was wearing black dress pants and a crisp white button-down with a thin black tie, but at the last minute he couldn't stand the feeling of the cuffs buttoned tightly at his wrists, and so he'd rolled them up to just below his elbows, trying to keep everything still looking clean and nice. He couldn't quite get the sleeves to be the exact same length, and it was bugging him.

The door flew open before he had a chance to knock, and he glanced up to see Micah in the doorway. She was wearing a sparkly silver dress that draped softly over her curves, looking somehow like she'd been dipped in liquid metal. It went down to the floor, but there was a slit all the way up her thigh, showing a glimpse of her tattoo when she moved. He could see that her feet were still bare.

"There you are," she said, like she'd been looking for him.

"Here I am."

Her gaze swept over him from head to toe, and she gave him a smile that let him know she liked what she saw. "If you even knew what it does to me when you wear white. You look like an angel."

He remembered her saying something that first time they'd seen each other, at that meeting at the record label. He hadn't known how she'd meant it then—whether she was commenting on the color of his shirt in a good way or a bad way. It had seemed like such an odd thing to notice. But he liked thinking that it had done something to her even then.

"I'll throw out all my black T-shirts," he said.

She looked genuinely alarmed. "No, don't do that. It's the *contrast*, the surprise of it. I like seeing you this way because I feel like I don't often get the chance."

He could understand that, because it was part of what took his breath away now, seeing her in that full gown. And then she turned around, and he saw that it was backless all the way down, showing off her smooth skin, the delicate curve of her spine down to where the fabric draped right at the top of her ass.

"Everything okay?" she asked, which was his only sign that he must've groaned out loud.

"Yeah," he said, then remembered the box he was holding in his hand. "I, uh, got you something."

Her eyes lit up. "You did?"

He opened the box to show her the corsage nested inside, a simple pink rose surrounded by a few smaller white flowers and some sprigs of greenery. He'd had his heart set on a peony, but he supposed he was lucky they could do anything at all on a cruise ship where they couldn't just have any flowers they wanted sent at a moment's notice.

"It's supposed to go on your wrist," he said. "But I know that'll be hard to play with, so you don't have to actually wear it. I just wanted you to have it."

"Pink," she said, touching the petals of the rose gently, almost reverently. "My favorite. Help me pin it in my hair?"

He had no idea how to do that, but she sat in front of the vanity mirror, positioning the rose at her temple and holding it in place while he grabbed a few bobby pins from where she indicated. When she was done, it looked like she'd planned it as part of her outfit all along, sweeping one side of her hair off her face while the other side fell in soft waves past her shoulders.

"It's beautiful," she said. "Thank you. I feel like I should've gotten you something."

"Nah."

She rifled through her makeup bag until she came up with a short black pencil. "I could do your eyeliner? I mostly use the liquid stuff now, so this has never even been used—see, it still has the little plastic on it—so no risk of an eye infection, I promise."

"Sure," he said. "Go for it."

He sat down on the edge of her bed, and she spun on the stool so she could face him, scooting closer when she was too far to get a good angle. At one point, she braced her hand against his thigh, leaning in until he could see the shadow between her breasts, could smell that rose in her hair. He drew in a ragged breath, and she paused, her fingers still pressing against his brow.

"Almost done," she said. "You have such pretty eyes."

"Yeah?"

"You have very *kind* eyes," she said. "It was one of the first things I noticed about you. Why do you think I felt bold enough to just talk to you out of the blue like that? I could tell you wouldn't be one of those boys who laughed in my face or made me feel weird or made me feel silly. I could tell you'd be easy to talk to, and I wondered what you'd have to say. You were always reading or using homeroom to actually do your assignments, which was *wild* to me."

It had been hard for him to concentrate at home. Even when nothing had been happening, he'd always felt like he had to stay vigilant. It had made him grateful for any time he could get to himself in class or on the bus, not wanting to waste those precious moments of quiet.

"Look up and to the left," she said, going back in to continue her work. It felt strange, that slight pressure, but he was determined to be good for her and sit still. He followed every direction she gave him, until eventually she told him to close his eyes. He felt the soft pencil tip sweeping once more along his lash line, and then she blew gently on his eyelids.

"There," she said.

He leaned over her to get a better view of himself in the mirror behind her, but then he used the excuse to press a kiss to her hair, careful not to disturb the rose. "Perfect."

She reached down to unroll his left shirt cuff a bit, smoothing it into a clean line before folding it back up until it matched his right one better. "*Now* it's perfect," she said, and smiled. "Let me finish my own makeup and get my boots on and then I'll be ready to go."

CHAPTER

THIRTY-TWO

THE MAJORITY OF prom was handled by a DJ—not a member of the Silver Cuties this time, since they'd played a short set to start the night off, but someone else who understood the assignment to play all nostalgic songs of that era, especially ones that had been featured on the show or that were good to dance to.

Micah would've loved to dance with John, to enjoy the prom just like they'd discussed last night. But she was conscious that even in this area that had been turned into a makeshift backstage, they were still visible, and there were already people snapping not-so-stealthy pictures of the two of them in their outfits. She tried to sip her water, pretending she didn't notice, while John kept picking up one of the acoustics and strumming it before seeming to remember that he wouldn't be able to hear anything over the music anyway, and then setting it back down.

The sign that they were about to go on came when the techs came to grab the guitars and set them up on the stage, together with two stools and the microphones. Micah felt almost preternaturally calm, but she could tell that John was nervous. Finally she went over to him and gave him a brief hug from behind, pictures be damned.

"It'll be okay," she said. "It'll be great."

He reached up to touch her hand, a ghost of a touch as she'd already started to pull away. But then they got the signal that it was time to take the stage. He was supposed to enter first—as silly as it had seemed to her at times, she'd always been the last one onstage, because it inevitably built the anticipation and got the crowd to scream even louder. But she wanted to go together, and so she walked up with him, until she felt the heat of his hand against the bare skin of her lower back.

They took their seats, and Micah lifted the acoustic guitar where it had been set up next to her, settling the strap around her and grabbing the pick that had been stuck between the strings. *You Rock My World* this one said, and she glanced over at John just in time to see a smile pinch the corner of his mouth before he got set with his own guitar.

She'd thought maybe she would say something when they were ready to perform. Something more about how much this entire cruise had meant to her, about how proud she was of this song, about how glad she was that ElectricOh! had had the chance to be a part of something this special. But she'd already said most of that during their first concert, and she was conscious of being on a knife's edge, emotionally, and not wanting to risk getting too overcome to even get through the song.

So she settled for just looking out over the crowd, all the people wearing their costumes and their sparkling dresses and their tuxedos, some faces she'd started to recognize from seeing them around the ship or during their impromptu sing-along the night before. She even saw one of her bracelets on a woman's arm, and she smiled down at her.

The sky was dark and clear and beautiful, the stars out like they knew it was a special night. She couldn't see the water from where she was, but she felt very aware of it being out there, of existing in this suspended moment of sky and stars and ocean.

She looked at John, half expecting him to be taking it all in, too, but he was watching her. She leaned into her mic, her eyes still on him as she said, "This one's for you."

She strummed that first A minor chord, and she swore she gave herself goose bumps. But then she went from somehow outside the song to completely in it. Everything faded away—the crowd, the cruise, all of it, leaving only her and John.

Usually she would've sung most of the first part with her eyes squeezed shut, but she couldn't do that because she didn't trust herself not to lose her place on the guitar somehow. Instead she kept her eyes on John, and she thought maybe she'd watch his hands, tracking them to make sure she was keeping the rhythm of the song, changing chords when she was supposed to. But she didn't need to do that. For one thing, *she* was setting the rhythm of the song. He'd told her that a thousand times in practice. She could play, and he'd be right there with her. *If you speed it up or slow it down*, he said, *I'll be there. Just play through.*

For another thing, she preferred to look at his face, his warm brown eyes so distinct, ringed with the eyeliner, his tongue touching the corner of his mouth as he concentrated on the buildup to the first chorus. When he started singing, she suddenly became aware of the crowd again, the way she could *feel* their energy, like they knew this was something special and different.

She ended that first chorus with a high, wistful note that she would've never thought to add if not for him backing her up.

By the time they got to the bridge, she was barely even consciously thinking about playing the guitar anymore. It was just an extension of her hands, of her body, and she didn't feel like she could mess up anything more than she could mess up breathing. She was *very* conscious of the lyrics to the song, though, which she suddenly felt like she was singing for the first time. *I was dreaming while awake / Then fell asleep and can't remember / Things won't ever be the same / Are you gonna come over?*

The weird thing about writing songs is that they could be so personal to you in the moment, but then years went by and they no longer meant the same thing that they once had. You performed them over and over, for radio shows, tour dates, festivals, various filmed specials and showcases. She could sing something that had made her cry when she'd originally written it, that felt like ripping out her own heart and putting it on the page, and by the hundredth time she'd be thinking more about how hot the stage lights were or if that was a crackle in the left monitor. She'd be thinking about whether she'd been flat on that last chorus, if her mic pack was coming loose. She wouldn't necessarily be thinking about the *words*.

But this was the song she'd written with John. The song she'd written *about* John, when it came down to it. It was all about longing, wishing things could be different, dreaming of a future you didn't know was possible. She'd heard that in the music and so she'd responded with words, trying to express what she knew she could never act on.

And then the song was over, seemingly almost before it had even begun. She sang the last line, her voice low, a hitch in the note that was half on purpose and half pure emotion. John let the last chord ring out, giving her a smile so sweet that it made her chest physically ache.

"Thank you," he said into his mic. Then he stood up, setting his guitar down on the stool so he could turn to her, clapping the whole time. The entire crowd was cheering, and she lifted her own guitar off her so that she could stand, too. She could've taken a bow, or she could've turned to John and led her own round of applause for him.

But all she wanted to do was go to him—to touch him, to share this moment with him. So instead she wrapped her arms around him in the tightest hug, squeezing him until she felt his arms come up and wrap around her, too, his hands on her bare back. It felt so good to be in that warm embrace, and she could've stayed that way forever.

"We did it," he said into her ear.

"Did you have any doubt?"

But she didn't let him answer, because then she was kissing him, her hands at his cheeks, all her love and everything she'd ever wanted to say in the feeling of her mouth on his. She was only dimly aware of the reaction from the crowd as he lifted her slightly, her toes in her favorite platform boots almost leaving the stage.

"Whoa," she said.

"My thoughts exactly," he said, squeezing her one more time, giving her a kiss on the corner of her mouth. "Should we get off the stage?"

"I think contractually we're supposed to."

He grinned at her, taking her hand, not sparing another glance toward the crowd as they made their way down the steps.

Micah knew they were about to be stopped by a bunch of people—not just other cruisers or *Nightshifters* fans, but possibly photographers, press, their fellow bandmates, members of other bands—and she just didn't want to deal with any of them. She wanted to get John alone, where they could really talk, because suddenly she thought they had a lot to talk about.

CHAPTER
THIRTY-THREE

ORIGINALLY, JOHN HAD thought they'd hang out at the prom a little longer, find Steve and Frankie, enjoy the music. But Micah was a woman on a mission, and all he could do was follow her as they made their way up to the top deck of the ship. The weather was the most mild it had been on their trip, but it was still a little chilly, and he wished he'd thought to wear a suit jacket if for no other reason than to be able to offer it to Micah. She had to be cold in that dress.

She didn't seem like she even noticed the weather, though, as she turned to him once they'd found an isolated spot by the rail.

"Come to L.A.," she said. "You can stay with me, however long you want to. I don't want this cruise to be it for us."

He didn't want the cruise to be it for them, either. But he also couldn't help but fixate on her word choice. What did that mean—*stay* with her? Like she wanted him to move in? Like she thought of him as a guest, a friend crashing on her couch while they saw the sights?

"It would be fun," she said. "I've *missed* you, John, and I don't want to miss you anymore. And I know you have your own thing in Orlando, but it seems like you might be ready to make a change. Am I wrong? *This* could be your change."

He ran his hand through his hair, trying to even imagine it. All he'd ever wanted was to be with Micah. He'd always thought he'd take her in any capacity she'd give him. But he did have a life he'd built for himself, very carefully and very thoughtfully, and it might not be perfect but it was *his*. He was scared to leave that behind for something so uncertain, when he still didn't even know how Micah felt about him.

Micah was watching his face, something desperate around her eyes. "Say something," she said. "And I know you always think before you speak, but *don't* think, it makes me nervous when you think. Just say it."

"I want to make music with you," he said, because that was truly the first thing that came to his mind. He hadn't even fully realized it until he said the words aloud, but he knew immediately that they were the right ones.

"Is that what we're calling it?" she said, giving him a flirty smile as she reached out to touch his wrist.

"Don't do that," he said, his voice tight. "You know what I mean. I want to write songs together, and I think I want to actually try to put them out. I want to play shows with you again. Separate from anything to do with ElectricOh!. Something new."

She withdrew her hand, tucking her hair behind her ear. Her fingers brushed against the rose, which had started to droop a little, sliding down until it was hanging in her hair rather than pinned up into it.

"I think I'm done with that part of my life," Micah said. "But you know I'd support you in anything you wanted to do. L.A. would be a great place for you, actually, if you wanted to get back into the scene—"

"I don't care about the scene," John said. "I want to do this with *you*."

Something sparked in Micah's eyes, and she took a step back, crossing her arms over her chest. "So those are your terms," she said, then gave a little laugh, looking up at the sky. "This is exactly why mixing music stuff with relationship stuff never works. They get too tangled up in each other, and then you can't pull on any of the threads without it all coming undone."

"That's not fair." John knew she was referring back to Ryder, which—if she couldn't see the ways that this would *not* just be a repeat of that debacle, then there was no point in continuing to have this conversation. "I'm not trying to set terms with you, or rules, or whatever else. We've done the all-or-nothing thing before and I don't want that, because I don't want *nothing* with you. But I'm also all in, Micah. I do want all of it—the relationship stuff and the music stuff. If that's not what you want, then tell me that. I'll still be your friend because I'll always be your friend. I've never liked the phrase *more than friends* because your friendship is already a lot, it's the most precious thing in the world to me. And music has always been precious to us, I think you need it the same way that I do. So yeah, I do want more. I can't do this in-between, where we're friends with benefits, I can't live in the liminal state of this cruise ship forever. I want everything. What do you want?"

She just looked at him, and if it made *her* nervous when he thought before speaking, then this silence was absolutely crushing. He knew Micah cared about him. He knew she was attracted to him—god knows if nothing else had come out of this whole experience, it had proven to him that sexual tension had *never* been their problem. But either she wasn't capable of committing to him, or she just didn't want to.

She'd also started to shiver. He stepped closer to her, rubbing his hands down her bare, goose-fleshed arms.

"This is a lot to figure out on a cruise," he said. "When we're still under the influence of all those virgin piña coladas."

She laughed, leaning into him, her forehead resting on his chest. "I've been buzzing since that first sip of fruit punch."

"We don't have to have all the answers right now," he said. "Maybe we just go back to our real lives and see how things go."

"Ugh, our *real* lives," Micah said. "Do we have to?"

He stroked his finger down her spine, from the base of her neck all the way to the dip of her dress, until he felt her shiver again from the featherlight touch. "Not until tomorrow," he said. "We still have tonight."

She turned her head to kiss his throat, looping her arms around his neck until it was like they were slow-dancing, even though their bodies barely swayed. "Then I say we make the most of it."

THEY HAD TO separate the next morning to pack their stuff in their respective rooms, sign off on where some of their larger gear was being shipped back to. John saw the couple he'd gotten the masks from down in the disembarkation line, and he thanked them again, taking several pictures and getting their address so he could send them something from the band since they hadn't connected at prom.

He stood with his luggage, not wanting to leave until he'd had his chance to say his goodbyes, scrolling through the number of notifications on his phone that had stacked up in the time he'd been away from cell service. Mostly it was his housemates' group chat that had been popping off, and he saw a few choice messages—JOHN YOU ABSOLUTE FUCKING LEGEND!!!!!!! was one from Kiki that made him smile—before he slid his phone back in his pocket to deal with later. He really did miss his housemates, he realized, and was excited to see them again after these days away.

"Hey," Micah said from behind him, and he turned. He already missed *her*, even though there she was standing right in front of him. For a second he wanted to rewind back to the night before, wanted to just say, *Yes, I'll come to L.A., I'll stay with you for as long as you'll have me.* But he knew it wouldn't fix any of their problems. It would just delay the inevitable conversation, and he didn't want to engage in delay tactics anymore.

She had her silver suitcase and her bag, together with her guitar case, which he presumed was empty unless she'd used it to pack more of her clothes. Which, come to think of it . . .

"That's my shirt," he said.

She glanced down at her T-shirt, black with white jagged letters spelling out the band name FINAL REVELATIONS, before glancing back up to grin at him.

"I underpacked for this trip," she said. "And you seemed to have shirts to spare. I figured it was the least you could do for keeping my guitar so long."

"You should take it," he said, sliding the case off his back. He meant it—the guitar had been a gift for her, he'd always wanted her to have it—but he still expected her to turn it down. She had an expression on her face like she was about to. Then she reached out, grabbing onto one of the straps and hefting it on the opposite shoulder from her purse.

"If you think this means I'm going to whip your shirt off and give it back to you, I'm not."

He twisted his hand in the hem of that shirt, pulling her closer to him. He still couldn't believe that he could touch her that way, much less so publicly without worrying that someone would catch them out. He still felt dizzy with it, although some of that might be the sensation of standing on solid ground again after five days on the sea.

"Damn," he said. "That's too bad."

He wanted to say more to her—he had so much he almost didn't know where to begin—but then Steve and Frankie walked up, dragging their own luggage behind them.

"The gang's all here!" Steve shouted, leaning in to snap a quick selfie of the four of them together with his phone. "That was some performance last night, mate. Didn't know you had it in you."

"Yeah, I don't sing much," John said, deliberately misunderstanding him. He didn't really want to get into the kiss now.

"You sounded good," Frankie said. "You both did. Micah, that bridge—I got chills, for real."

"Thank you," Micah said. "And thank you all, for . . ." She seemed to be having trouble gathering her words, and John stroked his thumb along the warm skin of her waist where he'd left his hand. "Thank you for sticking up for me with Ryder. I know I'm the one you were angry at, I know I deserve it, but it meant a lot to me, you all having my back like that."

"That shit was a long time ago," Frankie said. "And Ryder was being a dick right now, in the present, in a way he just did not need to be. I'm sorry if we didn't have your back more when he was a dick to you in the past. I just didn't want to get involved in whatever that all was, but I never meant for you to think you were alone."

"He was bad vibes," Steve said. "But that punch was some *Street Fighter* shit. I'll remember that every day for the rest of my life."

He mimed like he was setting up some jabs into a right hook. Micah laughed, but John could also see her rub the knuckles of her right hand as if in memory, and he knew that she wasn't ready quite yet to treat everything as a joke. Maybe one day.

Something caught her attention, and she glanced over before looking back at the group. "My ride is here," she said. "To take me to the airport. So I guess . . ."

John felt panic rise into his throat. She couldn't be leaving already. She couldn't be leaving like *this*, when they didn't even have a private moment to themselves first. He watched her hug Frankie and Steve, saw her look at him uncertainly before he finally snapped out of it and set down his own luggage so he could grab the handle of her suitcase.

"I'll help you to the car," he said.

He spent an almost inordinate amount of time settling everything in the trunk of the car, waving away the driver as he worked to make sure the electric guitar was on top and nestled in enough not to slide all around during the trip. And then he closed the trunk, and there was nothing else to do but say goodbye.

She looked at him, and he could see that her eyes were a little shiny. And then she wrapped her arms around his neck and pulled him toward her in a hug. If he'd thought the one she'd given him onstage had been tight, this one was *tight*—it knocked the breath right out of him, but maybe that was all of it, everything about the last five days, not just the hug. It felt so good just to hold her, to have that full-body contact, and he wrapped her up, too, like he never wanted to let go.

"Johnny," she said into his ear. "Don't be a stranger."

He kissed her cheek, the corner of her mouth, which tasted a little salty, like maybe she'd started to cry. His mouth found hers then, and he kissed her with all the feeling of a last kiss, even though that couldn't be what this was. He refused to believe it.

"My number's the same," he said. "I never changed it."

She kissed him again, and then she climbed into the back of the car, and he shut the door behind her, giving her a wave. He was still watching it leave when his phone vibrated in his back pocket, and he pulled it out to see a new message from a 213 area code number.

M: Hi <3

He grinned before typing his response.

J: New phone who dis

The three bouncing dots appeared for only a second before her text came in.

M: You're such an asshole

He wondered if she'd still had his number programmed in her phone, or if she'd memorized it from all those times they'd talked. Even now, he could rattle off the phone number to her dad's house, had thought about calling it several times over the years just to see if the number still worked.

J: Sorry, autocorrect. I meant to type: hi <3

CHAPTER

THIRTY-FOUR

OVER THE NEXT several weeks, Micah texted John every day. She sent him pictures of stuff she saw on her walks—the reservoir, her favorite lemon tree, a typo on an ad printed on a street bench that made the slogan something really unfortunate. He'd sent her a picture of him with all his housemates, so she could know who they were, and sometimes he said stuff like Kiki said we're both clowns for our pineapple-on-pizza opinions or Elliot has been listening to So Much Promise and says there are a lot of bops. It always gave her a warm and fuzzy feeling, just to think that he was talking about her with his housemates, that she was able to be a part of his life even in some small way.

They also sent each other things in the actual mail. It started when Micah asked John for some music recommendations, and he'd mailed her a mix CD just like they'd made each other back in middle school, the tracks labeled on the shiny silver surface in his bold, familiar handwriting. He asked her to send him a CD to get him into Elvis, and what had begun as her just trying to figure out a way to even burn a CD anymore had somehow led to her spending hours narrowing it down to fifteen tracks, designing and printing a zine to go along with the CD, making a bespoke friendship bracelet she could slip into the package, **CHICKEN TENDER** spelled out in tiny beaded letters.

She'd been obsessively tracking the package since she sent it, so when he called one night just as she'd climbed into bed, she knew he would've hopefully had time to listen to the CD and read through the zine earlier that day.

"Hey," she said, a little breathless.

"Hey," he said. "Sorry—did I wake you?"

It was late for him—one o'clock in the morning—but relatively early for her. She'd been trying to regulate her sleep schedule a bit more, both because she liked being up more of the day when John would be, but also because she knew it was healthier for her.

She assured him that he hadn't, and they spent the next hour talking about Elvis and then veering off into other topics, karaoke song choices and the time one of his housemates had done an emotional rendition of "Blue Christmas" and whether ElectricOh! had never played in Louisville or if that was a fever dream. They'd talked on the phone before since the cruise— he'd call her when he was running errands, or she'd call after she'd woken up and was watering her plants. But they hadn't talked like this, late at night before bed, and she wondered if that had been on purpose. The sound of his voice, the low intimacy of it directly in her ear, did dangerous things to her.

"Do you still think about the cruise?" she asked at one point, where what she meant was *Do you ever think about being with me? Do you think about it as much as I do?*

"I think about all of it," he said. "I think about it every night."

"Just at night?"

She could hear him smile over the phone. "Sometimes in the morning."

"I—" She knew they were talking under something, over it, around it. They were tracking on multiple channels, and she wanted to turn certain ones up in the mix but she didn't know how, or maybe she was just incapable. "I really miss you."

John's long exhale was audible. "I miss you, too."

She swallowed, was trying to gather her courage to say more, to say whatever it was that had felt like a weight on her chest since she'd gotten back from the cruise, that wasn't going away no matter how many lighthearted text exchanges she had with John.

On the other end, she could hear rustling, like he was moving around, and when his voice came it sounded a little far away at first before landing close to her ear again. "It's late," he said. "I should probably get to bed."

"Oh yeah," she said. "Me, too."

"Good night, Micah."

After that conversation, she'd wanted to go to sleep, hadn't wanted to risk falling back into her old insomniac patterns. But she'd found it difficult to settle down, and so something had made her dig out a copy of *So Much Promise* she kept in a box under her bed. It wasn't like she couldn't have listened to the album any time she felt like it—it was available on streaming platforms, there were music videos on YouTube, there were no shortages of ways she could've revisited the album. She'd just never wanted to.

But now she put it on, sitting in the middle of her living room holding the Discman she'd bought just so she could listen to John's mix CDs, letting the music wash over her through her headphones. In a way, it didn't sound like her. She could almost appreciate it like it *had* been someone else, could better hear the places where the music was pretty good, actually. In another way, she could hear every bit of pain and sadness in her voice, melancholic artifacts in even the most upbeat, dance-y songs. Maybe that was why the album hadn't taken off, maybe it had been too strange. But she was proud of that aspect of the record now. It felt like the most honest part.

She fell asleep on her couch and woke up to black-and-white reruns playing on her TV, the Discman discarded on the floor next to her, popped open to show the CD inside. She didn't even bother to pick it up before going to her closet to retrieve the guitar case that John had given her when they'd left the cruise. It *smelled* like him, somehow, which didn't make any sense—it probably just smelled like wood and strings and guitar polish. He'd always taken exceptional care of his instruments. Truly, she was glad he'd had custody of this one as long as he had.

There were still a bunch of the suggestive guitar picks hidden away in one zippered pocket, and she smiled when she saw the one she pulled out. *Give Me a Lick.* She used it to strum down the strings, which were woefully out of tune.

She ended up getting so involved in what she was doing that she was jolted by a knock at the door. It was just past noon—well within her sanctioned hours with Mr. Li downstairs, and she'd been playing the guitar without an amp—so she didn't think it could be him. Then she remembered, and set the guitar down on the floor, wincing at the thud and buzz from the vibrating strings.

"Shit," she said. "Sorry, sorry, I'm coming."

She opened the door to see Tatiana Rivera standing on the other side of it, a pair of giant sunglasses on her face.

"I tried to text you," Tatiana said, holding up her phone. "We're still doing lunch, right?"

Sometimes Micah thought that her rediscovered closeness with John was the most surprising thing that had come out of the cruise, but then that didn't feel right. In many ways it didn't feel like a surprise at all. It felt almost fated, like of *course* that was why they'd been on the cruise in the first place, of course they were going to find their way back to each other.

In which case, maybe the most surprising outcome of the cruise was her newfound friendship with Tatiana Rivera. It had all started when Micah had reached out to her on social media, worried that she'd somehow been so distracted by her insecurities and jealousies on the cruise that she'd come off as rude. But Tatiana—true to form—couldn't have been kinder about the whole thing, and said she was hopeful that they could hang out before she had to leave for a film shoot next month. Since then, they'd gotten together a couple times, and Micah found that it was really nice, having a reason to get out of the apartment, sitting across from someone way more famous than she was in a public space where Micah could realize it didn't have to be that big a deal, actually, if people recognized them or came up to talk to them.

"Come in," Micah said. "I just need a couple minutes."

Tatiana seemed to take in the whole scene—the guitar lying in the middle of the floor, the stereo, the notebook of scribbled lyrics. "We can reschedule," she said.

Micah didn't want to do that when she knew Tatiana would be out of town for so long. But at the same time, she truly did feel like she was in the middle of something magical, and she was afraid that if she stepped away she'd lose it. "I can take a break," she said. "But would you mind if we just got something to eat here?"

They ordered burritos from Micah's favorite local place, and while they waited for the delivery to arrive Micah played Tatiana a tiny bit of the song she'd been working on, too shy to share any more of it. When Tatiana indicated toward the notebook, obviously asking for permission to take a peek, Micah pushed it toward her, chewing on her thumbnail while Tatiana read over the words.

"My handwriting's terrible," Micah said.

"It's fine," Tatiana said. "Your handwriting, I mean. The song is really good. Have you shown it to John yet?"

Micah was still debating whether she wanted to let John hear it at all. Of course she did—it was the entire reason she'd written it in the first place. But it had also been so long since she'd written any music, and the idea of sharing *this* felt almost painfully vulnerable. She was worried her lyrics were stupid and obvious. She worried they weren't obvious enough, when she had so much that she wanted to say.

"He told me he was in love with me," Micah said. "On the cruise. He told me that he'd loved me since we were kids."

Tatiana didn't look surprised. If anything, she looked . . . oddly *pleased*, like she'd had something to do with it. "And? What did you say?"

"I said . . ." Micah thought back to that moment between them. She'd thought about it a lot, in the weeks since. She thought about the intimacy of that darkness, the way she'd been extra conscious of the heat of John's body, the sound of his breath, every single nerve ending where he touched her. She thought about everything he'd said, how he seemed to see her in a way that she worried wasn't true, that she *wanted* to be true in the worst possible way. She thought about that overpowering, overwhelming orgasm—she could still get herself close thinking about it, even now. She thought about how, afterward, she'd broken down and cried, too overcome by emotion to do anything else.

"Nothing," Micah said finally. "He told me he loved me and I said . . . nothing."

"Why?" Tatiana asked. She said it like the most obvious answer—*because I don't love him back*—was off the table, and weirdly Micah appreciated that. It was off the table, although she could of course see how John had no reason to know that, how much she'd hurt him by not being able to express how she felt.

"I think I've just always been so afraid of failure," Micah said. "In the past, when I've put myself out there . . . every time, I fuck it up somehow."

Tatiana looked down at the notebook still in her hand. It was basically what the song was about.

"You're not afraid of failure," Tatiana said. "You're afraid of success."

That didn't make any sense. When Micah thought back to the biggest accomplishments in her life—the record deal, when "If Only" had gone platinum, that final performance on the cruise—she felt good about them. Sure, that feeling got complicated, even warped sometimes, but she still chased it.

"Maybe I need some exposure therapy," she joked. "Once I'm successful at something again, then I'll see how I feel."

Tatiana gave her a look like *You're making my point for me.*

"You're not afraid of failure because you expect it. If anything, it makes you feel like the universe is working as it's supposed to. The success part scares you because you're always waiting for the other shoe to drop. You're so convinced that it *will* drop that you don't want to allow yourself to even go for it, because then you think you're setting yourself up for inevitable disappointment. You play games of *what if what if what if*, but like, what if everything was just . . . good. What if it did actually work out. What if you allowed yourself to accept that John loves you, what if you allowed yourself to love him back."

Micah sat back against her couch, legitimately struck completely silent by Tatiana's speech.

"I've been in a *lot* of therapy, if you couldn't tell," Tatiana said. "And what are friends for if not to swap around each other's therapeutic insights until we can cobble together something close to comprehensive mental health care."

Micah laughed. "I'm in therapy, too, believe it or not. But yeah, my guy is . . . not very good, because you just did more for me in two minutes than he ever has. He's really fixated on my dreams. He always makes me describe my dreams to him."

"I can refer you to my person, if you want," Tatiana said.

Micah picked up her guitar, idly strumming a few chords while she thought about that. She was starting to feel in her gut like she wouldn't be sticking around L.A. long enough to make switching therapists worth it. "Thank you," she said, meaning for the offer but for everything else, too. "I'll let you know."

THIRTY-FIVE

J: YOU READY?

John had started texting Micah when his house was all sitting down to watch their favorite dating show, because sometimes she cued up the episode at the same time and they texted back and forth afterward to discuss. John tried really hard to stay off his phone during the episode itself, not wanting to be rude, but sometimes he couldn't help himself. Like now, when his phone lit up with a text.

> M: This guy's lost every job he's ever had but it's
> not his fault

John grinned, picking up his phone to send a stealth text.

> J: His favorite band is The Used

This was one of the games they liked to play—speculating

about a contestant's favorite band, the only rule being that you couldn't say Nickelback because the joke had been done to death.

> M: You fucking love The Used, don't even try to front

> J: A band can be beloved and still included in the game. Last week you said that guy with the bowlcut's favorite band was The Beatles, and they're the most popular band in the world.

> M: The point was that bowlcut would be the type of person to SAY The Beatles because he doesn't know any other bands—it's like saying The Great Gatsby is your favorite book

> J: The Great Gatsby is a banger. I'm all about that green light.

> M: I can't talk to you when you're like this

> J: You love it <3

"John!" Kiki said. "Do we need to have a basket that everyone puts their phones in during family time?"

"Sorry," John said, sliding his away from him on the couch. "I'm paying attention, I promise."

He loved being in more regular contact with Micah again. It felt *right*, having her there in his phone, where he could text her about his day or ask her about hers. It felt so good to have her friendship back in his life. He still thought about that possibility of something more than friendship, of course he did. He was pretty sure Micah did, too. She'd made him a zine to go along with a mix CD that was practically a love letter; there'd been a moment on a phone call late one night where he'd been sure she was going to tell him she loved him. But he also had to enjoy what they had without wanting it to be something else or he'd go out of his mind. He had to meet her where she was. Micah didn't seem ready to be serious about him in that way, and he was incapable of being anything *but* serious about her in that way.

The episode ended and everyone split off into their separate activities—Elliot to go work on an article they had due by midnight, Kiki out to the gas station to pick up some drinks, Asa to his and Lauren's room to log into his crisis line shift. Everyone except John and Lauren, who was curled up on the couch with her accounting textbooks out, studying for some exam she had coming up.

"Can I ask you something?" John asked.

"Sure," Lauren said, putting her pencil in the middle of her textbook to save her place before shutting the cover.

He'd had the sudden thought that, of all people, maybe Lauren would be able to give him some insight on Micah. He hadn't known Lauren very well when she and Asa started dating, but he'd known she kept a lot to herself and could be hard to read. It had really pushed Asa's buttons, how hard she was to read. But somehow Asa had cracked through those barriers she put up, and John just wondered *how* he'd been able to do that.

"This is personal," John said. "You don't have to answer."

She smiled a little, which was just more evidence of how much had changed since he'd first met her. If he'd said that to her in the beginning, she would've looked alarmed.

"Okay," she said. "What is it?"

"When Asa told you that he loved you," John said. "What made you say it back? Did you say it right away, or . . . you know what. No, never mind. This is stupid."

"I said it first, believe it or not." Lauren laughed when she saw the expression on John's face. "I know, I was surprised, too. Asa was definitely surprised. It just kind of came out. But in retrospect, I think . . . I knew how he felt, you know? He'd shown me that he cared about me in a lot of ways, so it felt safe enough for me to say those words. Not that I knew that at the time—it was all terrifying then."

John wondered if he was getting hung up on words, if he *was* rushing Micah into something before she was ready, just like he'd always said he wasn't trying to do. He'd just never felt *sure* of anything growing up, and he wanted to feel sure about her. Not only that she cared about him, although that was a big part of it, but also that there wouldn't be anything holding them back from being their whole selves in a relationship. He needed music to feel complete, and the Micah he'd always known had been the same way. But maybe that wasn't true anymore, or maybe he just had to let go of being sure about anything. Right now, the only thing he was sure of was that the most important relationship of his life was confined to a phone, and he hadn't felt whole since stepping off that cruise ship.

"Did that help?" Lauren asked.

"Yeah," he said. "I think it did."

———

EVER SINCE HE and Micah had started up a regular correspondence, he always looked forward to the mail arriving. So when Elliot brought in a stack that included a small bubble-wrapped package on the top, John was right there to receive it.

"This one's not poster-shaped," Elliot said. "But I'm open to other merch."

Ever since Elliot had gotten low-key obsessed with *So Much Promise*, he'd been waiting for a signed copy that Micah had promised to send. She was also going to dig up other artifacts from her time as a pop singer for Elliot, including a poster from a show she'd done with Carly Rae Jepsen that she said she could see if Carly would sign.

"Carly's touring in Japan right now," John said. "Which you know, because you keep sending me links to watch that I can't even open."

"Your commitment to not having a single social media account waffles between Thoreau-level shit and Kaczynski-level shit every day."

"Meanwhile he doesn't even know how much social media *loves* him right now," Kiki put in from her spot on the couch. "I've seen so many videos of that kiss on the stage it's fucked up all my algorithms and now I keep getting ads for some nostalgic emo music festival in Las Vegas."

John had to admit he'd watched *that* link. He'd even had Kiki show him a way he could save the video on his phone. It embarrassed him even as it thrilled him a little.

"It'll die down," he said. "So we kissed after an emotional performance. We've never been shipped like that."

John could practically hear the record scratch as Elliot and Kiki both looked at him. Even from the kitchen, where Asa and Lauren were cooking dinner, John heard the sound of a lid being slammed down on a pot.

"What did he say?" Asa yelled from the kitchen.

"He said that he and Micah have never been shipped!" Kiki called back, her voice filled with glee, like she knew she was about to start some shit. Kiki loved nothing more than starting some shit.

"Dude," Asa said, leaning out from the kitchen doorway, a wooden spoon still in his hand. "I don't even know what you're talking about. We were able to follow everything on that cruise in real time and let me tell you, the internet was screaming crying throwing up. There's footage of you guys playing together, where she touched your hair?"

Okay, he'd seen that video, too. He'd had to watch the entire live performance—just to see how it had gone. And save it to his phone, in case he needed to revisit how it had gone.

"The beach pictures," Lauren put in.

"Oh my god, yes," Asa said. "You looked cozy as hell when you were sunscreening each other. And there are whole comment threads on the fight, where you and Ryder threw down over her."

"That wasn't how it went," John said, for the hundredth time. Asa had *loved* hearing about the fight.

"The shuffleboard tournament, the casino, the sing-along," Asa said, listing them on his fingers. "I'm just saying, you were not subtle. You were shipped all over the place."

"Any other places?" John asked. "Or were those the only ones?"

Kiki was the one who clocked that he'd asked the question with a bit of genuine trepidation, and from the way she cackled, he knew he'd never live it down.

"The point is," he said, wanting to change the conversation, "before the cruise. I was never the one anyone wanted for her. Which was fine—I mean, obviously it doesn't matter what anyone else thinks. But I'm just saying that people will move on."

Elliot frowned, pulling up their phone and typing a few things in. "Okay, obviously I always tried to respect your cone of silence around the band," they said. "But unlike you I am *terminally* online. I am also dedicated to the truth and actually no, that's not the truth. The Tumblr pages alone, your mind would boggle. Some people tried to get *Jicah* to take off, but that's a terrible name so it never caught on. There are forums where people identify themselves in their signature lines as MJs or MRs—or actually I think you might pronounce that one like *misters*, I've never heard it aloud before—and you'd be surprised how many MJs there are. They also tend to have better internet literacy, which. Feels appropriate."

Elliot moved as if to hand their phone to John, but John didn't take it. It did shift something, knowing that he'd been thought of as a viable option for Micah all along. It shouldn't, maybe, but it did. It was a tiny piece of validation he'd never even known he needed until he got it, that he hadn't always played a secondary role in the band or in her life.

But he didn't need to see any of it. At the end of the day, it didn't *change* anything. His and Micah's relationship was still just about him and her, and no one else.

John looked down at the package in his hand, Micah's return address written in her distinctive handwriting, starting out neat and then devolving into something spiky and a little rushed by the end. "She asked me to come to L.A.," he said. He'd never told his housemates that, after the cruise, and he didn't know why. He was afraid they'd be upset, tell him all the reasons why he couldn't leave. He was afraid they'd encourage him to go.

"Ah." Asa looked suddenly very serious, which always meant something because Asa was usually one of the most unserious people John knew. "You didn't not do it because of us, did you?"

"No," John said. "Well, maybe a little. This is my home."

They were his home. Day to day, it was easy to focus on all the trivial stuff, the shows they watched together or the chores they assigned and then reassigned when people complained. But if John actually let himself think about it, he got emotional about how hard he'd worked to find this kind of place, how much he'd needed it. The idea of leaving it behind did scare him, even if it was for a future he'd always wanted.

"Sometimes home is just a place to land for a bit, until you find something else," Asa said. "Lauren and I have been saving up to move out around when we get married. Elliot still talks about moving back to Jacksonville."

"My family's there," Elliot said. "That's the only reason."

"I'll be here," Kiki said. "Because nothing about my life will ever change. But yes, Asa's point stands. You should go to L.A. and be with Micah, if that's what you want."

"This house was never meant to hold you back," Asa said. "You just have to promise to come home for Christmas, that's all I ask."

John swallowed past the lump in his throat. "Of course I would."

"And bring Micah," Lauren said.

"See if Micah can bring Carly," Elliot said. "I'm just kidding, obviously. Unless . . ."

John smiled, saluting all of them with the package in his hand. "I'll see what I can do."

He shut himself in his room to open it up, because past experience had taught him that it was always better to open Micah's packages in private. Once she'd sent him a copy of her *Playboy* issue, a Post-it stuck to the front that said *Don't just read the articles!* She sent him Polaroids, too, nothing that salacious but still pictures that he liked to look at when he was all by himself and could study for as long as he wanted, taking in every detail of what she was wearing, what part of her apartment she seemed to be in, the expression on her face.

This time it was another CD, which made him smile because he loved when she sent him music to listen to. There was no zine to accompany this one, just a folded piece of notebook paper stuck in the front as a makeshift album cover, a few words written on it in black Sharpie. **EP = Extended Play (not Elvis Presley).** John inserted the CD into his old laptop and put his headphones on, cueing up the first track. He noticed that there was more writing on the inside of the folded paper, and so he opened it up to read.

TRACK LISTING:
1. heart x 3
2. fruit punch
3. only if

That was it—no further explanation or message. But he knew what it was before he heard the first notes of the first song, which had him holding his breath. Even before her vocals came in, he recognized the tone of his guitar—*her* guitar. The melody was simple but catchy, with a breathless chorus that ended with her laughing a little bit, clearly a mistake that he was glad she'd kept.

The second song was about the cruise, somehow managing to capture the vibe of a situation where anything could happen, from a spilled drink to a right hook. She'd even added electronic drums, which impressed him. There'd been a lot of work in crafting these songs, writing them and recording all the parts, either dusting off old equipment she had or sourcing new stuff.

But it was the third track that really put John's heart in his throat. It was the most stripped-down of all of them, just piano and her voice. He only got a couple of lines in before he had to pause, take a couple deep breaths, and then start the song over again. Her vocals were low, a little dreamy around the edges, but once again he was struck by just how much like *herself* she sounded when she sang. That might seem like an obvious thing to say, but it was something in her voice he'd always admired— the fact that the Micah you got on the phone and the Micah you got on a record felt like the same person. He'd never felt any distance from her when she sang, and now it felt like she could be sitting on his bed, performing this right in front of him.

> *I've been trying, trying to tell you*
> *Just not in so many words*
> *If only I*
> *Could close my eyes*
> *And show you everywhere it hurts*

This ache in my bones feels like touching you
This heartbeat in my chest will let me try for you
I'll try for you
I'll try for you
I'll try for you

When all I wanted was a dream
Only if they made it true
It was a lie
It's fucking mine
And you gave it to me new

You know you've always been my best and oldest
    friend
So please say that we can, let us start again
I'll start again
I'll start again
I'll start again

It was unusual for Micah's lyrics to be this direct, for you to even fully know who or what she was singing about. There had always been lines, here and there, that had snagged at him, like a jagged nail sticking out of a doorframe. *Are you gonna come over?* That was what she'd asked him almost every day, had made him wonder if there weren't parts of "If Only" that were about *him*. But then there would be other parts that felt like maybe she wasn't talking about a person at all, but the feeling of being on that back porch, writing a song for an album that could change their lives in ways they didn't even know yet. Then she'd bring the lyrics back around again with a bridge that was big and romantic, that filled your chest with air and then took it all away, and he'd be left wondering again, *Who is this song about?*

The bridge for this one sounded like it had been recorded as a voice note on her phone, the vocals mixed a little lower so he had to press his headphones to his ears to make sure he was catching every word before she came back in at full volume for the last chorus.

> *Well, maybe you still can't hear me*
> *Maybe I'm talking in code*
> *Maybe I'm letting some notes drop*
> *Under the noise on the phone*
> *Maybe I know that my signals*
> *Have always been smoke*
> *Maybe you'll think that I'm brave*
> *Until you get me alone*
>
> *But I'm not afraid of the past or present, oooh*
> *The future that I see, baby, it's all you*
> *I do love you*
> *I do love you*
> *I do love you*
>
> *I do*
> *I love you, too*
> *I do*

For a minute John just sat with the silence after the music had finished. He knew he'd end up listening to it a hundred times, but for now he just wanted to let it take root inside him. He thought back to that first time she'd talked to him in homeroom, the times they'd sprawled out on her bed listening to music and talking about everything and nothing at all, performing with her with ElectricOh!, seeing her again after so long at that first meeting for the cruise, all the moments they'd shared on the cruise itself. He thought back to the way she'd cried, that night he'd told her he loved her, and he thought maybe he understood it better. It *was* a lot, this feeling. He leaned back in his chair, took a deep breath, and pressed play again.

CHAPTER
THIRTY-SIX

MICAH PULLED HER car into the first street parking spot she found near her apartment, but she didn't immediately get out. She pulled out her phone, checking for a text message like she'd compulsively been doing for the past couple hours, but there was still nothing. It wasn't like John to go half a day without texting her back, but he was probably just busy.

The last message from him had come at an ungodly hour of the morning his time, which meant that she'd been asleep. He'd asked what she had going on that day, and she'd told him the boring answer—cleaning her apartment, grocery shopping—and then asked what his plans were. That had been six hours ago, and he'd never responded.

It had only been a week since she'd sent him her EP, and they'd had a really good conversation afterward. He'd told her how much it had meant to him and had said very kind things about her songs, which she still felt weird and prickly even talking about, although it was getting easier. She was gratified that he seemed to notice all the subtle details in the production she'd tucked in there just for him, that he was obviously still listening to the songs and thinking about them when he'd text questions about the choices she'd made. Music was always one language she'd shared with John, and it felt good to have that back.

But she knew there was more they still needed to discuss, including the fact that even her saying she was "cleaning" her apartment was a little disingenuous. She just didn't want to jinx anything before it was final, wanted to get a sense of the time-line before she brought her idea to John.

Micah must've had John so much on her mind that she was seeing things, because as she walked up to her apartment with her groceries she could've sworn she saw him, talking to Mr. Li downstairs. There was his distinctive curly dark hair, a bit of scruff on his chin, the muscles of his back moving under his black T-shirt as he gestured toward her apartment.

"The one with the hair," he was saying, bringing his hands up to his own as if to demonstrate. And that was what really did it—the sound of his voice, so dear and familiar, so much of a *relief*, like she'd been waiting to hear it for a hundred years.

"John?" she said, setting her groceries down on the side-walk. "How did you—"

She wanted to go to him, wanted to fly at him and wrap her arms around him so hard she knocked him over, but she felt rooted to the spot.

Luckily, he seemed to have no such issue, and he said some-thing else to Mr. Li that she couldn't hear before he headed to-ward her, stopping when they were toe-to-toe on the sidewalk.

"I took a flight from Orlando," he said. "With a connection in Phoenix."

She laughed, the sound bubbling out of her almost hysteri-
cally. Obviously she didn't mean literally *how*—she knew how
air travel worked. She just couldn't believe he was here, like this,
standing in front of her.

"I was in the mood to be a bit presumptuous," he said. "Like
I didn't bother booking a hotel, so I was hoping your offer to
stay with you was still open."

"Yes," Micah said, hiccuping a little. She hadn't known she
was crying until John's hands came up to her face, wiping at the
dampness on her cheeks. "Yes, of course. For how long?"

"How long will you have me?"

"Forever," she said, and then she did wrap her arms around
him, her hands clenching at his back, his shoulders, any part of
him she could touch. "I love you, John. God, I love you so
much, and I'm sorry I couldn't see it for so many years, I'm
sorry I couldn't *say* it—"

He leaned back to look at her, his hands on her face again,
holding her so gently she thought she might really lose it.

"I realized I knew you did," he said. "Even before your song,
although that was the biggest gift. I've always felt your love, Micah, in every form it's taken. I don't take it for granted."

She appreciated that, but she was still going to get all the
words out, because she'd thought about them so much in the
last couple weeks and she wanted to make sure she actually said
them. "I think when things seem too easy, I don't trust them.
Even our song—'If Only'—for years I've felt like it was *too* easy.
Do you know what I mean? The way it came together, the way
it blew up like it did. I didn't feel like I deserved it, I didn't feel
like I'd *earned* it."

John started to say something, probably to assure her that of course she'd earned it, to remind her of how hard they'd worked at every part of their early career. But she was worried she was going off track already, and she didn't want to get any further derailed.

"When you told me you loved me, it just seemed like . . . fuck, it can't be this *easy*, can it? There has to be some catch, some pitfall that I'm just not seeing. Maybe *I'm* the pitfall. It can't be as easy as just . . . being with you."

"Micah," John said, giving her a crooked smile. "You have to know that, when it comes to you, I'm incredibly easy."

It was obviously meant as a joke, something lighthearted, but she shook her head because that was exactly what she wanted him to see. "That's the thing," she said. "My whole life, everything has felt like . . . I don't know. A closed fist. Like I'm trying to hold on so tight, like I'm on the defensive, ready to throw a punch. But *you*, you've always made me feel like I can just . . . let go. Uncurl my fingers. Open up my hand. Does any of this make sense?"

His eyes were a little shiny, and he had to swallow before answering when it was clear she was waiting for him to. "It makes sense."

"You're the best person I know," she said. "You're kind and thoughtful and funny and warm and honest, you're a great friend, you're so talented—I love every part of you, John, and I *want* every part of you that you'll give me."

He raised his eyebrows. "Especially my—"

She reached up to tickle his neck right under his ear, where she knew she could get him to squirm. "The twenty-four hour rule is still in place," she said. "And I *really* want to take you upstairs and have my way with you, so please don't ruin it."

"I won't," he said, still laughing. "I'll be good. Fuck, I just really love you, Micah. I have for so long."

She pressed a kiss to the corner of his mouth. "Then it's a good thing you're here," she said. "Because I really fucking love you, and I plan on loving you for a very long time."

"Speaking of a long time," John said, gesturing down to the grocery bags at her feet. "Is that ice cream? We should put it away before it melts."

She liked the way he already said that—*we*. He ended up grabbing his luggage while she handled the groceries, and she led him up the steps to her apartment, balancing one of the bags against her leg while she dug through her purse.

"Oh, one more thing," she said as she finally got her key out and inserted it into the lock. "I should probably warn you—"

When she pushed the door open, it was to reveal the disarray she'd left her living room in, piles of stuff everywhere, stacks of boxes in one corner. She still had her couch and TV, but she'd already given away her dining table and chairs, so there was a conspicuously empty space where they used to be.

He set his luggage down, seeming to take it all in. "You're moving?"

"I fell for a guy who lived across the country," she said. "California seemed too far away."

John ran a hand over his face, giving a little laugh. "I guess this is what we get for both wanting to surprise each other, huh? A real 'Gift of the Magi' situation."

"Don't even bring that up," Micah said. "Why did Mrs. Allen always assign the *most* traumatizing stuff?"

"She was an emotional sadist," John said, but he already sounded distracted, looking around at the remnants of her life from the past decade. There was a shelf filled with records, a picture of her and Hailey propped on top of it. She'd painted the walls a warm pink, and she had a row of her most sun-needy plants lined up on the south-facing windowsill. She'd spent so long thinking of this apartment as some kind of tower room, where she could isolate from the outside world, that she sometimes forgot that it had also been a haven. It had been what she'd needed it to be, a safe space that was hers alone. She was proud of the home she'd made.

John reached down to pick up the grocery bags at her feet and took them into the kitchen, where he started unpacking everything on the stovetop.

"So when do you have to be out?"

"End of the month," she said, automatically grabbing each item to put it away where it belonged. "Mr. Li actually bought the apartment for his son and his family. They just had their first baby, so Mr. Li will get to see his grandkid every day. I know he's really excited about it."

She glanced over to give him a sideways smile, but he'd moved to stand in front of the fridge, still holding the pint of ice cream in his hand like he'd already forgotten why he was there. He was looking at the picture of them she'd stuck to the front of the fridge with a magnet, and he touched his finger to where her teen self sat cross-legged in the grass, then to his own laughing face.

"I wonder what we were talking about," he said.

"What were we *ever* talking about," she said, reaching around him to grab two spoons out of the drawer, then taking the ice cream from his hand. "Probably music."

"Always music," he said. "Speaking of which, I had an idea for that first track on your EP—a way we could get a little cheeky with some pop production stuff. If you were open to it. Obviously it's your song."

She opened the ice cream and handed him a spoon, leaning back against the counter as she took her first bite. "I intended them to be *our* songs," she said. "And I would love to work with you on them, and write more together. Once we, you know, figure out where we're going to live. Is your room back in Orlando still available?"

John dipped his own spoon into the ice cream, which was the perfect level of softness to let him easily scoop a generous amount. "I'm pretty sure Asa was measuring it to put a drafting table in there by the time I was at the airport."

"Well, I wouldn't have just invited myself into that situation anyway," Micah said. "I'd always intended to get my own place. We can still do that in Orlando, or stay in L.A. if you'd rather. What do you think?"

But John just pressed his spoon to her lower lip, leaving a dab of ice cream there. "Oh," he said. "You have a little—here, let me get it."

He touched his warm tongue to the cold spot on her mouth, licking the ice cream off her.

"There," he said. "That's better."

She rolled her eyes, although she was smiling. "Now that that's settled, we should—"

John pressed his spoon to her lip again, leaving even more ice cream smeared there. "You just can't seem to get it in your mouth, huh?" he said. "Don't worry, I've got you."

He started kissing her, but she was too busy laughing, her open mouth against his. "John," she said in between kisses. "I'm trying to be serious here."

He took the pint out of her hands, setting it next to them on the counter. With his arms bracketed around her, he leaned in, his gaze dropping to her mouth before lifting again to her eyes. "I'm always serious," he said.

Of course she'd seen John's goofy side, she *loved* seeing that side—but she knew that he typically had been the serious one, when they were kids and then later in the band. He was steady and strong and true, and that was what she saw in his eyes now when he looked at her.

"What are we going to do?" she whispered. She hated to think she'd already messed something up in their brand-new relationship, created a stressful situation with their living arrangements.

John nudged his nose against her cheek, pressing a kiss to her temple that she worried gave him more a mouthful of hair than anything else, but he didn't seem to mind. "Whatever we want, Micah," he said. "We'll do whatever we want."

EPILOGUE

Winter

"**HEAR ME OUT**," Micah said, coming down the stairs and pausing for dramatic effect. "A cruise to the Bahamas actually sounds *perfect* right now."

John leaned back in his chair, pushing the headphones that had already been off one ear down his neck. "You explicitly said if you ever went on another cruise again, it would be too soon."

"That was the first night," she said, dropping into the chair next to him. "You can't hold anything I said the first night against me. How are *you* handling this winter thing so much better than I am, Florida boy?"

John laughed, taking her bare feet in his lap and rubbing them until she could feel the warmth start to tingle back into her toes.

"For one thing," he said, "I'm wearing socks, which I would highly recommend."

"Mmm. It's too bad, because I love your feet."

They'd enjoyed her L.A. apartment in the limited time they'd had it, hanging out and listening to records and having sex and finishing packing up all her stuff. And then they'd led a somewhat nomadic existence for a while, traveling around and spending a couple weeks back in Orlando with John's housemates. He wasn't wrong that Asa had already moved some art supplies into his old room, but the bed was still there and it wasn't a bad place to crash. Micah had felt so shy about meeting everyone, knowing how important they were to John. But they couldn't have been more welcoming, and she quickly felt like part of the group.

They'd discussed going back to L.A. or staying in Orlando, and they'd even discussed moving somewhere else entirely, but in the end, it had seemed inevitable that they'd find their way back to Ohio. Micah wanted to be closer to her family, and John joked that it wouldn't hurt to be closer to a reliable, hard-hitting drummer. They'd bought a house only twenty minutes away from Steve and were renovating the basement to be a recording studio and rehearsal space.

Now John was sitting in front of the monitors they'd set up for playback, leaning forward as he adjusted something on one of the scratch tracks he had up on the computer. She still had her feet in his lap, close enough that she could look over his shoulder at whatever he was doing. He'd unplugged his head-phones and taken them off so that the music played in the room for both of them to hear.

"Isolate that one," she said. "The backing vocal."

He muted the other tracks until the only one still playing through the monitors was the harmonies she'd recorded a couple days ago.

"That note isn't right," she said. "I'm flat."

"It's your timbre," he said, scrubbing back to play it again. "I think you're on pitch, actually, it just *sounds* off."

"Well, if it sounds off, then it's off."

"Not necessarily," he said, leaning forward like he was suddenly excited by something. "It adds a little depth to it. Hear that?"

He'd added back in her lead vocal, playing them together until she could hear the way it *was* more interesting, actually, for that subtle feeling of something being a little strange. John had such a good ear for those kinds of things, and she felt like she got better at appreciating them, too, the more time she spent listening to him talk. She loved the way his eyes lit up when she really *nailed* a take, when she played him something new on the piano, when they finalized the arrangement of a song. They had more than enough demo tracks for a full album and were starting to record parts for final versions. Whatever they'd end up doing with them still remained to be seen.

"Fine," she said. "We'll call it an innovative new sound instead of me being flat as shit. I guess I should be happy to have a complete take—that day felt like all I was good for was fucking up."

"Hey," John said, squeezing her foot. "Don't talk about my wife that way."

That had been their most impulsive move, although it also felt like the most deliberate thing they could've done. "Hey," John had said one morning while they were waiting for their café order. "Do you realize that today is the twentieth anniversary of when we first met?" Micah's tea was still hot by the time they'd come up with the idea and booked a quick weekend trip to Vegas. They'd found a twenty-four-hour wedding chapel that boasted the Strip's best Elvis impersonator, and were married before the clock struck midnight. Micah didn't know if the middle-aged man wearing a crooked wig and a too-tight white jumpsuit was the *best*, but then he'd crooned a pretty decent "Can't Help Falling in Love" while Micah and John slow-danced under a ceiling dotted with twinkle light stars and she'd thought it was all perfect, actually.

She still got a thrill, seeing the ring around John's finger when his hands were on her like this, when he was playing guitar, when they were at the sink doing dishes together, when he reached for her first thing in the morning when they woke up. She couldn't believe he was hers, that she got to live this life.

She rubbed her foot in his lap, gratified when she felt him getting hard beneath her.

"Steve's going to be here in fifteen minutes," John said. Their old bandmate had agreed to record drums on their songs—he'd been charmingly excited about it, had said a lot about how good it was to have a music *scene* again, as though two people could possibly be a scene.

"I can be quick," she said.

He'd gotten up from his chair to lean against hers, his hands braced against the arms of the chair as she tilted her chin up for a kiss.

"I know you can," he said, kissing down her jaw. "And it certainly would be one way to get you warm . . ."

"See," she said. "These are healthy choices. Don't you want to make healthy choices, John?"

But just as she'd started to pull him down onto her, they

heard the doorbell from upstairs, followed by Steve's distinctive shave-and-a-haircut knock.

"Fuck," John said.

"Why does he use the doorbell *and* knock?" Micah said. "I never get it."

"No idea," John said. "For a drummer, he also has the worst fucking timing. But we can't just leave him out in the cold."

She wrapped her hand around the back of his neck for one more kiss, then pushed at his chest. "Go," she said. "We survived all those years of will-they-won't-they sexual tension, I suppose an extra few hours aren't going to kill us."

"Says you," John said, but he pressed a kiss to the top of her head. And then he went to answer the door.

LINER NOTES

This book was me telling myself a lot of things about art and creativity and bravery and joy that I really needed to hear. I won't belabor them here, since I put them all into the 300+ pages preceding this—with the exception of the meaning behind Micah's *iteration* tattoo, which felt right to leave out of the book itself but which she'll tell you one day. Also, John does want you to know that, canonically, *his* favorite song off Saves the Day's *Under the Boards* is "Kaleidoscope."

As always, there are so many people who helped take a draft document and turn it into the book you're holding in your hands, and in particular I would like to thank Laura Bradford, Kristine Swartz, Mary Baker, Kalie Barnes-Young, Kristin Cipolla, Nick Martorelli, Christine Legon, Alison Cnockaert, Jennifer Lynes, Hannah Andrade, Taryn Fagerness, Colleen Reinhart, and Jenifer Prince.

Thank you to my friends and family. Thank you to readers, especially ones who've reached out since *With Love, from Cold World* to ask if we'd ever get John's story. (Here it is!!!) And thank you, most of all, to anyone who creates something new where there was nothing before, and puts it out in the world. There's such power in that, no matter what you end up doing with it or what ends up happening with it. Promise me you'll let yourself feel that.

Keep reading for a preview of Alicia Thompson's

WITH LOVE, FROM COLD WORLD

CHAPTER

ONE

LAUREN FOX HAD the most boring job at the coolest place. Literally, the coolest—it said it on the website and everything. If you felt the sudden urge to build a snowman or ice skate in Central Florida, Cold World was the place to do it. Lauren was Cold World's bookkeeper, meaning that she was mostly holed up in her office, which was kept just as frigid as the rest of the place, reconciling bank records and paying vendor invoices and making sure the Zamboni didn't get repossessed.

She loved her job, though. There was something so satisfying about entering numbers into spreadsheets, sorting the data into different permutations, and keeping her filing cabinet like a finely manicured garden of color-coded folders. And there was something just a little magic about stepping into a blast of winter every Monday through Friday, no matter how humid and gross the Florida air was outside.

Like today, the first day of December, clocking in at a muggy eighty-three degrees. Lauren had dressed in her usual uniform of skirt, tights, button-up, and cardigan, holding her arms slightly away from her body in hopes of staving off the sweat until she could reach the relief of a central air-conditioning system that set Cold World back four figures a month in the dead of summer.

It hit her in a wave as she walked through the front door, the air frigid with a slight whiff of cinnamon. They'd been decorating for Christmas since before Thanksgiving, because it was obviously their biggest holiday. The front ticket counter was draped with garlands, and giant ornaments hung from the ceiling. Life-sized reindeer statues, spray-painted with glittery silver and gold, stood watch in one corner, and the finishing touches had almost been put on the twelve-foot tree they put out in front of the gift shop every year.

The converted warehouse building opened up to the right of the ticket counter, holding the Snow Globe, an enclosed area kept even colder with real, actual snow on the ground. (It was a little icier than people expected, and not the *best* for snow angels, but hey, it felt miraculous when you could drive an hour away and be at the beach.) Then there was the small ice skating rink, and Wonderland Walk, a lane flanked by stands selling hot chocolate, warm cookies, and various artisanal goods.

Lauren didn't have much reason to go right. The administrative space was to the left—the Chalet, as they called it for the decorative faux ski-cottage front that hid the entrance to the offices, the break room, and the storage space. That was where she spent most of her day, and thank god, because it was at least moderately warmer than the rest of Cold World.

It could never get *too* warm, though, or it threw the whole balance of the building off, hence Lauren's ubiquitous cardigan. Even thinking about it made Lauren superstitious that the unit would fail, and as she entered the break room she kissed her fingers and pointed at the ceiling, a tribute to the air-conditioning gods.

"You find Jesus last night?"

Lauren startled in the act of reaching for coffee, dropping the K-cup on the floor. Normally, she had a couple hours to herself before most of her coworkers showed up to begin their shifts. But from the low, sardonic voice behind her, at least one person had decided to make an early morning of it.

"If Jesus is certified for commercial HVAC work," she said, bending to pick up the small container filled with lifesaving coffee grounds. "Then yes."

She liked the people she worked with. She genuinely did. Except . . .

Asa Williamson just got under her skin for some reason. Like now, he was leaning casually against the supply closet door, his eyes crinkle-smiling at her over his coffee mug, and she knew, she just *knew* that he was laughing at her.

He was tall and lean, lanky in a way that should make him seem awkward. But instead he always seemed easy, effortless, and comfortable in his own skin. His arms were covered in tattoos, which she couldn't help but notice because he wore short-sleeved shirts even when everyone else on the floor layered long sleeves under their baby blue Cold World polos. He was always doing something different with his hair—it had been long when she'd started two years before, down to his shoulders, and now it was short and dyed a bright aqua blue.

He'd been there ten years, longer than anyone else who wasn't the owner, Dolores, or her son Daniel. Maybe that was why he always felt like the Cool Kid around the place, or maybe it was because he was genuinely friendly with everyone. He was even housemates with Kiki, one of Lauren's closest friends at Cold World. Not that Lauren had ever gone to their place, which they shared with another couple of people she'd only heard about. It was important to have boundaries at work, she thought.

Of course, that was probably one reason why Lauren had never been one of the Cool Kids. Not back in school, not anywhere she'd worked, and definitely not here.

She resented that about Asa, just like she resented that little pinch he got at the corner of his mouth, like he was always thinking about some inside joke. He didn't take anything seriously, and that was something Lauren couldn't stand. She took *everything* seriously.

"Why are you here?" she asked now, the question coming out more churlish than she'd intended as she slammed the top of the Keurig over the K-cup.

"The meeting?" he said. His eyebrows shot up at her confused frown. "The first of December. Holiday season. The planning meeting. Did you forget?"

She *had* actually forgotten. Which was totally unlike her. Lauren lived her life with lists and systems and plans. Three months ago, she'd Googled "best skincare routine" and clicked through the results until she found one that was numbered and affordable and easy to follow, and now she did it every morning and night. She updated her Goodreads page religiously, not to leave reviews but just to ensure that she had some kind of record of every book she'd ever read. It annoyed her to get the biannual postcards from the dentist's office about her next cleaning, because she'd already put a reminder on her Outlook calendar at work to follow up.

"Shit," Asa said, squinting at her. "Is there a problem with your programming? I knew we'd see the effects of Y2K eventually."

"I didn't *forget*," Lauren muttered, even though by now it was obvious she had. She'd already hit the button to brew a cup of coffee, but it wasn't lighting up, so she hit it again. She could hear the churn of the machine as it started to heat the water, but still no coffee. If she was actually a robot like Asa loved to tease her about being, shouldn't she have more proficiency with the stupid thing?

"And you saw all the extra cars in the parking lot and thought, what?" he continued, ignoring her denial. "Maybe it's overflow from the Waffle House?"

She hadn't even noticed the extra cars. She'd been on auto-pilot, lost in her own thoughts. Scarily, she only had vague impressions of the twenty minutes it took her to get from her apartment to Cold World. She had a volunteer engagement after work, and even though she'd been preparing for it for months, *planning* for it, now that it was here it still tied her stomach in knots.

"I have—" *A lot on my mind*, she almost finished, but she didn't have that kind of relationship with anyone at work. And if she was going to start confiding in someone, it certainly wouldn't be Asa Williamson. She stabbed the Keurig button again with her finger, mentally urging the machine to start already so she could extricate herself from the awkwardness of this moment.

He set down his own mug on the counter, reaching over her to fiddle with the machine. Not for the first time, Lauren couldn't help but notice that he smelled good. Like, *really* good. It was one of life's true mysteries, because she felt like she'd know his scent anywhere, but she couldn't quite place what it *was*. Some mixture of cedar and citrus, not overpowering, never burning her nose like some colognes did. But always *present* whenever he was nearby, and sometimes she'd catch the tail end of it when she entered a room he'd just been in. She lived in fear that one day he'd catch her inhaling a big whiff whenever he was close, and she'd have to quit her job and move to North Dakota.

"There," he said as the Keurig whirred to life, dispensing a steady stream of coffee into her mug. As far as she could tell, all he'd done was lift the top and place it back down again. Of course he'd make it look easy.

"Thanks," she said grudgingly.

He settled back with his coffee. "No problem."

This might be the longest Lauren had ever spent one-on-one with Asa. They hadn't exactly hit it off right away, despite his ability to charm his way into friendship with everyone else. Lauren wasn't even sure of his technical job title—he seemed to do a little bit of everything. She'd seen him working the gift shop with Kiki, serving hot chocolate wearing an apron the same color as his hair, even skating circuits around the rink, making sure everyone was traveling in the right direction and no newer skaters needed help.

And it was Florida, so they often needed help.

She'd started at Cold World only days before the staff holiday party two years ago, which was an awkward time to be the new person. She'd still been reeling from her job interview. It had been pretty standard until Dolores mentioned the need to get Cold World's books more organized. Somehow, that had set

Lauren off into an impassioned speech that, embarrassingly, had brought actual tears to her eyes. When she'd finally come up for air, she thought she'd blown it. She must have seemed unhinged. Instead, to her surprise, Dolores had told her on the spot that the job was hers if she wanted it.

Since she hadn't been there long enough to *know* anyone at the holiday party, she'd spent most of it taking note of ways to cut costs at the next shindig. It was part of what Dolores had hired her to do, after all. Lauren thought they could dial back the sandwich platters since there were tons of leftovers, she figured a closed bar would be more money-saving and probably more responsible, and if there was already a Secret Santa she saw no reason for Dolores to separately give gift cards to each employee.

"Those come out of my own pocket, dear," Dolores had said when she brought it up, patting her hand kindly.

But one of Lauren's best—or worst, as in this case—qualities was her tenacity. For some reason, she had a hard time letting it go. She'd turned to the person next to her, who was piling his plate high with two each of the five different types of cookies. She hadn't learned his name, and normally someone with that many tattoos would've intimidated her, but there was something about his eyes that had seemed kind.

"It makes no sense," she said. "If you think about it, if everyone buys a twenty-dollar Secret Santa gift, and then they get a twenty-dollar gift card, doesn't it all come out a wash? If the gift cards are going to mean something, why not cancel Secret Santa?"

"Bold move," he said. "Running on a platform of *cancel Secret Santa*. How long have you worked here again?"

She'd felt her face heat. "Three days."

He'd pointed a cookie at her. "Love your initiative, though," he said. "Keep at it and by March we can get all the toilet paper down to one ply."

He held the cookie in his mouth and walked away, still facing her, one hand holding his plate and the other holding up crossed fingers as though he were actually hopeful. The most infuriating thing was that his tone hadn't even sounded sarcastic. It wasn't until a full minute after he'd walked away that it hit Lauren that there'd been a spark in his eyes as he'd left, and it hadn't been kindness. And a week later, she'd received her generous hundred-dollar gift card from Dolores along with everyone else, and a token coffee mug from Kiki as a belated Secret Santa present.

"This is a regift because my aunt gets me a new one every year," Kiki had said. "So don't feel bad that you didn't get anything for anyone."

"The holidays are kinda . . . intense around here, huh?"

Kiki shrugged. "Dolores thinks that we work so hard to make all our guests' holidays special, so we deserve something special, too. She's a little eccentric, but she's a sweet boss. You'll get used to it."

"Ah." Lauren ran one finger along the rim of the mug. It was white, printed with a rainbow and flowers and an aspirational quote that encouraged her to **BLOOM WHERE YOU ARE PLANTED!** "It's nice," she said hesitantly. "That she arranges the Secret Santa thing and goes out of her way to get everyone in on it."

"Oh, that's all Asa," Kiki had said. At Lauren's questioning expression, she gestured to her shoulders, as if telling a stylist where to cut her own bleached strands. "Long hair? Tall? Tattoos? When it comes to Christmas, he doesn't play. Secret Santa was totally his idea."

The guy she'd vented to at the party. Great.

Photo courtesy of the author

ALICIA THOMPSON writes romance novels, reads whatever she can get her hands on, and plays a mean "Bad Moon Rising" and not much else. She lives in Central Florida with her family.

VISIT THE AUTHOR ONLINE

AliciaThompsonBooks.com

🖸 AliciaBooks

Ready to find
your next great read?

Let us help.

Visit prh.com/nextread

Penguin
Random
House